Ember of a New World

Ishtar Watson

Published 2023 by Dark Elves LLC, Virginia.
600 Princess Anne St. #7695
Fredericksburg, VA 22404

A previous edition of this book existed using the same title but was authored under my old name. This edition is the definitive edition and contains significant changes from the original.

eBook ISBN   978-1-960683-01-4

Paperback ISBN   978-1-960683-02-1

Hardcover ISBN   978-1-960683-00-7

I hereby dedicate this book to…

To the spirit of humanity, peace, and the freedom for all forms of human expression. May we learn a little humility and compassion.

To the LGBTQIA+ and Neurodivergent people of the world. We have always existed, and we always will.

To the archaeologists of the world. Without your dedication and skill, I would have been lost.

And to my spouse… thank you for being who you are.

Ishtar

DEAR ARCHAEOLOGISTS

I am professionally a computer scientist and an archaeology student. I have spent fifteen years studying the Neolithic and Late Mesolithic. At first, this was an effort to create the proper setting for my story, but it soon evolved into a full academic effort. I have a university background in archaeology, anthropology, and computer science, and I have engaged in experimental archaeology to understand and properly depict the ancient world as accurately as possible. For example, I grew flax, then harvested, processed, spun, and wove the flax into linen using only Neolithic tools and techniques, including wearing period clothing. The purpose of this six months of work was merely to write a few scenes involving flax farming accurately. Our understanding of the past is ever-evolving, and some details from my story may be incorrect, given time and research. You may disagree with my treatment of the Neolithic, from religion to clothing, but please know that any mistakes you find were made in good faith and not for lack of research. Additionally, some gaps in our understanding required a bit of conjecture to create a proper narrative.

~Ishtar

INTRODUCTION

Units of Measure

The modern era has established units of measure, such as the Le Système International d'Unités Meter or the English Foot. In ancient times, it is a reasonable assumption that measures were roughly standardized to the apparent mean lengths of arms, legs, the distance a person could walk given an average period, or by the seasons. The entire book is detailed in measures that correspond to this hypothesis. The choice to use these natural units, such as the length of a hand, is designed to bring the reader into the Neolithic world and help the reader appreciate the wonder that is standardized measure, one of our modern era's most overlooked achievements.

Nudity

Many of the characters are depicted in various degrees of nudity throughout the Ember series, from wearing no apparent upper garment to wholly nude. While this may come as a shock to many people, it is by no means out of place for the period in which the books are set. In our modern culture, nudity has become associated with sexuality, but the extreme nature of this relationship is a modern – recent – association. Social attitudes and the sexual relationship with nudity have arisen through historical, cultural, and religious means.

In the sixth millennium B.C.E., nudity was depicted in art in such a manner and frequency as to infer that it was not out of the ordinary nor taboo. At the dawn of the 21st century, several cultures still exist where little or no clothing is worn. Within these cultures, nudity and partial nudity are not considered sexualized elements, nor are they looked down upon as any form of depravity. It is important to cast aside our modern notions of modesty and sexuality when considering the social norms of an ancient society.

Misogyny

Misogyny has been a consistent component of humanity for much of recorded history. While certainly an attitude that needs to be eliminated, it would be dishonest not to portray it as it likely existed. To that end, many characters display varying degrees of misogyny, and some misandry, from all genders. It is important to remember that these individuals likely grew up in a society that shared these views. Be thankful that we have a society that is slowly progressing so that we can identify misogyny and be displeased by it. With luck, one-day misogyny may no longer exist other than as a conversational piece in a history class. May we live to be so fortunate.

KEY PRONUNCIATIONS

Kaelu	Kay-loo
Brig'dha	Brig-da
Aurochs	Aue-rocks
Kanter	Can-ter
Pak	Pack
Calpano	Kal-pon-oh
Rosif	Ross-if
Gar'ath	Gar-eth
E'lyse	El-eye-s
Kat'ja	Cat-ya
Tor'kal	Tork-ale
Ven'Gar	Vin Gar
Borjk	Bor-sh-k
Ana	Anna
Ena	In-ah
Aya	Eye-ah
Kis'tra	Kiss-tra
Zhek	Zeck
Sv'en	S-veen
Nor'Gar	Nor Gar
Duruth	Da-Rooth
Peerth	Peer-th
Inn'bry'th	Inn-br-eye-th
Isen'bryn	Eye-sin-brin

PROLOGUE

The warriors approached the edge of the peaceful village by the Great River as the first motes of light broke the horizon. They had traveled for many days from their village in the South. It was never a good idea to raid a village too close to one's own, as you might again meet those same people face-to-face at a harvest festival, a morbidly awkward run-in. The lead warrior felt confident having brought twelve young, strong men, each armed with a wooden war club, a sharp stone attached to the head of each weapon. Across their backs, each raider carried a freshly strung bow and a quiver of arrows, and a sharp stone knife at their side.

Before them lay a small slash-and-burn field of mixed crops. Eight villagers labored picking weeds and cleaning debris in the early morning. The weather was not hot, but the villagers worked diligently to complete their work before the Sun rose too far. It was the early barley harvest season, and the temperature shifted wildly between cool and hot. Two women had brought their children, leather wraps holding the babies against their chests so they could feed while their mothers worked.

Not far from the field stood a young man with a spear, his body clad in red ochre, and obviously standing watch. Sometimes, animals would stray from the woods in the early morning. It was always a good idea to have someone nearby to scare them off. Unfortunately, he would have to die first.

Winterborn awoke with an odd sense of foreboding, having thought he heard a sound outside the longhouse where he and his wife East lived. The old structure had a musty smell, a mixture of mildew, leather, and dried herbs. The early morning air was moist and cool, the fire having burned down sometime during the night. It was not common, but deer had been known to occasionally wander through the village early in the morning before anyone awoke. Ignoring the sound, he rolled over on their bed of furs, placing his hand upon the soft hip of his young wife, East. He casually brushed a few of his long, waist-length red hairs from her nude form.

They had become joined only two harvests before, and already a child lay on a bundle of furs just within reach of her mother. Turning his attention from the woman he loved to his infant daughter, Winterborn could not be happier. The baby girl had been born early that very warm season and was barely two moons age, yet already a small puff of red hair grew upon her tender head. She was a beautiful, healthy child. She had the same rich emerald green eyes as her father and was much more well-behaved than many babies, tending to sleep a good portion of the night. What gods they had pleased for such luck, he could not say.

Another sound just beyond the wall caught his attention. This time it sounded like somebody wandering through the village, perhaps someone heading out to relieve themselves, or potentially a small animal foraging. Again, Winterborn felt a strange sense of foreboding, yet he couldn't reason why. Noises were part of village life. Snoring, romance, arguments, and more were unavoidable in a village, yet something was… off.

Beside him, young Ember lay sucking her tiny pink fingers. She needed feeding and would probably start to fuss if not attended. With East still exhausted from her previous long day and their joy-filled night, he gently lifted little Ember and delicately placed her to rest against her mother's breast so she could drink her fill of the precious milk. It was well known that a baby should be allowed to feed as often as it would take milk. A full baby was a happy baby, and a happy baby was a quiet baby. As Ember found the life-giving breast, East made a slight noise, though she continued to sleep. Winterborn lay beside the two most important people in his entire world and felt at ease once more.

He was beginning to drift back to sleep when again he heard a strange noise as though somebody was traipsing around outside of the longhouse. This time, he sat up, alert, suddenly concerned for reasons he could not quantify. He reached for his prized obsidian dagger, a beautiful and sharp weapon made of some of the strongest obsidian he had ever seen. Its edge could cut flesh quicker than any other blade he had used. It had been a gift from his people before he had left to join East's people. Tying its sheath around his waist, he stood ready to peek out of the longhouse and make sure all was well. The temperature outside would be unpleasantly cool when nude, but the snow had not yet fallen. Hopefully, all would be well, and he could return to the warmth of furs and East's side.

Winterborn reached for the heavy leather flap door to the longhouse when suddenly it burst open, and a man stepped in, forcing him back. The intruder wore a sleeveless leather top, with leather leggings strapped tightly to a woven cord, a pair of heavy leather boots, and a long leather loincloth adorned with shell beads. His skin was lighter than Winterborn, typical of river people, like East and most tribes along the Great River. But what first caught Winterborn's attention was the heavy war club in the man's hand, the end wet with a slick of blood. In a split second, he realized that the man standing before him was none other than a raider, a man from another tribe whose sole intent was likely to steal and kill.

Before the raider's eyes could adjust to the dim light of the dying embers in the central hearth, Winterborn rushed the man with his dagger, plunging it deep into the man's stomach just below his shirt where a line of skin was visible. With his other hand, he grabbed the club, forcing it aside as he repeatedly plunged the blade into the stunned man's gut. Obsidian blades were meant for slashing, not thrusting, but the soft exposed skin of the raider's gut made for one of the few viable targets on a human, when stabbing.

The man let loose a scream of anguish as both men collapsed to the floor. They had entered into a sort of grapple, yet the mortally wounded raider was running on pure shock and adrenaline. He was younger than Winterborn, perhaps only becoming a man recently, yet his strong body was fading fast. This had likely been his first and now his last raid. In his desperate attempts to free himself, the raider rolled atop Winterborn momentarily, pinning him in place. The raider was losing blood at a frantic pace and would soon be dead, momentary upper hand or not.

East awoke to the nightmare of a raid upon her tribe, the Great River People. Before her, Winterborn rolled on the floor in a perilous battle with what looked like a raider. The younger man's body and face were painted striking black and red, the colors common of river people, the Neolithic farming tribes who lived along the rivers, one day known as the Linear Pottery Culture. Her husband, Winterborn, was a "Forest Person" from one of the tribes to the North. His people would one day be known as Mesolithic people.

Suddenly, the door flap opened anew, and a second raider entered. The next man was also painted strikingly and carrying a blood-stained adze, likely having lost his weapon, and taken the first tool he found. She began fumbling for the small flint knife she kept behind her reed sleeping mat, the only defensive weapon she had. In her other arm, she held little Ember tight, unwilling to let go of the precious child at such a dire moment. She would defend her child and husband, no matter what the odds.

The second raider stepped into the longhouse, finding what looked like one of his companions atop a wounded man, judging by the blood. He suspected his companion had quickly subdued the oddly red-haired man with the dark skin of a forest person. Before him lay a woman clothed in bed furs holding an infant. Behind her, a dozen people were waking in shock, obviously caught off guard. Among them, he saw only old women and young children. He smiled, having been so fortunate. Perhaps he would toss the child aside and take the woman. A young woman who had proven herself able to bear children and had survived her first childbirth would likely give him many strong sons.

He ambled forward with an adze in hand, a specialized tool used for removing bark from a tree, ready to tear the young baby from her mother and cast it aside, then leave before the rest of the extended family chose to intervene. Unexpectedly, the woman revealed a small flint knife, holding it before her. The raider had very little time for this and lifted his adze, ready to swing it sideways and knock the weapon from her hand. A woman who fought back was far less desirable. If she persisted, she would be a problem the entire way back to his tribe, though hopefully, her defiance would break quickly. Behind him, he heard what sounded like his companion getting to his feet.

The woman oddly looked more defiant by the moment, but that was easy to fix. He swung the adze to strike her knife hand. A broken hand would give her something to think about and make fighting back much more difficult. Suddenly, a firm hand caught the weapon and halted its plunge. The raider glanced to his side, coming face-to-face with all-to-unharmed Winterborn. He opened his mouth to speak when the robust redhead punched him square in the face knocking him back against the wattle and daub wall, cracking the mud-plaster. *Monologue will get you killed,* Winterborn thought in anger.

It took a few moments for the stars and blackness to leave his sight, but the raider shook his head, clearing his vision. He glanced back and noticed that his companion was lying in the fetal position holding his gut and jerking in agony. The raider removed a long flint dagger from his waist cord, needing to end this fast. An average forest person stood nearly a head taller than a river person, the sort of opponent he had not expected to find when they attacked this small river tribe. Worse, the man was quite muscular and stood supremely confident in his abilities, but the raider had a few tricks left for such a man.

As the raider stumbled back, Winterborn turned for just a moment ensuring East and little Ember were safe. Behind them, the longhouse had awoken, but none were in the condition to fight, which left the defense of the longhouse to Winterborn. Seeing the opening, the raider lunged forward, swinging his adze high in a brazen, yet over-committed effort. Winterborn heard the sound and turned in time to catch the deadly weapon when suddenly, he felt a solid blow to his abdomen as though he had been punched. He hadn't seen the man's other hand in time.

Winterborn backed away, looking down to find the raider's dagger protruding from his abdomen. The pain felt sharp and cold, and the wind was momentarily knocked from his chest. Behind him, East said something, but he was too shocked to understand. Winterborn sank to his knees when suddenly the raider slammed into him. The pair collapsed to the floor in a grapple. Tearing the blade free, the raider tried to stab Winterborn's face, but the mighty redhead still had some fight left in him. He grabbed the raider's hand to begin wrestling over which direction the dagger would point, the adze knocked harmlessly to the side. Winterborn was losing blood fast and, with it, his strength. Behind them, East screamed in vain.

The raider began to smile as the blade edged closer to Winterborn's neck. Soon, the foolish redhead would be dead. He would kill the child, bind the woman's wrists, and take her back to his village as a proper spoil. If he had time, he might even grab another woman from those in the longhouse. It wasn't as though women would put up much of a fight... Suddenly, the warrior felt a bizarre sensation in the back of his neck, a mixture of sharp pain and cold numbness. He rolled off weakened Winterborn, clutching his neck and finding a small flint knife protruding. Just behind him in complete horror stood East, her right hand bloody and trembling, her crying child held tightly in the other.

Before the raider could act, Winterborn rolled back onto the man with his giant obsidian dagger and plunged it with all his remaining strength into the man's side, though it bit more muscle than anything else. For a moment, it was a struggle of wills as Winterborn's last energy faded. He had to kill the man before he died, yet he was so weak he could barely rip the dagger from the raider's side. Then, suddenly, the raider cried out in horrific pain. The raider twisted to see the damned woman on her knees at his back holding his discarded adze, her baby in tow.

Anger and fear drove her as East dug huge gashes into the man's legs, swinging the adze as she had harvests before when she had helped make the family longhouse. His flesh tore from the bone just as the bark from the trees which had made her home. Just then, Winterborn freed the dagger and plunged it anew. The raider screamed in abject horror at the unimaginable pain caused by the tool-turned-weapon as both wife and wounded husband tore him apart. Finally, his screams became nothing more than a gurgling sound as blood erupted from his neck.

With both raiders soundly defeated, Winterborn rolled onto his back, blood gushing from his wound. His vision slowly darkened with speckles appearing at the periphery. His final actions had been fueled by adrenaline and the drive that every parent had to save the people they love. But as soon as that was exhausted, so too was the last of his strength. His vision faded, and he could barely hear as his blood pressure collapsed. Nevertheless, he had enjoyed his life, and he had made the most of it, leaving his tribe as a youth and setting out into the world to find adventure. His greatest find had been a fun and loving river people woman he had eventually married.

Looking down at him, he saw the fading visage of East crouching above, young Ember in her arms. She seemed to be crying in anguish. He could feel her warm tears against his skin. He tried to lift his hand to caress her soft face, but his hand would not respond. East and baby Ember would live.

He would trade his life for theirs, and so he had.

CHAPTER ONE

SUNRISE

Neolithic houses were quite sophisticated structures for their time. Far from the caves, which many, unfortunately and incorrectly, associate with prehistoric peoples, Neolithic people constructed complex houses of many materials, including mudbrick, stone, and wood. Some houses were quite large, housing entire extended families, while others had stables for livestock built within. Neolithic houses could be found on stilts near the water, buried partially into the ground or the sides of hills to aid in climate control, and even stacked upon each other into a city-like community of buildings.

The long and rectangular longhouses of Ember's village were sturdy wooden structures designed for the harsh winters of Europe and the occasional flooding of the rivers her people so often lived beside. The sides were a lattice of wood and bark caked with mud to keep out pests, often with small ditches dug just beyond the walls, perhaps to catch water runoff. Packed dirt floors were covered with dried mud and worn animal hides. The roofs could be propped open in the warmer summers to let heat out and covered with extra mud and thatching during the cold winters.

Our story starts in one such longhouse where a teenaged girl sleeps happily on a set of woven reed mats and large red deer skins. Her longhouse is old and smaller than the others, only housing a handful of people, unlike the much larger longhouses of the village. Her dreams were interrupted by the sudden and uncommon sound of silence...

As she awoke, Ember immediately knew something was amiss. The usual cooking sounds and the smell of reheated pork strips and beans had been replaced by an eerie quiet. Ember breathed in the warm, earthy scent of the longhouse and its accompanying mats and skins. As she sat up, she began to understand her situation, sleep leaving her. This was the morning before the Great Lunar Festival, a festival of epic proportions, which kept most of the tribe occupied with preparatory crafts. This was a time to give thanks to the gods for the world's bounties, receive blessings for good hunting, and for a good harvest before the cold season.

Some tribes prayed primarily to the Sun during this time, while Ember's tribe worshiped the Moon Goddess more strongly. Ember had heard of other tribes who worshiped different gods, but never of a tribe that did not plead to their gods to aid in their harvests. A full and rich harvest would see a lucky tribe through the cold season, but only if the gods saw fit to fertilize the land with their life-giving blessings. Conversely, a poor harvest could mean death. As a result, the entire tribe had awakened early, for much had to be done. Well, everyone but Ember, of course.

Linear Pottery Culture Longhouse

Blowing a few long red strands of hair from her face, Ember sat upright. She had slept late, again, and missed whatever food had been prepared. With a touch of embarrassment, she dragged herself out of bed, reed mats covered with warm red deer furs, and started her morning with a yawn. She always slept on deer fur with her head pointed toward the place where the deer's head had been. This kept her from getting "fur burn" when her soft skin rubbed against course fur the wrong way.

As she stretched, Ember's hand brushed against the side of the longhouse. She withdrew it, mid-yawn, in surprise. She had never bumped into the wall before while practicing her lengthy morning stretches. This was a reminder that she was no longer a girl but a budding young woman, though she was not sure that she really felt like a woman. In truth, she didn't feel like a girl, either, though her body had filled out in the way of a woman, despite her reservations.

Ember pulled the deer fur aside and fumbled with her clothing, which she had placed beside her sleeping mat the night before. She picked up a loosely woven knee-length bark fiber wrap skirt made from the bark fibers of a limewood tree. Old lady Oakwood had woven the garment several seasons before and given it to Ember in exchange for her help gathering various plants and materials for her crafts. She was an excellent weaver, perhaps the finest, but far too old to brave the deep woods searching for materials. Lucky for the both of them, Ember loved a good adventure, even if it was just a walk in the local forest.

The skirt was not Oakwood's finest but strong enough for work. The garment wrapped around her waist and fastened by a simple leather thong, a thin cord of leather. Clothing, costly of time and skill to make, could become damaged while sleeping and was often not worn within a family longhouse, especially during warmer seasons. Ember quickly secured the skirt, ensuring the tassels at the bottom were untangled before she finished.

The still air was slightly musty from the morning dew though the longhouse felt fresh and comfortable. A delicious smell of wood, soil, and leather filled her nose – the smell of home. Ember stood beside her woven mat bed and took in her familiar surroundings. The room was nearly 15 lengths of a man's arm in length and a third that distance in width and height. The walls were wooden beams bound by fibrous cord or sinew and caked with dried mud and grass. The mud and grass held fast the heat of the hearth in the cold seasons and repelled the glaring Sun in the warm seasons, making a highly efficient insulator.

The roof was made of delimbed and tightly lashed tree branches, with reed mats firmly attached to their outer surface with fiber cord. The reeds were bound, running perpendicular to the ground so water would run down and not into the building. Ember wondered how other tribes dealt without reeds. Traders from other tribes told of lands far from the water where leather was a primary material for clothing and roofs were thatched with tall, dried plants.

How strange other people could be, she thought. Reeds were a staple construction material for her tribe, the Great River People, or "Dau apu meg'denn," in her language.

Ember's longhouse featured three center log poles, each separated by about four lengths of a man's arm, which helped support the roof. The interior walls were adorned with various trappings of her family, including reed cooking mats, several decorated clay pots with beautiful, incised line artwork, and several colorful reed baskets. Near the rear of the longhouse, where Ember's bed lay, small animals had been carved into the walls during the long and dreary cold season. She had been yelled at for the damage, but soon other images had been carved elsewhere as cold seasons tended to be long and very dull. Many fresh herbs, dyed wool yarn, and freshly cut leather thongs hung from the center pole, which ran the length of the dwelling. Here and there, the inside had been decorated with colorful paintings of various designs, many of Ember's own doing. This was home.

The entire structure sat atop a slight hill no more than two arm lengths above the normal height of the surrounding land. The dirt was additionally pushed up nearly an arm's height around the perimeter of the house. This had the effect of keeping animals, smaller unwanted house guests, the cold season drafts, and surging river water out. Unfortunately, the dirt barrier required constant maintenance as rain would erode the soil.

Ember advanced to a reed cooking mat and knelt before the clay pots and reed baskets which held the family's ready food supply. Strawberries, softened cabbage, dried barley cakes, various tubers, and lentils were kept for many days. Meat had to be dried or eaten within a day or two to be safe. If meat were kept for too long, mischievous spirits would try and inhabit the flesh. As a result, consuming such meat could make one quite ill, requiring a major ritual to purify and heal the sick person.

Ember had heard of a man who had died from old meat when she was very young. Though she had never spoken to the man and remembered little of him, she had learned a valuable lesson. Such stories were either passed from tribe to tribe through visitors or taught by elders. Many were not so much true in story, but true in fact, helping keep people safe by imparting important lessons. Humans were storytellers, learning from verbally shared experiences.

With that and several other random thoughts, she opened each container and examined its contents, knowing that one contained "the perfect breakfast." She located the clay pot that held small strips of dried and salted pork with a quick sniff. Her mouth watered at the thought of all the salt, her favorite food. Salt was an essential commodity. Every season, traders came and traded the precious substance for other finery. Without salt, a person would soon get the sweats, and eventually, they could die. Salt was used for rituals and sparingly as a preservative because of its value. Luckily, the previous season's traders had come with many large pots and sacks of salt. After a few moments, she had selected several choice pieces of dried pork and a small clay pot full of lightly salted peas, which had been sculpted from clay to look like a human face was coming from its edge, a common motif.

"Mmm, salty!" she mused as she licked her fingers clean of the tasty mineral while walking toward the hearth. Unfortunately for the tribe's salt supply, she consumed many times as much salt as her peers, much to her mother's chagrin. Now it was time to heat the food before eating it.

Longhouses had two hearths, one on each end, yet only one was generally ever in use at any given time. Ember found, to her dismay, that the working hearth had been allowed to burn down and now merely smoldered. She struggled blowing and fanning the fire back to life, at one point becoming light-headed. In her native tongue, her name "Kaelu" meant "Ember from a fire." Regrettably, her name came from her beautiful waist-length fiery red hair, not her poor fire tending skills. Ember was more likely to burn herself than strike a blazing flame. Even though she was mildly proficient with a fire bow, a tool used to make fires, she had earned a bad reputation for her inability to light the hearth on many occasions.

Ember snatched a few of the long sharpened and fire-hardened twigs used to cook meat and let the pork lay across the small fire. The flame kissed the meat with tiny pops and crackles, producing the blackened crispy pieces at the tips that she loved. Of course, eating too much of the burned parts would cause an undesired trip behind a tree, but only a little wouldn't hurt. She needed a tasty start to her morning on such an important day.

The pork quickly sizzled and roasted over the open fire, with the salted peas staying safely in their pot far from the heat. She plucked the pork from the fire and tossed a piece in her mouth, soon regretting her haste, for she had burned the inside of her mouth in the process. Luckily, several of the clay pots contained drinking water. After a few gulps, she sat back against a center pole savoring the oily taste and thinking the entire breakfast was wonderful. She had grown tired of porridge each morning, a boring dish made of grains and salt.

After the meal, Ember went about her daily preparations before entering her village's busy world. She usually wore her soft doeskin shirt, a remarkable piece of clothing given to her by her grandmother just that past cold season. The shirt was incredibly soft and loose, far more than most leather shirts. It had been painted with black spots, each half the size of her palm, producing a beautiful pattern. Around the bottom, aurochs teeth were hung for decoration, creating a lovely clicking sound when she moved. The shirt was said to have come from the skin of a young female deer felled by a blow to the head. Ember loved soft leather, hard to come by in larger animals. Soft leather required special tanning and beating to "break the will" of the leather, as the tanners in the village told it. Unfortunately, the warm season had grown far too hot for shirts.

Gazing into a broad and shallow fire-blackened clay dish filled with water, she considered her hair and face in the reflection. Ember had long flowing red hair the color of fire and lightly browned, tan skin slightly darker than most of her people. Red hair was not common, most having dark hair colors, and most redheads in her tribe and nearby tribes were not so richly colored. Others often had a lighter color, approaching either blonde or brunette. Ember's hair color was quite rare, being vibrant and thick with many different hues of red, while her eyes were emerald green, giving her a striking contrast.

Unfortunately, as with most young people, she saw only imperfection. Her face had a few minor bumps, which were hard to hide and painful to remove. Her grandmother had said that everyone got such bumps and that they were merely her body growing too fast, as most people got them early in life and kept them until at least fourteen to eighteen harvests age when they became adults.

Ember's hair was also quite oily from a long day of work and a long hot night of sleep. Even when she washed it, her hair always retained a little oil, but this kept the hair in good condition. Water was one of the ways tanners removed hair from hides, and she always wondered if over washing could cause the same effect. She pulled her hair behind her head into a loose ponytail and secured it with a leather thong. She would wash it at the river when time permitted. She might coat it with red ochre after cleaning it, though she wasn't sure.

Lastly, she decided she needed to add a dash of color on such a special day and a way to hide her red bumps at the same time. She applied a small amount of red ocher paint to her face. The ocher covered her skin, smoothing out imperfections and giving her a generally uniform look. Delicately, using her pinky finger, Ember added four small black dots below each eye, running horizontally, made from a paint of fish oil and animal bone ash. As she did this, she sang a short song, a prayer to the fish spirits for good luck at the river, her next destination. Spirits enjoyed the attention, and she might find luck in their joy.

Most of the tribe painted their faces and bodies. Indeed, as far as she knew, painting of the body was widespread among most river peoples. Various designs could signify a person's tribe or rank within the tribe or even a ritual significance. But mostly, body painting and design were up to the artist and merely decorative. But most importantly: it was considered indecent not to be painted in some way. Satisfied that she could face the day, and with a warm meal in her stomach, Ember grabbed her flint work knife by its leather wrap handle and a small reed basket, and headed out to greet the morning.

CHAPTER TWO
EMBER'S WORLD

Ember is a teenager living in a medium-sized tribe of about 170 people, broken into perhaps a dozen extended family groups. In such a close setting, everyone would know each other by name and face. This may sound pleasant, but there are serious problems with a gene pool when the total number of people is too small. As a result, it may have been commonplace for marital exchanges of people between villages, known as exogamy. Members of Ember's tribe probably intermixed with the tribes of the local region, and perhaps even Mesolithic people, such as Winterborn. Interactions between peoples consequently led to exchanges of ideas and culture. Perhaps similarities of cultures within specific geographical areas owe to this fact.

Based upon contemporary pre-industrial cultures, it can be fairly supposed that people sometimes traveled to other tribes to find spouses, yet the exact protocols and rates of exchange are unknown. Ember is becoming a woman soon, and per her tribal customs, she will need a spouse. Perhaps she will choose one from among her local tribe or perhaps from afar.

As she opened the leather flap covering the longhouse door, Ember was hit by a blast of warmth, as well as the intense light of the morning. It was the late warm season, so some warmth was expected, but this sort of heat was uncustomary. Its effects showed on the faces and clothing of the first few people Ember saw. Sweat rolled down their hot faces as their skin gleamed wetly from labor. Ember could not believe the heat this early in the warm season, perhaps the hottest day she could remember. The people of her village had shed as much extra clothing as they could, some even stripping entirely.

Men tended to wear loincloths or nothing at all when the work was laborious enough, such as the emmer harvest, which had thankfully just ended. Women often wore wrapped skirts of leather or, occasionally, textile, or soft deer skins tucked into waist cords and draped down their fronts from waist to knee, the excess folded over the waist cord a hand's length or more down the front. Garments were sparse, yet each was carefully decorated. For example, a leather wrap skirt might be painted at the bottom with ochre or berry pigments, with perhaps a few dozen to several hundred beads of bone or antler and deer teeth adding decoration, the garment held up by a woven fiber belt with a clasp of shell or bone.

The older girls and younger women wore woven fiber aprons signifying their coming of age or availability. Aprons were garments that hung from a waist cord covering the front waist of the wearer. Each apron was handwoven by the girl wearing it both to advertise her availability as well as display her crafting skills. Ember was supposed to wear such a garment too, but the effort was too much, in her opinion. Besides, Ember had yet to find any interest in joining. So instead, she tended to wear either her lovely bark skirt or a loincloth and shirt, the latter being more common, though not exclusively, of men. Ember was hardly one to follow gender roles, a constant source of friction with her mother.

Ember saw a man walking by complaining about the heat while fanning himself with a reed fan, as she stepped into the hot sun. This was going to be a tough day, it seemed. She would need to head to the river before she started complaining as well. As she walked through the village, the signs of people trying to keep cool were all around. Her people were just not used to such heat. Luckily, they had a river nearby to cool off, as well as to irrigate crops and provide fish for the tribe.

Her people lived on a slightly raised portion of land that overlooked the Great River, known as the Rhine River, one day. The trees had been painstakingly cleared by hand using stone axes, small fires at the bases of the trees, and sometimes a combination of the two to create a wide meadow for the tribe. Controlled fires were also set to remove the brush from the land.

The fires used to burn the ground clear were also very useful in growing crops. One night when she was a young girl, Ember had listened to her grandmother explain how the Goddess of the Moon wept for burned lands and quickly caused plants to grow upon them. This made sense to her, though she had always wondered why plants did not grow in the cold season. Did the Goddess not mind the lack of flowers then? Was she only bothered by burned land? Ember was always full of questions, though few could answer her.

To complicate things further, Ember's mother had explained that fire also told the plants that it was time to regrow. She had examined flowers very closely, following her mother's proclamation, even speaking to them on occasion, but they never showed any signs of intelligence. Ember wondered how they could know to grow or how two completely different stories could exist for why fire resulted in new growth. She supposed both stories could be true. Ember's mind was always a chaotic mess of questions and thoughts, and rarely focused on the task at hand.

As she passed the next longhouse, she stepped past an old stump many used as a chair. In fact, the most challenging part of land clearing was always the removal of stumps. She had watched the men work for days on a new plot of land to be used for crops. Stumps required fires, digging, and all manner of work to remove if they could be at all. Ember had spent an entire evening bringing water and food to the men as they cleared the land for farming, only last warm season.

The whole village meadow was nearly four fallen trees in length, circular, and well protected from the weather by a ring of trees at the perimeter. Unfortunately, the trees blocked the wind a little too well, and everyone suffered in the unusual heatwave. The worst hit by the weather were the women working near the central hearths, surrounded by the village's sixteen longhouses. As Ember passed the central hearths heading for the river, she glanced at the poor women melting in the heat.

Eight women were working by the hearths, firing clay pots, cooking lentils, or fanning themselves with whatever could be found. The women had mostly discarded their clothes in the heat, though they were all painted, for modesty, as some standards couldn't be discarded, no matter the heat. Their skin had been carefully coated in red ochre and white clay, common among women. Beside several women sat clay pots they were decorating with sharp stone pieces, microlithic pieces of flint, large enough to use as tools. Flint was a precious commodity and never discarded until too small to be used.

Around them, happy unclothed children played free from the worries of adults, too old to be swaddled but too young to be put to general work. A few industrious mothers had taught their children a game called "fan mommy with the reed fan and win a prize." Ember recalled those happy days when she had seen barely five harvests and the fun she would have had on a day like this. Those were blissful days where she ran free as a bird flew. But unfortunately, everyone eventually grew up.

As she strolled through the village, she became excited by thoughts of the festivities to come. People worked frantically painting longhouses with fresh designs, creating delicious food, and a multitude of other tasks to properly honor the gods. Not far from the hearths, men worked with round flint tools cutting open freshly killed animals to clean and prepare. There would be roasted meat en masse for the tribe tonight and hopefully plenty of salt. Ember smiled at the thought of the food to come.

Near the busily working men, a younger woman stood obviously trying to pick up a partner for the coming events. She wore an elaborate twined apron of wool with an eye-catching design. Their tribe had no sheep, but the closest tribe to the North did, so she had likely traded for the soft fiber. She had decorated her hair in thick braids with flowers throughout. Her light brown skin had been painted white with clay, and red streaks of paint ran from her forehead down her body to the ground. As she stood, she smiled at one of the men who seemed to notice her.

It's a bit late to find a date for the festival, Ember mused, though she suspected the pretty woman might succeed. The paint and flower effect were quite impressive. Ember found the woman quite beautiful to look at, but unfortunately, that particular woman was far too annoying in person. Ember shook her head just the same. Such relationships never lasted as many men would leave for other tribes, and new men would arrive. Of course, this meant new chances for the women of her tribe, but perhaps, that was the point.

Girlish musings aside, Ember considered the reality of inner tribal dating. It was hard to find a mate in the same tribe who was not closely related, which was the main reason for inter-tribal exchanges. Additionally, new men brought new ideas and new skills. On rare occasions, a few women would arrive from afar. Sometimes, traders would purposefully bring their daughters to wed in the village, securing their future and a close link for trade. There were tribes all along the Great River, and people journeyed quite often between them. Most of the larger tribes were to the East, where another great river ran. Ember continued through the village, heading towards the Great River, and her chores for the day. She wondered what those other river people were up to on such a hot day.

He squatted beside the shallow, rectangular grave, having just finished refilling it by hand. He had the use of a small hand ax he brought for digging, but the entire effort had taken much of the night. Pak, son of Ran, son of Torn, sighed with finality before sitting beside the grave. Just to his side he watched as a wasp flew by, obviously inspecting his work. Pak was the youngest member of a trio sent by his village to scout the Western lands for trade and any competition which had taken root since the last cold season. His group had been headed west, following the Great River for several days when they had encountered a ruined village. He adjusted his leather leggings as one did when squatting and combed his fingers through his long, dark hair to clear his bright blue eyes.

Pak had initially considered burning the bodies, per custom, but their leader, Rosif, had forbidden it. A burly man who never shied from a brawl and had the bulk to win his fair share, Rosif was nearly twice Pak's age or more and a veteran of many such scouting trips. Rosif was by far the leader of the group. He was huge and imposing but not so well kept. His muscles were old and gristly, but he was still a dangerous man to cross. He wore a leather shirt opened on the sides and fastened by a leather thong. About his waist, he wore a roe deerskin wrap, leather leggings, and woven fiber shoes. His dark hair was never quite in order, and his skin featured many scars in intricate patterns displaying his prowess.

Rosif boasted that he wore a scar for every predatory animal he had killed. In fact, it had been many seasons since Rosif had claimed a wolf that came too close to the village. His sheer size and mysterious blue-gray eyes held back all who would question his prowess. Only the fiercest practiced scarification and Pak was not yet up to the task, though it would be expected if they returned with good trades. He shuttered at the prospect of his flesh being carved, yet traditions were traditions.

Pain, suffering, just like this trip, he grimaced. Personally, Pak suspected Rosif spent so much time away from their village because he was barely welcome. Between the men he picked fights with and more than one woman who claimed he had taken advantage of them, Rosif wasn't exactly a respectable member of society.

"Hey, you used all of the ochre," said the third member of their group in a nasal tone. Calpano stepped forward holding a now empty leather pouch that had once contained the group's red ochre paint. Calpano was a rough man with a remarkably introverted personality. He was not much older than Pak, yet he had already participated in several scouting and hunting trips, mostly because he liked to be away from the village. He had achieved greater things than Pak in a shorter time, which unnerved Pak more than a little. Calpano had taken a mate, a young brown-haired woman from a neighboring tribe, and already had a child on the way. Pak had always liked the woman, Faja was her name, and she seemed to like him too, but that was a relationship which would not be.

If Calpano ever failed to return, it might be... he thought, and Faja would be better off in my arms. As suddenly as he thought it, he waved the notion aside. Such thoughts poisoned the mind and would never come true. He returned his attention to the blonde-haired man with a bone earring in his right ear, a trait more common to the Eastern rivers.

"Sorry, I needed it for her," Pak said, nodding at the grave. Only a half day's walk from the destroyed village, they had come upon the desiccated body of what looked like an elderly woman. The body had mostly rotted to the bone, but her woven nettle fiber skirt with ample beads and discarded walking stick had given her away as likely an older woman, probably an elder. The village had obviously been struck in the colder seasons, judging by the clothing found on the bodies, at least what little remained. Pak supposed the elder had fled during the raid, likely from inside a longhouse into the cold, given her lack of proper cold-weather clothing.

An elderly woman fleeing during a cold day on foot with only a woven skirt wouldn't have lasted long. Moreover, she had a half-rotted arrow protruding from her back. Such a wound likely wouldn't have killed her outright, but the pain would have been unbearable as she fled into the cold night and certain death. Pak could only guess why, though he had a reasonable suspicion.

"She wasn't one of The People, so she didn't need our ochre or your time," Calpano added before returning to their small camp for the night. 'The People' meant their tribe. Pak had accepted that burning the entire destroyed tribe was neither their job nor feasible, yet this had been an elder. Elders were supposed to be honored, no matter where they came from. If Pak's guess was correct, this elder had fled to her inevitable death to protect something, likely the tribe's sacred item. Many tribes maintained relics and religious objects which were protected, no matter what. It was the only reason he could see for running into the wilds to die. With an arrow in her back, she could have laid down and died in peace much closer to the village and likely been left to do so. Instead, she had braved half of a day in agony.

"Find the next world and rest," he said, standing to return to the camp. He'd done what he could to help her find the next world. He had dug a grave, placed her body in the proper direction and position, and even covered her remains with red ochre in the proper way of burial. That had been tough without his trusty antler mattock, a sort of pickaxe-like tool made from a wooden handle and a deer antler pick. His only regret was that Rosif had likely taken whatever object she had suffered to protect. He'd seen the older man looting her body before calling him and Calpano to come to see what he had found near their camp. Pak would likely never know what the item was, and he doubted Rosif would take well to being asked. With another sigh, he returned to camp.

ɔ ɔ ɔ

The Great Lunar Festival was usually a significant event, but this one would be more important to Ember's family because Ember's cousin Heather was to be joined with a man from a neighboring tribe. Heather was named for a flower that bloomed purple and gave the grassy meadows some needed color in the late thawing season. The lucky man, Vance, would probably come to call Ember's longhouse home and ally himself with her tribe. Both Heather and Vance would stand before the tribe and agree to live as one. This was an exciting and wonderful event that happened once or twice a harvest, at best.

Ember momentarily considered the eventual day when a man might choose her from another tribe. Would he join her tribe, or would she be forced to leave her home and venture elsewhere? The thought scared her, yet her fear brought a sense of exhilaration as well. Ember had always been excited by the prospect of adventure, and soon she might just get it. This was not only the Great Lunar Festival or even a joining, but also the day chosen as Ember's coming of age. On this day, she would become a woman. She had put off even thinking about it until this moment, but the intrusive thoughts eventually wormed their way back into her mind.

Ember continued her alterations between fear and exhilaration as she left the village and strode down the small but well-worn, dirt path which led to the river. Behind her, a token palisade of wooden poles and several ditches kept the village's boundaries in order without really gaining much security. Tribes farther away from the river, who relied on farming more heavily or mining, required better walls and traps to discourage raiders. This was not as critical to Ember's people, who fished and gathered much of their foodstuffs from the river. The collected foodstuffs could quickly be replenished and did a raiding party little good. Not only did the river provide a passive form of protection, but the river was the mainstay of the tribe providing water, food, and building materials. Houses were patched with reed, mud, and clay. The bellies of those workers were filled with shellfish, amphibians, fish, and animals lured to the water.

The river was the center of most of the tribes' activities. In the morning and evening, the younger men and women would fish, primarily for sturgeon and salmon, using simple spears. Many would use nets to catch the numerous varieties of small fish that swam in schools close to shore. The older women would clean clothing and gather reeds for weaving as the children helped and played. At the end of the day, villagers could often be found cleaning and dressing the animals they had hunted earlier that day.

Aside from working by the water, nearly everyone in the tribe bathed each morning, and sometimes at night, on any day warm enough to do so. Every tenday from the start of the cold season until the beginning of the hot season, a large fire would be set by the water, and those who needed extra cleaning would take a quick dip in the cold waters or wash by hand. The fire would provide the required instant warmth to allow such cleaning during the cold season. When the worst of the cold season came, the water would become too cold for anyone, fire or no. Washing was then performed by hand, one body part at a time. Ember's land could be a cold place, but the People of the Great River were hearty and robust.

Besides the fishing and gathering, the tribe grew many simple crops on several small, demarcated squares of land. However, nearly half of their food still came from hunting, fishing, and foraging. One of Ember's favorite dishes, boiled lentils with salt, came from those fields, and every few days, her turn came to spend an entire day working them. In this way, the work was distributed among the people just as the resulting crops.

With thoughts of boiled and heavily salted lentils on her mind, she skipped happily down the path feeling the cool soil on her bare feet. Most people were barefoot unless the weather was cold. Footwear was costly in time and resources to make, and usually saved for harsher weather.

Along the way to the river, she ventured off the path and behind a copse of trees where she found the small bushes of red-colored "sour berries," as they were called, which she picked each warm season. She squatted with her reed basket and began selecting the best berries, those free of insect damage. The berries were warmed by the Sun and ripe for the picking, bees and butterflies flying about liberally, though the berry bush's flowers had long withered. She quickly placed nearly as many berries in the little reed basket as she stuffed in her mouth and trotted off down the path toward the river. Her stomach grumbled from the tartness, but she didn't care.

Ember always made the worst work of harvesting. She generally stuffed herself with the majority of what she had picked. As a result, her duties often included fishing, which she was good at, and finding flint pieces along the river shore. Her mother probably doubted that she would stuff a live fish in her mouth, though she had done this so many times with small shellfish she had found. She paused for a moment to savor the memories of tasty river mussels. She often found them in the mud by the banks and ate them raw. The taste was sweet but chewy. Her mother seemed more amused by her daughter's inability to forage, with any net return, than angered by her antics. With a smile, she burped loudly and continued to skip lightheartedly down the path towards the river where she knew her mother would be working. Perhaps the rest of her family was there, too.

She heard the river before she saw it – the rushing sound of water mixed with the muffled sounds of children playing and women laughing. Then, as she rounded the bend, the river came into view in all its glory. It was a vast expanse of water nearly twice as wide as the village with pebbly shores and gently moving waters. At the shore, women cleaned caught fish and herded the children out of the more dangerous deeper waters and into the small shoals where they might look for the finely colored stones which could be crafted into trade wares. Just to her right, a large pile of mollusk shells stood piled. An older woman with a lovely bear claw necklace knelt next to them cooking river mussels over a small fire while a young girl carried a fresh basket of shellfish for cooking.

Most of the women wore woven bark fiber string skirts, leather hides draped from waist cords, and an occasional woven plant fiber skirt or fish skin leather clothing while the children ran about the same way they entered the world. Some of the younger women, hoping to catch the eye of any men from neighboring villages who might wander by the river or even tempt a local man, wore fine necklaces of multicolored beads made from the pearls of a spiny mollusk one day known as a Spondylus, or even a colorful bird feather in their hair. Their faces were painted with more striking patterns, zigzagging lines or dots, than the married women. Ember thought they looked pretty and their finery quite beautiful, if not cumbersome, in the water.

In the deeper water, several of the older boys could be seen with small spears catching fish. The older boys and younger men stood nude, unlike the women, though some opted for thin animal skins wrapped around their waists or a loincloth. The younger men were hoping to catch the eyes of women with their fishing skills, each trying to outdo the next. Ember watched them for a moment before she continued her quest for her mother. Their antics were also amusing as they each tried as hard as they could to spear a large fish, preferably when one of the unmarried women was looking.

Ember tended to spend her warm days in the deeper water fishing for larger fish, like the boys and younger men. But most of the time, it was too cold, and she would have to rely on a fishing spear with a tether to retrieve it from the bank. Luckily, the water was warmer than usual from the warm temperatures of late. Often, she would watch both the younger women and men, yet she never did more than look. One day, she would be forced to choose, but she would avoid that day as long as possible.

After a moment's scan of the bank, her eyes settled upon her mother, East. She sat upon the ground cleaning a fish not ten lengths of a man from the path where Ember stood. She looked up and smiled at her daughter, who quickly walked over and knelt beside her. East was cleaning a large salmon with a thin flint blade. The blade was probably a small flake from a flint knapper, someone skilled in the craft of creating tools from flint or obsidian. Such flakes were kept and tooled using firm pressure to shape them into tiny but useful knives. Today, the flint was being used to dress salmon, a favorite catch because of their delicious meat.

Gutting was required for any animal before it could be cooked and eaten. The entrails would first be removed and discarded. Eating entrails or allowing any of their "poisons" into the body could make one very ill. This was common wisdom passed down from mother to daughter. However, many of the organs were kept and eaten for their nutritional value. Great care was required when removing and separating these organs from entrails and other discarded pieces. This was a task at which East was quite proficient.

"It's always nice when you awaken merely to see how the rest of us work," she said sarcastically. Ember shrugged and let the comment roll off her. She had been guilty of sleeping late many times in her life, and she wasn't about to let her mother get to her.

"You will have to be more considerate of others when you become a woman. Or do you plan to remain a girl for your entire life? You could even start by sitting down beside your tired mother and helping her with these fish. They don't gut themselves, you know," she said, gesturing to a few eels and several fish of different sorts beside her. Ember held back a smile as she thought of a self-gutting fish, causing East to frown. Then, changing the subject, Ember held out the small reed basket and sat it beside her mother.

"You're right. I should be more considerate. I picked some sour berries for you on my way over because I know how hard you work." Smiling to herself, Ember's smug expression drew an incredulous look from her mother, who was not fooled a bit by her daughter's weak explanation.

"Well, at least, you always know how to talk your way out of any situation," her mother said, eyeing the delicious gift. "Here, make yourself useful and carry these fish back to the village for the festival," she said, indicating a reed mat-wrapped bundle of small, cleaned fish and organs. Salmon were usually relatively large, though these were small fish, each being no longer than Ember's arm in length and the width of her leg.

"I'll get right to it, but first, the water calls!" Ember said as she leaped up and broke into a run toward the river giving her mother no time to reply. East merely sat there shaking her head as she flicked another fish onto the pile.

When will that fool girl ever take anything seriously? She's just like her father, East wondered, her thoughts drifting back toward her long past Winterborn. She wondered if that was one of the reasons she always had such difficulty staying mad at her wayward daughter.

Ember stripped her clothing as she ran, leaving her bark fiber skirt and leather wrap-handled flint knife in a small line headed to the water. With a great leap, she flew into the water, causing a vast splash, drawing the ire of everyone fishing nearby. She could hear several people shouting angrily.

Perhaps they are just jealous. My swimming is pretty good, she mused.

Ember took a deep breath and swam beneath the water. Though it was the late warm season, the water was only mildly warm on the surface and became quite cold as she touched the river's bed, her body gliding just near the bottom of the shallow bank. Ember swam out from the shore into water just deeper than a man stood tall. Any farther, and she would have to deal with the stronger current. Several times before, she had been pulled away by those stronger currents and had to swim her way, slowly, back to shore. The last time, just a tenday ago, she had drifted away from her laughing friends, a frowning smirk and rolled eyes the whole way.

After a moment, she opened her eyes under the water to have a look. The river was silty and hard to see in, but Ember kept scanning the bottom of the river for the telltale reflection of high-quality stones. Usually, the river was decently clear, but the lack of recent rain and the very uncommon wave of heat had lowered the level of the river, producing a much siltier swimming experience. In the darkness of the silty water, Ember felt a sense of wonder and fear.

Atlantic Sturgeon

To her right, she caught a glimpse of sudden movement. A closer look revealed what was most likely a sturgeon nearly half her size. The giant fish quickly swam away towards the deeper part of the river.

Hello, fish! How's the water? I am going to eat your friends tonight! She usually tried to keep her mind free and lighthearted, but there was always an ever-present edge of danger when swimming in the river. Coming up for a much-needed breath of air, she laughed and then dove deeply once more. If she were a bug or small fish, she would have been frightened, but a sturgeon was not likely to try and chew on her. They would both be stuck if it did, for only about half of her body would have fit. Instead, the fish would find itself with half of a girl protruding from its mouth.

She choked back a laugh at the thought, causing her to lose her recently acquired air. Water insects and even a curious duck parted way as Ember reemerged from the water and once more took a deep breath of warm air. In her mouth, she tasted the pleasant motes of a cooking fire, likely preparing the night's meals. Momentarily blinking as she watched the annoyed duck swim off, she again dove deep toward the black and silty depths.

As she reached the bottom of the river, Ember extended her hands and felt through the silty bed for smooth flint pieces. The cool current of the river and the dark depths of the water made each dive a small adventure. Then, a gleam of light caught her eye, ending her musings. She reached out for the object which produced the reflection. It was a small yet overly heavy piece of stone. She palmed the stone as her lungs began to burn. She continued for a moment longer, feeling about the silt when her right hand rubbed over something smooth and large.

Hello my prize, she thought. Her lungs cried for air, and her body forced her to the surface. Then, with a few quick breaths and not even a moment spared to examine the first find, Ember dove again to recover what she had just felt in the silt. Once more, on the bottom of the river's edge, she reached into the dark silt and again felt the same smooth object. Its surface was hard as stone but as smooth as shell. Her fingers probed through the cold, silty bed, trying to dig under the object. She quickly confirmed what she had found, the smooth side of a large piece of flint.

The suction created when removing rocks from the silt always made the large rocks a multistage dive. On her next dive, she retrieved the large piece and tugged it to the surface. The stone was heavy and difficult to carry while swimming. She slowly emerged from the cool river, soaked but with a smile on her face. Ember waded out of the water with her large flint piece, twice her foot size, and the small but overly heavy stone. This was much more fun than cleaning fish.

On the shore, she took a closer look at her two finds. The first was not an ordinary stone but a yellowish, shiny, dense, and malleable rock that some villagers had shaped into pendants for necklaces or even exchanged for goods with traders from the East and South. The yellow stone weighed nearly four times what a rock of the same size should have weighed and was the size of a baby's balled fist. The quick, excited dives and sight of Ember lugging something from the water had attracted the attention of children playing nearby. Several of the children gathered around her to see what she had found.

Among them, she noticed her little cousin Fox. Fox was young, having seen a mere nine harvests, but she already had the beginnings of womanhood and a pair of striking blue eyes. Ember was quite confident Fox would grow into a beautiful woman in not many harvests' time. Smiling, she placed the heavy yellow rock in Fox's hand and gave her a wink. Fox giggled and ran off with the other children chasing her to see what she had been given. Unfortunately, such stones were not of much worth to her people. Ember had already collected a few over the harvests. If she traded the stone to a southern trader, it would fetch something of quality, but today the flint find was worth much more.

Ember picked up her knife and skirt, reattaching it quickly to save a little of her dignity. She then knelt to examine the large piece of flint which she had found. It was a tan color and nearly as large as a child's head but shaped more like her foot. As she removed the silt and mud, she realized that she had truly found something valuable, for this wasn't a regular piece of flint; this was a large flint nodule. A nodule was a large piece of high quality and very workable flint which, in the hands of a skilled knapper, could be transformed into incredible knives, arrow or spearheads, or even tiny pendants used to channel the power of the gods. East looked up from her work to regard her oddly lucky daughter.

"So, you did it again... woke late, skipped on your chores, and still returned better than you started, aye? One last time, dear?" East yelled from her pile of fish. Ember smiled back with a mockingly toothy grin. After some stern looks from the other women who regarded her actions as childish, Ember walked back to the village with her flint under one arm and East's fish under the other, leaving wet footprints along the path. A flint nodule was indeed a worthy achievement for any day. Ember couldn't help but relish the delightfully jealous looks from the other women as she passed. She had awoken late and not even caught a single fish, yet she had just discovered a wondrous item which surely pleased the gods and would place her in excellent favor with the Elders of the tribe. Unfortunately, this was also the sort of behavior that got her into the most trouble.

Oh well, too bad, she mused.

CHAPTER THREE
THE GREAT LUNAR FESTIVAL

Neolithic clothing has long been underappreciated by much of archaeology for several reasons, including the scarcity of material evidence and an odd perception that fashion is purely aesthetic and contributes little to understanding a culture. In fact, clothing and adornments are critical to understanding many aspects of culture. This view has finally gained traction in archaeology. Unfortunately, many museum exhibits and illustrations of Neolithic people continue to depict them wearing cloth tunics, often of styles and complexity, which would not be seen in Europe for another 3000 to 5000 years. While the scholarly data almost universally supports a completely different view of Neolithic clothing, its depiction to the general public remains mostly inaccurate: the "noble savage" trope. In short, when you see a Neolithic Person wearing a textile robe, full-length dress, or full cloth tunic, this is most likely wildly inaccurate.

Ember's people, the Linear Pottery Culture, often abbreviated as LBK, after their German name, Linearbandkeramik, are considered an early Neolithic culture in Western Europe. However, the Neolithic had been underway in other parts of the world for many thousands of years beforehand. LBK clothing would likely have appeared much the same as Late Mesolithic clothing in Western Europe, owing to similar technological capabilities and nearly the same materials and environmental pressures. While limited textiles would have been used, as they were also likely used by Mesolithic people, the predominant materials would probably have been leather, fur, and grasses. Garments would have been heavily layered, made of smaller pieces combined to create larger ensembles. For example, a wrap skirt of leather with an optional leather or fur shawl or vest-like upper garment would have been worn instead of a single-piece textile dress. Instead of pants, leggings connected to a waist-cord and a loincloth would have been worn.

As the Sun settled low on the horizon, Ember returned to the family longhouse to prepare for the festivities. She had spent much of her day gossiping with her friends and enjoying herself. She never could keep on task and was often just allowed to do as she pleased. Such antics were the way of children. But she was no longer a child. Her hands and feet were dirty from the riverbank, and she felt like she needed to tidy up a bit before the festivities. She generally attended such events merely to have fun and eat her fill of tasty snacks. However, on this night, her ascension into womanhood, she would have to put on a better appearance. She wasn't sure what she might wear, but perhaps she could borrow something from her mother.

As she lifted the leather flap of the longhouse, she noticed that more of the family had returned after the day's chores to prepare. Her mother East, her grandmother Blue River, known to most as "Na Na," and several of her extended family, including her very young cousins Red Flowers, Fox, and Fox's mother Blue Skies, were sitting on reed mats preparing for the event. Fox's father and Red Flowers' family were nowhere in sight, but they probably had tasks preparing for the event. Fox took note of Ember as she searched for the missing family members.

"Everyone else is getting ready," Fox said in a matter-of-fact tone. This was indeed the case, for Na Na applied white paint to her and Fox's face while Red Flowers applied small feathers to Na Na's white hair. Red Flowers was quite shy though she was merely eight harvests old. She had similar red hair to Ember and always wore a smile. She liked to spend her days with Na Na watching her paint zig-zag lines on the pottery made by the younger women. Much of the tribes' pottery was made of brownish clay with white and black lines applied to the neck or grooves cut through the clay. This pattern identified the tribe, as well as the family who owned the pot.

Na Na often added a ring of small dots around the neck. The dots represented the strength of her people and were also worn by any warrior or hunter of the tribe in times of danger or when the strength of the people was needed. Ember had borrowed this simple pattern as a personal style for her facial paints, which she usually wore on special occasions, but had recently started wearing almost every day.

Ember noticed that her mother was sifting through a basket of clothing, searching for the correct garment to wear. East lifted a woven nettle-fiber skirt dyed red and compared it to a linen skirt adorned with feathers in her other hand. Both were her best, being very valuable and easily damaged. The correct choice of garment was critical for a major festival, at least for social reasons. It wouldn't do to have one's choices critiqued for the next tenday by the rest of the tribe.

EMBER OF A NEW WORLD

"Well, I just don't know. I like the linen, but it's just too stiff. I'd beat it soft, but the feathers would be damaged," East said, giving herself a worried frown.

"Choose the nettle skirt. That stiff linen hurts worse than feeding twins if you dance long enough in the chill," said Na Na with a cackle of a laugh. East carefully folded the linen outfit and placed the red nettle fiber skirt aside for the event. Poor Na Na had mistaken the skirt for a shirt, though East wasn't going to correct her. The comment had reminded her, however. The temperature fell at night just enough that she would prefer a shirt, which she began digging for. As she finished, East noticed that Ember had entered the longhouse.

"I suppose you want to borrow something of mine," she asked? Ember nodded, reaching for East's clothing basket.

"No. Not this time," East replied with a tone of ire, drawing a confused look from the redhead. All around, others bit back laughter and smiles.

"But I don't have anything nice to wear!" Ember began to protest, but East spoke louder, cutting her off.

"Why don't you wear your apron?" East suggested.

"I never made one," Ember replied, a bit confused as everyone knew this and her lack of textile skills had been the center of much teasing.

Well, I guess you won't become a woman this season," East chided, repressing a smirk. Ember frowned, though she didn't snap back a reply. In truth, the idea of being a woman never felt right to her, yet it was expected among her people. There were men, women, and wergene (plural), a third gender. There had been no signs she was a wergena (singular), at least not enough to warrant her proclaiming this, yet the older she got, the less like a girl she felt. Could she be a wergena? There were no wergene in her tribe, yet she had met them when they traded from other tribes. Her easily side-tracked thoughts snapped back as Na Na spoke.

"Well look at this, it seems our Little Fox wove an apron and didn't tell us," quipped Na Na, nodding to a new basket beside Ember's bed, one she had never seen before, and using East's pet name for Ember. Her apron? Had the entire longhouse gone quiet with anticipation, or was it her imagination? Ember approached the basket, kneeling before it and opening the lid. Inside lay a green-dyed, woven garment neatly folded. She removed it, holding it to the flickering firelight to examine. It was a gorgeous, woven apron. The single square panel of twined cloth was nearly two hands wide and three long, with tassels hanging two hands below that. It had been woven to show a series of V shapes down the center, a typical pattern of river people. The woven V shapes were further embellished with bone beads at regular intervals. Along the bottom, various red stone beads had been tied. It was a marvelous garment of exquisite beauty, the sort of garment an older girl or young woman wore before joining.

Below the apron lay a red fur fox tail with a braided loop allowing it to be attached to the apron, providing a covering to the otherwise open back and matching her long, red hair. Together, she would have not only a similar style of garment to the other girls but perhaps the grandest of all. Usually, a girl would spend many seasons learning to weave and manufacture such textiles. Were they just handing her such a prize?

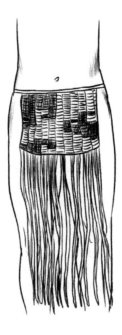

A Typical Neolithic apron garment

Ember nearly fell to the floor as her legs became weak. She had never seen such a beautiful tunic. How had her mother procured this marvel? The garment may have taken a good weaver and beader part of a season to make. She looked at her mother with teary eyes and asked that very question with her stunned silence. East smiled at her awed and rarely speechless daughter, truly a marvel, and waited for Ember to sink to her knees on the matted floor before explaining.

"This past thawing season, when the traders came from the South, I traded for the apron. Your grandmother and I added the beads while you were off searching for flint, fishing, and otherwise not doing what you were supposed to be doing. You should not be surprised. Just two of those yellow rocks were more than enough for the trade. You may spend your days acting like a boy, but tonight you will have the proper apron of a woman."

Ember, still stunned, looked back at the apron. She would be the most beautiful girl – wait no, on this eve she became a woman – she would be the most beautiful woman in the village. Ember stood and rushed to her mother so fast that East nearly fell backward. Ember squeezed East as hard as her arms could. She was not a member of a major family of the tribe, but she would surpass them all that night. Afterward, she hugged Na Na, though with a bit less force, less she crush her beloved grandmother.

"But why? I didn't work to make this? I'm not exactly a great daughter," she finally asked. East shook her head, but Na Na was the first to reply.

"You are terrible at being a girl and barely know the ways of a woman, but you are who you are. You are great at being Ember. You did plenty of work, just not in the ways of others. You hunted, gathered flint and shells, and even helped with repairing the longhouse. You did your part, just differently. So, we took care of the rest," she said with a toothless grin. Ember had trouble, for the first time, expressing her gratitude. In fact, she had never been any good at doing what a girl was supposed to do in her society, but that had never seemed to bother Na Na or East. They had mainly been angered by Ember's innate laziness more than anything else.

"Thank you," she said, too overwhelmed to say more. Releasing her grandmother and stepping backward, Ember took a deep breath and carried the apron and a clay pot of water to the back of the longhouse where she might prepare in privacy. If she had stayed, she would have burst into tears. A moment later, she sat on an old deerskin and removed her skirt, taking care not to touch the clothing against her dirty feet or hands any more than could be helped. Ember next poured some of the water into a large shallow clay dish and washed her hands. Afterward, she applied her feet to the water, one at a time, carefully cleaning each foot and removing the water from her feet with drying sand. Scrubbing with sand made the skin soft and very clean, as long as the sand was fine.

She wiped a tear of joy and continued, trying not to become overwhelmed by the lovely gift. After discarding the water through the small back entrance of the dwelling, she set to work preparing her hair. Ember spent the next few moments brushing the tangles from her hair, starting with a long piece of wood carved into a smooth, single shaft as thin as a finger, about two hands long, which removed the nasty tangles. Afterward, she used a five-tooth comb made from finely polished driftwood, a trinket from a trader from the East nearly two harvests before. Combs were time-consuming to make and delicate, so great care was used to ensure they didn't break.

Some of the oils had washed from her hair as she swam, leaving it clean and fresh. Once she was convinced her hair was combed free of tangles and in generally good order, she proceeded to fasten several tiny bird feathers to it at varying lengths using small pieces of plant fiber as thread to tie them. She glanced over her shoulder to see her mother giving her a nod of approval. She swallowed a lump in her throat as the excitement grew.

Just like you taught me, mother, she thought as she finished her hair. East had just donned her own garb and was about to step out, presumably to help prepare the feast. Ember smiled a warm farewell, though she noticed that Na Na and the girls had already left.

"Don't be late tonight. For the first time in your life," East said with a half-smile leaving Ember to work.

Making myself beautiful is a time-consuming job, indeed, Ember thought, though she wondered why she had become so enthusiastic about the celebration.

Tonight, she would stick with a classic look. She began by smearing her body in red ochre. Once completed, she used a mixture of twice burned wood and bone ash mixed with nut oil to paint horizontal black stripes around her entire body. The look was striking, she hoped, though it was traditionally the design worn by younger men. She suspected that would be noticed, though she didn't care. Just because she was becoming a woman did not mean she had to act like one.

Ember used plenty of paint, applying rich coats to her face and down her back. Painting her own back was a difficult task. Had Fox remained, Ember would have asked her to help. Instead, she used a thin strip of soft leather to rub back and forth across her back, smearing and staining it with paint. Ember took a moment to inspect her arms and considered how striking she looked. She might not fit in, but she would definitely leave her mark on the village.

Using the same blackened pot filled with water from the morning as a reflecting pool, she applied several small black dots in a horizontal line, her personal design, below her eyes on each side of her face. Four dots under each eye. This time, she made the dots much larger. Tonight, she hoped to attract the attention of everyone. Perhaps, even the gods.

With her paint finished, it was time for the final touch to complete her look. She lifted the beautiful apron, marveling at its beadwork and lovely patterns. She placed it against her waist and wrapped its two free cords around her, taking a moment to ensure the foxtail was looped through before she tied the garment tightly around her waist. The soft tail hung behind, tickling her skin nearly as much as the apron fringe.

Oh well, if I am to be a woman, I might as well show everyone what that means, she thought as she spun, letting the apron and tail fly outward. Ember looked at herself in the blackened reflection pot and was overwhelmed. Was she already a woman? Tears welled as the rush of excitement built within her chest and tingled down her spine to her toes in waves. The anticipation of the night was overwhelming. She quickly got a soft leather rag to wipe the tears and fix her paint. Tonight, was a night to laugh and enjoy, not cry.

The night air was cooler than the day but still warmer than normal. She lifted the deer hide door and stepped out into the night. All around, fireflies lit the sky with little motes of light while the sounds of uncountable insects and frogs filled the night air as if competing with the distant sounds of the festival. Ember stood and stretched, preparing her body for the night-long dancing. If she didn't stretch her body, an injury was assured. As far as she was concerned, stretching was one of the more pleasurable things a person could do and a perfectly acceptable way to spend a hot afternoon.

To her right, not far off, was a large fire burning high into the night air, perhaps the height of a man. Ember watched as many of her people danced around the blaze, thoroughly enjoying themselves. At this early point, dancers of all ages mainly were just having a good time to the sound of music. Off to the side, many food items were laid out on thick reed mats for the taking. The fine foods included strips of roasted pork, various pâtés of meats and fish organs, roasted tubers, roasted deer liver, lentils with salt, Ember's favorite, and berries of many types. The grandest foods were the giant roasting spits with whole deer, boar, and small birds crackling and sizzling. Some of the younger men cut pieces for a line of people who couldn't stop licking their lips at the sight.

As Ember passed through the village, the wind reminded her how revealing her new outfit was. There was a sort of existential excitement to the feel of the warm night breeze on her bare skin and the promise of an exciting night. Ember could feel tingles of excitement and thrill dancing up and down her body, as she slowly approached the fires. Under her breath, she whispered a prayer to the fire spirits for an eventful and exciting night. Finishing her prayer, she took a moment to take in the sights.

Women, children, and men alike sat on the grass or on mats near the flame watching the dancing while eating the delicious food. Nearly the entire village was present, with only a few hunters guarding the village perimeter. Those hunters would eventually trade-off with a second group of men allowing all to partake in the rituals and celebration. In total, Ember's tribe consisted of about eighty men and a slightly larger number of women, not counting children. As far as tribes went, hers was of medium size. Ember had heard of giant tribes to the East where such ceremonial events could last days. She was glad for the shortness of her Lunar Festival, as the emotions and shear physical work involved were a bit much for her tastes.

"Ember! Ember!" called a voice. She turned to see her friends Fire Blossom and Kanter rapidly approaching. Fire Blossom, "Ehkne Aneha," in her language, was generally called "Blossom" by her friends. She was named for a small red flower that grew in the area. Ironically, Fire Blossom spent much of her time hanging around Ember, and jokes were often made. It was sometimes said, "Where there's an Ember, there's often a Fire." The jokes were entirely accurate. In fact, the two girls had grown up together and were good friends.

Beside Blossom strode Kanter, a young lad from the opposite corner of the village. Kanter and his mother had joined the tribe many harvests before after his father and uncle had been killed while the quartet traveled. Kanter was originally from a different tribe, and his name had some meaning in another language. She had asked him the meaning many times, but he had always dodged her questions. Kanter was very shy about his past and even his birth tribe. In fact, it was generally suspected that only the elder members of the tribe even knew the details. Ember certainly did not. Maybe one day he would tell her the meaning... or perhaps she had other ways of learning. She might be able to convince Blossom to coax the meaning of Kanter's name through any number of insidious means. Such manipulations took careful cunning and plotting, something Ember was less than good at. She shook her head, dismissing the amusing, if not ill-advised ideas.

Kanter was dressed in a soft leather wrap around his waist and many long hawk feathers in his hair. His face was painted lightly red with ocher paint, little black dots evenly spaced throughout. His chest and back had been painted with black horizontal stripes. Blossom wore a wide leather apron hanging to her knees and flowers in her hair attached at various lengths instead of her usual fish leather skirt. She wore red face paint, like Kanter, but darker and with subtle zig-zagging patterns. Tonight, wasn't Blossom or Kanter's night for adulthood, so they had dressed less spectacularly, though their times would come.

"Hey!" Ember yelled back from a distance as they approached. Kanter and Blossom were a pair, seeming more closely related to a joined couple than either of their parents knew. The following warm season would see them both become recognized as adults. Only time would tell if they would remain a pair, but for now, they were inseparable. Ember knew that such a union would bring with it the answers to Kanter's origins, but Ember would be forced to wait quite a long time. Her friends being closer to the fire, Ember had seen their outfits before they could see hers. When they did, Blossom's mouth fell open.

"How did you... You can't weave! Where did you get... that?!" she asked. Blossom turned, shooting a confused look at Kanter, which quickly shifted to an angry glare when she noticed Kanter was carefully examining Ember from head to foot. She poked him hard in the side with her pointer finger, which brought his attention back to her. She glared at Kanter, scolding him all the while, as she continued to speak.

"Did you make that?" she asked.

Ember smiled and blushed with embarrassment, not that it could be seen under so much paint. She quickly spun, letting the foxtail fly where it could be seen, drawing a shocked gasp from Blossom. Kanter worked to ensure his eyes remained fixed upon Ember's, lest he feel Blossom's fiery wrath.

"Well, I *can* weave, sort of. My mother traded for it. I guess all those yellow stones were needed elsewhere. Anyway, tonight only comes once. If I am to be a woman, I might as well attract a man. This should work, right?" Ember finished with a slight edge of regret in her tone. Blossom and Kanter both nodded, wide eyed. Ember had not really contemplated finding a lover, but she was open to the possibility, wherever it might be found. It was both an exciting idea, as well as a source of dread.

"If you need to attract one, that is." Blossom squeezed Kanter closer, indicating him with a smirk. The three friends laughed and journeyed merrily toward the large fire and celebrations. Kanter was significantly confused by the exchange between the girls but laughed anyway.

As the trio approached the fire, the shapes they had seen dancing around the fire took on faces and names. Ember called out to several of the partygoers, who waved back with enthusiasm. There were men and women wearing their best outfits and painted from head to toe with designs in brightly colored paint. Most of the dancing men had various headdresses, often resembling the antlers of deer or the horns of bulls, secured with leather cords. Many of the women wore string or woven skirts, as well as aprons and even a few feather garments. They decorated the rest of their bodies with paints, feathers, and their finest jewelry. All around, people danced enthusiastically to the beat of the drums and communal singing. Ember felt truly alive as she took in the sights, smells, and sounds.

"We should dance before we eat. Remember River Breeze last harvest? I've never seen someone eat so much before dancing!" Blossom said with a laugh.

"...and she was doubled over for half of the night afterward," Kanter added. Just then, Ember rounded on both, beaming a smile at each.

"Who cares what we do? We need to have fun while we still can. Don't you see? This is the last night I am still just a child. In a few seasons from now, both of you will be in my place. So, we should just let go... just for tonight." She was caught up in the moment, and her excitement was intoxicating. To this proclamation, Blossom gave Kanter a sly wink.

"I think you're on to something. Who knows where the wind blows," she exclaimed. Kanter stared at Blossom with a confused and slightly hopeful look. She knew what he wanted, but she would let him dangle as long as possible. Blossom's unquenched temptations had started as an essential act, for unjoined women didn't have children often, but now it had become a sort of sport, a game she played. Ember gave her a knowing look and shook her head. She could see the appeal, yet she felt a bit sad for poor Kanter. He really was a nice guy, if not a bit chaotic.

During the early part of the night, the tribe danced, ate, and made merry throughout the festival area. Ember, Blossom, and Kanter joined the dance, twirling and moving to the natural beats of hide and gourd drums, sound sticks, and singing. As Ember spun and bounced, her apron and tail flowed like a great storm around her body, tossing this way and that. Many of the people had come in their finest outfits, but none rivaled

Ember, and she knew it. The point was made nearly immediately after she started dancing when a girl with long blonde hair, though currently red as it was caked in red ochre, named Yellow Flowers, caught her attention.

Visible disgust and envy filled Yellow Flowers' eyes at the sight of Ember's impressive attire. Yellow Flowers was to become a woman that night and was generally thought to have the best chance to choose her partner. She was, in effect, the premier girl, soon woman, of the event. Ember was considered attractive by her people's measure of beauty, but she was not glamorous, nor was she flashy. Instead, she was lithe and toned from long warm seasons of running with the boys and swimming. To her people, a proper woman was supposed to be more rounded and carry a little more weight. Ember was just shaped too much like a boy. If her skinny form wasn't enough to cause her trouble, Ember's beautiful apron and boyish body paint were just too much for Yellow Flowers to accept. The lanky redhead was stealing her presumed role quickly as she danced in a whirl of feathers, beads, and the flashy appeal that only such a lithe dancer could manage.

Yellow Flowers was utterly outraged, and to make matters worse, there were several young hunters from other tribes here tonight, increasing the impact of their sudden rivalry. Yellow Flowers wore beautiful clothing, much like Ember's, but just not unique enough to set her apart. The sight of Ember's apron sent her into a fit of frustrated anger. She threw her hands aside and stormed from the dance with her latest ephemeral boyfriend following closely behind.

"I didn't mean it, Flowers! Whatever I did, I didn't mean it..." the confused boy said as he raced after her. Ember and Blossom laughed as the boy, about Kanter's age, chased after Yellow Flowers, making things much worse with his lack of understanding. Kanter watched the whole spectacle and realized that he would never understand women. He surmised that Yellow Flowers had left the dance for a reason other than her date. That was all he, or the majority of men and boys, could deduce, not being privy to the secret networks of women and girls.

Gods, please grant me the strength to handle them and the courage to keep my mouth shut, for they make absolutely no sense, he prayed to himself as he watched Blossom glide over to him with an oddly sly look.

The dancing continued for a reasonable length of time afterward and became more and more formal as time progressed. Special dance moves and lyrics were used as each member of the tribe who danced geared their collective dancing towards pleasing the gods. At a specific time, everyone in the dancing group fell to the ground or genuflected, as was part of the ritual of the song. Ember fell to the cool ground laughing and trilling and laid still for a moment with her eyes closed. When she opened them again, she was staring directly into a sky full of stars.

For a brief moment, she was struck by the beauty of those mysterious points of light. Her people called them the "Eyes of the gods." As she looked, she thought she saw a star appear and vanish, leaving a short streak of light in its wake. As she looked on, she didn't see anything like it again. She closed her eyes once more and held them shut for a moment until she heard people laughing and standing. She opened her eyes and quickly looked to ensure that her apron was in good order. Above her, she thought she saw another streak, but her attention was caught by a blue feather.

Not but a few hand lengths away, a blue feather had fallen. Ember touched the feather but then pulled her hand back suddenly, thinking that she had seen a snake. The "snake" turned out to be a root protruding from the ground. Ember snatched the feather and crawled aside, out of the way of the dancers as they resumed their joyful festivities and fastened it back into place. As she began to stand, she felt two eyes boring into her. Ember, still on her knees, slowly turned to come face to face with little Fox. Fox blinked her large, blue eyes. She smiled and pointed at Ember, accusation in her gesture.

"A root scared Ember! A root scared Ember!" With that, Fox ran off making fun. The encounter was quite strange, though slightly amusing to the random redhead.

Children... I was never one of those... she thought.

As the dance began to wind down, the Elders came forward to perform rituals. The Elders were half a dozen old men and women who controlled the tribe in an executive fashion. Each elder was elaborately painted and decorated in their best clothing. In addition, each sported various necklaces and other adornments indicating special merit and status. The leader of the tribe was a wise old man named Aurochs. He stepped forward with a semi-serious grin on his face.

An aurochs was a large and powerful bovine, almost like a larger version of a bison, that some tribes actually kept and bred for food. However, the variety kept by tribes seemed to be smaller and tamer. The man Aurochs was a bit like a bull, being quite muscular and imposing. Aurochs had the look of a mighty and authoritative hunter about him, someone to fear. He wore a wolf pelt over his back like a cape and a thick and well-constructed leather shirt. His legs were wrapped in leather leggings, a linen loincloth between them. Ember thought Aurochs was overdressed for the occasion, but that was the way of the mighty Aurochs. She doubted he would ever be defeated by an enemy, though he might die from the heat.

Mighty he was, but intimidating? Ember knew better. She had secretly watched the mighty hunter as he knelt on the ground and played with his granddaughter. He had held a small rabbit fur doll in his hand, and the two of them had played for a long time. Aurochs used his size and robust frame to keep those in line who needed a good enough reason or to force the hand of reluctant traders. In most affairs, Aurochs would defer to the other elders and merely back their decisions. This powerful but amenable disposition had seen him rise to the leader of the tribe, a man of true character.

Among the other elders in the group was Na Na, or Blue River, her real name. Na Na wore a fine wool wrap skirt with beads set into the cloth at varying lengths, and a shawl of bark fiber. The clothing was dyed pale blue, likely from the small yellow flowering plants that made a rich blue dye when ground and mixed with urine. Blue circles were painted down Na Na's arms, the tribal symbol of unity and strength. Around her neck, she wore necklaces with the symbols of various important gods and spirits etched into them. Na Na smiled at the sight of Ember and gave her a little wave.

The elders entered the circle around the fire, walking around the dance area where the edge of light radiating from the fire faded off several times while chanting. Each elder held a ceremonial stick adorned with feathers. As the Elders chanted, they slowly circled the fire in a large swinging radius from the center. They screamed and chanted, driving away any evil spirits and other nasty things which might hamper a proper ritual. During this time, they were cheered on by the tribe. After the prolonged and loud circumnavigation of the dance area, one of the elders, Dark Rock, approached the oldest female elder, Morning Dew.

"We have walked the dance with pure moves. Is the dance clear?" Dark Rock asked, to which Morning Dew entered a thoughtful pose. After a moment, she began to walk around the dance area, moving her hands this way and that way as if sensing for evil thoughts or spirits.

"She never finds anything bad," Blossom whispered to Ember.

"That's because your cousin Frog scares everything off," Ember replied, nodding at a board-looking boy not far from the elders. His name wasn't "Frog," but many thought that he somewhat sounded like one, so the name had stuck.

After a moment, Morning Dew looked around, as much at the tribe as at Dark Rock, and yelled, "The dance is clear! Let the ritual begin!" To this, the tribe let out nearly 170 breaths as one. Rituals were always a scripted affair with thanks to the gods being given the same way and with the same speeches by elders each time. Ember wondered if the gods might one day become bored with the repetition and find somewhere else to go. When she was a child, East had explained to her that the gods cared more about intent and less about the exact words. However, Ember knew that this was not a view held by all tribes and that some tribes considered their survival contingent upon the rituals' perfection.

The elders gathered in a circle around the fire and bade the hunting dancers come forward. Within moments, the elders and the fire were encircled by dancers holding favored weapons dancing in time with a fierce beat. The weapons were carefully wielded to prevent accidents, and some were not even genuine weapons, being ceremonial entirely. Given a correctly performed ritual, the coming cold season would be full of fresh game and warm hides. Ember truly didn't understand why the gods required so much fuss over some simple deer and game, but that was the way of things.

The affair was not without humor. Some of the smallest children wore little rabbit or bird costumes as they ran around the outside of the fire area. The costumes were merely rabbit pelts or a reed construct of feathers with small and quickly constructed ears or beaks. The hunters had trouble dancing as they laughed at the little children bounding in such funny costumes and making silly noises.

The most important parts of rituals were readings and signs. A pronounced sign or vivid reading could not be ignored, especially if the gods were to look favorably on the tribe that cold season. The gods had not called for anything to be given to them or any special tasks in a long time, but the tribe still offered the coming-of-age tasks, a task each newly created adult must perform, as a quasi-offering to the gods. A poor harvest or harsh cold season could devastate the tribe, and people could die, especially the old and the young. This was especially noticeable when the average life expectancy was only a little over thirty harvests if one counted from birth, though that was partly due to infant mortality. Counting from five harvests, life expectancy was a bit longer.

"I wonder what task they will give you?" Blossom commented.

Kanter smiled and whispered loudly enough for both girls to hear. "I heard from a trader two harvests past, and he looked truthful too, I can tell... anyway, I heard him say that a tribe to the far south sacrificed a person each harvest for good crops! I heard they took the blood and..."

"Be quiet, Kanter. Ember doesn't need anything to worry about. Besides, we don't do such things," said Blossom, quite annoyed. Sometimes she wondered if Kanter would ever mature into a normal man. While his overly childish musings were annoying, they were also often humorous and one of the reasons she loved him so much. She frowned at him, but deep down, she was glad he had stayed by her side for harvest after harvest. He was going to make a good husband, and probably sooner than he thought.

After a short time, the hunters left the area, and those with spiritual business came forward. There were couples seeking blessings for a child, a man seeking to heal from an injury, and finally those to be joined. The elders performed minor rituals for each of the people who came. For the couple seeking the blessings of a child, the woman to become pregnant was touched by each of the female elders and other women nearby. The woman's stomach was painted with a deep ocher paint, and seeds were placed into the thick ocher. Na Na came forward and chanted for the injured man as she applied a coating of mud to his wound. It was known that fresh mud could cause death, but when boiled with magic ingredients, the mud actually aided in healing. Ember suspected that the magical ingredients were the real reason and that boiling the mud was just for show.

The last to come forward was a young man who wished to join with a local woman. Everyone held their breaths as Vance stepped forward. Vance was a hunter from a close village to the East. He had short black hair and dark eyes, and a strongly defined face. Vance wore a finely crafted leather vest and leather wrap around his waist, as did many men at the dance. His face was painted with a single dark streak of paint from ear to ear, the custom of his people. This declaration from Vance had been anticipated for quite some time, and many waited eagerly to see what would happen. It was said that Ember's cousin Heather would be the woman Vance chose.

"Great elders, I have need of you this night," he called bravely.

"Oh... do you now, young hunter? Step forward and tell us about it," Black Rock said, unmoved by his words.

"I am Vance, son of the hunter Bael. I come from Deep Forest village to the East. I have come to join The Great River People as a hunter and to take a wife. What say you?" Behind Dark Rock, a young woman stood in the crowd, quite worried and anxious. Behind her stood an older and very impatient woman, her mother.

Get to it... you take too long, Dark Rock, the older woman thought. Dark Rock came upon Vance suddenly and with a fierce expression. Vance was visibly shaken, but he held his ground in the face of the mighty old hunter. Dark Rock's eyes belied a touch of respect for the younger man.

"You need more than skill to join our people. You need a link that binds your loyalty!" the older hunter said. Heather's impatient mother, West, Ember's aunt, had told Dark Rock to keep it quick and straightforward. The decision to allow Vance to join the tribe had been made the previous day by the Elders, in secret, and the theatrics now was causing Heather unneeded stress. Heather was a shy woman and far too nervous for anything too long. Dark Rock directly addressed the mass of people with the scripted words of the ritual. Behind a group of people, Heather waited with her mother for the coming moment. The entire ritual was choreographed, but the meanings were entirely true. If Heather became scared and ran, it could prevent Vance from joining.

"Is there a woman here who would take this man as a husband?" Dark Rock asked, skipping several common steps in order to expedite the ritual. Silence. Knowing that Heather had likely lost her nerve, Dark Rock continued, flipping the script.

"Have you a woman to call out, Vance of the Deep Forest village?"

"I have!" Vance announced. He turned and looked to where he knew Heather stood.

"Heather, daughter of Dargen and the potter West, will you be my wife? Will you stand beside me now?" he asked with as much gusto as he could muster. For a moment, nothing happened as a bead of sweat rolled down his face, and then Heather shyly stepped forward from the crowd. She wore a long leather wrap with painted black stripes and the circle pattern of the tribe painted down her chest. Heather had long brown hair let loose, as was the marital custom. Around her waist, a simple leather thong with attached river mussel shells was fastened. It was said only a virgin could wear the shells without them breaking or falling off.

Ember didn't know where the saying came from or even what it meant. Virginity was a bizarre trait to promote, in her opinion. So many rituals emphasized fertility and motherhood, which made the fixation upon virginity seem at odds with the fundamental values of her people, yet the custom had continued. Ember had fashioned such a waistband a harvest before, and she and Blossom had both worn it without issue. The custom had been adopted by other tribes and had become a fad of sorts in the region. Ember then noticed Yellow Flowers watching, and her naughty mind could not keep silent.

I bet she can't even lift a shell. They probably turn into powder in her hands. Perhaps they will paint them on her when the time comes, but would the paint run? Ember nearly laughed and caught herself. Such naughty thoughts were a fine delicacy.

Heather stepped forward to stand before Vance as she spoke, "I... I will stand with this man. He is a hunter... and will bring us good luck. We can plant our crops and eat fresh meat," she said nervously and almost too quietly to hear. Morning Dew stepped forward and nudged both Vance and Heather together, not wanting to let Heather's anxiety fester. Some people were simply different from the majority, such as Heather. The tribe loved her just the same and accommodated her anxiety and shy ways as a family.

"Vance, son of Bael, and Heather, daughter of Dargen and West, do each of you understand that you will now vow to live as one for the rest of your lives? Is this your choice?" Morning Dew asked, more terse than usual.

"Yes," both blurted in unison. Vance spoke so loudly that Heather's soft words weren't heard, yet everyone saw her lips move. West looked as though she might melt into the ground, her eyes welling with happy tears. She had been waiting for this moment for at least as long as Heather, and she had been ever so worried that her daughter wouldn't hold her nerve long enough to seal the bond.

"Then it is so. From this night forward, Vance is a hunter of our people and joined with Heather. May the gods bless you," Morning Dew proclaimed. Vance and Heather embraced passionately as the tribe cheered. She clung tightly to the hunter, likely warding off an entire tribe of onlookers, at least in her mind.

Meanwhile, Kanter was just glad it was over. He turned to say something but found both Ember and Blossom staring with wide glistening eyes and longing expressions. As the people cheered, Heather was lifted off her feet by Vance and gently carried away to some secluded place where they would consummate their joining, as well as be free of so many people. This was the way of things, and with any luck, a child would come by early thawing season. As Heather, carried by Vance, passed Ember, she gave her younger cousin a nervous smile.

After much dancing and talk of the new couple, the boys and girls to be declared men and women were called to the circle as the Elders returned. Sometimes, there would only be one boy or one girl, sometimes a few. On occasion, someone would be declared adult yet not man or woman, a third gender. No one of this gender had existed in her tribe for as long as Ember had lived, but they were not uncommon in other tribes.

This harvest's festival was overflowing with children coming of age. The unseasonably warm weather, coupled with the massive number of children and other "signs," which the elders had seen lately, suggested that this would be a special festival. Perhaps one of the boys would be sent on a journey to some far-reaching goal, like another tribe or a distant place. This was not commonplace, and it was dangerous, but any boy who completed such a task would return a man – more of a man than many of the men already present. He might even return with a mate from another tribe. Many boys secretly hoped and feared such a task, at the same time, though it was rare for such tasks to be very far-reaching.

Luckily, we girls get easier tasks. Who wants to go kill a deer or chew on a tree? Ember held back a laugh at her foolish thoughts. Her head was always filled with strange ideas and observations. She had made a habit of observing her own people and could often be found watching people doing their daily tasks. She had long ago learned that this was not the standard way of thinking among most people. But she supposed Na Na was right: she was good at being Ember.

A collection of four boys and two girls came forward to become adults. Each stood as tough and stern as they could, though fear and anticipation were easily seen in their eyes. The boys were the first to be seen.

Best for last, Ember thought as she strode forward to join Yellow Flowers, the other girl who was to become a woman. Yellow Flowers gave her a jealous look as she eyed the beautiful green apron, which contrasted Ember's red hair so well. If lightning could burst from her eyes at Ember, it would have. Yellow Flowers wore a lovely woven skirt of bark fiber, though a more earthy color and without beads or feathers. Over her head, she wore a flax fiber net with hundreds of tiny river snail shells forming a cap, her red ochred blonde hair just beneath. Yellow Flowers' family could have obtained a greater outfit but probably felt that it was not needed, given Yellow Flowers' well-known effects on any traveling men who came to the village.

In addition, she was nearly double Ember's weight and despite her youth, her breasts hung lower than most girls her age, both features considered highly attractive among her people. Ember couldn't match her weight and her own breasts had barely made their presence known, but that hardly mattered to the radiant redhead. She wasn't interested in finding a man, at least yet, and in her opinion, looks weren't everything. Besides, she'd love to see Yellow Flowers trying to run as fast and freely as she did. Ember held back a laugh as she approached the ritual area.

As the ritual continued, each of the boys was ceremonially brushed with a leafy branch by the elder women to "remove" evil spirits from their bodies. The tribe's markings, small circles, were applied to their faces, and a spear, or another such defensive weapon, was placed in their hand by elder men. Finally, each boy's name was announced loudly. Some changed their names from childish to adult, though not all boys opted for this.

"Where there was once a boy named Warm Sands, here now stands Strong Arm, son of Flint Blade, defender, and protector of the People," Dark Rock announced.

We are going to run out of new names, Ember thought. There are only so many different things to use as a name! Flint, water, east, west, north, south... Perhaps we might all choose two or even three names! No... Who could remember three names for each person? Maybe a family name, then a personal name? But maybe... Ember was always thinking and rarely about what she should be. Her thoughts were interrupted by a flash of light in the sky. It was another streak of light, just as before. The streak was short, and few seemed to notice. As she touched a pensive finger to her cheek, the ritual continued.

The eldest woman, Morning Dew, would come forward and touch the head and hands of each boy looking for signs or other supernatural indicators of particular tasks which must be performed for the gods. Generally, each new man or woman would be given a simple task to complete. Men often would be given the task of hunting at a distance, alone, or crafting an item of some quality. Women would be given tasks of creating beautiful works of weaving or pottery. On rare occasions, a man, or even more rarely a woman, would be sent off on a long journey to some distant place. Ember wasn't worried about a journey as it was uncommon for men and basically didn't happen to women. The last known time was a story told of a woman tens of generations before. It was a tragic story, and Ember recalled a bear being involved. She would most likely end up making some pot or other such object.

Ember waited with nearly unhealthy anticipation to see if any of the boys would be sent on some silly and dangerous task. There was a tribe to the Southwest where people found to have certain signs would sometimes travel to be ritualistically killed and offered to the gods. It was even said that some were ritually eaten, though this was something Kanter had said, so she wasn't entirely sure she believed it. Though the honor of being sacrificed to the Sun God or the Goddess of the Land was tempting to many as it guaranteed a prominent place in the next world. Ember wasn't so sure that she entirely believed the stories of the next world. She would live this life to its fullest, then worry about what came next.

Luckily, none of the men were found to have the sort of sign which might recommend their lives being given to a god or their bodies feasted upon. Each new man was given a hunting task, except for Strong Arm. He was the most accomplished of the new men and had already hunted many deer by himself. Morning Dew found various undisclosed "signs" on him. They told her that Strong Arm needed to journey to the East, to a nearby tribe, the same tribe Vance came from, and seek a brown-haired woman who would be his mate.

As it just so happened, such a girl was part of a traveling group that had stopped by the tribe just that thawing season. This was the way elders played their matchmaking game. In fact, Ember had caught Warm Sand's eye, or so Blossom had said. As the newly created Strong Arm, he could join with her if she was both amenable and wasn't already taken. She wasn't sure how she would react to such an event. Ember was open to the notion of love from any source, in general, though she had a distinct, if unlikely preference.

What ironic luck that there would be signs found by the matchmaker herself, old Dew, Ember thought ironically. For once, she would like to see a sign for herself. Where were her friends to discuss this? She looked back at Kanter, his mouth full of food, and Blossom, giving her an exaggerated wink. Ember wanted to gossip, but her turn was coming up, and she wanted to be on time for at least this event. She owed that to East, at least.

When the men were fully created new, they each hurried off to assert themselves as the new men they were, each immediately calling out a woman they had eyed for a time and starting their new tasks. After a few awkward interactions between the new men and several thrilled yet embarrassed women, two of the men had proposed their feelings successfully. By their right, the delighted women had accepted, leaving the third man to find a mate in a nearby tribe sometime soon and the fourth to do the same as part of his task.

A young woman, named Butterfly, agreed to an immediate joining. In contrast, the other woman, Cold Stream, opted for the next full moon. The second joining followed a similar theatrical ceremony as the first.

Afterward, everyone returned to the festivities as a young hunter carried his new bride off, presumably to the riverbank for joining bliss. Ember was sorry to see Butterfly go as she was a cheery person to hang around, but she was also happy for her. As she watched Strong Arm leave to prepare for his quest, she wondered why she had even considered the chance that he might call her out. Was she really ready to be carried away like Butterfly?

After a short recess, Dark Rock came forward and waved the two girls, Ember and Yellow Flowers, forward. As they approached, Yellow Flowers stepped ahead, nearly pushing Ember aside. Ember rolled her eyes and ignored the attack. The middle of their womanhood ceremony was hardly the time to slap the sense into the annoying girl, though that was exactly what the rancorous redhead would do if she tried something like that on any other day. Dark Rock, ignoring the pushing, placed a hand upon Yellow Flowers' head as he spoke.

"Yellow Flowers, daughter of Dancing Herd and Evening Flowers, you have been known to me for a long time as but a child. You have played and laughed at my feet, and yet I no longer look down to see you. Could you have become a woman while I grew old?"

Dark Rock paused, thinking he caught sight of something moving in the sky, but took little note of it. Returning his attention to the events at hand, he examined Yellow Flowers up and down with exaggerated movements meant to be seen clearly by the tribe. He "noticed" her wide hips and budding female features with a grunt here and a nod there. With a shrug, he looked back to Morning Dew.

"I have looked more closely, and young Yellow Flowers has bloomed into a woman. Come see for yourself, and read her signs that we may pronounce her a woman."

With that ritual proclamation, Morning Dew strode forward and touched Yellow Flowers' head as she babbled in some unknown language, looking intently at things only she could see. Within moments, she met Yellow Flowers' eyes and began her pronouncements.

"Before me stands no girl! This is Yellow Flowers, a woman of the people. By the next Lunar Festival, you should come wearing a fully beaded gown of your own design. Now go!" Yellow Flowers hugged Morning Dew and strode off with her new task in mind. Ember considered the impressive task Yellow Flowers had been given. The task of creating a single high-quality bead took quite some time and work grinding shells or tiny stones with sharp stone tools and sand granules. Even using bones, the quickest way, was a slow process. Before the beads could even have their holes ground, they had to be smoothed with oil, leather, and sand. The thought of so many beads made Ember's hands reflexively clench.

My outfit will still look better, she thought. Ember's mind was taken back to current events as she heard her name spoken in full by Dark Rock.

"Ember, daughter of East and the warrior Winterborn, fallen in defense of the people many seasons past, I have watched you dance and sing at ritual. You have brought me more flint and strange stones than any other girl, or boy for that matter. What brings you to the circle this night?" he asked, his eyes lingering on her body paint, the design normally worn by young men, a sharp contrast to her woven apron. With the theatrics only an elder would use, Dark Rock stepped forward and examined Ember as he had Yellow Flowers. He poked her shoulder and made a few odd noises.

"Hmm, I see..." he said before standing back and giving Morning Dew a level gaze.

"Dew, please come and see if my eyes are working this night, for I thought I saw the girl Ember, but this is surely a woman standing before me."

Dew came forward and placed her hands upon Ember's head to start her typical act when everything in the world suddenly changed...

The sky lit as day.

The dark of the night was shattered by the sudden appearance of a strange and wondrous object. In the sky above, a bright light appeared with a sudden radiance and a glowing trail behind it as it soared across the dark sky. The light was bright white in the center, with green and red pieces tearing off as it flew across the sky. Everyone had seen a star fall though no one knew why they did. This was more like a burning arrowhead streaking across the sky and faster than anyone thought possible.

As the red and green falling star blazed through the sky, it suddenly became significantly brighter. The light became more orange-red and nearly blinding. The heat from the light warmed the skin of the people, causing many to scream. The sight was breathtaking, yet also frightening. Some dropped to their knees, genuflecting in awe, while others prayed and chanted to the gods for mercy. Most screamed, and a few ran in terror. Morning Dew merely stared at the sight, much too jaded to run. If the end of the world had come for her, she was far too old to do much more than watch. Beside Dew, Ember watched the bright streak fly over her with a sense of foreboding.

Aeeya... she thought, a common curse word which fit the moment.

Well, that is just great... It had to be now, and the colors had to be red and green. Great... I'll get stuck making the largest bead ever or killing a wolf with only my hands or something for this... Aeeya! Aeeya! Aeeya! Ember thought sarcastically as she let go a great sigh.

As the tribe stared, the light flew across the sky from one end to the other, heading in a westerly by northwesterly direction in line with the Great River. The light promptly broke into many tiny pieces, which disappeared over the horizon. When calm returned, the entire tribe stood in silence and stared at the cloudy trail, which seemed to follow the path of the lights. For what seemed like a long moment, no one said anything.

All seemed to be over for many long moments when suddenly a boom was heard, startling everyone. Ember could not imagine why she would hear a loud sound, presumably from the falling star, so long after it had apparently exploded overhead. A long moment after the boom had left, many started to realize that the event was truly over. Ember sighed once more as the tribe fell silent. For a few breaths, not a sound was heard. Even the frogs and insects were quiet. Ember stood with a slightly sad, if not resigned, look about her. She knew it was coming…

The silence was broken as Morning Dew, calm throughout the entire encounter, suddenly let loose a cackling scream and fell to her knees before Ember. The effect was stunning, many nearly jumping out of their skins at the sudden sound. She looked up into the night sky and babbled, much more frantically and loudly than normal, in that language only she seemed to know. Finally, after several moments of intense, "otherworldly" rant, Morning Dew slowly regained her senses and stood. She stared at Ember for a short time, an incredulous look on her face. Next, she rounded upon the tribe with her arms and fingers extended.

Go on... say it, you know you want to… Ember thought.

"It was a sign!" she proclaimed.

Here we go, Ember mentally groaned.

"A great sign! At the very moment I prayed to the Moon Goddess for the correct task of womanhood. The skies themselves spoke their will!" Morning Dew stated.

East stood just beyond the ritual, casting Ember a fearful look. Then, before she could consider what might come next, Morning Dew looked from Dark Rock to Ember, then back again, and started speaking once more.

"Ember, you are directed by the very sky and the gods to seek a goal to the West. You will journey at first light two days from now, along the Great River by boat and seek the farthest edge of the world, many tendays travel. There, the gods have something planned for you!"

There were gasps and looks of shock all around. Ember stood with her mouth open, a gawking stare. What was going on? Was she not supposed to make a basket or decorate some stupid pots? At worst, she might be sent to a neighboring tribe as a wife, but a quest? Quests and journeys were the lot of men, and only experienced hunters took on such a task. This was an epic quest. Ember was not alone in her thoughts as much of the tribe stood in various states of shock.

Dark Rock turned from Ember to East and then to Morning Dew. He placed a hand on Morning Dew's old shoulder.

"Are you sure of this? This sign was seen by all, but surely this is a grave task. Perhaps there..." but Dark Rock was cut off by Morning Dew's sudden retort.

"How much clearer must a sign be?! Her father, the warrior Winterborn, came from the Northwest so long ago. This is the work of fate and the gods. Are the signs not there?" Morning Dew looked at each set of eyes of the tribe as she made her case.

"What color was the light? What color is Ember's hair? What colors are her eyes and her clothing? Such a journey needs luck! Who has found the most flint? Who has collected the most of the yellow stones? What of the unusual heat and the strange crops in the Western fields? She has been given a task, and she must follow it or be a child forever! This is the way of things!" With that final statement, Morning Dew left the stunned circle and strode toward her longhouse.

Ember had been effectively damned by those words. If she chose not to take the task, she could probably be made a woman by another elder, but there would always be the stain of an unfinished task. Worse, if the harvest went badly or something unfortunate happened within the next few seasons, Ember would most likely be blamed. It would be said that she had upset the gods. There was no escape.

I have to go... she thought... she knew.

Ember stood very still with everyone gathered before her, the loud sound of the fire in the sky still replaying in her memory. At first, she thought she might start crying, but then she caught sight of East. Her mother had a mixed expression of both fear and admiration. It gave Ember strength in the moment and steadied her before she could cry. Instead, she simply turned and walked slowly toward the safety of her longhouse. As she passed through the throngs of people, the hunters one by one gave her a short bow of their heads, a sign of respect usually only offered to warriors and hunters. As she passed them, Ember filled with pride – as though she were reborn.

She passed a stunned Yellow Flowers without a single word. Ember felt dazed, yet she also felt an odd sense of amusement at the look on the girl's face. Yellow Flowers looked like she might wet herself with shock. Somehow, that brief touch of amusement, so non-sequitur, helped Ember keep her composure. Adrenaline and her inability to fully grasp the events of the night did the rest.

Emerging from the people, she paused and allowed herself a moment to collect her thoughts. She always had an odd way of looking at life. Her views were based on a sort of self-humor and an uncanny ability to see herself plainly and beyond her own immediate situation. Ember, sad, afraid, and generally overwhelmed, smiled as a single tear escaped. Then, she turned to the expectant people and forced a larger smile.

"I will journey in two days to the ends of the world, to the West. I will face whatever the gods have dealt me, and I will return. Until then, let the festival continue!" It felt like someone else spoke as the words left her stunned lips. With her forced smile and the exclamation, much of the tribe let loose yells, trills, and whistles. Kanter and Blossom both ran forward and grabbed Ember in an all-too-tight embrace. The night had become surreal as Ember lived in a daze. After a few moments, the three friends found themselves heading toward the mat where the sacred drink was poured. Ember was in too much shock by now to cry. The actual insanity of her predicament had not yet fully sunk in. Kanter gave Ember a poke in the ribs and offered what he considered his impressive advice.

"Now that you're leaving for a while, you had better drink up tonight! Wouldn't want to leave without a bowl full, right?"

Ember gave Kanter a grimace and nodded, accepting a shallow clay pot with some precious, sacred brew. She brought it up to her lips and drank down the bitter-sweet drink. Fire arose in her stomach and her skin bead with sweat. The drink always had that effect. Offhandedly, she wondered where East had gone? She had expected her mother to come to her, yet she was nowhere to be seen. She sipped more of the drink, letting her fears evaporate as the brew melted reality away.

The liquid was made from water, honey, herbs, and a little fermented porridge. If consumed before it had time to sit for a tenday, the liquid could make one very sick or cause the mouth to become red and irritated. Luckily, the sacred drink was always given at least two or three moons to age. Ember was quite sure a squirrel would willingly attack a wolf if given enough of the fiery liquid.

It might even win, she thought as she lay on a reed mat next to Blossom and Kanter, absorbing the night. As she lay on the warm grass, Ember caught sight of a few smaller falling stars. She laughed sarcastically.

Curse you, fate... she tearfully mused.

CHAPTER FOUR
THE GREAT RIVER

"The Great River," what is now called the river Rhine, has been a vital waterway for European peoples for millennia. The river generally flows south to northwesterly, through various parts of Europe, meandering between east and western directions. The river starts in the Swiss Alps as runoff from glaciers. It flows thousands of miles from Switzerland to the Netherlands, passing through Germany, Austria, Liechtenstein, and France. As a result, many ecological environments exist along the Rhine, from thick forests to wide-open fields.

Our heroine encounters the Rhine in what is now southwestern Germany near the present-day city of Mannheim. As the story progresses, so too does the river, changing from thick forests and deep valleys to vast open fields with tree-covered banks. The only feature which remains is the steady flow of water and travelers. The Rhine has cut deeply into the land and into the heart of humanity.

To navigate such a mighty river, people needed boats. Unfortunately, boats were tough to produce for Neolithic peoples. The most likely boat available to Ember would probably have been a dugout boat made primarily from a log. The center of the log would be dug out, hence the name, using adzes and small, controlled fires. The digging leaves an inch or two of wood on each side and perhaps a little more at the bottom. The outsides would be sanded with leather and grit, and the bow angled.

Ember awoke the following day to a throbbing head. She lay on a reed mat with a deer hide covering her. Her apron had been removed and hung on the wall nearby. She looked around and noticed East by the hearth cooking some sort of meal. Her head spun, and she felt a little ill, but her stomach ached with hunger. How long had she slept?

Breakfast! she thought. Her wits came to her slowly as she shook off the sleep and a pounding headache. She vaguely recalled staggering into the house and removing her apron, then falling flat on the mat. Apparently, East had found her and helped her to bed. Ember was still painted black and red and smelled of sweat. She would need a trip to the river before long, but at least she had survived the sacred brew.

"I see you're awake," said East in a stern tone, causing Ember to flinch when she turned, yet the look on her mother's face was calm, if not a little sad. There was something odd in her expression, emotions Ember couldn't pin down. She had not seen her mother since the ritual, which had been odd. She felt slightly guilty over running off with her friends instead of finding her mother, but the young often made such mistakes. It was simply part of living and growing.

"If I were about to do what you are set to do, I would have been just as intoxicated as you were when I found you last night," East said, forcing a smile. Her emotions were masked just below the surface, and Ember could see her efforts to hide them, though she was doing a poor job of it. How could she not be emotional about her only daughter leaving on a dangerous journey? East stood and brought forth a wooden tray of polished driftwood with food and sat it beside Ember. Her behavior continued to be odd, as though her movements were forced. Something was deeply troubling East, and Ember was pretty sure she knew what it was.

The wooden tray held a shallow reed basket full of roasted bird meat with salt and a few small tubers with a sauce of wild onions and salt mixed with the drippings of the birds. Ember was surprised both by the fancy breakfast and by the way her mother was treating her. She sat back and ate her breakfast quite hurriedly as East sat beside her with a worried look. When she was finished, Ember put aside the tray and started to speak, but before she could, East interrupted. She had obviously been waiting for the right moment to say what was bothering her.

"These many seasons have been hard for both of us. Life is never how we expect it to be. If you do not follow the will of the elders, know that I will always love you." She placed her hand on Ember's head and gently stroked her hair in silence for a while the way she used to do when Ember was young. Ember stifled a tear at the words.

"I know, mother, but what if the harvest fails? What if the gods really do want me to go?"

East wanted to say something profound to her daughter, something that would fix everything and make her feel like she was helpful in some way. This was one of the moments when a mother was supposed to give her daughter advice and make everything better. Instead, all she could do was stroke her daughter's hair with one ever so slightly quivering hand. In her heart, she had long ago given up hope in the gods. After her husband had fallen, her devotion to them had died with him. He had been killed by raiders so suddenly that she had never had a chance to say goodbye, if she ever really could have.

Winterborn was so much like his daughter. He had long red hair and those same bright green eyes. East used to sit and listen to him speak his funny musings of life. He was so adamant about fixing the wrongs of the world, the injustice, the pains, to the glory of the gods. But gods didn't help him as he lay dying. Now, they supposedly schemed to take her one and only child. She would curse the gods until her dying day, and then again to their faces, if she met them in the afterlife, but her animosity was a private thing.

East kept her thoughts to herself. Ember believed in the will of the gods, at least on some level, and she wouldn't share her doubts with the girl. Her spirit was so similar to the fire she had seen in her beloved Winterborn. East wanted so many times to say what she thought, but her daughter's green eyes held too much innocence to taint with her own secret grief. In the end, she knew what Ember would choose. She held a part of Winterborn's spirit within her, and she would travel to the ends of the world just as he would have. She couldn't fault Ember either, as it was simply in her nature. One could no more curse the Sun for shining bright.

She might never return, promises or not, and the thought terrified her. Exploration was another trait of Winterborn, the reason he had journeyed and met East in the first place. It was just their nature, she supposed. Was this really any different than if a man from another tribe had asked Ember to leave and live with his people? It was natural for a child to grow up and leave the nest. At least, this time, East would have a chance to say goodbye. As though she could read her mother's mind, Ember caught her eye, tears on her young face.

"I will come back or at least let you know I am alright. It might take a few seasons... maybe even a few full harvests, but I will see you again. You saw the sign; the whole world saw it..."

"I know, my little fox. You had better get cleaned up and prepare yourself if you are to do as the elders say," East said with a forced smile, barely holding her composure as her lower lip quivered.

"Don't worry! I'm sure I will find the end of the world and return. The gods willed it, so why would they let me fail? I love you, mother," she said as she embraced East in a hug. Whatever East used to keep her face neutral faded as her composure broke. Ember scampered off with her clothing to the river to clean and prepare for the day. As she left the longhouse, East collapsed and burst into sobbing tears of uncontrollable pain and grief. East remained in the back of the longhouse for the first part of that day, sobbing and cursing the gods for conspiring to take her husband, and now, her only daughter.

We are our own gods, and our fates change with the winds, she thought in agony.

A short time later, Ember burst from the cool waters of the Great River, having swum to clean herself. Diving in the shallow water and scrubbing her body with silt and sand had left it clean and exfoliated. Stepping from the water, she noticed her body was still slightly red with ochre stain, though the ash had come off. The ochre was enough for now, but she would need more paint soon. Standing nude by the river wasn't a concern, but to be seen without at least some body paint was indecent, if not wholly scandalous. She donned her bark fiber skirt and considered her next two days. She would need to say goodbye to her friends, extended family, and mother. It wasn't going to be permanent, but it was still a significant change.

I'll be returning within a season or three, so it's not a big deal, she thought. But, deep down, she wondered how truthful that was. She quickly shook such feelings away and walked toward the riverside of the village where Blossom's family lived. She would need to spend some time with her cousins and perhaps even go for one last swim before returning home. There was so much to do and just not enough time, something she normally had little concern for. For her people, time meant very little. Entire tendays would drift by with no significant deadlines or goals, other than harvests and planting, with a few rituals here and there. Time was one thing her people usually had in abundance.

As she came upon the longhouse, she spotted Blossom and Kanter sitting on a log bench talking. They looked and acted more like a married couple every time she saw them. She wondered if they would join before she returned, yet another downside to what was likely going to be a lengthy trip. Kanter noticed Ember immediately and waved at her with a broad smile. It seemed they had fared better with the sacred brew than she had.

"Hey! Come on over here and see what Blossom has!" Blossom was sitting with her back somewhat to Ember and oddly seemed, perhaps angry or agitated? It was hard to be sure, but as Ember skipped over, she heard her friend whispering angrily to Kanter.

"I told you to keep quiet! I don't know why I tell you anything," she ranted, suddenly turning toward Ember and standing. Her tone and expression changed far too quickly to happy. It was a forced "innocence" which screamed of deceit. Something was amiss, and her hands were now behind her back, moving as she did. Worse, Kanter was staring with open anticipation. Ember already held a smug enough look that Blossom was unable to retain her mock innocent demeanor. Before Ember could voice any objections, Blossom swung her hands forward, thrusting them into Ember's face quite suddenly.

"Here! I have a present for your journey!" She opened her hands to reveal a moon goddess pendant made of deer antler. Goddess figurines were quite common adornments as they provided blessings, though Ember thought them more likely just ornamental. Typically, bone and antler figurines were toys, while clay was reserved for proper ceremonial figures. The little pendant was the size of a man's thumb and intricately carved with a hole for a leather thong for it to hang around a neck.

"My mother gave it to me when I was young," she continued.

"But I can't take this! It's special and..." but Blossom countered Ember's worries with an outstretched hand of dismissal.

"Take it! When you return, you can bring it back with you and with my present from far away! You are bringing us gifts, right?" Blossom finished with an inquisitive smile.

Ember wanted to point out that she might not return. The thought had occurred to her the night before and again that morning by the river, but she had been ignoring it. Mortality was something everyone was acutely aware of in a small tribe. Every full season, at least one person died. Death was a predator who stalked the village and could never be driven off.

"I..." Ember stuttered.

Ember was interrupted now by Kanter seizing upon the moment to add his opinions. He was well-meaning but very haphazard, somehow even more chaotic than Ember, which took extra effort. Though she fussed at him often, Blossom seemed to get along well with the boy when they were alone. It almost seemed to Ember like their bickering was a strange species of flirtation.

"You'll only be gone a season or two. Next warm season, you will be back with stories to tell! You will be as respected as a hunter, maybe more. You'll immediately be in line to become an elder... but that will take a while. I bet that..."

"Kanter!" Blossom interrupted before he could go off on a tangent of some sort.

"He's right, though. You'll be back soon enough," she said.

"I guess... I wonder what the end of the horizon looks like?" Ember wondered aloud, changing the subject. She wondered if the world merely ended or even started anew. What would she find? The world was obviously flat, as anyone could see. Did the river just fall off the edge? If so, where did new water come from? She was brought back to reality as Kanter started openly pondering the same questions but in his own odd way.

"I bet there are giant bear people, or talking fish, at least," Kanter said, matter-of-factly.

With that, the three friends spent much of the rest of the day talking and saying goodbye in their own ways. As the evening came, Ember, Kanter, and Blossom visited each of Ember's cousins and friends. The village was a little larger than she had recalled, but she rarely visited each of her extended family all in the same day. When she finally returned to her longhouse, she was pretty tired and in need of rest. She had waved a huge good-bye to her friends, smiles all around, and spent every moment with them. She now took careful inventory of her memories as she approached the hide door, ensuring that she could fully remember each face. She hoped she would see them again.

As she opened the hide door, the tasty smell of a vast array of foods struck her. Before her, Ember's entire immediate family sat laughing, talking, and waiting for her before a grand meal. That night Ember, East, Na Na, Heather, and Vance, her cousins Red Flowers, Fox, and their parents all sat around the central hearth eating a large family meal. East had made it a point to make Ember one last giant dinner, and everyone had helped. Ember was known for her love of food and might not eat well for many days to come. This was an excellent chance to "fatten her up," it seemed. Na Na had even guilted one of the village women, whose husband was a consummate hunter, into giving up a fully roasted deer rump and legs.

The deer provided enough meat for everyone to have their fill. East had made boiled lentils and salt with roasted tubers, a sauce of chopped turnips, deer liver, salt, coriander imported from the South, and mashed peas. For dessert, roasted early nuts, a nut that was harvested in the warm season. East only had a small pot of coriander for which she had traded ten blue stone beads. The use of exotic spices from the South and East was reserved for only the most important events. To East, this was worth the trade. The family dined, talked, and laughed long into the night.

As the family settled in for the night, East was left again stroking Ember's hair as her daughter drifted to sleep beside her. East was worried, deeply worried. Perhaps her daughter would return, even if it took many harvests. If any woman could brave the world where only men dared tread, it would be her Ember. Yet, there were so many dangers, so many ways she could... She was so much like her father.

A short life is the fate of those who burn bright, she thought with great sadness.

East wept.

The following day Ember awoke to find her mother lying beside her, sound asleep. She sat up, quite disturbed, for she had awoken before anyone else.

Well, at least, I did it once before I ran off to be eaten by Kanter's "giant bear people" or whatever lives out there, she thought sardonically. She spent the next few moments carefully stretching. She adored a good stretch after a long night of sleep. She flexed each arm and leg until she felt relaxed, perhaps her favorite activity, aside from swimming. This was what made life worth living, in her opinion.

Ember stood and wobbled, still very sleepy, over to the family's food stores. She loved to eat more than most, and today she had leftovers to "help" clean up. She plopped some dried meat and turnip pieces from the previous night onto cooking sticks, loading each stick with alternating meat, turnip, meat, and started a fire. The rest of the family awoke that strange morning to the unprecedented sight of Ember cooking them breakfast. Truly, the gods must be crazy or at least in a humorous mood. East awoke and rubbed her swollen eyes.

Brightly... she burns so brightly, East thought with both sadness and love.

After breakfast, East, Na Na, and the rest of the family went to the river's edge for a quick bath and hair washing. Ember missed this communal cleaning most days. Instead, she opted for solo swims when the water was warm enough, for she normally overslept. Regardless, cleaning was still vital, and even in the cold season, cleaning was normally a group exercise. Ember stood by the water, whipping her head about, causing her waist-length hair to sling back and forth, freeing the water. This was a way to help aid in drying, but there were also side effects... As Ember became dizzy, East put a hand on her shoulder to keep her from falling.

"Watch yourself before you fall over. You shouldn't whip your head that hard. Try letting the hair sling more than your head," East said with a laugh to hide her sorrow. East was living in the moment now, escaping her fear and sadness by occupying her mind with what she was doing, but even this only helped a little. Her only daughter was preparing to leave, and each activity – each moment – brought her one step closer to leaving. Ember didn't notice the sad look in her mother's eyes, being simply too excited and overwhelmed by her own anxiety and fears to notice much else. At least she had her final goodbyes to keep her preoccupied.

Her last day was full of family bonding and farewells. Ember met with many of her extended family and friends once more. She was becoming nervous and wanted to start the journey as soon as possible. The longer she waited, the more time she had to think over what was to come and the harder the goodbyes became.

That final night, Ember slept as East gently stroked her hair one last time. East was now starting to accept what was to come but was still frightened for her beloved daughter. If she never saw Ember again, she could go on as long as she knew her daughter was okay. If she met someone and fell in love, perhaps she might choose to remain with them. This was natural and happened all the time, yet it was so sudden. That night as she knelt beside her daughter gently stroking her long, red hair, she prayed for the first time since Winterborn had died, whispering under her breath. She had to try, if only for Ember's sake.

"Goddess of the night, lady of the Moon, listen to my plea. Protect my little Ember and see her safe return or at least give me a sign that she is alive and well. Take what you want for this request but not from her. All I care for in this life is her happiness. Moon Goddess, protect her." East doubted the gods listened and often doubted they even existed. She hoped she was wrong.

ᐤᐤᐤ

Ember awoke with a start. She sat up and stretched, though a sense of foreboding permeated the longhouse. After a quick meal of leftovers, it was time to prepare. East and Na Na approached, ready to help Ember paint and straighten her hair. The trio knelt before the central hearth and began the task of preparation. East and Na Na chanted a song of courage and protection as East painted and Na Na removed the tangles from Ember's waist-length locks. This sort of ritual was the same used when someone prepared for battle, a disconcerting thought in Ember's opinion.

"My little fox," East said, holding back her tears and forcing a smile as she finished adding red ochre to Ember's face and painting the black dots under her eyes, reverently. Ember's upper body was painted entirely red with ochre, with black lines of ash creating bands, very much like her paint the night she became a woman. The day was already hot and bare skin was generally painted, per custom. Behind her, Na Na affixed two hawk feathers to her hair. Some tribes considered feathers to carry special meanings, such as status or achievement, or even religious significance. Ember's people wore them more for decoration, though children were generally not permitted to do so.

Next, Ember packed a large hide bag of sorts containing roe deer leggings, woven flax fiber shoes, leather and bark fiber frame boots, an old rabbit fur coat, a long grass cape to ward against rain, her bark fiber skirt, and her precious doeskin long shirt. Besides this, she packed various cords, flint tools, and a few odds and ends. Given the heat, she had opted to wear a roe deer leather loincloth with long tassels hanging to her knees and secured with a bark fiber waist cord. While her clothing was really more suited to a man, it seemed to her like the best choice, given the heat and her now painted body.

Attached to her waist cord was a small leather bag with her best pieces of unworked flint, quality pieces, pure of color, and with the perfect shapes for pressure flaking. In that same bag, she placed Blossom's goddess pendant wrapped in a thin leather scrap. She planned to create a nice, braided necklace for the pendant on the long boring ride down the river as she roasted under the Sun. On the other hip hung her father's obsidian dagger, a beautiful weapon with a leather-wrapped handle nearly half the length of her arm. It was the largest obsidian blade she had ever seen, given to her by East only a few harvests before.

She was painted and dressed like a man and had been sung the chants and preparations of a warrior, an interesting thought. Women rarely wore loincloths except under other clothing, and during their pains, though it wasn't unheard of. An apron was more comfortable in the heat, but her exposed butt would hurt from sitting in the boat, something the loincloth would alleviate. Her body paint and large dagger made her look like a warrior, off to fight her people's foes. There were stories of women who had been great hunters and even warriors. If such stories mentioned clothing, which they rarely did, the woman in question was usually painted and garbed similarly. Ember's amused thoughts quickly faded when she recalled the usual ending to such tales.

With a final look around the longhouse, Ember left her home for the water. Her mother and family followed, carrying some additional supplies. As Ember began walking toward the river, other people began to follow her, leaving their work behind. When Ember passed the central hearth, women lifted their children and followed, forming a long procession. As she passed, people touched Ember on her shoulders as a sign of reassurance and respect for her choice to honor the gods' will.

Ember was doing this as much for herself as for them, and they knew it. She had always been curious about the world and daydreamed of adventure. This would be her big chance to live that adventure before returning and settling down to join and raise a family – a fate cursed upon her by accident of her feminine birth. This expectation always lingered like a foul odor. Besides, following the gods would ensure a safe, mild cold season, and the people of the village knew this too. She was risking her life for them. Either way, there had only been one correct choice.

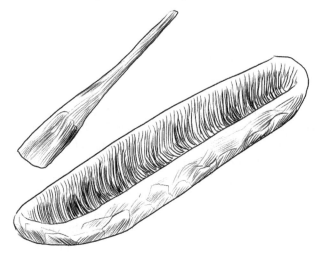

Dugout boat

Ember approached the riverbank with most of the tribe at her back. Before her, several men had prepared a small boat that would take Ember on her journey. The little wooden boat was about one and a half times the length of a man, made from the hollowed-out trunk of a tree. The sides had been carved to a width of one-half of a finger's length, and the front had been angled into a bow. The boat was very sturdy, made of one solid piece of wood, but heavy and hard to control. Many who used such a boat would fight hard against the river's currents, incorrectly using brute strength. Ember had used such a boat before and knew that only a soft hand could coax the boat into the currents and keep it straight and right. The trick was to find the best path down the river and allow the boat to be swept along that path, not fight the water's will.

Inside of the boat were many leather thongs lashing items in place. The villagers had packed the boat with gourd-shaped blackened clay jars full of water as well as leather sacks of dried meat, tubers, and some assorted supplies. The entire boat had even been blessed by the tribal elders that very morning, evidenced by flowers and various painted markings along the hull. It was perhaps the best small craft of her people, and now it would be hers, though the price was quite steep.

Darkwood, one of the best hunters of the tribe, was finishing the boat loading by adding some reed mats. He turned with the other men gathered at the water to regard the daring young woman who now approached. He noted her choice of clothing and paint, dressed as a ritual hunter or a warrior. His people had no dedicated warriors, nor did they raid. In times past, some had been called upon to fight other tribes, though this had not been the case in a long time. To see the spunky and carefree girl he had watched grow into a brave woman, filled Darkwood with pride for his people.

"Best of luck, Ember. Me and 'stubs' have gone west many times before, a tenday once. It's not so bad. Just stay close to the water," Darkwood said as reassuringly as he could. In truth, he feared for her, but she was also under divine commandment, so what wrong could come to her?

"I... I will be fine. If the gods wish this, why would they allow harm to come to me?" Ember said, more to convince herself than Darkwood, though the hunter seemed in agreement. Several of the men nodded their heads as well. It appeared to Ember that the tribe was still in as much shock as she, and many were still unsure of the wisdom of this journey. Darkwood looked deeply into Ember's green eyes, just as he had so many young men before their first solo hunts. He could see her fear.

Good... Be afraid, and let that fear guide your hands to less daring deeds. The gods gave us fear to counter stupidity and to make sure we stayed alive, he thought. Darkwood had seen what happened to those who were too brave.

They don't call my friend "stubs" for nothing, he thought, considering his friend who had lost his hand many seasons before in a tragic accident while gathering wood. It was a terrible nickname, though the man had come up with it himself and insisted on its use.

Several of the elders, including her grandmother and most of the tribe, were starting to wonder if Morning Dew was still of sound mind. If she questioned the elders, Ember could probably get out of the trip, even now. But, if she did, the confusion and a split among the elders might cause a rift within the entire tribe.

Besides, I really want to see what exists at the edge of the world, she thought with both irony and a little truth. Perhaps Kanter's bear people or where the water went. If she could look over the edge of the world, what would be below? Her mind was racing, trying to avoid the fear and sadness over leaving. Finally, after a moment, she inhaled and turned to confront the truth that this was her final moment before leaving. It had all happened so fast. Ember turned to see her teary-eyed mother and grasped her tightly in an embrace to which her family joined.

"I love you, mother," she said to a speechless East.

"I will return, by the gods' will, maybe next warm season!" Ember announced to the crowd, showing much more bravery than she felt. What more was there to say? Was this how warriors in the tales of old felt before they left to fight another tribe? So many of them wouldn't return. Was this the same for her? Her mind was overwhelmed with fear and curiosity, strange bedfellows.

Quickly now, before you lose your nerve or start crying, she thought as she smiled and turned toward the boat. She stood for a moment merely staring at the craft when suddenly she heard the faint sound of East beginning to chant a song. East chanted a song of strength, her voice rising in the morning air. The Great River People were singers and dancers at heart. One by one, the entire tribe joined East, lifting their voices as one. With the whole tribe now singing and chanting behind her, Ember mustered her will and climbed into the small dugout wooden boat, tears welling in her eyes. She settled her traveling supplies and a fishing spear, then took a deep breath.

Before her, the Great River flowed. Once, the river had meant home and family, but now it carried her away, filling her with fear and adventure. She had lost herself in thought for a moment, but the sound of a change in the chanting drew her back. With a final whisper to the gods for aid, she glanced over her shoulder to her mother. East's eyes were red and wet with tears of both sadness and admiration. East gave her daughter a short nod, a final send-off.

Ember was almost glad to start. The anticipation of such a quest could do more to unnerve a person than the actual quest. Several village men came forward to help push the little boat into the water with a resounding splash. Behind her, she heard East, Blossom, Kanter, Na Na, and even little fox calling to her for luck. Ember breathed deeply and set to work with her small steering pole, long with a flattened end, which she would use to steer the little boat through the river.

Floating down the river was a sort of controlled chaos. The more you tried to fight the river, the more the river fought back. The most you could hope for was to use a small pole or oar to steer the boat away from the bank and rocks toward an open path in the flow of the river. It was a laborious task, at least until the boat found a good current. After that, one merely sat back and let the river do the work. Unfortunately, returning would be significantly harder, but that was something to worry about later.

Behind her, the sounds of the chanting and singing became faint. She couldn't bring herself to look back for fear she would start crying or lose her nerve. Instead, she concentrated on the river. The boat was small and splashed from side to side as it rolled through the choppy waters of the Great River. For a while, Ember watched the shore for landmarks. She could see the familiar places near the tribe slipping away like the last glints of sunlight at the end of a day, along with everyone she loved and her entire life until that moment. Soon, the little boat had traveled so far that she no longer recognized the land.

She spent the remainder of the first day watching the slow change of scenery along the riverbank. The thick trees with their emerald canopies and deep ground cover were slowly replaced with more reeds and smaller trees, as the land slowly changed. She lived in a heavily wooded part of the world with dense trees and dark forests, another reason why the river was used for trade. Traders said patches of open area and even high valley walls were not uncommon along the river, though she had never seen it.

She had never really seen anything beyond her tribe. Traders and the few hunters who had journeyed to and from the Far East, like Darkwood, said the forests were greater and deeper as they had traveled beyond the river, while fewer people were found beyond the banks of rivers. Those they met were a different sort. They were forest people, usually a little taller, and with much darker skin. Many were said to have blue eyes and some of the finest leather clothing available, though they also wove beautiful bark fiber garments. Ember hoped she might meet some as they sounded amazing and typically peaceful, if the stories were true.

Those who had come from the South described forests giving way to lighter wood, such as the banks she now passed, as well as more stones coming from the ground. Of all the directions a person could explore, the West and the South had always interested Ember the most. The South held large villages and exotic peoples. The North and West were mostly unknown lands. Now, she too would know the strange lands where the Sun traveled each evening. She wondered if it slept someplace. Perhaps she could see it sleeping.

After a while, Ember opened her leather bag and removed some dried meat and a boiled tuber. She chewed on the food while sipping from one of her four clay pots of water. She would need to fill them each night when she pulled ashore and heat them by fire to make the water safe to drink. It was said that fire cleaned the wayward spirits from the river. Failing to remove these wayward spirits might allow them into one's body, causing sickness, though people often just drank directly from the river, if the proper prayers were made.

The first day rolled along and Ember spent the time singing to herself. As the songs became repetitive, she relaxed, entering a state of half-awake daydreams. She had always been one to lose track of what was happening, quickly slipping into the world of her quirky mind. Her daydreams and the lazy river slowly rocked her into a stupor. She once nearly lost the pole dozing off.

The water sure is dull. Fish must sleep all the time, she mused.

When the evening settled in, Ember directed the tiny craft toward a small, sheltered bank. Good campsites were always important. A protected bank could often be found at a bend in the river or where some thick natural feature sheltered the land. Perhaps the best were giant rocks and boulders. Powerful rock spirits imbued many large boulders with the strength to hold back the river, creating small, ephemeral ponds aside the shore, an excellent place to fish, and semi-sheltered for a camp.

The Great River will one day claim these boulders, but not without a fight! she thought with a bit of mirth. Ember sat up high in the boat and held her arms wide, yelling a challenge to the river.

"Bring forth a mighty storm to destroy these proud boulders, Great River!" With a laugh, she dug the pole deep into the water to maneuver, feeling the bite of the current. With a bit of luck and careful motions of the pole, Ember steered the boat up and onto the bank, a bank created by just such a large boulder. The boat actually slid halfway up the bank with the force of the impact. Ember stepped from the boat into the ankle-deep water. Her skin had been warmed by the Sun all day, and the cool flow of the river water and the smooth pebbles beneath her feet felt delightful.

She stood for a moment in the cool river stretching her arms. The water felt as refreshing as always. It was these existential moments that brought her the most joy. After a moment of stretching, she set out to securing the little boat, quite a difficult task. She pulled as hard as she could, losing her footing several times before slowly dragging the boat ashore. Boats must be pulled from the water and secured to protect them from the weather. After securing the boat to a sapling, she bent low in the boat and removed the three reed mats Darkwood had placed with her gear. She used one to cover the opening of the boat, keeping out rain and animals. There were simply too many items in the boat to flip it upside down the proper way.

Ember turned to see two rabbits standing on the bank not far from her. They both sat in a perched manner, watching her intently, as rabbits do.

"Well, here I am, rabbits!" she announced suddenly, to which the rabbits answered by scampering off.

"Fine, leave me by myself..." she said. The rabbits didn't reply.

The darkness was rolling in as the air grew a little cooler than it had been during the day, yet not unpleasant. Tonight would be mildly warm, but she still wanted a fire for protection and food. She walked a short distance inland, finding a small grass clearing, abandoning the rock in the pleasant weather.

This will make a good camp, she thought. The other two mats were placed on the ground as a sort of bed. With a campsite selected, Ember began looking for kindling and wood for a fire. Luckily the Great River always provided. Rivers often had piles of tangled wood and fallen limbs from storms, conveniently left on the shore to dry. She found one such woody tangle and removed many choice pieces for her fire after a quick prayer to the snake spirits for bothering their domain. Though she still kept an eye out for snakes, just in case. As she returned, she noticed the boulder forming the inlet where she had come ashore.

"I thought I told the river to wash you away. I guess we're not having a storm tonight, then." Ember laughed, returning to the camp with her wood. She placed the large pieces of wood in a crisscross stack and stuffed the kindling and leaves into the holes, leaving enough room for air. Fire spirits were known to love air and the wind as much as they loved wood and leaves. Fire without proper holes for air would quickly fail if it even started at all. This made sense as her body became warm when she ran, and she was forced to breathe harder. Of course fire spirits, being the hottest, would need to breathe the most.

Before a fire could be lit, some food would need to be secured. The strips of salted meat and boiled tubers were not very tasty and really more of a lunch-on-the-water sort of food. The only problem was that Ember was not much of a hunter. She doubted she could catch any animal on the land, but the water offered a large selection of tasty fish. The elders wouldn't have let her leave if they had thought she couldn't find food. All women from her tribe could fish, gather, and trap with decent skill, and many could hunt, though not Ember.

She removed her loincloth and tossed it on her reed mats. Her skin was the best attire for the water. Mostly, she just couldn't help getting into the water. She had all the time in the world and really nothing to do, aside from her quest. Luckily, the unseasonably warm weather had given her more swimming time than ever and she was going to use any excuse for a swim and fish.

Though she had brought a good fishing spear, it was lashed to her boat. Creating a quick spear from a stick took but moments. Ember selected a long stick, as tall as she, and quickly sharpened the end with her obsidian blade. The bark and wood simply slipped off as though they were not even attached, so sharp was the blade. Obsidian, volcanic glass, was black with a smooth, dull shine. Obsidian could slice razor-sharp cuts with very little pressure. The blade, a dagger really, was heavy in her small but nimble hands. She carefully used the dagger and slid it back into its sheath. The dagger had belonged to her father, Winterborn, and had been in his hand when he fell defending her mother. Ember was proud to carry the dagger on her long journey.

Bare from hair to toe, she strode into the water with an ad hoc fishing spear. The task came to her naturally but only due to a lifetime of practice. Fishing with a spear was a complex task that required time. Performing the action in a pond or lake was very difficult due to the fish noticing the huntress. A river always moved, allowing her to remain still and let the fish swim near her. The problem was seeing the fish and hitting it. Luckily, she was an excellent fisher, one of the few tasks she didn't regularly mess up. The light was leaving fast when a fish finally swam close enough to spear.

If only a deer or rabbit would swim by, I'd have a real meal, she thought with a laugh.

Rivers were populated with many spirits. Spirits of the dead, spirits of animals, and of the water element itself. The water spirits tricked the eyes, making you think a fish was in a different place than it really was. Being an experienced spear fisher, Ember knew not to aim for the fish but for a place next to it, where the fish really was. Even better, she would place the tip of the spear into the water, just a little. The spirits couldn't recognize the spear for what it was and would play their illusions with the spear, too, showing her where the spear would really strike. To ensure that her efforts were enough, Ember whispered a fishing song to the fish spirits. The song would comfort the spirits and help weaken their resolve. With any luck, she might have fish to eat.

She thrust her spear through the fish and hauled the arm-long trout from the water in a smooth, practiced motion. She flung the fish overhead and onto the land where it would soon die. Small fish were easy to kill, but large fish required additional beating from a cudgel. The peaceful singing didn't match up well with the beating, so Ember kept her songs short.

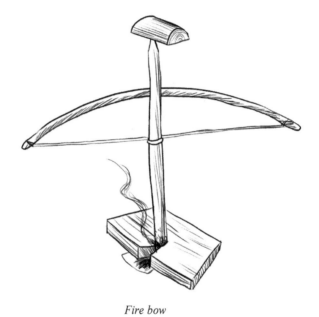

Fire bow

Now, how to cook the fish, roasted or blackened? she pondered. Ember strode from the water and considered what she needed for her fire. From her bag, she removed a fire bow used to start fires. Other methods existed, such as striking a flint and pyrite stone, but the bow was her favorite. Now, Ember merely needed a small stick with a point, about half as long as her arm. She would point the small stick straight down against a piece of dry wood and rotate it rapidly using the fire bow, generating friction, which would create heat for a fire by sawing the little bow back and forth, its string wrapped around the stick, causing it to rotate.

Ember pulled the bow back and forth, rotating the vertical stick until smoke trailed from the piece of wood. With that, she dropped to her belly and gently blew onto the tinder. She kept her hands cupped around it to keep the tinder from blowing away. Long, slow breaths brought life to the fire, which suddenly flared into a tiny flame. She used dry leaves and grass to set fire to the wood and kindling. Within a short time, a small but steady fire burned. Ember wished she had been named for skill with fire and not her fiery red hair. She had seen many of the women of her village perform this same feat in moments, much faster than she.

Leaving the river, she checked the fish to ensure it was dead. Killing a fish was one thing, but burning it alive was totally different, and Ember didn't want to anger the spirits of the fish by being so cruel. She stared at the fish for a long moment and saw no movement. She poked it several times, again without movement. Then, using her dagger, she slit open its stomach and spilled its innards into the river. She was careful to keep the liver, eyes, and heart. She would eat these as well, tiny as they were. It was known that these tiny little bits of the fish could keep the body feeling well, even when fish was all there was to be found. Eating the meat alone was not enough to sustain a human. She cleaned the empty cavity, careful not to leave the guts behind as they could make a person quite sick and placed a stick in the fish's mouth.

"There you are fish. Sorry, but your guts must go. At least, I killed you first." She had heard hunters tell of wolves and their prey, often not entirely dead before they started eating. She shivered at the thought of wolves, a sudden and primal instinct for she wasn't the dominant hunter in the forest. Suddenly, the fire really seemed like a good idea. Ember felt more alone at that moment than she had all day. With a glance to ensure she had enough wood for the night, she moved closer to the fire and prepared her meal.

The stick was placed into the ground at an angle allowing the fish to cook over the fire. Every few moments, the stick was rotated a quarter turn. While she waited for the meat, she used a tiny twig to roast the organs and quickly ate them. She always liked the taste of fish hearts, though they were so small that often they were missed when cleaning fish. East had been good at never missing a single heart and she had always saved them just for Ember. The thought brought a smile as she savored the tiny morsel.

As the night rolled in, she knelt before the fire and gave thanks to the gods for her good fortune and the large fish she had caught. As she knelt, she lifted her arms toward the sky, palms out, and slowly lowered them to rest upon her stomach. The fire crackled, and the heat radiated over her bare skin, bringing relaxation. Such simple rituals were commonplace in the tribe and nearly second nature. Thanks were generally given in the mornings, before eating, and at night. Besides, the camp was lonely, and she couldn't see more than four lengths of a man beyond the fire. She could use the extra security her beliefs afforded her.

With her cupped hands, she "pulled" the badness from herself, symbolically, and let it burn in the fire as her hands moved quickly through the flames. She hummed the words of a short song of blessing, an old habit by now. The fish had fully cooked by the end of the ritual, and she moved it away from the fire to cool. After a few moments, she sank her teeth into the crispy skin of the fish, tasting the succulent, if not delicate, meat. Trout was not very oily, but it tasted almost as good as salmon. Some fish produced bones that could be used for various purposes, such as charring for black pigment or even bone needles. After her meal and a few near misses with such bones, Ember walked to the edge of the water to clean off before bed.

The water's edge was just barely visible from the fire. Ember's skin crawled with fear as she suddenly realized how vulnerable she was standing bare-skinned, without even her dagger, by the water's edge. She was far from her people and even her small protective fire. Ember cleaned off very quickly and returned to her fire. Much of her body paint had come off, leaving red-stained, light brown skin. It was still painted enough to be decent, but she would need to apply more in a day or two.

"Run! For the monsters of the night love a tasty girl!" she scolded and then laughed. She pulled her doeskin shirt over her waist and laid back to watch the stars in the sky. The wind was warm and felt incredibly good as it lazily drifted over her bare skin, the sounds of frogs, crickets, and cicada filling the night. If only she could sleep like this every night, she thought as she slowly drifted into sleep. A warm breeze rolled in, growing in humidity and strength as the night drew steadily forward.

The next morning, Ember awoke to a deep red sky and warm winds. With her fire having long ago died to a smoldering heap, she found the warm breeze welcoming against her skin. She lay under the rich, blue sky and spent a short time simply stretching each limb. The feeling of her muscles being gently stretched always sent waves of pleasure through her body and left her in a much better mood for the day. After the blissful stretch, she sat up and rubbed the sleep from her eyes.

The red sky was often an omen of a coming storm, and she considered the wisdom of having challenged the Great River spirits the day before. She had been teasing, yet she knew that the spirits were real and didn't always have a sense of humor. Perhaps they would show her their power. That thought was unsettling to someone about to venture forth in a tiny dugout boat. She considered being a little humbler around the river and perhaps even giving the river a few offerings over the next few days. She decided to spend the day pondering these and other helpful activities as she traversed the Great River.

As the morning broke, Ember walked down the pebbly riverbank and set about washing in the river. The temperate water was always welcome as the river was often too cold for such aquatic pleasures. However, this season had been particularly warm, so much more than others, which allowed for such special indulgences. Ember's people were generally always clothed outside, and the chance to trot about without modesty or worry was relaxing. Even if her paint was wearing off, who would see?

After cleaning her hair, she caked her skin in the soft clay, which could be found in patches near the bank. She sang as she worked with the clay, remembering songs her mother had taught her. Ember's hands sank deep through the silt and pebbles into cool, thick pockets of mud and clay. The clay was nearly as thick as that used to make pottery and readily stuck to her skin. Within a few moments, she was totally covered in a thin layer of the stuff, giving her a gray appearance. The clay would keep the insects at bay, keep the Sun off of her skin, and leave her incredibly smooth when it flaked into powder, probably before she left. With cleaning taken care of, Ember set to work making breakfast. With the quick grind of her fire bow, she soon had a small fire in the same place which had burned the previous night. Fire often started more quickly where one had before burned. All around her flew butterflies, midges, and a few mayflies.

Using a straight twig, she heated a strip of dried deer meat and a large tuber. She longed for some roasted deer liver and fresh heart. The meat was filling, but a diet of meat could only sustain a person for so long. After the simple meal, she cleaned her hands in the river and made the boat ready for travel. She pulled the mat off the boat's top and slowly pushed it halfway into the water. The clay on her skin had dried, mostly, and much of it had flaked off. Quickly, Ember donned her loincloth and doeskin shirt, tossed her dagger and items in the boat, and gave one final stretch. The iron rations were loaded along with some twigs to fiddle with and pebbles to toss during the long, tedious trip. She was ready for her journey after a quick "natural" moment leaning against a tree in a squatting fashion.

The majority of the day was uneventful, with not much more than birds or a jumping fish to interest her. The valley walls she passed were decently high in some places, but this did nothing to block the sunlight. She sat back and nibbled on her lunch while lazily keeping the boat moving straight. On the nearby shore, a large brown bear was having a cool sip of water while bevers worked their dams. Ember and the bear regarded each other for a short moment. She had already seen plenty of birds and animals, too numerous to count in the forest.

I really should be able to hunt something. The men do it so often. Besides, fish are starting to get boring, she thought, tossing some semi-boiled turnip pieces in her mouth.

During the period of "high sun," where the Sun was at the highest point it would go during the day, she passed a place where people had recently been. Large wooden poles protruded from the water in series around an overused bank, a sort of river inlet. As she passed the inlet, the tops of longhouses and village structures could be seen from the river.

"A village!" she said excitedly. Ember was struck by the sound of her own voice. It had been nearly a day since she had uttered a single word. The thought of a quick stop at a village sounded like a good idea. Maybe she could trade one of her flint pieces for some deer heart or something else good to eat. She used her steering pole to move the boat closer to the shore to have a look. As the boat approached the shore, she began to notice that something seemed amiss. Along the shore, discarded pots and baskets were left here and there. A pile of fish had been left to rot and were now nothing more than strewn bones, picked clean by animals. Discarded wooden poles and other debris were scattered in the sand. Something was wrong with this scene.

She steered the boat toward the edge of the bank where she might come ashore and see what had befallen these people. The tough little boat steered an angle with the river's force behind it and slammed into the shore with speed. Ember jumped out into knee-deep water and hauled the boat onto the land. Was it her imagination, or did the Great River seem to have picked up its current a little? She pulled the boat ashore and straightened her doeskin shirt. It wouldn't do to be unpresentable if she found people. She wished she was more painted.

Often, a village would be abandoned if the resources in the local area needed time to recover. The tribe would simply leave and move to a different place. She had heard of tribes that made this journey every few seasons between two or more locations, moving to one site for the warm season and returning to another place every cold season. This problem of having to move was more common with tribes who farmed. Many of the tribes near her people hunted for their meat but either fished or grew crops to make up for the rest.

Maybe they ate bad meat the night before, and everyone's finding a quiet bush, she mused. A look around the village would determine the truth of the matter. As she approached the village, she took a closer look at the bank, which revealed pots and baskets of decent quality strewn about. They were left where they fell haphazardly. This made no sense to Ember. She could understand broken pots being left, but the quality hand-woven basket with an intricate decoration, which she now stood over, simply wouldn't be left sitting on the ground to rot. The basket held rotted tubers as though it had been placed on the ground to dry after washing and just left.

She walked up the path from the shore towards the village. This village had a high bank of dirt separating it from the water. This had a wind-breaking effect as well as granting a measure of safety if the river flooded. Ember's village used the same sort of wind-breaking wall as well as wind-breaking trees.

As Ember crested the hill, she realized that something was wrong, very wrong... The village stood before her with perhaps twenty longhouses and central hearths. All throughout the village were possessions left unattended. Many of the houses had entirely burned to the ground. As she looked around, she began seeing what looked like arrow shafts buried in many surfaces. She froze in place, instantly realizing what had befallen these people. Before she could even consider what that realization meant, she saw the first body. Beside one of the longhouses lay a half-decayed body, now mostly a skeleton with what looked like a broken spear stuck partially inside of its rib cage. The body lay face down as though it had just come out of the longhouse before being impaled from behind. Ember held her hand to her mouth, eyes wide. This village had been attacked.

She sank to her knees, overcome by the horror. As she knelt on the ground, she sang a short and mournful song for the dead, a custom of her people. The words were pure, and her voice held steady, but she felt tears as they fell. She was letting her emotions take hold, and the song was amplifying this. The sight of the carnage had overcome Ember before she had realized it. After she had finished the prayer song, she stood and took a few deep breaths to regain her composure.

Raids were a common enough occurrence. Generally, only a few warriors would rush into a village, quickly stealing food or animals, and perhaps even a few women and children. Rarely did anyone die. The point of a raid was to obtain food and resources but typically not to kill. Worse, given the size and location of this tribe, Ember had probably met some of its inhabitants before, traders from local villages were common enough, and this village was on the extreme edge of such local trade.

Ember carefully walked around the village with her obsidian dagger in her hand, more for self-assurance than for any foe. By the look of things, this raid... this massacre, had happened not long after the end of the last cold season. She checked each of the bodies she found around the village. The decayed corpses, mostly skeletons by now, still wore their clothing. Those who had been disrobed and looted had their clothing lying nearby. She could generally guess the sex and often the age of the people, in terms of young, adult, or elderly by their size and style of clothing.

Ember carefully entered each of the houses finding the same basic scene in each. They had been looted entirely, and anything of value had been taken. Though she found some female corpses among the fallen, she found nearly all dead to be male. This made some sense given a woman's value to a tribe, harsh and reductive, though that might be. These women and many of the children may have been taken by the raiders as slaves. Ember shuttered to think of the kind of men who would take women and kill their men.

A stolen woman was often a prize for a young and budding warrior from one of the more aggressive peoples. She could expect decent treatment as the mate of the warrior, but she would never truly be free. As terrifying as that was, it was still nothing like the wholesale bondage and slaughter of an entire tribe. Ember kept reminding herself that she had no proof that the missing women had all been taken captive. She had to consider the possibility that many had merely fled.

After a while, she came across the body of what was presumably a raider. The body lay face down, much like most of the dead. His soiled loincloth and decayed leggings were about the same as the others, but he wore a now mostly decayed leather shirt with a design Ember had never seen before. She stood in disgust and kicked the decayed body. The skull rolled away, leaving the jaw behind.

"You worthless beast! Now you'll have no head in the next world!" Unfortunately, she knew that the head needed to be removed just after death to miss the journey to the other side with the body. She hoped he would, at least, feel it, wherever the dead went. She wondered why the enemy had been left on the ground with the dead of the village. Was he the only enemy to die? If not, where were the bodies of the other dead raiders? She walked around to the forest side of the village.

This village is a tomb and no place for the living, she thought. Ember needed to decide what to do next, and her options seemed more limited by the moment. The sky was becoming darker, and the wind was growing. She was starting to worry about a coming storm. Normally she would not have dared to go farther down the river, but how could she sleep all night in this destroyed village with the spirits of the dead? The thought nearly sent her into a panic. It was said by some elders that the dead who were not properly buried could rise, especially at night, and wander the forests. She gulped at the thought. Finally, she decided that she would try and put as much distance between her and this village as before the storm came.

Ember stood still for a moment and asked the gods to watch over the fallen people of this lost tribe in the next world. The more she thought about their fate, the more pain she felt welling in her chest. Ember gave the village one last look and brushed back a tear as she pushed the little boat into the water.

What if the Raiders had come to my village? she thought. This had been a bigger village, and she knew it was assuredly better guarded. When she returned, she would discuss the matter with the elders.

"If I return..." she grimaced.

When Ember sat in the boat, she noticed the water becoming choppy and the wind blowing more steadily, yet still, she pushed the boat into the current with her steering pole. She had two choices: keep the boat close to the bank where she could quickly get out of the river if the rain started or move towards the center of the river where the current was the fastest. She might put more distance between herself and the dead village before the storm, at the risk of being too far out when the storm hit. She chose the latter of the two and maneuvered the boat into the center of the river. The thought of the dead village adding fear to her every action.

The boat was constantly tugged by the water as the wind picked up. The current made controlling the boat harder, but images of the half-decayed skeletons were still on her mind. She was glad she had worn her doeskin shirt as the temperature began to fall. She knew the rain was close at hand, but she hoped to get a little more distance before it came.

The wind blew ever stronger while the choppy waters became a rough, treacherous current as the little boat bobbed about, barely controllable. The sky had become dark, suddenly, and the wind was really picking up fast. Though the boat bobbed about, buffeted by the winds, she still felt that she had some control. She started to maneuver the boat toward the shore, expecting to abandon the river for the night soon. She was quite familiar with steering the little craft as she had grown up using such boats for fishing the deeper waters, but all hopes of continuing vanished when the first blast of lightning hit the opposite shore with a terrifying crash.

The sound pained her ears, and she was temporarily blinded. After a moment, Ember regained her sight and realized, to her horror, that her paddle pole was gone. She must have dropped it into the river as she reeled back from the blast. Panic ensued, and a cold rush of fear danced up her spine. The storm was not getting closer; it was on her now. Ember had misread her environment and taken too great a risk. Her blood ran as cold as the suddenly chilling air. A boat without a paddle was a feather falling in the wind. She would have no control over where she went or upon what she landed.

The boat was already starting to turn slightly sideways, a dangerous event as the boat would soon capsize. She noticed the small fishing spear lashed to the boat and removed the leather thong holding it in place. Using her fishing spear, she could try and control the boat in the ever faster-moving river. She dipped the spear handle into the churning water and pulled hard against the current. The effect was noticeable, but the boat continued to grow increasingly hard to control. Drag in the water created by the rounded spear handle couldn't compare to the pole oar, which had a flat paddle side. The boat started drifting into the dead center of the river, where the current was strongest.

Ember couldn't believe how fast the river had become deadly. This was not the way the river behaved, normally. The storm had come from the West, which meant the river shouldn't have filled with water so fast. How could a storm from downstream cause water to flow more greatly? Little did Ember know that the storm was a massive front moving north by northeast. A larger portion of the storm system had already dumped a massive amount of water east of Ember. Only by happenstance did she now encounter the rise and rush of water at the same time as the storm. This truly was a very odd weather pattern. Somewhere not too far up the river, a boulder fought a deadly duel with the onrush of water. The proud boulder seemed to be winning.

Water rushed, and the rain fell hard as Ember rode her boat through what resembled a tidal bore. She was suddenly thrust aside as a hard knock from a hidden rock sent the little boat tumbling to the right. She dropped her spear in surprise, feeling her body lurching to the right as though an unseen hand pushed her. Then, reacting instinctively to the fear of the rolling craft, she threw her weight to the left in an act of desperation. The boat halted its starboard roll, but her sudden movement sent it tumbling the other direction, aided by the rushing water.

The little boat rolled from right to left too fast to stop. The water and the hull's rounded shape forced the boat too far over, causing it to capsize. Over rolled the boat, and into the cold rapids went Ember and all her precious supplies. The end of her perilous run had been around a major turn north in the river. There, the water was forced around a bend in the river, the water passing over rapids at either bank.

She fought hard against the current and struggled to orient herself, but the water wouldn't allow her freedom. Down she was dragged as the river held her, tumbling end over end. Her saving grace was the feel of the cool, soft silty sand against her feet as she hit the riverbed. She must have capsized in the shallows of the river, she realized, but how? She had been in the center of the river when she lost her oar. Had the boat moved into the shallows while out of her control? The rock which turned her boat over had to have been in the shallows.

Her lungs burned for air, wiping any thoughts from her mind, yet her arms were not strong enough to pull her from the water's grasp. Ember knew she would have to allow the river to have its way a moment longer. She allowed the river to win and stopped struggling, letting her body glide to the bottom fully. Her feet made solid contact before springing upwards with all the force she could muster. Ember could see the water becoming less dark as she sprang upward, but the effect diminished quickly as her eyesight began to darken from lack of air. She let the air from her lungs leave her mouth, needing them free if she emerged from the water for even a second.

Suddenly, her head broke the surface, and she inhaled air furiously before she was again thrust under. Suddenly Ember's face became free from the river once more, and she gasped more air. The river was indeed forcing her up and down, but she could see that she was nearly ashore. She swam with all the energy she had left, which was not much. As she started to feel the sand in her grasp, she felt her body give way to the strain. The water still had her, and she was being pushed and pulled without any control, her body giving out from a lack of oxygen. She took another half breath, but she had used too much energy in her burst of swimming and was giving in to the water now. This time when she was tugged down by her exhaustion and not the water, she gave in. The light of the evening slowly faded into darkness as Ember just simply let go.

CHAPTER FIVE
ALONE

There really isn't much evidence for large-scale combat in early Neolithic Europe. Armies, warriors, battlements, and fortresses arose much later in history. There is evidence for raids, but wholesale slaughter and total war were not commonplace for many reasons, such as the lack of nation-states and the massive resources needed for such warfare. Individual peoples may have practiced raids for food, tools, or cultural reasons. These would have been local events, and fatalities were probably more incidental than routine. However, massacres did occur on rare occasions, such as the Talheim Death Pit in which 34 bodies were found, possibly murdered.

The sight of an entirely destroyed village with dead everywhere and mass murder would have been abhorrent to Ember. Such raids would not become common in Europe for perhaps another five or six thousand years. Regardless of the reduced threat of violence, Ember grew up in a time when childbirth was very risky, when a poor harvest or a bad winter could kill an entire people, and when harmony with nature was still required for life.

Ember opened her eyes and saw darkness. She was dead, and the river had carried her body away. Perhaps she would drift along the river and decay in some dark place. She felt no pain now and hoped it wouldn't come. The strange thing about dying was the stars all around her. She did not move for a short time, only watching the stars, when suddenly a shooting star caught her eye and snapped her from her daze.

Did the dead float in the sky? she wondered.

As she slowly became conscious, she realized that she had not died but had apparently washed ashore or finished her swim? Ember was lying strewn along a pebbly bank with one of her legs still in the water. All around she heard the song of frogs and insects. She couldn't remember anything past blacking out. The sky was dark and had become night, but the rain had subsided, leaving a mostly clear sky. A slight wind fell upon her skin. Looking down, Ember took a quick and half-dazed inventory of her person. She still wore her precious doeskin shirt, though it was pretty wet and muddy. Ember carefully propped herself up on her elbows and looked around.

A quick check revealed that she was alone on the pebbly riverbank with none of her supplies to be seen. She pulled herself to her feet and stumbled off of the beach toward the brush farther ashore with great effort. Her loincloth had come quite loose, and she tucked it back into place, nearly falling in the process, as she was very weak. The cord was almost broken, but she could worry about that when she had regained her strength. She feared it might break but then realized what little it would matter.

What a silly thing to worry about! she thought as there was probably no person within a day's journey, and of course, the rabbits and deer don't worry about such things as modesty. Thankfully, the well-made shirt had survived, it seemed. Her mind slowly began to go blank. The swim and her ordeal had tired her out much more than she had expected. As she walked up the bank, she nearly toppled over several times from weakness. Dazed, she struggled to walk farther and fell limply into the brush. Finally, she curled into a tight ball against the wind and shivered back to sleep.

That night, Ember dreamed that she was a raven. She took to the night sky and flew high with the stars. Below her, she saw dark forests for as far as the eye could see but dotted with tiny points of light. Each point of light was a great distance from the next. She flew towards one of these points and came in low for a look. The lights turned out to be central hearth fires from small villages. Below her, people walked around talking and living their lives.

Ember, the bird, landed on a wooden post and watched the people. One couple of merrymakers came from a longhouse in each other's arms, laughing and speaking romantically, though Ember couldn't understand them. As they approached, she realized the woman was her. She was perhaps a few harvests older, but the long red hair and green eyes were a giveaway. In her arms, she embraced what looked like a dark-haired woman. Her older self had a necklace with a large shiny yellow pendant and a large dagger at her waist.

Older Ember carried herself as a warrior wearing the loincloth and leggings of a man, though her bosom spoke of womanhood. Her body was painted in dark stripes, with dots below her eyes. As the couple wandered off for some romantically secluded spot, Ember suddenly felt alone. Who was the woman, and why wasn't it a man? She couldn't seem to get a good look at the mysterious partner. She had transitioned from a girl to a woman and ended up on a wacky adventure, the apparent will of the gods. How would she ever go about being a woman when she really didn't even feel like one? She took to the sky to contemplate these questions.

Ember woke to a welcoming sun warming her skin. She was covered in mud, dirt, a few insects, and a bit of vegetation. She slowly sat up and took better note of her surroundings. Her boat was missing and would likely never be found. Given the rage of the storm, her boat was probably halfway to wherever she was supposed to go, by now. A pang of fear and loss hit her, but she forced them down as she had more immediate problems. The throaty sounds of a distant male red deer returned her to the moment.

She was sitting on a large pile of drift brush by a deceptively calm river. Above her flew vultures and a single hawk, while insects hung closer to the ground filling the area with their impossible numbers. Something small scurried in the brush nearby, obviously alerted to the larger animal by her movement. Sitting up, Ember poked a large brown spider which sped off her chest and back into the brush. As she slowly stood to head to the river's edge to clean herself, she caught sight of a massive meg'vahen, one day known as an Irish Elk, on the opposite bank, a rare sight indeed. The world teamed with animals, and they all seemed to be in better shape than the ragged redhead.

She removed her doeskin shirt and stepped tenderly into the same water, now calm, which had nearly been her end just the day before. The water was slightly warmer with the Sun, but the Sun's rays upon her skin made the real difference. She placed her hands on the river's surface and closed her eyes. She said a prayer to the river spirits, thanking them for letting her go, or at least for not taking her.

With her ritual thanks given, Ember dove beneath the water and ran her fingers through her long hair cleaning the debris from it. With a second lung full of air, she dove and scooped handfuls of mud and clay from the bottom of the river. Her mind was still cloudy, but she was starting to recover with the help, ironically, of a good swim. She emerged from the water and began to spread the mud on her skin. She recalled her mother making a special paste from tubers and some other plant she couldn't remember. The paste allowed her to clean her hair more effectively, but the river would provide for now.

After a short while, she had covered her entire upper body with the mud. She feared for her missing supplies and boat, but she could look for them after she cleaned. Ember proceeded to rub the mud vigorously over her skin before diving into the water again and removing it. The mud had an exfoliating effect which left any who used this method feeling clean and refreshed. Standing at ankles depth in the shallows, she washed her lower body using the same method. She removed her loincloth and rubbed it clean in the water. Afterward, she came ashore, took her doeskin shirt, and beat it against a large rock until much of the dirt was removed. The Sun had done its work, and the dried mud and the debris merely fell from the shirt.

Sitting on the bank, she repaired her waist cord, creating a knot from the damaged length of cord. It wouldn't do to let it break when she was walking. Ember replaced the shirt and the loincloth when suddenly she remembered the leather bag and dagger. She had expected her boat and supplies to be lost, but she had not considered the precious dagger and pendant. How had she forgotten those?

A feeling of fear and foreboding dread trickled down her spine. Then, like a startled rabbit, she was off running barefoot down the riverbank, looking for her possessions. She clearly knew the possibility was remote, but she had to look. As best as she remembered, her capsizing had occurred in the shallows at a bend in the river. Much of her possessions would have been lost as she swam ashore. Perhaps some had been washed ashore or were merely left by the water when she awoke, tired as she was. The ground around her had telltale signs of having been submerged recently. Perhaps the river had flooded, and she now stood on what had been underwater the night before?

Regardless of her hopes, Ember needed help, and she had an idea how to get it. Dropping to her knees on a patch of wet sand, she traced a long, wavy line with her index finger. She placed her finger at the end of the wavy line and made a big dot, the head of a snake. She knew that the image was simple and would probably not interest the Snake Goddess or any snake spirits near enough to see. Still, she hoped she might garner some favor in her search from her crude effigy. Gods and spirits tended to like their own images or symbols drawn. In fact, many elders spent much of their time perfecting the addition of such symbols to longhouses and anything her people decorated. She quickly spoke a prayer to snakes, slithery creatures who tended to find their way into unexpected places.

"Snake Goddess, snake spirits, here me. The gods wished me here, and I need my dagger, at least, or I will surely die! Please help me find the dagger." She knew snakes were very chaotic and as likely to bite as to help, but she also knew that a snake lived to cause mischief, and what better sport than to defy the fate of the mighty Great River? Perhaps with some luck the snake spirits might hear her prayer and aid her.

How long would she be searching before she found flint to make another clean edge, though not as good as her obsidian blade? It had been her father's dagger, taken from his stilled hand by her mother all those harvests before. He had used that dagger to defend those he loved – she had to find it. Besides, Ember was not a skilled knapper. Her ability to shape flint came from randomly flaking pieces with a rock, called percussion knapping, or pressing against the edges with a pointy stone or antler piece until pieces came free, called pressure knapping. She was terrible at both.

After she had finished her prayer, Ember stood and moved to the place where she had come ashore, wasting no time. Arriving, she searched the sandy pebbles, looking for any sign of her items. Ember turned and walked northwest along the bank with a weak heart, following the river with little hope. The bank was strewn with branches, and other debris washed ashore by the storm. The river ahead turned sharply, producing a small inlet of sorts.

While river inlets afforded calmer waters for swimming, an inlet also worked as a trap where water was forced with great pressure during such storms. Her people often set nets and traps within such an inlet to capture fish and anything else that wandered into the protected area. As a result, the inlet was full of beached wood and even a few dead fish from the storm.

What a great torrent must have come through here last night! Maybe the river overran the inlet's bank. That might explain the way the ground looks, she conjectured, talking to herself as always.

She approached the far side of the inlet and noticed a giant tangle of brush-covered with debris. It looked fresh, as though it had collected the night before. This was the exact sort of scenario Ember had hoped to find. The destroyed brush covered the piece of land which stuck out into the river and formed the wall of the inlet. There was a muddy trail from one side of the land to the other. This was solid proof that water had indeed overrun the inlet. The water might have flowed over the brambles and driftwood, working as a net and catching anything in the water, like Ember's possessions. Even more, the spot where she now stood seemed like it was directly in line with where she had fallen into the water. Anything falling from her could have been forced into the inlet and over the beach by the water, she hoped.

A surge of hope-filled her as she dove into the brush and started pulling large pieces of wood away and casting them to the side. Ember dug and tore at the wood and brush for a long while, moving from pile to pile without luck. Finally, she stood from her fourth such pile and walked over to the last pile. She dug with reckless abandon, throwing wood in all directions. She was starting to accept that she had truly lost everything. She would have to find stone to shape new tools, but how could she hope to replace her dagger?

Ember caught a glimpse of a stick that was twisted in an odd curly shape. As she reached for the stick, it suddenly sprang at her. She recoiled instantly as the "stick" struck at her with a hiss. The stick was actually a snake. Had the snake been fully coiled, it might have had the range to bite her hand. Luck was with Ember as the snake which nearly bit her was a sort her people called a Black Snake, what would one day be called a European Adder. These little black and gray-colored snakes were vipers, having two long fangs and a venom that could kill a small animal. The snake slithered off deep into the pile of debris, obviously offended. Ember sat back on her butt for a moment leaning back on her hands, a wide-eyed expression.

How could she have been so stupid to search a wood and brush pile without taking care for the creatures that could be found in such a place? Though the little black snake probably wouldn't have killed her outright, she would have been in great pains for days, and without food, she might still have died. When alone in the wilds, one only had to become wounded to die. The wilds would finish you themselves and without the need for the mercy of a quick death.

Suddenly, she caught sight of a familiar-looking object near where the snake had just been. With a gasp, Ember realized the item trapped in the mud and debris was a quality piece of flint. She reached, carefully this time, into the brush. Shocked, she lifted the piece of flint from the brush and examined it. This was a piece from her sack of flint, there was no doubt. She held the flint close for a moment, and with renewed vigor, she dug through the driftwood with greater care.

As she dug, she began to lose hope as no more flint was to be found. When she finally removed her hands from the debris, she brushed against some of the caked mud, which fell away, exposing the tip of a leather thong. She grabbed the thong and pulled free a large clump of mud from the brush. As she removed the mud, she realized that the flint must have fallen free from her bag, which she now held. The little leather bag had been so caked with mud that she hadn't recognized it. Moreover, the bag was tied to the longer leather thong she used for a belt. That same belt also carried the sheath in which her obsidian dagger was kept.

Sure enough, the dagger was still bound to the belt firmly with a small leather cord. She pulled the entire assembly free from the mud and stared at it with disbelief. Then, overwhelmed with relief, she inspected her father's blade for damage, noting that the sheath was still filled with water. The blade remained intact throughout the ordeal, and the little bag had only a small opening at the top from which very little could have fallen out. Inspecting the bag, Ember found much of her flint pieces and the goddess pendant.

I haven't broken my promise, Blossom, she thought, holding the pendant tightly.

What marvel was this but the fate of the spirits and gods? What wonders of delight and terror could they work, and why? Ember spent a long moment just sitting on the gently warming pebbles and sand, pondering the chances of having found her lost items in a massive river and how close she had just come to a bite which surely would have left her in a sorry state. Then, after a few moments of introspection, she became aware of her tears. Not for the first time, she considered the wisdom of the elders in sending her out by herself into these dangerous lands where even the hunters from her village traveled in groups of no less than three. At that moment, she both thanked and scorned the gods for their double-edged obsidian-sharp "signs."

But not the snakes… The Snake Goddess had come through for her, and she wouldn't forget that.

Pak watched as Calpano ambled along, stooping in the bent-forward fashion of a man tracking small game. Calpano was by far the best tracker of the group, and he had again spotted something to eat. Thoughts of the rabbits returned to him with abandon, and Pak let himself fall deeply into his memories to fight the boredom of the current tracking, which might yet take significant time. The previous night had been wet with a major storm. The storm had forced the loss of half of a day of walking, but they had luckily found a cave just before the rains had fallen.

Caves were not numerous nor easy to enter, and often contained a very angry animal with a greater claim. Three men would be hard-pressed to kill or scare off a bear. Caves were also an indignity only the weakest tribes faced when driven from their own lands. His people lived from farming and only a little hunting, so a cave was discordant with his people's ways.

With no food but the dried meat they carried, the night had been quite solemn. Pak's bored thoughts returned to the cave and last night's rain which had driven them inside. The storm had lasted for a long time, and the wind had blown heavily. Without anything to do and only the company of the two most inhospitable men of his tribe, Pak had taken to looking around the cave for points of interest. He fondly remembered the investigation of the previous night as he mindlessly followed along the trail behind Calpano, tripping every now and then.

It had been cold and wet when the trio had found the cave near the river. Rosif had quickly made a fire from driftwood near the entry. He had equally quickly fallen asleep with the understanding that the two younger men would keep the fire tended. Rosif snored loudly by the fire and Calpano whittled away at a piece of beach driftwood he had found. Pak had taken it upon himself to explore.

The cave had not been deep and quickly became too narrow to pass. Pak had continued to move toward the back of the cave, examining the walls and crevices for anything strange. The back walls became dark as they faded from the fire's reach, but soon, they had shown clearly with his torch of animal oil and plant fiber. The walls were made of dark stone, smoother than he had expected, with small outcroppings of disorder.

As he let his hand drift down the rock, Pak noticed an image. At first, he retracted his hand before realizing the human nature of the picture. It depicted some sort of deer and a man chasing it with some kind of spear, Pak suspected. The picture was crude and faded but clearly visible in the torchlight. After a time, he happened upon a handprint on the wall which looked as though someone had blown pigment over their hand, leaving a "shadow" outline behind. Such images were not too uncommon to find in caves though most were barely distinguishable from the rock.

Some said they came from spirits or even from animals living in the caves, but Pak thought them more likely the work of people. How long had they been there? The images appeared very old and depicted hunting techniques primitive compared to what Pak used. Never did he see a bow, but always those spears. Who hunted large prey with a spear? Surely, only a fool approached a large animal with a spear. Large animals were herded and shot with arrows or trapped. Spears were reserved for small game, fish, and other humans.

He had slid down the wall in the cooler, darker part of the cave and allowed himself to slowly drift to sleep. Just as sleep had come upon him,

Pak had wondered if he would ever be remembered in the distant future by other hunters, much as this nameless hand's mark had served its owner. Nevertheless, he had slept reasonably well that night.

Thoughts of a night spent in the cave mildly entertained an otherwise board Pak as he followed Calpano. He couldn't have known that he was quite right about the use of spears or that the crude drawing had omitted the use of a smaller handheld shaft, perhaps half an arm's length, to which the spear was attached. This acted as a lever propelling the spear at greater speeds. Instead, this stick figure used an Atlatl, an ancient weapon long since fallen out of favor and replaced by the bow and arrow. Though it should be noted that even with an Atlatl, only a fool would attack anything larger than a small deer.

ↄ ↄ ↄ

Ember strode along the riverbank for a long while, following the river's flow, but at a much slower pace than travel on the water had afforded. She was slowly making her way north by northwest without any idea of what might come next. She had lost much of her supplies and had now only what she could carry in her hands and attached to her belt. She pondered her current predicament over and over as she walked down the pebbly bank. She had lost her leggings, shoes, apron, coat, food, water, and nearly everything she needed.

Her stomach finally ended the indecision with a deep grumble. She knew she would need some food but not how she would obtain it. Perhaps some small game would do, but first, she would need the means to capture and kill. The skills of basic trapping of small game were known to Ember, like all most members of her tribe, but traps could take days to catch animals, and she would need thread. Ember was hungry now. She would need to make a quick weapon and find some small game if she wanted anything but plants. She searched the bank for a short time before finding a stick nearly as long as she was tall, with a generally straight shaft.

This weapon would need to be more robust than the short-lived fishing spear she had made the night before. She knelt on the dirt and removed her bag. From the bag, she took a long sharp piece of flint that would make an impromptu spearhead. Ember took a bit of flint with a sharp edge and sawed it back and forth over the end of the stick until there was a decent groove. Then, she forced a sharp, flat rock into the groove, splitting it open.

93

Next, she took a larger stone and hammered the first stone, using it as a wedge, into the groove until the stick split, just a little. She removed the stones from the split and inserted the flint head. Using a thong made from the dwindling excess of her belt, she secured the head in place as tightly as she could. Perhaps she would craft a more quality weapon later, but she would use this crude spear to quench her hunger for now. Ember headed off toward the brush, alternating where she searched from the sandy pebble bank to the grassy meadows beyond.

Rivers attracted many small animals, and if a hunter, or huntress as it were, looked about, they were assured of finding something small and furry. Fish was one of her favorite foods, but she was in the mood for something different. After a time, she spotted her quarry, a small brown rabbit happily chewing grass on the shore just a stone's throw ahead. Almost immediately, the rabbit stopped chewing and stood ready to bolt. Ember slowly walked around the rabbit as though she would merely pass a few lengths of a man behind it. Unfortunately, she was not a hunter and had little idea how to do this. Her only hope came from the younger men she would watch returning to the village with many rabbits. Perhaps a rabbit would fall for this most human style of trick.

That's right, rabbit. I'm just passing by. Nothing to see here... she thought. The rabbit was very wary and suddenly ran before she could even lift the spear. She stood there with her arms limp at her side and a grimace. Not even a single sarcastic comment was issued. Then her stomach made a comment. Off in the woods, she watched a small sounder of boar heading to the water to drink. The thought of roasted pork came to mind, yet she knew better than to taunt such a powerful animal. She didn't even have a wad of birch tar gum to chew... then her stomach rumbled once more.

After additional fruitless searching, Ember decided to try the river for food. She strode into the cool water and began her search for dinner. She noticed a large crested newt, but that would just make her sick. Nearby, a group of pond turtles sunned themselves on a rotting log, their yellow spots reminding Ember of her favorite face paint design. Why had she tried to kill a rabbit? She was no good at that sort of hunting. However, fishing had always been her skill. Within a few moments, she noticed several fish swimming a mere arm's length away, the water so filled with life one could simply watch the water for a moment and often see movement. *Such tasty movement*, she thought.

If only rabbits would swim through the water, I could eat piles of them, she thought. Laughing to herself, she slowly moved the spear tip through the water toward the fish. She kept the tip below the water to fool the river spirits, overcoming the distortion they caused. As one of the fish presented its flank, she drew the spear closer. Suddenly the fish kicked its tail to flee the approaching spear, but Ember's quick jerk was faster. *Fish warrior, most feared by the fish,* she mused, impressed by her own skill.

She walked along the riverbank with a still wiggling fish on the end of her crude spear. For the first time in a day, a smile crept onto Ember's face. She had been depressed at her lack of hunting ability, but her actual skills came to light when she entered the water. There was something about having a proficiency, no matter how simple or small, and being good at it delighted her. She was terrible with most of the commonly woman-oriented skills and not so great with many man-oriented skills, but she could find things and was nearly a fish in the water.

With practiced skill, she flung the fish through the air onto the land. When she looked at the gasping fish, she recalled her own drowning and suddenly felt a touch of remorse for the poor creature. To that, she swung her spear, butt first, holding it near the pointed end. The butt of the spear smacked the fish hard on the head, effectively braining it. She twisted her mouth sideways and smirked. Perhaps that was the strangest sort of pity she had ever shown. She shrugged.

Hey, at least, it was quick. Ember renewed her fishing. After a good while, she had captured three fish and picked a handful of tasty river mussels. She walked ashore and knelt on the warm pebbly sand to clean and dress them. As long as this uncommonly warm weather lasted, Ember would be safe from starvation. The problem was that warmth lasted only a short time, and soon, the cold season came. That last notion lasted in her mind as she eviscerated and then cleaned the fish.

With cleaned fish, she merely needed a fire, and she would be hungry no more. She longed for her fire bow. With it, she would have had a fire in moments. Unfortunately, only the gear attached to her when she fell overboard had been found. The bow had probably detached as she swam close to shore. Without a fire bow, the old ways would have to do. Tired and weary, Ember was thankful for the ample driftwood on the riverbank. Without delay, she selected several choice pieces which had been dried by the Sun.

Ember placed a small, particularly dry wooden stick against another piece of wood with some tinder, made from small twigs and leaves. She put her hands on each side of the stick and rubbed them together, forcing pressure downward. This had the same effect as her lost fire bow, but it would take much longer to produce fire. After a short time, sore palms, and several hurt fingers, she had a small fire smoldering. She dropped to her belly and cupped her hands around the tinder, blowing as gently as a morning wind. Within a few moments, a flame rose from the thick, white smoke. She added larger pieces of kindling and slowly created a fire. Ember roasted the cleaned fish over the flame with a long stick as the fire became hot and burned brightly.

Keeping a gutted fish on a stick was not easy. The tail was removed and a slit made from the belly through the tail muscle and out of the hole where the tail had been. The stick was inserted through the mouth and made to exit the hole toward the tail. A second stick, poking into the opened belly, would be needed to turn and control the fish as it crackled over the fire. The mussels were simply placed beside the fire where they could steam from the inside. Their tiny shells would slowly open, telling her that they were done.

Ember slid a fish, as hot as it was, but being very hungry, off its cooking stick and started eating it. The reckless redhead carefully licked burned fingers as she tasted the wonderful fish meat. Next, she ate each fish's heart, her favorite part, as well as other assorted fish organs. Her now oily fingers were a welcomed thing, indeed. She lay back on the pebbly sand and nibbled the inside of each mussel, chewing the sweet, succulent meat. If only she had some salt.

She would need new clothing, better tools, and supplies whether she continued her quest or headed back. Either way, she would need to set up a camp for at least a few days while she fixed these issues. Her food and water were secure, as long as she could stand fish, and the weather was warm, for now. What she needed most was thread. Thread was perhaps the most important tool humans had as nearly everything they made required thread, from arrows to longhouses.

Not far from her "camp" grew tall reeds that were strong and flexible, a great resource, and incredibly useful building material. Reeds, especially the wide, firm ones, often grew by the riverbank. They could be worked into clothing, baskets, and shelters. Ember walked to the bank and carefully selected some choice reeds, noting a crop of tall, green plants that grew nearby. These would be her next task.

She chose an armload of the longest and strongest segments and placed them into a pool of water by the riverbank. They would soak up water and become more flexible over the course of the day. Afterward, she took a moment to remove the large black and yellow striped reed spiders from her hair, making sure not to harm them lest they ask the goddess of spiders for retribution. Even a child knew not to anger the spider goddess. She felt good taking back some control over her situation. She was starting to feel a slight tingle of freedom replacing the previous dread.

She returned to the river a moment later, finding the tall green plants called Deke'aeleh, meaning "bitter biters," known as stinging nettles one day. As a child, she had grabbed one the wrong way and received many "bites," little painful stings from hair-like needles that grew from the plant. Ember quickly removed many of the green leaves, which could be washed and eaten as well as used to treat insect bites. Afterward, she grasped the plants from the root and slid her hands along their shafts. In this way, she removed the remaining leaves and branches, leaving only the long central stems of the plant.

Using her dagger, she cut the stems and took them back to camp to process. A short time later, Ember knelt on the ground by her fire, beating the thick stems, each half her height, with a round river stone to break the outer woody parts. Once broken, she tore the woody parts away by hand, leaving the precious fibers. After a short time, Ember had enough fiber to last her many days. She took the fibers to a nearby tree and hung them in the Sun to dry. Just like that, she had fiber to spin into thread.

With her building materials on the way and food supplies replenished for a time, Ember turned her attention toward herself. The ochre covering her skin had nearly faded away, and more coloring would be needed. Colored skin tended to repel insects, though this was the effect of the colorant used and not the color itself. Painted skin was also a custom of her people. If she were seen by travelers without her paint... Ember shuttered at the indecency of it. She supposed such hypothetical people wouldn't hold it against her, being lost in the wilds, but how embarrassing.

Ember would remedy her clothing issues soon enough, but she could start making a remedy for her body coloring first. She searched the river's edge until she found some quality smooth and pure clay. Scooping a good handful, she returned to her "camp" and placed the clay on a flat rock. Pulling the cool, light-colored clay slab apart, she removed a bit of the purest clay with a rich uniform color. As she pulled the piece of clay out from the slab, tiny bubbles of air and water squished from within the clay. Before she could finish, she found herself poking a finger into the clay and making a funny noise.

Pokee pokee... After a moment of this, she considered how silly she was being and resumed her work. The clay would make a light-colored pigment for her skin. Searching a little longer, she found a similar amount of red clay, which would provide a reddish ochre to contrast the white clay. Lastly, she would need fine ash from her fire, producing black paint when mixed with oil. She rolled the clays into thin tubes and placed them beside the fire to dry. As the clay dried, she checked on her two remaining cooked fish. It was important to guard your food against birds and small animals.

The day was still early, and she was still quite tired from the night before. Ember decided to leave the clay to dry, it was quite wet, and take a short nap while the reeds soaked. She relaxed on the shore for a while, periodically taking a drink from the river and eating some of her cooked fish. What a fine day this was. The Sun slowly warmed her skin, and Ember found herself almost feeling relaxed. As she lay by the water, she broke into a long and cheerful song. While she sang, she listened to her voice as it disappeared into the woods to join the birds and other animals. Her only friend now was the faint echo of her words.

As evening settled in, she sat beside her fire pit, preparing to make a reed mat for her camp. The reeds had soaked most of the day and were now quite flexible. With a bundle of reeds beside her, she hummed a tune as she wove several mats. These would become the floor and roof of her little home, at least for perhaps a tenday until she was ready to continue or return to her people. That was still a decision she had yet to confront.

Ember lay on the sandy beach by her now larger fire, using her shirt to support her head, and fell asleep. It had been a busy day, and she still had a fish for tomorrow's breakfast. The clay would probably be ready by the morning, and she still needed to construct a simple dwelling, but perhaps tonight, she could get some needed rest. The Moon was out, and the sky was a beautiful spray of stars. There were a few clouds, but they were far to the Southwest. She relaxed and let herself drift into a deep sleep. She was recovering, and soon, she would be firmly back in control.

Ember awoke to the sounds of chewing and sniffing. She opened her eyes to a dark sky, the Moon blocked by clouds. She started to wonder if the sound was a dream when she heard it again, this time from her other side. She rolled onto her back and quickly turned her head to look, too frightened to sit up. Not one length of a man from her stood a wolf. The wolf was very large with gray fur and bright yellow eyes, like the Moon. Just then, it slowly turned to regard her.

Staring a wolf in the face close enough to smell its breath, stole hers. She froze, unable to even blink. The wolf lifted its lips showing its fierce, sharp teeth, and issued a low growl. Tears ran down her cheeks, so frightened was Ember. There was no one to help her. Panic and horror danced along her spine as she froze. Suddenly, the animal made a snarling sound which struck Ember like thunder.

The moment of fight or flight came upon her, and she chose the former. Kicking her feet at the dirt before the wolf, she blasted enough sand into the air to disturb the beast. The wolf backed off a short distance and turned with a snarl, lowering its head and baring its fangs. Ember quickly stood on shaky legs and looked around for a stone. Quickly finding a heavy one, her nettle breaking stone, she hurled the tool at the wolf. The stone struck its hind quarter causing it to whimper and scamper off.

How had this happened? Ember's brain slowly began to take in what was going on. She had been so deeply asleep that she had let her guard down. She looked at her precious fire and saw, to her horror, that it was out. Fire would have thwarted the beasts, but she was extremely vulnerable in the dark of night with only her dagger. As if an answer to her thoughts, she heard wolves in the distance. This was a worsening situation, and she needed to react fast if she was to live. Suddenly, she realized why rabbits were so fearful.

If she could just add more wood and blow on the embers, the fire would restart. A moment later, several wolves emerged from the trees ending that prospect. There wasn't time to spend coaxing a fire to life. She turned and ran toward the river, fear filling her with primal panic. Behind her, she heard a wolf right on her heels. Terror struck her like a thunderbolt as the animal's sudden proximity horrified her. She dashed into the water, splashing in all directions, quickly wading in, waist-deep. She fought to move farther into the river, hearing the splash of a wolf right behind. As she felt the current tug against her waist, the sound of the wolf diminished.

Ember turned in time to see the beast leaving the water. Her vision was tunneled, though it slowly returned to normal. The wolf had only just placed its paws in the river, not wishing to go deeper than a finger's length. She stood shaking in the cool water with a crisp breeze blowing to make things worse. The season was warm, and she knew she could stand the water temperature for quite a while, but could she stand being in the river for the rest of the night? Even when people could swim in the Great River, it was still quite chilly. As if to punctuate that thought, three more wolves emerged from the forest edge, raising the total count of wolves to four.

This must be a pack, she thought.

Ember's options seemed a little bleak, but she had survived the river and was not about to be killed by some random wolves. People lived in villages for a reason, but a lone human was really outclassed by most animals. She would have to use her superior brain to defeat these skilled hunters. As the wolves slowly came from the forest to stalk by the water's edge, she made up her mind. She would try and walk down the river far enough to keep safe and hope the wolves would lose interest. As she walked, slowly due to the strength of the slow but mighty river, the wolves continued to follow her. For a while, she continued, and the wolves followed. She was becoming frustrated.

"Shoo! Go away! Stupid wolves!" The wolves appeared quite willing to wait her out, not good at all. A new thought occurred to her. What made her think the morning would somehow banish them? Just how long would they linger? Not far down the river, Ember decided on a new and more proactive strategy. She was at a standoff distance, and the wolves could not advance without braving a river, something she was sure they would not do. Ember might eventually become too tired and become their meal or be swept away, but they would pay and pay dearly in the meantime. She strode closer to shore where the water was shallow and stuck her arms underwater, feeling around for stones. The wolves approached her cautiously. When her arms emerged from the water, they bore a new arsenal of ranged weapons.

The gods had given the wolves speed and a powerful bite, but they gave Ember long arms, a good aim, and the understanding to use her environment as a tool. As she lifted the first missile, the wolf she had struck before turned and stalked away with its head down, low. She hurled a rock at the same wolf, hoping it would leave for good. The stone missed its target, but the wolf did scurry farther away. The others looked worried, dipping heads and pacing about, but they were not yet broken. Ember continued to hurl stones at each of the wolves in turn.

As the stone rain fell on the wolves, they lost interest quickly, several taking nasty hits to their heads. The warm seasons provided lots of animals to eat, and the need to hunt a single person was not worth being battered so much. Regardless, they remained close by on the edge of the woods in the event she was foolish enough to come ashore. Seeing their persistence, Ember lost heart quickly. As their distance increased, her aim decreased. As if noting this, the wolves moved even farther from the water. She couldn't hurl a stone far enough to hit them.

Ember was standing in the chill waters of the flowing river without a warm Sun and still quite tired as the water slowly sapped her strength.

100

Every now and then, she thought she felt something bump her leg, but she couldn't see what it had been as the waters were just too dark. Fear was starting to become ever-present as the night rolled along. She felt her will to stand in the water wane with still half of the night ahead of her. She slowly started her walk downstream again but was unsure if the wolves were following. Perhaps she could come ashore and climb a tree. From a tree, she could secure a place to rest, though sleep would be dangerous.

After much time had passed, when the wolves had not been seen or heard from in a while, Ember approached the shore. She brought two large stones, one in each hand, but she did not consider them anything more than a token against her own fear. Even if she threw them perfectly, which she would likely not, only two wolves could be wounded, at best. There were, at least, four.

Ember slowly placed her first cold foot onto the sand and then her second, moving slowly and cautiously, listening for any movement. The trees by the bank were small and not so firm. Farther in, a short dash, were larger, full-sized trees. Before her stood a massive tree with thick, sprawling limbs. She was pretty sure she could climb that tree, but she would have to run into the bushes and the start of the forest to get to it. That would leave her vulnerable for a moment, perhaps a moment too long.

Slowly she walked, as quietly as her feet could step, toward the tree line. Once, she thought she even saw the gold rings of wolf eyes. She kept walking, her heart pounding in her chest, heaving as it already was. Ember suddenly stepped on a dry branch snapping it and creating a loud sound. Then, in the left corner of her eye, she saw movement. With a burst of pure panic, she sprinted for the tree, only just ahead. Her feet pounded into the ground, and her arms pumped as she ran blindly, fueled by pure terror and adrenalin, her vision darkening for everything but the tree. Just as she was near to safety, she heard the low growl of a wolf right on her heels. This caused her to move even faster than she thought she could, a blind run.

Ember all but ran up the tree, planting one foot into the thick bark and the other right above it. The sharp bark bit into her skin as her momentum carried her up to her first-hand hold, then the second. She literally pulled her body up to the first branch with just her arms, a feat she couldn't have usually done but for her fight or flight panic. Her tunnel vision and adrenaline made her goal of the next branch above her all she could think of, and she ignored all pain. The first pull had hurt her arms though perhaps saved her life, but she couldn't pull herself up again, her momentum spent. Below her, the wolves jumped at the tree, snarling and growling. Floundering, Ember kicked with her feet while she fought for a better grasp on the branch she was holding. The thought of being eaten alive filled her veins with primal fear. She could nearly pull herself up, but her weight was just a little heavier than what her arms could lift.

So close... no! she thought.

Ember knew pure terror as she felt her arms slowly giving way and her body sinking toward the wolves. She was to be eaten alive. Her feet suddenly found a wet, furry face to step upon, and she planted all her weight on that face, a now yelping wolf. She reached with her weakened right arm and grasped the branch above. The leg-up from the reluctant wolf was all she needed, and moments later, she was in the tree sitting on a large branch. Ember held the trunk as tightly as a newborn held its mother. She quivered in fear as the wolves growled below. Their interest renewed by the meal so close and the droplets of blood and urine from above.

She sat there in horror for a while, watching the wolves. She had lost her rocks somewhere before the trees. If she still had them, she could have taught these beasts a lesson. After a short time, the wolves lost interest and stalked off; she was unsure how far. For a time, Ember held tightly to the tree, gently crying as fear left her. She had never been so frightened in her life. When she finally calmed down, she checked herself for damage. The throbbing in her feet told her the answer. Her feet had bit literally into the tree, catching the bark and holding fast by the force of the bark digging into the soft flesh.

Ember shed many a tear as she removed a few pieces of bark. Her poor feet would heal quickly, they always had, but she needed to stay in one place for a while, especially if a fever came. Sometimes wounds might cause a person to become very hot to the touch and even flush with color. Rest, removing debris from the wound, and heat were beneficial in reducing the chance of this.

She needed a good rest as well as some security. Mostly, she needed a boat. She decided that the following day she would build a proper camp. With a shelter, fire, and traps, camps would offer security and a warm place to sleep. As she thought about the fire and how she would make a boat, she slowly fell asleep, still clutching the tree. Luckily, humans had a long history of arboreal adventures, and true to her primate heritage, Ember snuggled against the tree, tightly, all night.

Each morning brought a new chance for life and a fresh look at the world. Ember awoke that next morning with a sense of hope. She had lived through the night and now would take measures to ensure that life continued. Her arms hurt from being wrapped around the tree all night, and her legs throbbed from springing to life from a dead sleep without taking the time to stretch. Worst of all were her poor feet, which continued to ache. Today she would take it slow and build a temporary camp to heal and rest for a few days. Perhaps she could construct a new boat, even though she wasn't entirely sure how that was done. However, she did know how to rig a camp. Camps generally had the same design wherever you went. A central fire to cook, provide heat, perform rituals, and ward against animals, such as wolves, a simple hut made of wooden poles and thatching, a bed of woven reeds, and defenses. Everything else was decoration or convenience.

Ember climbed down from the tree and walked the short distance toward the river she had run to and from so fast the night before. Her feet hurt from their cuts, but the wood seemed to have not wounded her as badly as she had thought the night before. Her right foot bled a little, but blood loss cleaned a wound and was not to be feared unless it became a great amount. Generally, Ember was in physically acceptable shape, but she was without footwear, fire bow, boat, or much hope. With a sigh, she set to work gathering sticks for kindling and firewood for the main fire.

After a short while, she had gathered plenty of wood and even found her hunting spear in the process. The spear lay on the ground near her previous campsite by her reed mats. As she examined her camp, she also kept a wary eye out for the wolves. Her butt hurt from sitting in the tree all night, but tonight she would not make the same mistakes. Ember set about fishing in the river for a quick meal, her previous meal oddly missing. In time, she would look for a more varied food supply and perhaps even dig for tubers in the forest or look for other edible morsels.

Drinking river water was generally safe, as the water flowed, though it was possible to become sick, and some did. Ember didn't worry much as she bent low, in between spearing a fish, and drank her fill, finishing with a prayer to the river spirits. When she returned to the shore, several fish lay in a pile, one or two still flapping about. Once out of the water, she applied her loincloth. She had taken it off to clean from the previous night. The stains on the leather reminded her just how horrifying the night had been. She hoped the leather would hold up for a few more moons as she didn't have a replacement.

That done, she returned to the fish. The wet fish on the bank would soon dry in the Sun and become inedible if not tended to. Fish needed to be preserved. In place of salt, Ember decided she would try and smoke them. Quick smoking might not work at all and wouldn't last for long if it did without salt, but she hypothesized that smoking might gain a day or two of longevity for the fish. In truth, she had never done this, though she had seen it done, and had no idea if it would work. With such thoughts in her mind, she began work on a smoking rack.

Ember placed two sticks with Y-shaped ends into the ground and put a pole across the top so the Y ends would hold the pole horizontally. This created a sort of cooking rack to place food over a fire. She put long sticks into the ground around the main smoking rack and pulled them together at the top, binding them with wet reeds. This created a sort of miniature cone shape to trap the heat and smoke. She trotted down to the river and grabbed another arm full of reeds. She carefully wove them in and out of the sticks she had placed around the rack until the tiny structure had a small reed top, resembling a little hut. They were stiff, having not been soaked, but they were workable. With her tiny smoking hut complete, she would construct a larger hut for herself later.

After a short while had passed, Ember had two fires burning: one to make charcoal from logs and another, smaller fire beside the tiny smoking hut to smoke the fish. On the rack within the smoking hut, six fish now hung by their tails with smoke and heat pouring across their flesh. Ember was unsure if this smoke method would work. She had only seen others doing it and had never actually performed the task herself. Without salt, it should still work, though she wasn't entirely confident. Within a little while, she would taste the *fish* of her labor.

Until then, she had other concerns. First, the sand must be cleared of debris that might attract unwanted guests. Secondly, grasses were required to make a place to sleep for the night until a hut could be made. Long grass made the foundation of her temporary bed. The cleaning, smoking, and preparations continued until the end of the midday. With her work now mostly done and plenty of the day remaining, Ember sat down for a quick rest and pondered the construction of a boat. She had seen men create such a craft before, but she was never paying much attention when they did.

Perhaps they dug into the wood of the log with stone tools, yes... that was it. Her mind was slowly recalling the missing parts, but it would take time to recall. First, she would need to find a good log.

As evening came, she sat down by the smoke hut and carefully removed one of the fish. As she suspected, the fish didn't really have the same consistency as properly smoked fish, but they had cooked and would most likely last a day or two without going too bad. Ember carefully removed the fish's skin. She squeezed the skin over the flat rock she had used for the clay. Small drops of fish oil fell upon the rock. Had she thought of this beforehand, she might have saved the fish livers, which contained much oil. Ember picked up a few fish bones saved from the previous camp, placing them on another small flat stone and set the stone into the fire. Tomorrow she would use the oil and fish bones to make herself black body paint.

She spent the rest of the late day and evening swimming and soaking in the healing waters of the river. The cool water soothed her muscles and numbed the pain in her foot. Thoughts of the wolves returned to Ember and caused a shiver down her spine. How close had she come to death? A hunter with weapons and fire was a formidable opponent to a wolf, and wolves rarely ever approached people... unless those people ventured deep into the wide-open lands, alone. Ember was sure she had even heard the hunters explain how wolves usually ate small animals like mice and rarely attacked larger animals. Their behavior had been odd, but it was what it was, she supposed.

Ember had escaped and now used her cunning and skill to prevent such events from happening again. Thoughts of her camp and the traps she would soon set brought a sense of control back into her mind. The waters suddenly felt cooler and more wonderful to the relaxing redhead, and she became acutely aware of their flow across her skin. Afterward, Ember came ashore, her body fully clean and her hopes restored. The water had made her foot feel much better.

I would have made a good fish, she thought.

The last task before bed was the setting of traps. Ember selected many small sticks and cut them with her dagger to have pointed ends. Each of the tiny hand-length spears was held over the fire until it had dried and hardened, which took a good time. Ember took the tiny blackened spikes and buried them around the perimeter of the camp. Each spike sat in a small bowl-shaped hole in the sand, pointed up. Over each of the little pit traps, just big enough for foot or paw, leaves and debris were placed. Ember carefully memorized the correct run through the tiny traps and into the water. Around the outside of the traps, she added many long but thin twigs. These twigs would break loudly if someone or something sneaked upon her. Ironically, she had gotten the idea from the loud twig, which had nearly cost her life the night before. Lastly, beside her fire, she placed a pile of perfectly sized rocks. She would hurt any wolves which came for her tonight.

The evening drew to a close, and night fell with a slight breeze. The weather was generally warm, and the nights were tolerable without the use of furs for warmth. Regardless, Ember couldn't get past the thought of a warm fire. Soon she had built up the second fire from a simple charcoal manufacturing operation to a raging flame. Beside the fire, many large pre-charred logs sat ready to burn. Her fire would last all night with this much wood.

She sat beside her fire wearing her loincloth as the shirt couldn't afford to be damaged from being slept in. She felt the fire's heat as it drifted across her skin as gently as the wind. She watched the little hairs on her arm stand when the cooler wind blew but settled down when the heat of the fire returned. Ember was never one to sleep close to the hearth, but she was starting to change her mind about this issue. The radiance of the flames was simply intoxicating against her skin. Only the occasional popping bit of hot material caused her concern. The warm wind blowing across her bare body was just too appealing. Perhaps being alone wasn't so bad. Ember watched the river flow slowly by while she drifted off to sleep.

She awoke the next morning to find that she had rolled around in the sand and was now lying in the gritty substance. Luckily, she hadn't rolled near the fire. She would need to place rocks between her and the fire for the next night. After a moment of carefully stretching her body, she stood and took in a deep breath of air. The large fire had long died, but the effect had kept animals from her fish, and she was rewarded with a quick breakfast. Today she would have to create a small hut to provide her shelter and perhaps obtain additional food. She couldn't eat fish forever.

She turned to the main fire and carefully touched the small stone with the now charred fish bones. The rock was hot but not so much that she couldn't lift it. She ground the little bones into black powder with a small stick and mixed this with fish oil. Within a few moments, she had a paste dark as night, a simple black pigment of oil and ash. She stood and walked to the river for a bath. She ran her hair through the water and cleaned her skin with mud. Within a short time, her skin was clean and smooth, as always.

Ember bound her hair tightly and flung her head backward and forward, slinging the water from her hair. This time, she let her hair fling more than her head, as her mother had shown her. She finished with a short jog down the river shore and back, allowing her body to awaken and dry off. The run was slightly painful for her sore foot, but she was careful to remain in the sand and away from the hard ground. She would need to keep an eye on her foot and ensure it healed.

Once she was mostly dry, Ember pulled her long red hair back and tied it with a thong into a ponytail, inserting a long black feather she had found. She returned to the camp and carefully painted her face and arms in the black, white, and red pigment. Using her fingers, she traced little zigzagging lines down her arms and her face as decoration, more out of habit than the thought of meeting anyone out here. The pigment immediately started working, keeping her quite warm in the Sun, but while it warded most insects, it attracted a few others.

That's what I get for using fish oil, she thought.

The rest of the day was spent looking for a log large enough and long enough to make another boat and a few large poles to make a lean-to hut. Ember remembered having seen the men burn the center of a log with coals as they dug with stone axes. Her memory had been working as she slept. Perhaps, in a few days, she might create a simple version of such a boat? Otherwise, she was going to have to walk the entire way northwest.

I guess I could sit on a log and ride it the whole way, she mused. It was a possible method, and some people occasionally used such means, but the entire trip with her legs in the water would be uncomfortable and possibly dangerous. Feet left wet for too long could make you sick.

As the day continued toward the evening, Ember took the now dried nettles from the tree and prepared them for use. She rubbed her hands together with the nettles inside, stripping even more of the thick outer material and leaving her with a pretty ample supply of fiber. Usually, she would have used a drop spindle, a fired clay weight called a whorl, which acted as a flywheel, affixed to a short stick. This spindle spun, aiding in the twisting of fiber into stronger thread.

Without the spindle, she would have to spin and ply the fibers by hand. She quickly spun a few times her length in fiber, enough to make her new home as the Sun sank low. Some lengths were easily spun, while others required a splicing method. Manufacturing cordage, thread, yarn, and twine were second nature to her people. From a mere four harvests age, Ember already knew these simple techniques.

Ember gathered the materials she had found. She removed the extra limbs and bits from long solid branches she had gathered. She placed them in the ground pointed up in a half-circle around a large tree trunk, much as she had constructed the smoking hut. She buried each "pole" a hand's length into the sand and gathered their tops together against the tree. Ember spent a long time that evening lashing the poles with her nettle twine and weaving reeds around the poles making a simple framework. As the Sun set, Ember was only halfway done creating the mats, which would be affixed to the framework and run vertically. These would stop wind and rain, but not tonight.

How long would Ember remain in this tiny lean-to barely big enough for her to curl up? She had to get to the West before the season changed, but wouldn't a boat help that goal? The longer she remained, the more likely she might find a log and make a boat, but the longer she stayed, the cooler the season would become. The cold season was death to the unprepared. Ember would need to kill a deer by some fashion and make cold season clothing, either way. Unfortunately, tanning took a long time, and rawhide was a short-lived answer to her problem. Many worries flooded Ember's mind.

That night was one of the clearest Ember had seen in many seasons. This was all well and good as far as she was concerned, given that her hut was still not complete, and totally dark nights could be frightening. The night brought with it a gentle, barely detectable breeze. The spirits of the wind often became tired after their most fierce outbursts, and clear skies were often soon to follow heavy rain. The sky was filled with more tiny points of light than Ember could ever hope to count. The biggest of these lights was the waning Moon.

The Moon was a religious symbol of her people's main gods, the Hunter and the Moon Goddess. The Moon was perhaps a place where these two gods lived? Maybe a round pool of water in the vast sea above? She wondered, though no one knew for sure. By contrast to the harvest gods and the Sun God, the Moon was more in league with Ember's current state, and she welcomed the massive light it cast upon her new, unfinished hut. Ember slowly slipped into a deep sleep, comforted by the gentle crackling of a warm fire blocking the only entry into her protective shell.

She awoke with a clear head and a new goal in mind. She had seen a large fallen tree high on a hill a good distance from her camp. She could only barely see it, but the odd shape it cast among the trees around it had caught her keen eyes. The camp was on the bank of the river in the harder, more packed sand close to where the grass started to grow. The tree had fallen on the crest of a hill just beside the river, not too far from where she was now but higher in elevation. Ember would journey up the hill and see what could be had of the tree. With some luck, she might even make a boat out of the trunk.

After an early morning swim and a reapplication of her new body paint, Ember spent the early part of the morning eating some of her fish and nettles. She longed for the quality paint that stained her skin and remained for many days. Her improvised paints were coarse, smelly, and just not to her liking. She was glad she had something, at least. Regardless of the paint problems, she needed to diversify her food supply. Foraging would provide new food sources as people who only ate one thing for too long tended to become ill. All of this could be done when she visited the hill to inspect the log.

The forest would often provide food if you knew where to look. Ember hoped to find some berries for their medicinal value and their ability to make beautiful body stains. The two main berries were Bitter-Berries, a dark-colored berry that could be mixed with nut oil, and Red Berries, which were made of little clusters of tiny red orbs. Red Berries were sweet and a favorite treat for Ember. Both could be used to make body stains, but she was more concerned with food than looks right now.

Aside from berries, a lucky forager might find Tuber Flowers. These purple flowers sprouted from a tasty tuber root buried beneath the ground. The root and the leaves were edible and added a lovely side dish to any meal. When she was a little girl, Ember would find these tuber flowers and pick them to place in her hair. Of course, her mother would scold her for this. Once the flower was picked, finding the tuber root was nearly impossible unless you knew where the original flower had been. Other available foods included Early Nuts, a small nut that fell in the late warm season, before the Spike Nuts fell in the harvest season, and a host of edible green plants. With thoughts of food in mind, she set out into the deeper forest.

Getting to the hill where the tree had fallen took Ember a good part of the morning. Cheerfully, she sang a tune as she walked toward her goal. Moving up a hill was always harder than coming down, and she had to walk extra carefully as she still had no shoes. Her feet were tough from a life of walking around barefoot, but this was the thick forest. She had some small cuts and hurts on her feet, which needed daily tending with water and drying by the fire to ensure they didn't become worse. Luckily, the deepest wounds from the bark were coming along well, though they bled a few times that morning.

Ember could not be too upset about a small wound with a bit of blood. She had seen men who had been wounded hunting or by accidents and had died in a very terrible way from superficial injuries left untreated. Fire truly cleaned everything, and Ember had spent the last two days with her feet propped near the fire as she rested, letting the heat melt away all that could make her wounds red and sore. More importantly, it prevented the red blotches. A wound left untreated might become red, then sore, and finally, little red blotches would flow from the wound towards the center of the body. Next, cold sweats would come, and the person would die soon after. Such a death was horrible to witness and likely worse to experience.

Na Na had explained to Ember that evil spirits could enter the body through cuts and wounds. Merely washing the wound was not enough. The spirits could only be driven from the body by the constitution of the person, medicinal plants, such as the use of White Flowers or honey, or from the purifying power of fire. In fact, one of the last possible cures, when all seemed lost, was to place the person between two large fires and allow the flame to heal them. The heat would be very intense, and the person would need to drink water constantly. Sometimes this worked, but most of the time, they died anyway.

The walking upset Ember's injured foot slightly, and she wished, not for the first time, that she had some White Flowers. The precious flowers grew in fields and open areas throughout the land. Their leaves could be ground or chewed and then applied to the wounds to cause them to stop bleeding and to heal faster. As legend had it, the flowers prevented the spirits from breathing, the reason they kept the wound clear. Ember suspected that the water also prevented spirits from breathing, a good reason to always soak the wounds.

As she stood finally on the crest of the hill, she was able to get a clearer view of the Great River's majesty. The river ran through the forest for as far as the eye could see. She was merely twenty lengths of a man above the ground, but her perspective revealed a good distance each way from the higher ground. From here, she realized just how far she had already traveled. There were none of the landmarks she knew and a forest which went on in every direction as far as the eye could see.

She finally found the tree she had seen from the shore. The fallen tree was very large and looked like it could be the perfect size to make a boat. She ran toward the tree and slapped her hands upon it in victory. The log gave way, and her hands moved partially into the wood. For a moment, she looked at her sunken hands in shock, which quickly turned to disgust. The tree turned out to be rotten and not usable for any sort of boat.

"Ahhh!" she screamed aloud. Ember sat on the rotted trunk and considered the consequences of this revelation. Without a suitable log,

110

she couldn't make a boat. She certainly didn't have the skill to fell a tree, and she was still not sure she even knew how to build a quick dugout boat. She would now be forced to walk northwest. As best as she could guess, figuring her speed on land, how far she could see, and the stories of traders, she expected that she might make the western lands before the cold came if she moved fast. This would require taking a break to finish healing her feet and to make some quality footwear, which would, in turn, require a hide or plenty of cordage. All of this took time, and Ember didn't really even know how far the lands to the West truly were, but she had to try.

She sat on the more solid part of the log considering the ways she might trap and kill a red deer or perhaps some rabbits when she suddenly noticed a thin line of smoke flowing in a long and slow path up from the darkest portion of a hill on the other side of the river, east of her current path. The smoke was so faint from this distance that she wouldn't have noticed it had there been any wind or had she not been up so high looking down against the dark background of the forest. Where there was smoke, there was fire, and where there was a small, controlled fire, there were people.

Ember was joyful and filled with relief. Finally, there were people she could speak with, trade some of her flint for hides, or even learn about the West. Then, with the sudden promise of a quick fix and the need to see people, she burst into a run. She ran most of the way, heedless of her feet, toward her camp. She would prepare to meet the travelers, all thoughts of berries forgotten. Based on the distance of the smoke, they could end up at the river by the evening or perhaps earlier if they were fast. As she made her way toward the little camp, she thought of all the hardships she had faced. She had been nearly killed by the river, eaten by wolves, and even found a village devastated by evil men from some distant land... and then the realization hit Ember like a branch to the face. She stopped running and dropped low, though pointless, as the people were much too far away to see her.

What would these people be like? Were they somehow automatically nice just because they seemingly came to her rescue, or had she been so afraid and longing for human kindness that she had forgotten that people could be either good or evil? For that matter, who said they would come to her rescue at all? They might not even come this way, and why would they want to trade with a young woman anyway when they could just take what she had? How could she even stop them? These questions bothered Ember as she made her way more slowly down to the camp.

Ember came to a hard decision after much thought. She would hide the traces of her camp, stowing the poles and reeds where the travelers would not see them, but where she could return and reclaim them afterward. She would watch the river that night from nearby and observe these people, should they even arrive. Then, she could make her choice with more evidence and less speculation. She would play it safe.

Ember spent the rest of the day packing up her poles and reed mats. She hid most of them within another rotten log near the camp. This closer log was very obviously rotted, and she had never considered it of use. The log was filled with dirt and debris from floodwaters. To remedy this, one of the stronger poles was inserted into the log, and a large rock was used to beat the pole through the log. Ember used this method to clear out the rotted innards, a tiring job indeed.

After what felt like the entire day, and mostly was, she had covered her tracks as best as she could. She now sat on the hilltop by the fallen tree awaiting the people. Ember placed one of her simple reed mats on the ground and lay upon it with her back against the tree's stump. As the long evening gave way to night, she became increasingly aware of what a friend a warm fire could be. She could hear animals of many types moving through the brush as well as insects dancing the night away, as insects should. Next to her, she had a supply of rocks and a spear.

Don't worry, wolves, I haven't forgotten you, she thought with a sarcastic smile.

Ember was carefully listening to the sound of a particular set of insects when suddenly they stopped. In fact, all insects had stopped. She rolled over and onto her knees. As she looked around, she noticed a large, four-legged shape moving slowly through the night not far from her. Ember's breath came in short, low pants as she tried to remain calm and quiet. As soon as she had seen the creature, it had gone. She fumbled with her magazine of rocks, finding a large smooth stone, and hurled her missile at the shape in the dark. She heard a growl and frightened snarl, and then the shape ran off into the darkness of night. She lay still against the tree, terrified for a long time before the stress of the encounter overcame her, and she fell asleep. Ember was genuinely starting to understand why rabbits were so fearful.

CHAPTER SIX
HUMANITY

Morality is quite fluid among humans if history has shown us anything. Usually, there is a degree of compassion for one's own group, but this compassion rarely extends far beyond even the slightest differences in race, religion, culture, and status. Being different, even just slightly, has been the basis for wars, conquest, and any number of human atrocities. Even in our modern era, we see this happening, from the persecution of Jews, people of color, and LGBTQIA+, to the marginalization of women, the disabled, and nearly any other group who does not fit the current ruling group.

What was moral at one point may be considered immoral at another. The Romans killed thousands of people, both adults and children, via crucifixion, while Hammurabi considered an eye for an eye, just. Within the colonial world, slavery was often considered moral, as was the burning of women as witches. It can be objectively shown that these practices were not moral, using the modern secular moral concepts of doing the least harm, but it is important to realize that they were, at one time, considered moral – though they were, in fact, not. Given the lack of modern laws and a system of authority to protect her, Ember is right to be fearful of a group of men from another people. What are their morals? What would they make of her, and what disposition might she have to them? If they chose to be hostile, what could she do about it?

Ember awoke in the early morning with a blanket of dew across her body and a crisp wind gently tickling her face. She had worn her clothing to bed, just to be safe as she had fallen asleep without a fire or protection, aside from a few stones. She scolded herself for her foolishness as she could have become dinner, but risks had to be taken. Her self-berating was interrupted by the sudden sound of men. Had she just heard a faint laugh in the distance, or had it been a dream? Had the wolf, or whatever it was, been a dream too?

She stood so fast that she became slightly dizzy, still not entirely awake. Placing a steadying hand against the fallen tree while her heart caught up with her actions, she gazed in the direction of the sound. Sudden movement caught her eye. Three men strode down the riverbank where she had set camp. Ember dropped to the ground and peeked cautiously over the cliff. From this distance, the chance of the men seeing her was minimal, but why take the risk?

She remained cautious because she had seen this hill and the rotted log from where the men now stood, so she couldn't be too careful. Ember was surprised that she had even heard them, not only because of their distance from her but the general fact that hunters typically didn't yell so loudly, giving their positions away for all to hear. Given their slightly different clothing, Ember assumed they bore no relation to her local people. Her heart pounded, filling her veins with the feeling of adventure and excitement. She was the hunter watching these men walk about without any notion of her presence. This gave an entirely new meaning to what Fire Blossom had called "man-hunting," her term for the never-ending ridiculous lengths the girls of her tribe had taken to attract the attention of a group of hunters who had visited a few seasons back.

She recalled those happy days with a pang of longing. Ember, Blossom, and another girl she liked named Pine had run about making mischief, giggles all around, for days until one of the hunters had scolded them. She laughed, remembering their very negative reaction to the scolding. Ember scooped up her knife and other belongings. If these men continued west, she might be forced to follow them for a while until she could be sure of their intent and her safety. They were currently her best bet for new supplies. Besides, they might even be willing to let her follow them.

For now, she would observe them before making contact. She crawled on her hands and knees away from the edge of the overlook and behind some brush from where she could more secretly view the intruders. As she watched, a light-haired man was standing near where her camp had been. She held her breath. What if he found something she had forgotten? Then these men would be on the alert. Ember was starting to feel more like a doe than a hunter. She nervously adjusted the black feather in her hair.

After a short time, a larger, dark-haired man waved at the other two men, and all three left the area heading northwest, following the river. Ember sat for a moment, considering her choices. She had to get to the West before the seasons changed, and she would likely never find a boat-worthy log in this area. The river had cut through the land as it moved northwest and the banks gave way to hills. If she clung to the shallow hills while following the men, she could determine their intentions as well as scout for a log. If she found a large enough log, she would abandon the men and create a boat. Abandoning her camp was a painful thought, given the work she had put into it, but she just couldn't let this chance go. People rarely encountered other people in the wilds without the luck of the gods. With her decision made, she felt another surge of courage.

I am the hunter now, she laughed.

Pak, son of Ran, son of Torn

Ember walked briskly across the hilltop, following the same heading as the men but staying behind them a good distance. As the day rolled on, the stalking became more dull than exciting. She thought they might have seen her several times, but if they had, they made no indication. She continued on her way north by northwest, each step becoming more confident as the men walked not far below, near the bank of the river, laughing and seemingly unaware. More importantly, she noted, they were walking the same way she was headed.

Her feet ached from their wounds, but they seemed to be improving, pain aside. For most of the day, the group followed the river as she tagged along. Even though she was technically hiding from them, walking with the men afforded her some company, if non-reciprocated. Further, the fire and noise the men created would ward her from most animals if she slept relatively close, she supposed. She had even found some edible greens, berries, and a few nuts along the way.

As evening fell, the party had become preoccupied with finding a campsite and had examined several small fields slightly inland from the river. Ember waited until the men had found a suitable spot and busied themselves with the work of preparing for bed.

The larger, older, dark-haired man with a permanent frown was obviously the leader. He would yell at the other two, though the younger blonde-haired man would occasionally yell back. After a while, she decided their "yelling" was more of a playful bickering, though more aggressive than she would have found comfortable. Ember supposed this was how men acted when away from a tribe. It was interesting, though a bit gruff for her taste. Never-the-less, the men seemed to enjoy it just fine.

The youngest was a dark-haired man who looked only perhaps a harvest or two older than she. He was actually rather attractive, she thought. He had shoulder-length dark hair and a well-toned body, though he was a bit skinny. Ember decided that he would feel warm if hugged, though it was just speculation. He seemed shyer than the others, sitting farther from their fire than the bickering blonde and the leader. Was the younger man brooding? It was hard to tell as he sat on a leather hide eating some game they had cooked. Ember watched him for a while until her own stomach cried for food.

Ember lay in a tuft of grass not too far from the men as the night settled in. She had found a pile of river mussels and nettle leaves, but she would need to either make contact with the men or catch and cook some fish the next day. Keeping up with travelers while staying hidden was quite a chore. At least she could be reasonably confident animals would avoid the camp. Of course, she could always call out to the men if a wolf did attack, though that might carry its own risk.

Her feet still hurt as they hadn't finished healing, and she needed to obtain leather for boots, something the men had. Ember slowly fell asleep to the sound of the men joking and laughing in the distance. She couldn't understand them, but she enjoyed the company just the same. Tomorrow, she would consider leaving them be or showing herself. That night she dreamed she was a rabbit running through a field. A hawk followed her from above. She ran and ran, but the hawk was ever-present...

116

Ember woke to the sound of a large twig breaking. She sat up straight and turned to see three startled men staring at her. Her mind was foggy from having just awoken, and the men were a bit startled to see a red-haired woman pop out of a grassy field in the middle of the wilds. The three dumbfounded men and the groggy woman stared at each other in silence for a short moment. Ember realized from their expressions that they had not seen her until she sat up and probably would have passed by had she not. She had just given away her location.

"Aeeya..." she whispered. Adrenalin surged down her spine like cold water and rebounded at her fingers and toes, flowing back through her as Ember's heart began to beat nearly twice the speed it had been not moments before. Suddenly, Ember was the rabbit from her dream. Her arms and legs tensed as her muscles became taut. For a moment longer, the men and Ember stared at each other in shock, then as suddenly as a frightened rabbit, Ember scooped up her shirt-turned-pillow and bolted. She tore off as fast as she could, hoping the men would not follow. Many of the girls in her tribe would find running a problem as they came of age, but Ember had come of age in a less pronounced manner. She could run with her arms pumping as fast as any man.

She ran through reeds and long grass as fast as a rabbit, bounding over felled branches and rocks. As she ran, she heard the men behind her yelling in some language which sounded a little like her own but with a different cadence and enough different words to make communication difficult, if at all possible. The only word she heard which was close enough to her own language sounded like, "Wait!"

She ran now, as fast as she could over the rough field, her bare feet slapping hard against dirt and tangled grass. Ember had never understood, until that moment, the benefit she had received, having grown only modestly in the chest, unlike so many other women. She thanked the gods for that gift as she continued to run, though she would eventually start to ache, as other women did if she kept this pace for too long.

Down the cliff, she ran toward the river. The wet bank would be constantly washed clean by water and hide her tracks, letting her escape. She might even find them again once things cooled down, as they seemed to be following the river. As Ember hit the sandy bank, she slowed to a jog. How had the men found her? No, they had not. She had shown them where she was when she sat up. But why had they even come that way? It wasn't in line with their path. Perhaps they were hunting small game? She shook her head in disbelief at the odds. It made no sense.

After a while, Ember rounded a small but abrupt hill by the shore, which raised at least two lengths of a man above the riverbank. The cool shade of the rise and a slope to lie against felt like a blessing, exhausted after running and then jogging for as long as she had. Perhaps she would thank some local god for her good fortune. The day had started off hot and promised only more heat. This was not a good day for anyone to run. Besides the heat, her feet were throbbing, and she was still quite hungry.

Ember rested against the rise and let her body cool in the gentle breeze. The breeze danced across her damp skin, cooling her as millions of years of evolution had wrought. Yet, even with the wind, she was still hot, and her skin itched from drying sweat and dirt from the grass tuft. She longed for a dip in the refreshing water once her heart calmed to a rest. Unfortunately, the men would still pass this way even if they had given up any pursuit. Ember briefly considered swimming to the far side of the river before throwing away that fantasy. The river was only deceptively calm. The waters were slow-moving, but their force was huge and unyielding.

Perhaps hiding in the shallow waters would be a smart idea, a fix to all her problems, at once. She guessed the men were probably not so far away, but she had not seen or heard from them for a short while. If she slipped into the water quickly, the men might simply pass her by. Besides, it would keep her cool, allow her to clean, quench her thirst, and hide her all at the same time. The Great River truly provided. Of course, she would need to keep her mouth just above the water, which would be awkward but manageable. Ember smiled at her own cunning, thinking herself a bit foxlike.

She would first stuff her shirt someplace, perhaps behind a rock, where the men wouldn't find it if they passed by. A bulky leather shirt would present a problem in the water and degrade the leather. Luckily, there was a rock near the water she could put the folded shirt beneath. She was starting to get the hang of being on her own. It was actually much easier than one thought, so long as careful thought and planning were applied. Even outsmarting three hunters was much easier than she would have expected. She smiled at her cunning.

Ember glanced down the riverbank where the men should come from and saw no one yet. She headed toward the safety of the water, her plan kicking into action. As she approached the water, she heard a noise not three lengths of a man behind her and from above. She paused and closed her eyes, regret and shock flooding her mind. How could she have been so foolish as to forget her own species' tendency for hunting from above?

Just as deer and rabbits never seemed to look up, Ember had fallen to the same and simple device.

They must have run too... she thought as she began to turn and look up towards the men she knew were standing behind her on the high bank. A million stars exploded in her head, quickly replaced by a growing darkness. Ember tried to speak, but nothing happened. She was vaguely aware of an arrow lying beside her. In her daze, she thought the arrowhead looked oddly shaped, rounded, like a pouch of pebbles secured to the end with a cord, instead of the typical triangular shape of her people. She had seen men use these to hunt rabbits, shooting them in the head and stunning them. Perhaps it had worked by hitting her temple, or maybe she had become a rabbit... her thoughts were becoming a blur. Ember felt her body falling into the darkness, and then nothing.

Ember became aware again. Her head hurt, and her left temple stung. She couldn't manage to open her eyes, so she tried to rub them. Her arms failed to respond. She quickly became aware that she was bound from behind. Panic filled her as she realized her predicament. She was sitting on the ground, hands and arms pulled behind her and wrapped around a small tree, bound at the wrist. She forced her eyes open and was greeted by a burst of light from the bright Sun. She was sitting upright and leaning against a tree in an awkward position. Her butt had fallen asleep, and her legs hurt with a tingly numbness, though nothing compared to the ache in her head.

When Ember examined her surroundings, she noticed that her obsidian dagger, pouch, and doeskin shirt were nowhere to be seen. Could the men have merely left them where she had fallen? She hoped not. Turning her head to the right, she saw the trio preparing a camp for the night.

It's night? she thought in panic. Her stomach was sore, and the ribs on her right side hurt. This told her that she had probably been slung over one of their shoulders and carried. Fear and panic took hold of Ember, and she started to pull on the ropes. What would the men do with her, she wondered? The blonde-haired man turned and took note of her consciousness. He spoke to the other men, each turning to regard the now awake woman. She immediately wished she hadn't made any sounds.

It wasn't until she saw them staring at her that she began to notice how naked she felt. Did these men seek her for themselves, or would they take her as a prize to trade at another village? Such acts were not uncommon, and she had heard the stories of entire trade groups being massacred for their loot, animals, and women. She had even come across such a looted village. The images of the bodies were still too fresh in her mind. It didn't seem fair how women were treated, and yet it was commonplace and simply accepted.

As they leered, their eyes bore holes in her confidence. She looked away from the men and started tugging frantically at her bonds. Her body had become a liability in the face of such men. Her wrists hurt as she pulled as hard as she could. Ember began to panic, fear renewing her fight or flight. She pulled furiously as tears ran down her face, yet the bindings held. Finally, after a short time, she relaxed and slumped limply against the tree, defeated by exhaustion and hunger. She drifted into a light slumber. Her body was still exhausted from running and her new and aggravated injuries.

The sky was dark when Ember awoke once more to find the youngest of the trio poking her stomach to wake her. She looked up at him with a mixture of fear and hate. He wore a soft leather loincloth with a large flint knife hanging from his belt and woven fiber shoes. The man was a few harvests older than Ember but apparently the youngest in the party. He leveled his bright gaze at her, meeting her eyes. She was taken aback by his bright blue stare. He didn't look evil or wicked in any way, but there he squat as she remained bound and captive. She was embarrassed at her captivity, and the presence of the young hunter, a man her own age, made this worse. She found herself looking down to avoid his eyes, bright blue or not. How could he just stare and not help her?

He stared at Ember for a long moment before he began speaking. Oddly, he wasn't exactly gawking as much as studying. It was a fine distinction, yet it oddly mattered to her. When he spoke, his words sounded strange to her, but she understood a few of them from their similarity to her own language. She picked out the words for "food" and "do" from what he had said. The man gestured to a freshly killed rabbit tied to a pole in the ground and some tools.

How ironic, she thought, mirthlessly, *two "rabbits" caught on the same day...* Suddenly, he produced her doeskin shirt. She had dropped it by the bank when she had fallen. Apparently, the men had found the shirt and kept it, or at least, this one had. Maybe they had kept the dagger too? The young man tossed the shirt across Ember's bare upper body, affording her a little cover. He then produced a small flint knife and stuffed it into the ground before her, giving her a nod. Ember understood clearly what she would be doing now – domestic work for these lazy men. At least, their current ambitions were founded in their stomachs and nowhere else. She hoped they would fall asleep after they ate, as many did, and stop staring at her. She swallowed and looked the hunter in the face as she gave him a curt nod of understanding. His weak smile, in return, made her feel disgusted. *You cannot make me like you, fool... so stop trying,* she thought.

The young hunter stepped behind her to untie the thong which held her hands bound. Once freed, Ember slowly brought her aching arms forward to a more normal angle and held her wrists for a few moments, rubbing them to ease the pain of having been bound. The hunter had unbound her completely and now stood over her waiting for her to finish rubbing her sore wrists. He regarded her for a moment and indicated the large dagger on his waist. Ember nodded once more showing that she understood the consequences of running. The man looked slightly uncomfortable as he handed her the small knife, and did so blade first, so she could not immediately run him through, she guessed.

He indicated the rabbit again. Ember slowly rolled over and started to work her way up to a standing position using the little tree she had been bound to as a crutch. Her legs hurt, throbbing furiously, and her butt tingled from sitting on the hard ground for so long. After a moment, she found that she could again stand, though she was weak. She stepped slowly passed him, very much aware that his eyes followed her as she did. Ember quickly donned her shirt and checked to make sure her loincloth was secure. She might have to work for these men, but she wouldn't give them a show.

Being semi-nude or even wholly nude was not uncommon among her people. Often, family members would wear no more than a fur wrap, like a blanket, when in a longhouse, and bare breasts were common in the warmer seasons. Children were often unclothed until they were older or the weather was cold, due to the complexities of making clothing. This wasn't much of an issue as it was ordinary, yet nudity was also contextual; something usually common for her people but uncomfortable in certain contexts. This was such a context.

For the remainder of the early night, Ember was made to clean and cook rabbit and some wheat porridge for the men as they joked and socialized. She went about her tasks with her head down and her heart filled with fear and dread. After a chance to relieve herself and a small bit of porridge, which she refused, she was again bound to the tree, a bit more loosely than before, by the same younger man. She would not look him in the face. This was not how things were supposed to have gone. Where were the gods to help her? What was to become of her? Who could help? The answer was: no one. She was entirely at the mercy of these men, and no authority in the world existed who would come to her aid, outside of her own tribe. She quietly cried herself to sleep. Perhaps tomorrow, her head would stop hurting.

The next day, Ember was awakened shortly after dawn and bid to cook fish for breakfast. Fish were most active in the early morning and the late evening, the best times to catch them. The blonde-haired man had caught the fish just before Ember had awakened, and now he sat there with the older man laughing and eating. The two made light of Ember several times. Their gestures and comments, she knew, were directed at her though she knew not what they said.

After breakfast, the blonde-haired man approached and grabbed her arm rather roughly. She gave a token resistance, but she couldn't help but be bound again. The man moved through the motions mechanically without any indications of his disposition. Her hands were tied with a thick leather thong behind her back, lest she become a problem as they traveled, she supposed. Ember wondered if he had a wife. If so, what would she think of this? Would she even care?

The blonde man removed his large leather satchel and placed the strap over her shoulder. So, she would become a beast of burden? Perhaps they would just work her to death. She had still not eaten, and weakness crept into her body like a sickness. The shame had not yet surpassed her fears, but it was close. Her stomach rumbled once more and she felt a little dizzy, yet she kept quiet, unwilling to cry out.

The youngest man had tried to feed you, the voice in her head reminded her. It had been a day and a half since she had last eaten, just what she could forage, and she was growing weak. She would either need to eat soon or let her body fail. Allowing herself to die from hunger went against every fiber of her being, but she felt that she could accept it should all hope run out. She had to be strong until she had no other options.

Ember had always been a rebellious and resilient girl. The story of her father's death had taught her to be strong in the face of adversity, but this was a more frightening experience than she had ever known, aside from the wolves. It was surreal and filled her with a gnawing sense of injustice. In her village, she had her family and friends, but here she was at the mercy of three cunning, resourceful, and physically stronger men, each trained to track and kill animals about Ember's size. There was no one to help her and no rules or authority to appeal to. These men answered to no one, except perhaps the gods.

Slowly, hate began to fill the place in her heart where fear had been so strong. Was it hunger clouding her mind? It occurred to Ember that her realization and acceptance of her fate, perhaps even death, had opened new paths in her mind that she had never explored. Acceptance began to remove the fear which had initially bound her. Slowly, the rabbit would become a fox. The tiny fire of innovation and determination lit in her as she started considering how she might escape. She would wait patiently and use cunning to free herself. So far, this was her main thought, though she had yet to determine how she might do it.

Ember pondered many things while she walked along behind the three men as they made their way northwest. Onward, the quartet walked, over open fields, beside a large forest, and always following the Great River. The walking was tiring, and Ember was very hungry, making for a poor combination. She tripped a few times but never fell, which was probably best as she couldn't have stopped herself if she had. Though the pace was hard, the men took breaks every now and then, allowing her to rest. Regardless, the walking gave her time to plot, and plot she did. For now, she continued to appear as frightened as possible, though it was less theatrics and more true fear.

The second day of walking had caused Ember's bare feet to blister and swell with sores. Seeing her limp, the younger man called for a break, or so it had seemed to Ember. The group stopped by the river's edge. The men let Ember cool her feet in the river while they situated themselves and constructed a new camp for the night. The younger man was by far the most compassionate of the three. Ember had taken note of each man's behavior and attitude, as the key to escape might be in manipulating each of the men. Her confidence in her ability to find a way out of this mess had started to rise. Unfortunately, she was beginning to fear the older man.

He had now twice given her a hungry look; the kind men gave when they gazed upon something they wanted. She would have to do something about this before the older man, or the blonde-haired man for that matter, decided to take out the frustrations of a long journey on her. There were few moral issues among even her own people that would prevent them from whatever they wished. She was a captive, which meant she was effectively their property by most peoples' ways.

She forced such disturbing thoughts aside and concentrated on her growing understanding of the men. The blonde-haired man seemed to be collected and calculating, very difficult to read. He was the unknown element to Ember. She knew the old man would react negatively to her, but she would feel much more secure if she could figure out the blonde-haired man. She didn't fear the youngest man. He had been the only one in their group to offer her food, which she had started eating out of need. He had also given her back her shirt and with it a degree of her self-respect and dignity.

Besides their personalities, she had also paid close attention to her environment. The quartet had made quite a good trek so far, traveling beyond the high cliffs and into a flatter part of the land where the river was nearly the same height as the ground, though still lower. The thick forests had given way to thinner pine trees and small hills, and Ember could see large forests in every direction. Did the world just continue the same way, forever? Was there an edge?

The night of her fourth full day of captivity, Ember was left bound but allowed to lie on the ground. Her hands were tied behind her and then to a small tree, but she could lie on her side and not against the tree if she wanted. It was a small concession on the younger man's part, which earned him a few dirty looks from the other two. That night, she sat waiting for the men to fall asleep. Instead, the oldest man kept his eyes on her for a while, thoroughly disturbing Ember.

I would pluck your eyes from your face if I could, she thought. She wasn't pleased with herself for such dark thoughts, but the anger helped keep her going. Without turning to anger, she would quickly slip into fear. She continued with her dark thoughts, lest she consider the enormity of her situation and how helpless she was.

She knew that grim thoughts were considered wrong, but she wondered how people knew such things were wrong. The creation stories didn't mention any reason why some actions or thoughts were right or wrong. Ember didn't remember her mother saying anything that might indicate why such thoughts were bad, yet she knew they were. She supposed that people just knew it was wrong to hurt each other because it was the only sane way people could live together. A tribe of evil people wouldn't last very long. But if that were true, why did these men treat her so poorly? Ember remained introspective as she waited for the men to sleep.

As the night grew darker, the men situated themselves for bed. The older man suddenly stood and approached her. She sat upright, suddenly anxious with a quickening pulse. The man smiled at her in mock friendliness. He knelt beside her and openly leered. He was certainly aging but still a formidable hunter, by all appearances. He had long shoulder-length, ragged hair, slightly balding in the front. His face was wrinkled with a few small scars and a scruffy, unkempt look. Several deep scars on his hands told the story of a man who had been in the wilds for longer than most. Perhaps he was a senior hunter where he came from. Often, a senior hunter would lead long-distance journeys.

All of this time out in the wilds, and you have forgotten what is right and wrong, she thought. As the older man sized her up, she thought of her home and her warm bed. She was in that bed sleeping about a tenday ago. Yet again, the absurdity of her "task" came to her. Her mind was acting as though it could run from the situation, but how could it?

Well, gods, thanks for watching out for me, she thought glumly. Her mind snapped back into the moment as the man reached and placed his hand on her hip. Ember's face froze in horror as he said something with mock thoughtfulness. Slowly, his hand slid down her leg. Ember's skin crawled at the violation, as fear, disgust, and hate fought for dominance within her. She wanted to scream; to lash out at the man in rage. She knew what he would do next. She had seen it so many times, but those women had been willing.

So, now you're ready for me, she thought. *Well, I am not quite ready for you.* She drew her leg back nearly to her chest, a testament to her dexterity, and kicked the man square in the chest. He choked up spittle and fell backward onto his butt with a loud thud. Ember recoiled her leg, ready to strike him between the legs, but he had rolled too far for her to reach. The blonde-haired man blew the water he was drinking from his mouth, nearly choking. He stood and laughed as hard as Ember had ever seen a man laugh. Nothing about this was funny to her. It was a terrifying experience made worse by the massive power imbalance and lack of consent.

The stunned expression on the older man's face quickly turned to rage. He stood ready to force himself upon her with all his strength, and she knew, bound as she was, she wouldn't be able to stop him. Her saving grace came from the blonde-haired man. He said something to the older man in a playful voice and with a rueful smile. The older man rounded on him in an instant and charged. The blonde-haired man backed away, holding his hands out. He had obviously crossed some line with his joking, and the old man was now too enraged to consider Ember.

The old man yelled at the other two men for a while and then stormed off into the brush, probably to relieve himself. The blonde-haired man walked a few paces towards Ember, giving her a wicked grin. He said something underhanded and then gave her a wink before returning to the fire and bedding down for sleep. The older man returned after a while without a word and fell quickly to sleep, as well. For a time, Ember sat utterly still, trying to make herself as invisible as possible. She had come so close to being raped, and the realization of just how close was terrifying.

How could someone do such a thing to another person? How could she have no way to prevent it? There was a casual injustice about it that filled her with rage. His despicable moment of pleasure would harm her, both physically and mentally. If she became pregnant, she and the child could die, as so often happened. Yet all he cared about was a moment of fun. Her emotions alternated between disgust at the violation, hate over the injustice, and fear. As she breathed, she began to calm, forcing herself back into the moment and away from the terrible thoughts. She would need her wits if she were to escape.

Ember's people were known for singing and dancing, but this dance was more delicate and dangerous than any she had ever performed. She was not entirely sure of what had happened, other than how close she had just come to knowing this man, this brute. She would have to act fast, or she might not resist him again. Initially, she had hoped either to make an escape or perhaps pit the men against each other, somehow. In an odd sort of way, it seemed like this was happening all by itself, but Ember would have to do more, and soon. For now, she lay back and slowly drifted to sleep.

On the fifth day, the group was less talkative than the previous four. The older man walked behind Ember much of the way, watching her, she suspected. She could feel his eyes boring holes into her back as she walked, which was supremely uncomfortable. Deep down, she was sure that she would either escape or be taken before the coming night ended. It was just so enraging. How could she be forced to bend to some man's will? Why was there nothing in the world to prevent this? Where were the gods? Was this what her own people's men would do to an enemy? Was this simply what women had to accept?

Her mind was dark with thought, depression, and anxiety as she marched along. The day was long and hot, and Ember's poor ragged body was not used to this sort of punishment. Ironically, the comfort her shirt had brought was also a liability in the heat. Still, she would rather melt in the Sun than give the old man even the slightest bit to see. She longed for a cold dip in the river and a midday nap, or maybe her father's dagger deep within the old man.

Why must they always push ahead at such speed? Why can't they just stop for a while? Perhaps it's because none of these men like each other? she wondered. The biggest question she had was what these men were doing out here in the first place? They didn't seem like traders, and

Ember had not seen any furs or wares about them. What could their motivation be? Ritual hunters were usually more decorated. Perhaps they were merely scouting far from the village. It did fit their actions.

By the time the Sun approached the horizon, Ember was totally exhausted. The four stopped in an area with many broad fields to make camp for the night. Her feet ached, and her wrists were cut in many places from the unending bindings. She saw a thick forest on either side of the fields. She could bolt for the forest, but she would still be bound, and she was already weak and in significant pain. Running with her hands behind her back would be difficult, especially through the thicker woods. If she ran, she would have to somehow evade the men when they came for her.

Ember had started to consider her surroundings in even greater detail since the previous night. She had become an opportunist with her fear of the old man ever present. She had even openly accepted larger portions of food from the younger man instead of only taking it after she was forced. She would need the strength to run when she made her break. After a time, the men had finished laying mats and clearing the area of debris. Their trip for the day had ended. After food and relaxation, the older man would likely try again. Ember's anxiety grew as the Sun sank lower in the sky, yet no opportunity to run had presented itself.

The younger man came forward and placed a large rabbit beside Ember, then gave her a nod and a half-smile, then untied her bindings, leaving her to make dinner. Even now, the older man was leering, his intent clearly evident. She had to do something and soon. A short time later, Ember stood by the river's edge with the rabbit carcass, trying to muster the will to make dinner for the men. She was frightened, and her time remaining to find an escape was nearly spent. Ember silently whimpered as she knelt, her face hidden from the men.

Did they not understand how hard it was to make a meal for those who enslaved you? She tried to push her terror aside as she worked to clean the rabbit. Tears flowed as she considered what was to come. Ember held the small flint knife she had been given, preparing to work on the rabbit. She considered slicing her wrists a moment later. She could rush into the water and let the Great River carry her lifeblood away. Dying in the water wasn't the worst way to go. She forced the thought back as a last resort, though the setting Sun told her such a choice was nearly at hand. Offhandedly, she wondered if they might get sick and die from the rabbit. Ember paused; her thoughts of suicide dashed by a sudden idea.

An undercooked rabbit could make a man mighty sick, she thought as a brand new plan began to form. It was a long shot, but she was out of time and too stubborn to give in to her self-doubt. Besides, she wasn't really sure she could take her own life. Instead, perhaps she would take theirs. First, she could retain a tiny bit of the innards from the rabbit and then add it to the cooked meat before feeding it to the men. Undercooked meat would take far too long to sicken them, if it did at all, but entrails were significantly more effective. The men would find that she could be as deadly as any hunter, maybe even a little cunning, like a fox. Ember wiped her tears as she started work with renewed vigor.

The cleaning of a land animal was similar to the cleaning and dressing of a fish but smelled much worse. Ember's fingers were wet with gore and oil from the carcass when she was finally done dressing the rabbit. The belly of the creature had to be sliced open, and the organs spilled out. Afterward, the remaining pieces would be scooped out by hand, and the carcass cleaned in water. The hardest part was removing the fur, which had to be done by hand in a tearing fashion.

The noise and feel always bothered Ember. Children in the village would sometimes vomit while first learning to do this but growing up beside your mother as she performed this act nearly daily lessened the effect when it became your turn to prepare dinner. She tended to have trouble eating the same animal she had cleaned, but otherwise, she tolerated the gore well. Ember smiled to herself as she considered the art of domestic homicide. In truth, she was not trying to kill the men, but if they became seriously ill, she would not be too upset.

She cleaned her fingers in the river with sand for grout. But before washing the rabbit, she let a small piece of the foulest entrails fall to her feet where she could retrieve it after cleaning the rabbit. The entrails were the nastiest and vilest part of the guts, including the intestine and fecal matter within. If they were left in the food, they could make a person sick, even if the food was cooked. If they were applied to already cooked meat, they might prove deadly. The effect would take perhaps part of the night or even the next day, but it could render the men ineffective at chasing her, and if she were lucky, it might even kill the old one. The more Ember thought about it, the less she felt that she would care if he didn't wake up.

The men were casually watching her, but mostly to prevent her from running. She washed water through the rabbit carcass to clean it further and brought the rabbit back to the fire. She held the small piece of entrail cupped in her left hand carefully between her index and middle finger, blending in well with her skin. Her slightly dark and tanned skin was starting to return as the remainder of her pigment wore off, unfortunately. She would feel even more vulnerable when that happened.

Ember placed the rabbit over a newly constructed spit to cook. She again noticed the aggressive old man eyeing her body with a hungry look. She shuddered and wiped the saved gore on the end of the spit, just away from the fire but within easy reach. The warm fire would speed up its decay, making it all the more deadly. She hoped her treachery would take hold before he had a chance to try again. It was a gamble, but really her only option.

Ember knew that a full person would generally sleep soundly. To ensure this happened, she spent a short time creating porridge of ground grains from a leather bag the men carried and some water. The rabbit was quite large, and she was able to cut a small piece for each man. She added the entrails carefully to the inside and burned parts hoping to mask the taste. Unfortunately, there were only enough entrails to spoil two of the pieces, so she decided to poison the older man and the blonde-haired man. She would spare the younger man, assuming this even worked.

Ember walked to each of the men and handed them a crudely woven reed "plate" with porridge and rabbit meat, her head down the entire time. Each of the men ate greedily as she watched. Her stomach rumbled loudly enough to be heard, and the large man turned to her and said something, to which he and the blonde-haired man laughed. The youngest hunter grimaced at the men, stood, and approached. He offered her his bowl with some rabbit and porridge remaining. She refused the food with her hands crossed over her chest.

Five days of captivity had not diminished her embarrassment at being forced into such indignity. The young man glared at her and thrust the bowl once more. She again refused, fearing to be too agreeable and feeling more confident in her choice of victims. After a moment, the younger man squatted before her and forced a weary smile. Ember glared at him in disgust, then returned to looking away. He tapped his chest and spoke.

"Pak," he said. He repeated this word twice more, his name, she supposed.

Well, "Pak," I will not so easily befriend you, but I will spare your life, Ember thought, praying silently to the gods that the food sickened the old man, and hopefully the blonde-haired man, too. In defiance, Ember slowly stood and walked to a little tree near the camp, where the men would most likely tie her up, and curled up to sleep. Each night they chose a spot with a small but firm tree close enough to bind her. Not far away, she heard the men laughing, and she hoped they would leave her be, at least for the night. Anxiety grew as the time when the old man might again try was nearly upon her.

After they ate and socialized, the men prepared for bed. Ember's fear spiked when the older man approached and roughly tied her hands once more. Afterward, he squatted before her and carefully let one finger trace a line from her cheek to her chin. Her skin crawled, and she let out a gasp of revulsion. Was this the moment? Had her time run out so soon? He said something that promised suffering but suddenly let out a small laugh and stood to go lie down. Ember breathed heavily as she held back her fear and tears. She felt so small and defenseless before him, a terrible feeling.

"You'll die for that..." she whispered in response, but if the old man heard her, he did not show it. He just merely strode back to the fire and fell asleep. Was that it? Was she safe for another night and day? If so, it would give time for the rabbit to work. She hoped the rabbit was working its dark magic. Ember lay against the tree, her hands now slightly looser than before. She was learning how to loosen them, but she was unable to get them quite open, yet. She hoped she might make it through the night without the need to relieve herself, an uncomfortable prospect, to say the least, with three men only a short walk from her.

With such sour thoughts, she slowly began to drift from her fifth day as a captive. She considered her promise of death to the older man and the poisoning of the food. What had this done to her? Killing in defense of oneself or others was morally permissible to her people, but until this moment, she hadn't actually considered the actual act of killing. She was causing and had actually set into motion the possible death of two men, or at least a sickness of great harm. Some might even call it blood magic.

Every day I die a little myself. You sons of wolves. No more! she thought. Why the man had spared her that night, she could not say, but she doubted he'd keep away again. Besides, the fear and anxiety from waiting were eating her alive. She promised herself that there would be no sixth night.

Ember awoke with an impact of a blanket on her face. She soon realized her hands were freed, and a pile of the three woven mat blankets they slept on the night before lay at her feet. So far, each morning the men had awoken her and then had her clean and pack their bedding. Oddly, for some reason, they had each awoken before Ember and were now preparing themselves. The oldest man gestured at her in a gruff accent, using the word "clean," which she understood. Ember stared back at the man with an angry sneer and dared him to force her. He glared at her for a moment in return and then suddenly came at her like a wild boar.

Ember stood and held her ground even as he swiped his arm, backhanding her across the face. She saw stars and nearly cried out, but she held her tongue and her gaze. The man's rage suddenly left his face, and he began to laugh at her with fervency. The laughter unnerved Ember, but she knew she had played her resistance far enough. She turned her head away from the burly man and picked up the mats. She had come so fast from sleep to being struck across the face that she had not noticed the change in the men. The older man looked uncomfortable, and the blonde-haired man was nowhere to be seen. She licked the blood from her lips as she considered these changes.

What's the matter, old man? Your friend is going off into the woods sick, and you don't know why? I do... she thought. Could her plan be working? Time would tell. Thoughts of slicing her wrists returned as she considered what she would do once evening fell if the men were not ill. Her body was exhausted from anxiety, but she had to try just a little longer.

During the last five days since Ember had reluctantly joined the group, the men had traveled in a northwesterly direction, moving with the Great River toward the setting of the Sun. Ironically, she was making real progress in the direction of her quest, though at the cost of her morality, sanity, and freedom. The general lay of the land began to slowly change from green and flat to slightly less green and much more rolling. The slight rises in the land were replaced by great hills and open fields. The journey west was somewhat beneficial, circumstances aside, but Ember just couldn't understand why these men were traveling so far. She knew of merchants who journeyed so far, but they carried their wares and occasionally a few animals in trade, but these men were armed for hunting with no such wares.

As she cleaned the mats at the river, she noticed the blonde man. He was sitting against a tree behind a large bush, making gasping noises and shuddering. She could not see what he was doing, but the sounds he made were quite expressive. Ember couldn't care the less if he died there. Her dark thoughts were coming more easily now, but what was she supposed to do when in such a dark place?

My arrows are slower but just as painful in the end, she thought. The blonde-haired man had the runs and was relieving himself behind the tree, it seemed. She smiled as she washed the mats. Unless he recovered quickly, he wouldn't make it more than a few days if he lived. Sometimes, bad food wasn't deadly, and fire and lots of water helped the person live. What worried Ember was the lack of the old man showing symptoms. Perhaps he hadn't eaten the poisoned areas, or maybe he was too nasty for even the rabbit's entrails. Ember nearly let out a giggle, the first genuinely amusing thought she had in perhaps four days. The feeling was strange – a drop of humor in a sea of fear.

When she had packed up the last mat, the blonde-haired man returned. She had heard him called "Kal-paw-no," or something close to that. Calpano, if that was his name, was slightly pale and sweating profusely. The other men gathered their belongings and loaded a freshly bound Ember with two satchels for that day's journey. She was tired of being a beast of burden and knew the time was upon her. Tonight, she would make her escape or die trying.

The worst-case would be if the older man did not become ill. Either way, she could be sure she had removed any risk of a long-term chase. The men simply would not be able to follow her too far with at least one of them becoming worse as the day went by. This made suddenly bolting when freed more reasonable a prospect. The old man probably couldn't run far, but the man called Pak was strong, young, and could probably follow her for longer than she could run. Ember continued plotting and thinking as she trudged along behind the group.

During the day, Calpano did become much sicker. Twice, he had stopped and vomited, and as many times he had suddenly run off into the trees only to return a while later, paler than before. The old man had looked a little ill as well, but he had shown nothing more than a lack of interest in lunch and a few uneasy looks. Ember could not tell if he was suffering from the rabbit or just tired from a long journey. Her fear was growing with each moment that he wasn't ill.

At dusk on her sixth day of captivity, Ember sat very still watching the young, dark-haired man, Pak, filling himself on pieces of dried tubers and some sort of dried meat. Calpano had taken to lying on the ground and groaning while the older man seemed to preoccupy himself with staring at her inappropriately or yelling at the youngest man. Now was the best chance she would likely get, and judging by how freely the older man leered, her last.

Days of patient waiting suddenly paid off when the group's youngest member removed a piece of flint from his pouch and used it to cut the tuber he was eating. Not long after he started, a large sliver of flint broke off the piece he used. He scooped up the large flint fragment, inadvertently leaving a few small slivers. With a frown, he examined the larger broken piece and replaced it in his pouch. Good flint was never wasted.

Ember saw this.

After a short time, she was ordered to tend the fire for the men as they sat and told each other what sounded like stories. Calpano seemed a little better, having emptied everything in him along that day's short trip, though he was still pale and shaking now and then. He wouldn't chase her far. Now she merely had to do something with the other two. While poking at the fire with a stick, she noticed one of the tiny slivers of flint that the younger man had evidently overlooked.

Her pulse quickened as she remembered how sharp such slivers could be. She silently thanked the gods for taking her boots from her, even though her feet were now adorned by blisters and hurts from walking so far, barefoot. Ember carefully slipped the fragment between her toes. She quickly finished loading wood into the fire for the night as the old man watched her far too closely. Trying to remain calm, she dispassionately walked to the tree to be bound for sleep. Anxiety grew as the Sun set, the time when the old man might act, now looming. The oldest man took note of her resigned look and seemed pleased.

Does he think he has broken me? she wondered.

"Oh no... no, you haven't broken me, old man," she whispered, hate mixed with fear. A moment later, he stood and approached Ember to bind her, she supposed.

Instead, he came to a stop and leered at her from head to toe before binding her hands rather roughly. This was definitely a good night to escape, she thought in panic. He stood again and said something to the youngest man, who was now trying to sleep. She supposed that he was going to go relieve himself away from the camp. He had done this nearly every night so far. Ember hoped she could finish her escape before his return.

She had wanted to escape at night while the men slept or let the rabbit sicken the two worst men, but she saw the hungry look in the old man's eyes and knew the time had come. She would have to settle for one sick man and one absent man, leaving only her bindings and the younger man to deal with. The older man would be gone for a while, for he liked to take his time at some tasks, but he would return and take Ember before he slept, she feared. He winked at her and then lumbered away from the camp towards the bushes by the river.

133

She slowly shimmied up the tree enough to maneuver herself around the trunk, placing her bound hands where she had dropped the sliver. After a short moment of careful wiggling and cutting, Ember had removed her hands from the bindings. Leather was robust and resisted breaking when pulled, but sharp flint sliced through leather like fire through the snow. Her now freed wrists were red and aching from abuse. The memory of the man's touch still left a bitter taste, somehow worse than even his strike. At least she was free, but there were still two men and perhaps half a day travel to escape them.

She couldn't allow the men to chase her. If she could, she would kill the blonde-haired man and wound the younger man so he couldn't follow. Murder... a strange feeling as the idea washed over her, but this was how far they had pushed her. How had she gone from fear and running to considering murder so lightly? Was this the culmination of so many days of fear turning to anger and a chance at vengeance? Was she a fool who should just run while she could? Perhaps she didn't need to kill anyone. If she could find her obsidian dagger, she might slit their bare feet before they awoke and then run. How far could a man with a long cut across his foot travel? Ember knew full well how much a wounded foot could hurt, for her own feet were still injured from the wolf attack.

Ember might escape two wounded men, but the older man was still a problem. She was truly living in the moment as she approached the sleeping men. If they awoke, she could bolt and head for the river. In the night, she had a good chance of letting it wash her away to safety, but also of drowning. Terrified, probably foolish, but stubbornly determined, Ember slowly stepped toward the large travel pack that the older man carried, hoping it held her possessions. The pack was the sole object the older man carried, besides his dagger and bow.

Ember placed one foot carefully upon the soft dirt after the other as she walked as silently as she ever had. She knelt and opened the pack with care not to make a sound. To her relief, her flint pouch and pendant were immediately visible. She removed the pouch from the old man's pack and pulled the drawstring tight. She was about to put the pouch down when she noticed a rabbit pelt-wrapped object deep within the pack. She slowly lifted the bundle and unwrapped it, her natural curiosity overriding her better judgment. She nearly swooned as she saw the item within, a large blue piece of ice twice the size of her fist.

The "ice" was surprisingly not cold to the touch. Could this be a tiny piece of hardened water? Over the harvests, traders had occasionally brought tiny fragments of shiny color with them to trade, most the size of a small pebble. Some said they were fragments of the sky, while others said they were frozen water from a distant and magical river. Ember didn't honestly know which, but she was taken aback by the sheer beauty of the object. She slipped the large blue thing back into the pelt and inserted it into her pouch, now overflowing. She carefully lifted the large man's bow and three of his arrows. She now had her flint, pendant, the old man's treasure, and even a weapon, but the younger man and the older man would have her soon enough if she ran now. She would have to ensure they never had a chance to find her.

She had never cut a man or anyone, and the thought scared her. With thoughts of her innocents dying with the first man she wounded badly or killed, Ember approached Calpano, slowly listening to his breath. Suddenly, her own breath was stollen as she realized what Calpano had lying beside him. The sick man wore none other than her obsidian dagger at his side. She had not seen it before, and yet, here it was. She knew she had to recover it. So much for her complex and well thought out plans. She had already changed her tactics several times since freeing herself. Anxiety danced through her as she considered how long this was taking, but his snoring gave her confidence as she slowly moved to take her weapon back.

As her hand grasped the handle, she became aware that the man had stopped snoring. She now sprang backward, taking the knife with her, though the sheath was still at the man's waist next to the bow and arrows she had put aside. Calpano awoke with a groggy expression of anger. He looked horribly ill to Ember, and he seemed to be fighting to stay awake. On impulse, she reached out and carefully stroked her hand as softly as she could over his scalp. As she gently stroked his hair, he quietly gave in to the relaxing act and slowly slipped back into his delirious sleep, something which normally would not have worked, but for his sickness. Her poison was doing its job well.

With Calpano out of commission, the young man was her last target before running. If he was wounded, she was pretty sure the old man wouldn't have much luck chasing her, alone. After collecting the sheath, Ember waited for a short moment, her chest heaving in fear and panic. Slowly, she approached the sleeping man, apparently named Pak. He was just a few harvests older than she. He lay beside the fire, his well-defined body painted in a dazzling flicker of firelight.

What sort of a name is Pak? Or Calpano, for that matter? she thought. He had a serene look which was hardly unpleasant, though Ember wanted to hate him. She placed the blade against his neck and

135

made ready to cut. She had opened the flesh of so many animals – dead animals. This was not a dead animal. She could feel his pulse against the dagger. Ember realized that she could not kill him as he lay defenseless. She rolled her eyes and moved to his bare feet. She placed the blade against his right foot and prepared to cut. She would cut him open so that he would not follow but would probably not die.

Ember placed the edge of the razor-sharp obsidian dagger against his barefoot, yet she couldn't seem to slice. Each time she tried to cut, she found it hard to act. She couldn't quite force herself to wound this man, the only one who had shown her any kindness. He was guilty, yes, but her empathy continued to stay her hand. Ember was now lost in introspection, a typical problem for the random redhead who had the time management skills of a tuber. As she sat there mulling over her convictions, she heard a noise behind her. With a jerk, she turned and saw the old man returning early and with a dangerous fury about him. Her blood ran cold as she understood that she had waited too long.

"Aeeya…"

☼ ☼ ☼

He had held back so far, but he was not about to let this girl threaten his men, pitiful as they may be to have been taken by surprise by a girl. He was the leader, and that meant she was his. She would need to understand this more plainly if she was to return with him and bear him children. He was old, but not so much that he couldn't still have a son. His wife had died long ago in childbirth, leaving him alone and without a legacy. This girl would do nicely in that respect. Being a captive would cut out the pointless effort to win her affection, which Rosif considered a waste of time. The animals didn't wed, nor did they demand extensive courting. They simply did what they needed to do, and so would he.

ɔ ɔ ɔ

Ember saw the look in his eyes and realized what had changed. She fell backward into a crouch, terror filling her. She began to panic over what she had done and what he would do when he caught her. As if fueled by her apparent fear, the man began to approach slowly, menacingly, and with that deadly look of raw anger in his eyes. Her veins filled with pure primal fear, and she felt like she might start to cry. Her mind told her to drop the dagger and plead for mercy. It would be over soon, right? She could just drop her dagger and maybe he would spare her. He was just so big and so close, and she wasn't a warrior or some large man. She could drop the dagger... she would drop it and...

But she had a dagger, didn't she? Warfare was so far from her experience and life that she had not even considered that she was armed. That dagger was the same weapon that her father had used to save her mother. It had killed two raiders, men probably equal to this one.

Ember fought back sheer panic to hold her nerve, knowing full well that if she broke now, in the face of this man, she would never escape. Ember hated bullies, and that was what this man was. She thought of the injustice of this moment, concentrated on the anger and pain, forcing herself to fill with rage. She focused on the injustice, toying with it, using it to stoke flames of anger. What had she really done to deserve what had befallen her? Were women just property? She knew it wasn't true. She was sure he would kill her if she didn't fight him and win, but she was afraid... afraid to die.

And then it clicked... As suddenly as she had become frightened, a new emotion filled her, hate. How come she was made to fear this man? Had she not braved the river by herself and fought off wolves? Ember sobered as she realized that she was his prey only because she let him control her. Sure, he was larger, but she was smaller, quicker, and armed. Her fear began to transform into pure rage. Ember would not let him dictate the rules of this engagement anymore.

Summoning all the anger, hate, and courage she had left, she forced a smile, a broad and toothy grin born of manic desperation. At the sight of her smile, the large man paused his approach, seemingly confused by her change in demeanor. He wasn't the only one who could intimidate with body language. Ember had little idea how to fight or what to do, other than to charge and slice her dagger. As she looked, she remembered fighting older boys when she was a child. They had out-massed her then, too. There had been one consistent strategy that worked, yet this wasn't a boy and they weren't playing. The idea came to mind and she simply went with it, giving not a moment to second guess. This was her one chance and adrenaline would carry her to victory or see her fall.

Before the man could even react, she sprang to her feet and began her desperate attack against a foe more than twice her size. She would use her dexterity and speed in place of weight, strength, and skill. Screaming loudly, she dashed at him on pained feet. Ember prepared to leap high in the air before stabbing him, her moves wild and easy to see. At least, she hoped they would be. She would show him exactly what he expected.

☼ ☼ ☼

In all his life, Rosif had fought many men and even seen a few women fight, yet he had never seen a woman come with such a brazen and ill-conceived attack. She was young and inexperienced, probably only a season or two past becoming a woman, at the most. He doubted she had even killed a deer, let alone fought a skilled man. She would try and bring the dagger down from high, and he would simply knock such ideas from her with a single hit.

He slid his right leg forward, ready to kick out and knock the silly girl to the ground. The kick to her stomach could actually kill her as she came in a blinding rush. But if she didn't die, she would permanently know her place as his new wife. Three strides brought the woman to the man. He smiled in anticipation of what was sure to be a complete destruction of her will in one painful kick. Afterward, she would be in a much easier state to enjoy before bed, he thought with a smile. Then, just as her right leg landed in the last step of her stride, exactly where Rosif expected her to start her leap, she instead fell forward into a nimble dive, tumbling low and raising the dagger overhead as she tucked and rolled.

☾ ☾ ☾

Ember barely thought as she tumbled forward, holding the knife overhead. This was how she used to avoid the older boys when she played tag as a child. A larger person with a wide stance made an easy target to avoid when you were small. The large man kicked out in what would have been a devastating body blow, catching nothing but air as the younger, more agile woman rolled between his now wide-open legs and out behind him. She held the blade out above her head as she rolled under him and felt it catch something, biting deeply.

The man grabbed at his loins and fell to his knees with a shrieking wail louder than a woman giving birth. Ember recovered from her tumble and turned, wide-eyed to see blood on her blade. The old man held his ruined crotch in shock and disbelief. Calpano, semi-conscious, and the suddenly awake Pak looked at Ember and the old man in turn. Without any real skills with a knife, Ember had merely held it straight up when she rolled under him. Unfortunately, he had not worn his loincloth under his hide wrap, which might have saved him. Perhaps he had thought it unnecessary, given what he had intended to do next.

Bad move old man, she thought, her heart pounding in her chest. The obsidian blade, volcanic glass, was as sharp as anything known, and the blade had bit deeply into the man's groin. The razor-sharp edge rendered flesh and let spill his masculinity lose and free, along with a lot of blood. The old man fell into the fetal position, wailing in agony.

The other two men gawked at the sight which befell them as organs which should have remained safely bundled together now hung free from what had been his scrotum. Their leader lay on the ground holding himself in an undignified position, tears welling in his eyes and high-pitched whimpers trailing from his mouth. Not far away, the young woman they had captured slowly stood holding a bloody obsidian dagger in her hand. Her bright green eyes caught the firelight, each painted in fear, shock, and vengeance.

Calpano laid back down without the ability to do anything about the situation. Still, he held his original flint knife in hand. If the woman came for him, he would be ready. Pak quickly lifted his bow and nocked an arrow, ready to shoot. The girl, a young woman perhaps, reached down and lifted her leather pouch, which had fallen during the fight. Pak stared at her in disbelief as she slowly held the dagger pointed at him, blood dripping from her hands. For a moment, they both stared with mutual respect, if nothing more. He was a wolf, and she was a fox.

"Kehd ke?" she said in her thick accent. Pak was unsure what to do. His loyalty was to his group, and he supposed that meant he should capture or kill this woman. On the other hand, he despised his group and felt guilty for what had happened to her. He could have perhaps done more to prevent her mistreatment and had not. He found himself unable to loose the arrow, consumed by a mixture of astonishment and guilt. Rosif had tried to rape her. Pak had talked him out of it several times, but would he have stopped the man? Could he have stopped Rosif? He simply stood with his bow ready to fire, should she attack him. He would let her go. None of them, not even Rosif, had acted immorally per their cultural norms, yet somehow, Pak knew he was in the wrong.

⊃ ⊃ ⊃

Ember slowly left the camp with her face locked on Pak. She hoped he wouldn't loose his arrow and kill her. As soon as she left the firelight, she started running as fast as she could along the riverbank. As she ran, she cried tears of joy and fear. She would be free this sixth night. The fox escaped and rushed into the night, alone and free.

Pak stood quite still for a while, his bow now pointed down. He had just awoken to find his leader semi-emasculated by a young woman, a woman whom they had tied to a tree not long before. Pak looked at the dreadfully ill Calpano, both exchanging glances. Neither man seemed upset over the larger man. He had always been such a bully. The men stared for a moment and then turned to their fallen leader. With great effort, Calpano lifted himself to a sitting position.

"We will... need to stay here for a while and recover. You are in charge while we heal... His wound will need to be treated. I'll leave that to you," Calpano said with a weak smile. Pak turned to the pained leader and knew what must be done. A short while later, Rosif was bound to the same tree Ember had been strapped to. His hands were bound, and a stick was placed in his mouth for him to bite. His legs were spread wide and lashed to a pair of impromptu steaks in the ground. Calpano could be heard by the fire softly chuckling while Pak finished splicing the bast fiber cordage he would use next.

The obsidian dagger had cut Rosif so severely that both of his testicles had to be removed. Performing the act nearly caused Pak to wretch. Rosif had even blacked out for a few moments from shock and pain. He would personally have chosen death before this. Now it was time for the final act of pain. Rosif had felt true agony, humiliation, and a loss of control while tied naked to the tree. It was quite the reversal in Pak's opinion, though the old bastard deserved it, he figured.

I guess you should have listened to me and treated her better, huh? he thought, though he still felt personal guilt over her treatment.

"I'm sorry, but the bleeding won't stop without this," Pak said. Calpano used his weak arms to lift his head enough to watch what followed with an unhealthy interest. After the pains Rosif had put him through over the seasons, this was something he simply wouldn't miss.

"The pain will subside in a few days," Pak said as he pulled the loose skin together and tied the cordage tightly, cutting off the blood flow.

CHAPTER SEVEN
FREEDOM

Freedom is often underappreciated until you lose it. As Ember ran from her captors, she experienced a terror few encounter in the modern, developed world. In the contemporary world, a frightened person can run until they find more people, some sort of civilization, or a person of law enforcement, perhaps. In Ember's world, there was no one. She was a lone woman surrounded by millions of square kilometers of mostly empty land with only a few tribes of people, here and there. The world's population in Ember's time was likely a few million people, perhaps a thousand times smaller than today. Worse yet, the population was mostly gathered near the equator and in small, dense tribal groups.

If Ember even found another tribe or a group of people, she could not ensure that they would protect her. Freedom, fundamental human rights, and equality are modern achievements. Having grown up in a world with these precious gifts, the true enormity of Ember's escape cannot be readily appreciated by many of today's people. This is a testament to the society which humans have forged from a hostile world, yet its very need is a condemnation of our worst tendencies.

Ember ran as fast as she could for what seemed like an eternity. Whenever she felt that she might slow, she would hear a noise behind her and push herself even more. Once, she even thought she heard a woman screaming in the same direction from which she had come, but the sound was far in the distance and probably a phantom of her fears. Though she wore her doeskin shirt and leather loincloth, her arms and legs were bare and were quickly cut and scraped by brambles and other sharp objects she could not avoid while running in the dark.

If Ember's body had only minor injuries, her feet were an entirely different story. Her feet ached and even bled under the strain of walking those past few days. She was now running through thick bramble and sand. Her body was quickly growing weak due to the sudden and extended physical exertion. Her vision had slowly become blurry, and she had begun to feel lightheaded. Fear was her primary source of energy, yet she was running out fast.

Ember ran over what looked like a grassy mound just as she exited the thick brambles and dashed into a clearing. As she reached the top, she tripped on a rock and stumbled down the other side of the mound, rolling for a moment and coming up hard against the dew-covered ground. She rolled onto her back, dazed and breathless. The last thing she saw was the starry sky as the blackness of unconsciousness took her. Perhaps she should have eaten more.

When she awoke, she immediately noticed that the Sun was nearly halfway across the sky. She had been lying on the ground for a night and half of a day. How far had she run from the men, and would they follow her? Surely, they would hunt her for revenge after the wound she had given their leader. Running as she had, Ember knew that she could be easily tracked. She rose to a crouch and examined her surroundings for signs of pursuit. Her feet were bruised and bloodied with dozens of tiny wounds, and her legs bled from countless scratches and cuts. She stood and walked slowly, cautiously, to the river. This time, she looked up.

At the river, Ember soaked her feet for a short while before preparing to run again. The river provided reasonably safe water to drink and some small shallows in which Ember found some mussels, which she smashed open with a small stone and ate raw, something which could be done with shellfish. The mussels were slimy, but the taste was tangy and sweet, and Ember quickly filled her stomach with as many as she could before moving off and away from the river. She would have to return later when she was sure the men could not find her. Before leaving, she paused and simply cried for a moment.

Ember spent the rest of the day resting in a small thicket near the river. She sang prayers to the gods of the forest to hide her from the men and heal her wounds. Song was crucial to her people, and many of their prayers were made in simple repetitive chants sung for extended periods. Ember found the songs soothing and relaxing as she quietly sang them, nearly at a whisper. Finally, as night came, the ravaged redhead covered herself in long grasses to hide her body and fell asleep. She hoped the men and wolves wouldn't come for her because she was simply too afraid and tired to run anymore.

The next day was filled with half-heard sounds, anxiety, and an ever-present fear as Ember made her way through the woods near the river shore. She had only slept for about half of the night, giving in to mental exhaustion, then walked and ran only a little farther before sleeping again. Sleeping in the open and without fire, crying, eating what she could find, and growing weak, Ember was becoming worried that her luck might run out. What she really needed was a chance to rest and heal.

She was extremely haggard, having only eaten small raw tubers, the leaves of the tuber plants, grubs from a rotted log, mussels, and berries as she had found them. The fresh tubers came from beneath beautiful reddish-blue flowers. Most of these flowers bloomed many tendays before and were now harder to locate, but Ember happened upon several. She had been afraid to catch fish in the river because this was where the men were likely to look for her. Worse, the fire needed to cook them would produce light and an odor that might be detected.

Each night, Ember had climbed into a tree with an armload of stones to sleep. Truly she was a wild thing, sleeping like an animal and foraging in the bushes like some furry critter. Ember had endured much at the hands of the gods and their "signs." At this point, she had decided that she really needed to find someplace to weather the coming cold season and heal. Her body was young and strong, but she had abused it for over a tenday, and the wear was showing. She had experienced significant back pains after multiple nights spent sleeping in trees. Her bottom was scratched and itched from the bark, and she had additional pains from her legs losing circulation for extended periods.

Ember sat on her tree branch during the early part of the third night since having escaped capture. She considered what had happened and what she might do about it. Her wounded body was coated in drying river mud to conceal her from anyone who might wander by. Ember carefully flicked away dried mud from her hands and peeled the bark from her tree branch as her mind fought to reconcile the pain she had endured. She had concluded that she did not hate the younger man who had captured her, but she couldn't say the same for the older ones. Of course, the one she had sickened might not still live.

She felt an odd sense of power at having escaped in such a martial manner. Somehow, it had felt good to have escaped using a weapon and her own skills. She was starting to feel that she was not merely a leaf in the wind. She had a voice, and she would be heard, though she still needed time to cry and resolve some of the fears she had faced. She had nearly been raped and possibly killed. It was hard to put something like that aside. It was a violation that tainted her thoughts, but she was starting to feel like she might be alright.

As the tree branch began to run out of bark to peel. Ember wiped her fresh tears as she came to a conclusion of what she would do. She would give up the indignity and safety of the trees and sleep on the ground. The next day, she would start putting herself back together and regaining her control. Hiding was necessary, but so too was a stable food supply, clean water, and a good spear in her hand. She needed to start acting like a human again and not a wild fox.

During the early morning of Ember's fourth day since her escape, she was awakened from her tuft of grass, where she had napped, to the screech of an owl. She sat up, immediately worried the men had found her. Though the Sun had only just started to rise, owls were generally rare to see at this time of the morning. She looked around for the source of the noise, slowly standing and walking toward the river. After a short time, she found the offending owl. It was perched upon a freshly killed mink by the river. Even an owl would leave a nearby tree during the day if a foolish mink happened too close. Mink was one of the largest creatures that an owl could kill and the meat would keep the owl for many days. But Ember was hungry too, and she needed some fresh meat. The owl was a powerful and skilled predator, but she didn't care. The thought of cooked mink meat was simply too great to be ignored.

Ember quickly looked around for stones to use as missiles. This morning she would feast upon roast mink. With an armload of smooth river stones, she approached the owl. Upon seeing a competitor for the food, the owl promptly began flapping its wings and screeched at Ember, unwilling to leave such a grand prize. In response, she hurled a stone at the owl, hoping for a second meal. The owl screeched a few times in defiance, but when a rock blasted through its wing feathers, it took the hint and surrendered the mink to the wide-eyed and larger predator. Ember walked, painfully on sore feet, to the mink and stood victoriously over the body. *Great... now I'm a vulture*, she thought.

The mink had been struck in the head and neck, leaving the remainder of the body intact. The body was still warm and would remain fresh long enough for her to cook. The body would need to be cleaned and some of the organs set aside for cooking. She was glad she still had her obsidian dagger. With the mink in one hand and a discarded owl feather in the other, Ember strolled on sore feet down to the river's edge.

A short while later, she sat by a pile of driftwood and dried leaves briskly rubbing her hands together with a stick between them, forcing the stick in a downward motion. She was weak, and the stick slipped from her hands several times before the first motes of puffy white smoke smoldered in the dry wood she had used as the base. She quickly applied dried leaves and blew. Within a few moments, she had a small fire of kindling and sticks. She carefully nursed the flame into a full cooking fire.

She moved the mink near the fire to guard against scavengers and left for the woods to gather some wood and long grasses to construct a cooking frame and make a spit.

Ember sat on the ground that midday by the now raging fire with a full belly and oily fingers. She had fully skinned the mink and roasted it over the fire. She had initially intended to keep some of the meat, but she was simply too hungry. The mink meat, giving her strength, would do much to help her get more food. The organs had been carefully cleaned and cooked. They provided Ember with much-needed nutrition as well as some extra food in her stomach.

Toward the evening, she decided she would discard the mink hide due to the difficulties of tanning it and the owl talon marks preventing scraping the hide effectively. If the mink were in better shape, she could have stretched it on the ground using wooden steaks to hold it while she scraped the inner flesh from the skin. This would require making a scraper stone from some flint, which she would also have to find, though she could use her dagger if she had to. Crushing the mink's brain and mixing with a little water would make a liquid that could be spread over the leather causing it to tan in a short time as she scraped a tool, such as a smooth stick, over the leather to help it soften. Other tanning methods existed, such as bark tanning, but these were even more complex and impractical for a single person alone in the wilds.

Mink was generally of use in making small, soft, and delicate leather goods. However, what she really needed was the hide of a larger animal, like a deer. Sadly, she left the mink pelt and remains a short walk from her new camp, where the owl might find a small meal. Ember hoped that the owl spirits would not be too angered, but she had to eat too.

That night, Ember sat with her feet by the fire, letting the radiant heat heal them. The fire had always been helpful for healing wounds. She didn't know why the flame cured people, but she knew that a cut would be less likely to become red and sore if it was held near a fire for a time. As the fire raged, she sang aloud a song to the fire spirits asking for their healing powers. She had not sung loudly in many days, and the sound of her voice was somewhat foreign to her. It took a long while to get into a rhythm, but eventually, Ember let loose a powerful healing song. If her feet had not been injured, she would have danced the healing dances. She only hoped that the fire spirits heard her.

That night she slept by a warm fire with her cleaned and pampered feet on the mend. The wind was cooler, and somehow she knew that the colder seasons were not so far off. The end of the warm season meant that the water in the river would be the warmest it would be, but soon she would have a real need for better clothing and protection. She would sleep with her clothing on tonight. Hopefully, before the cold season fully set, she would find her way west and conclude whatever foolish "destiny" there was for her.

The more she thought about the whole ceremony, the more she wondered if the "sign" had not really been meant for another. Maybe Yellow Flowers? She had pushed Ember aside to go first. If she had not, maybe Yellow Flowers would have been sent. Poor Yellow Flowers wouldn't have made it. Ember very much disliked the arrogant woman, but she wouldn't have wanted her eaten or captured. Of course, Yellow Flowers wouldn't have encountered the men because she would have likely died in the storm, she suspected.

Ember thought once more of the men who had taken her and how she truly felt about what had happened. The thoughts kept returning, refusing to be banished. She had cried many times, and even come to terms with parts of what had happened, though she wondered if she would ever truly be the same. Some things changed a person. This was not always entirely bad, and sometimes bad events helped one grow. Her encounter had not been a positive event, but she had learned how strong she actually was and that even she could stand against a violent bully and win. But she had also come so close to being... She pushed that thought aside, unwilling to consider it.

Her trouble was with the younger man, Pak. He had seemed different from the others. Perhaps he was a flint in the rough, as the expression went. With thoughts of the ridiculousness of her journey in mind, Ember slowly drifted off to sleep. As she slept, an owl circled overhead several times, giving Ember a strange expression before settling by the mink body to feast on the remains.

CHAPTER EIGHT
THE OTHERS

Humanity is often more compassionate than cruel. This is a mechanism of humanity's social nature and a powerful evolutionary trait for any social species. The fundamental and intrinsic secular moralities found in social species exist because members of a social species who do not exhibit them tend to not perpetuate as well as those who do. For this reason, most of the people Ember meets display various levels of basic, reciprocal morality. They understand the concepts of what is socially beneficial as "good" and what is detrimental as "bad." Beyond the most basic of concepts, good and bad exist as relative terms and are defined by each society and by individual preference.

Given this moral complexity, it is hard to entirely condemn Pak for his part in Ember's capture. Pak grew up in a world where gender roles were codified into very distinct behaviors and likely rigidly enforced, as is typically the case in contemporary lithic cultures. From his culture's perspective, capturing and returning Ember to what Pak's people would consider her normal social condition would have been moral within the context of their society. But, of course, from our modern perspective, his actions were blatantly immoral and objectively so from a do-least-harm perspective. It should be noted that, even by the standards of his own people, Rosif's actions were immoral.

For the next two days, Ember remained by the river at her new makeshift camp, constantly vigilant and with a clear plan of what to do if the men came. She had prepared a place to run and hide if attacked and even set traps as an extra precaution. Around the perimeter of her camp, she had dug little holes in the wet sand and placed upright-pointing sticks she had sharpened with her dagger. She covered these traps with the same leaves and grass which littered the shore.

Ember had heard of such a technique from a story told by a trader long ago. She had already used them once before, though the spikes had never been put to the test. Still, she hoped they might be effective. Stepping on one of her traps would impale one's foot with the sharpened stick. Near the traps and her camp, she placed as many dried twigs as she could. If anyone approached, they would possibly injure their feet gravely and certainly break many a twig in the process, alerting her.

The traps were all she knew how to make. She had seen better defensive traps crafted by people of her tribe, but she wasn't really so good with traps and trapping. So, she was forced to use the only trap she knew. She was no hunter or warrior, and she was not really violent by nature. Yet, she was starting to understand that she would have to take matters into her own hands if she wished to survive. Other animals were not bad or evil, and yet they fought tooth and claw to live. Her own mother and father had killed two raiders, according to East. Ember was growing up in many ways.

It had been seven days since Ember had escaped the men, four spent in a tree and the last two in her small camp. Her feet had healed reasonably well from seven full days of either resting or light walking. Ember had even fashioned a pair of nettle fiber woven shoes. They had taken three days to make from cutting and processing the nettles on the first day, then drying and weaving the next two days. They were far from quality, but they made walking much easier. She had even used a poultice of the leaves as medicine for her wounds. With her injuries on the mend and her belly full of fish, shellfish, and amphibians, Ember decided to leave her camp and continue her travel northwest along the river.

Before she permanently left the camp, Ember removed the spikes and left them on the ground as a warning to the men if they passed this way. She was starting to suspect they were not following. Revealing one of her traps might be a bad idea, but leaving a warning to the men might possibly deter them entirely. More importantly, Ember didn't want to risk animals or other people falling victim to the traps long after she was gone.

She walked for a long while through warm sunlight, reflecting upon her recent encounters. She had truly lived an adventure beyond anyone of her tribe, and yet she had still not finished her journey. She was also starting to have serious concern over the mental state of Morning Dew for giving her such a task. Why did a falling star have anything to do with her? Couldn't lightning, falling stars, or other such events occur randomly and at the moment of some great speech or event? Why did a sign actually have to be a sign or specify her? Wouldn't other people have seen it and interpreted it differently?

Nettle fiber woven shoes

She often threw rocks at the water and other such acts of fun when she was bored. Couldn't the gods just be bored, throwing their own sort of "rocks?" Why couldn't the gods also have a sense of humor? Reflecting on her trip so far, perhaps they did, and a dark one, indeed. She did not even know how far she was from her goal. Ember walked along the deer trails near the river, deep in her thoughts but always far enough away from the river that she wouldn't bump into anyone walking along the banks. Ember wouldn't soon find herself once more at anyone's mercy, if she had any say.

Sometime near the setting of the Sun that same day, she heard the sounds of laughing and talking. The sounds bore a distinctly feminine sound, though the language was foreign to her. Ember dropped low and remained close to the tree-line as she approached the river bank where the sounds emanated. There had been no evidence of women, or anyone else, traveling with the three men. Besides, women were never generally found far from a camp, something Ember had never really considered too deeply before today.

"Well, that is not always true, is it Ember..." she said, more to hear herself speak than for any other reason, quickly laughing ironically. Ember was not far from the river and promptly made her way to the bushes and bramble just before the bank. She kept low, concealing herself behind a large tree trunk and gently parted the branches of a small bush to have a better look at the scene by the river. She kept her dagger in hand, just in case. The feel of the handle brought a sense of security and control over her environment.

Before her, eight women stood waist-deep in the river water holding small spears, obviously fishing. The scene was quite familiar to Ember. She could easily have been one of these women, spending long days fishing or gathering reeds and shellfish by the river before it became too cold. It was more refreshing a scene than she had hoped for, a return to something she knew and an odd feeling of safety. She relaxed as she knelt for an extended look at the fisherwomen.

The women were mostly nude, typical for those who worked in water. Leather simply couldn't handle the water without later smelling bad and disintegrating. They were adorned with feathers and necklaces made of antler and bone beads with a few full antler points and stone beads. Beside the river, a pile of clothing sat ready for their return to wherever they lived. While nudity was fine in the water, it was uncommon within a tribe without a purpose.

Each of the women wore a unique design of paint on their faces, mostly ash. Their designs were similar, likely all belonging to the same people. Their skin was significantly darker than Ember's, and they seemed a little taller, with darker hair. These were forest people. They inhabited most of the lands west and north of the Great River. Ember's people traded with them from time to time, though they mostly avoided each other. The elders' stories said they were the first people, created by the gods before Ember's own people. They were not greater or lesser, simply different.

As she watched, the women worked and socialized, seemingly relaxed and cheerful. A few of the women caught Ember's eye, though the vicarious joy of their laughter was equally inspiring. Ember noticed that the youngest woman was barely of adult age, but not more than a season younger than her, while the oldest was perhaps ten harvests older than she. This confused Ember. If this were a whole tribe, where were the older women? There were also no children, very odd for a village. Nevertheless, she continued to stare at the women trying to learn their secrets.

On the beach, there were small wooden frames set up to hang caught fish, as well as baskets to hold the cleaned fish, and a few odds and ends left by the women. During the cold season, fish were generally dried from such racks using salt and smoke, or even flash-freezing when cold enough. As she sat watching the women, Ember soon recognized this gathering for what it was, a small hunting and gathering group from a tribe elsewhere.

Such groups were commonplace during the warm seasons, such as hunting camps, groups gathering important resources, and entirely nomadic peoples. Fish, common throughout most rivers that crossed the lands, was not a reason for an outpost or encampment of any size. Ember wondered what the actual interest of these people was. She decided to sneak closer and observe the women longer. Perhaps she could join with them for a time and evade the men, who might still be following her. But, before she would reveal herself, she would ensure that these were good people who wouldn't see her as a threat or resource for exploitation.

She crawled on her hands and knees from bush to bush, slowly approaching the laughing women. She noted that her arms and legs, though slightly tanned, stood out from the brush too easily. Worse, the black paint she had applied many days ago had long worn off. Finding several muddy patches on the ground as she crawled, she smeared the cool mud on her bare arms, face, hair, and legs. With luck, she would be much more challenging to see. Ember hoped she wouldn't be caught with the mud all over her, creeping around in the bushes as she was. It simply would not do. She imagined herself being found and what she would say sitting in a bush covered in mud.

It's not what it looks like! I swear, she mused.

Now resembling a woman-shaped bush, Ember crept closer and got a better look. The women were fishing for small fish and doing an excellent job of it, too. Every short while, one of them would announce a catch and deposit the fish in a pile on the bank with a toss from her spear.

At this rate, you will eat all the fish in the river before you return to your own lands, she grumbled, but she might have just been a little jealous of their skill. All eight women were laughing and talking as Ember finally got close enough for a real peek. Ember, the bush, was hiding behind a large berry bush barely ten lengths of a man away, casually chewing on a berry as she listened and observed. She would make contact if they continued to appear friendly, though she was curious how their men behaved. She suspected there were men, but she had just not seen any. Either way, it felt to her that the act of being near these people was restoring a little bit of what made her who she was. She wanted to stand up and rush to the women and say "Hello," but she was fearful of the results. No, she would have to wait and see what more could be learned.

The women were laughing and chatting. Every now and then, one would wave her hand dismissively at the others, and then laughter would ensue. Though she didn't understand their words, their demeanor was about the same as the women in her village. The thought made Ember smile and feel her first sense of calm in a while. Their language was slightly guttural, with no words that she immediately recognized, aside from a few similarities in some of the word sounds. For example, when a woman threw a fish, she might say, "Un da'fek," which sounded like it could mean "I have one" or "I got a fish," though she could not hope to learn their language in a few moments of watching them, or even in a tenday, she supposed.

Hearing the words of another people was common enough when traders came, but never to any exceptional detail. Most people understood the trade language, a standard set of words that traders used. Perhaps she would try the trade language if she spoke to one of them. She had heard that the trade "language" was really "languages," and varied by region. If these people were technically from the same region as she, they might be able to communicate.

She noted one woman not too far from her. The fisher had rich dark skin the color of oiled wood, and bright blue eyes. Her long dark hair had been drawn into a long braid down her back and secured with a string. She wore a lovely, braided cord around her waist with little stone beads at finger lengths. Her knees and elbows were bound in oiled leather cords, almost like bracelets, whose purpose Ember could not surmise. Her shoulders and calves had been tattooed with black dot patterns. Ember found her beautiful and a tad exotic, at least compared to her own people. As she watched, the woman stood with a spear watching the water for fish. Her dreamy stare was suddenly interrupted when a man stepped from the trees yelling a greeting to the women, she guessed.

"Hssa-ook-herr!" he yelled, exaggerating the word, to which the women all replied in the same way with a few variations. The man had shoulder-length dark brown, curly hair and what looked like nearly gray eyes. He looked like he had seen at least twenty seasons and wore a leather loincloth covered in mud but with a familiar gold sparkle to it. His body was otherwise covered with dirt and the same golden-colored sparkles as the leather. Ember watched as the man stepped towards the water and removed his clothing as the women giggled and teased. He laughed at them and dove into the water scaring the fish away. This caused many of the women to yell unflattering things. Ember didn't need to understand their language to understand that.

The golden speckles partly answered the question of what the people were doing here. These people were gathering the heavy yellow stones that traders sometimes valued. The rock was useless as a tool, being too soft, but that same softness made it exceptional for jewelry. Such jewelry was extremely rare and typically only came from the southern and far eastern traders. But that couldn't be their only reason, as the yellow rocks were just not valuable enough by themselves.

Ember's people had found a few handfuls of the rocks in her lifetime. Many of the rocks had been ground for use in medicines or traded for quality textiles, a particularly expensive commodity. But, as valuable as the yellow-colored stones were, there were more important things to obtain, such as flint or animal furs. Ember felt like a sneaky fox as she crawled closer, very close, for an even better look.

As the man swam about and the women talked and splashed water at him, Ember became enthusiastic that she might be able to stay with these people for a time. All she had was a good obsidian blade, a small bag of flint pieces, Blossom's goddess pendant, worn clothing, and the warm ice to trade. Besides her flint pieces, she really wasn't keen to trade her other possessions with how little she had. Maybe they would let her trade labor? She hoped that would be all they asked for, if anything.

Suddenly her attention was returned to the scene as one of the women was pulled beneath the river, issuing a short, squeaky noise as she plunged beneath the surface. A moment later, she popped out of the water, bonking the man on the head as hard as she could while he stood there, accepting the bonks while laughing quite hard. The gathered women burst into intense laughter at the sight. Even the dunked woman started laughing after a few moments. Being nude, she wasn't inconvenienced much by being submerged, but the incident appeared to have startled her. Ember caught a gleam of affection in her eyes toward the man. If she had been dunked, Ember would have slapped the man, but she supposed they were lovers.

After a short while, the man emerged from the water and replaced his garment. A moment later, two more men approached the bank. Both were around the same age as the first man and wore leather leggings, loincloths, and leather shirts. However, they were not as dirty as the first man and had the look of men dressed for hunting about them. One of the men made a short announcement. As he spoke, he was sober-faced. His expression quickly became a broad grin as he finished. What he had said seemed humorous to the women, many of whom laughed. A joke, Ember guessed. With the last few laughs, the women left the water and donned their clothing.

Such amusing people, she thought. Several of the women spoke to the joking man using what sounded like a name, "Ssv'ee'n," or something like that, Ember decided. Within a short time, the group had packed their fishing spears and gathered the fish to venture back, presumably, to their camp. The group packed their gear and moved toward the trees. Two women carried the fish in a large basket-like structure made of reeds. Ember, the bush, sat watching as she nibbled another berry. She realized that she had been casually eating berries from the bush while she watched. They had stained her fingers red, which is why they were often used for dye. She would need to remove the mud and apply a more proper color. It would be required if she were to approach these cheerful people, assuming she did.

Ember gathered a few handfuls of the berries and placed them on a flat stone, always easy to find by a riverbank. She crushed the berries with a smaller, smooth rock until they became a reddish smear, ready to apply. The forest people had left, probably for the day, given that the Sun was low on the horizon. Ember sneaked from the bushes toward the shallow waters at the river's edge. She needed a bath to remove the mud before she applied the stain. Removing her garments, Ember slid into the water for a quick dip. The cool mud and sand felt terrific as she dug her toes into the riverbed. She would miss these fresh baths when the cold weather came. She swam as much as she could every warm season, then spent the cold season longing for her next chance to swim.

After fresh mud had been applied and removed from her now smooth skin, Ember remained in the calm waters, just letting the water soak in. Over the last few days, she had worked hard to restore her body and mind to the way they were. The wounds on her feet from the wolves had scabbed and were healing, as were most of her larger cuts. If she continued to soak in the water and allow a fire to warm her at night, she could expect to be fully restored in a few more days.

Ember remained in the water until the Sun was fully setting. She only came out then because the remaining sun-warmed air would be needed for drying her body and hair. While she dried in the still warm air, Ember sat on a rock in the dimming light and applied the berries. She painted her entire body with a mixture of purple and red berry pigment. This sort of stain was common and would last a few days unless she washed a few times. Finally painted, she had returned to decency as an unpainted body was offensive to her people. Offhandedly, she hoped the forest people didn't return and find her.

"Sitting nude on a rock is a welcoming custom of my people," she imagined herself saying if caught. She doubted they would believe such a dumb story, but what else would she say? Though slightly nervous, the thought nearly made her giggle. At least she would feel more normal if she met with the people.

"Unless it attracts insects like it did that one time!" she joked to herself, remembering how she ran through the village with insects chasing her after applying the wrong herbs, just a few harvests before. As a result, she had red bumps for a tenday.

After painting herself, Ember tied to her hair with nettle fiber the owl feather she had saved from a few days before. The feather was quite beautiful, having black stripes and intricate designs. Best of all, it complimented the dark feather she already wore. She wished she had a few more feathers to add to her hair, but for now, these would have to do. She wouldn't be at her aesthetic best, but she was wandering the wilds alone, so perhaps she was being too hard on herself.

With the Sun finally set and the cover of night upon her, the time had come to see the people in their temporary camp. Ember secured her loincloth, woven shoes, and her soft doeskin shirt. The shirt was tough and still in generally good shape, but she had started to notice wear from the brambles and the ground. Sadly, the painted black spots were mostly faded, but those could be repainted if she obtained some oil for paint. If the shirt became too damaged, sections would be removed, and doeskin patches replaced, and holes sewn closed. Leather wore out after a time, but much could be done to repair it, as well.

With her body clean and painted and her spirits lifted, Ember stepped through the bushes and small trees in the direction the people had gone. It was not long before she came upon their encampment. The light from a large fire lit the otherwise dark forest around a set of six small makeshift huts. In between each hut were pit stores of food, bladders and wooden bowls of water, and various hanging goods. Around the camp, cordage hung between huts allowing drying of plants. She crept closer to get a better look, staying low in the brush.

Being seen stalking around a camp was not a good idea, but the Sun had just set, and Ember was confident she could keep herself hidden. As she crawled in for a closer look, she stepped behind a large tree and bushes, much as she had when she had first watched these people. The growing darkness and her new purple-red coloring allowed her a closer look at the group without being seen, she hoped.

Before her stood a ring of little huts, each made of long wooden poles and reed mats. They were constructed like her simple camp hut but much larger, the biggest probably able to hold five or six people. The ends of each of the poles had been fire-hardened to last many seasons, but the mats looked like they were in bad shape, as though they had been poorly made and not designed for prolonged use. The main telltale sign that this was a temporary camp was the lack of color. People always painted and decorated their possessions and dwellings, but these little huts were quite bland.

In the camp center, twenty-one men and women sat around a fire talking and laughing while they ate a meal. The oldest of the group was a man who looked nearly too old to be away from a proper village. He was wrinkled, and most of his teeth and hair were missing. Ember supposed he was very old, perhaps fifty-five harvests or more, but his eyes held a sparkle of youth. He sat beside the fire, telling some sort of elaborate story while the rest of the people laughed and ate. As he spoke, he would use a stick in his hand to draw little pictures in the dirt before him. This sort of storytelling was commonplace in any village, and Ember had grown up spending portions of each evening listening to elders tell tales.

Quietly, she slithered around the camp perimeter, watching from various angles. Then, seeing that the people were thoroughly engrossed in the story, she began to approach the forest side of the camp. There, she came across a set of small leather sacks hanging from a pole frame. Carefully, she removed one of the small sacks and examined its contents. The sack contained a small handful of tiny heavy yellow rocks. Her suspicions had been correct: these people had been gathering the strange yellow rocks. Near the bags, Ember found a stack of deer hides and smaller furry pelts of high quality. She cautiously made her way to the pelts leaving the worthless yellow stones behind. Actually, a trader from the South would probably trade a good flint nodule for a bag that big, but they were nowhere near as useful as the pelts unless you traveled south to trade them.

She placed her head longingly against the pile of what looked like fox furs, feeling the soft fur against her cheek. How she longed for a warm, comfortable place to sleep without fear. She leaned against the furs laid upon two sets of reed mats and let their softness comfort her as she watched the people. Finally, after what must have been a decent stretch of time, the people seemed ready for sleep. One by one and two by two, they drifted away to the huts. Ember lay on the furs and watched as a couple left the dying fire. They were the last to leave, and they were heading for the hut near where she lay. She was sure they wouldn't see her from the furs, and she carefully kept low as she watched.

The man was the same person who had come to the river earlier that day and announced what must have been "dinner," she supposed. He was no more than twenty harvests old with dark, curly hair. He now wore a leather wrap tied with a thick leather strap and a fur cloak with leather boots. He walked hand in hand with a woman who looked a little older than Ember. She had the same dark hair, though straighter. Like most forest people, she was taller than those of Ember's tribe, as was the man. Both had significantly darker skin as well.

As she passed, Ember recognized her as the woman the man had pulled under the water, the same she had seen fishing, before. She wore a soft leather shirt, looser than Ember's and with more seams. The shirt ended just below her waist. Below this, she wore an ankle-length bark fiber skirt. The skirt was made from two cloth panels, sewn to allow slits up both sides, though the woman had a leather piece hanging at her waist in the front to keep the skirt intact as she worked. In addition, she wore leather boots much like the man. Ember decided that she was pretty and had good taste in fashion.

While they walked, the man spoke of something while the woman gave him catty side glances. Before they could reach the door to the hut, the woman spun and moved to block the man. She playfully tugged at his arm and spoke words Ember didn't need to understand to appreciate.

"Zhek... pente appa'orre, daen... Zhek," she purred. Though her body language needed no translation, her words were still foreign. Ember supposed the first word, "Zhek," was the man's name, by the way she had said it. The last word, "daen," reminded Ember of an old word she heard some of the elders use for distant rivers, "Da'ani." The woman hauled the ever-smiling man off into the woods, ignoring their hut. Ember followed from a distance, but she had already guessed their destination as they approached the riverbank.

The Moon was still waning, and the river was dark, but what light remained reflected off the water keeping the bank visible enough even in the dark. Within a few more nights, the darkness would be too deep for anything to be seen. The Moon came and went in cycles, which aided people in determining the best times to hunt and fish.

Just as they stepped onto the sand, the woman halted and turned upon the man once more. Ember could see her face clearly from the bushes. The woman whispered something to the man and giggled. She slowly removed his cloak and then his wrap, letting them drop to the sand. As she finished, he stepped forward and kissed her with the fierce passion of a man who had been awaiting this moment since he awoke. A moment later, the man removed the loose shirt from the woman pulling it over her head and tossing it on his own clothing. She stood before him, her breath coming fast as their mutual anticipation built over what they had been waiting for all day.

As the kissing continued, Ember started to feel warm and slightly embarrassed. The way the man's hands moved so slowly, with such care... the way the woman's body caught the Moon's light... Ember let out a held breath. A moment later, the bark fiber skirt spilled onto the sand, and the woman again wore only her braided waist cord. She looked down, worrying that she shouldn't be watching so intimate of an encounter. She had seen people this way before, not so uncommon in a longhouse without much privacy. But those times were not intentional, and something about just staring felt wrong. She looked back just in time to watch the lovers sink onto the sand and become one.

Before turning away, Ember noticed something else. Both the man and woman wore matching necklaces made from a leather thong with a large shiny pendant at the end that caught the Moon's light. The pendants were made of the same yellow rock the people had been gathering. Ember crept back toward the camp. She gave one last look back, seeing the man and woman on the ground in a deep sandy embrace. Blushing, she sneaked through the woods, still able to hear the two lovers halfway to the camp, likely the reason they had chosen seclusion. She hoped she might one day find out just how wonderful a lover's embrace was. She sighed at the thought as she approached the now quiet camp, remembering the strange woman from her dream not so long ago. Finding a lover was difficult and even more so if your tastes were uncommon.

She found the pile of furs and decided to lie back upon them for a short time and relax before finding a tree in which to spend the night. The softness of the fox furs was simply too much to resist, and Ember had plenty to think about. She flopped upon the furs and began to consider what type of lover she might one day find. Would she look for a strong hunter? Perhaps a talented artisan or dancer? Ember spent a good while thinking the fluttery thoughts of first love and romance. One day, she hoped for such love, but first, she would have to complete this foolish task.

If I make it to the West, the end of the world, and find nothing... I'm going to be very angry, she thought. She lay back on the soft furs and pondered many thoughts. Unfortunately, the fox furs were very relaxing.

CHAPTER NINE
THE FOREST PEOPLE

The Pleistocene epoch ended approximately 12,000 years ago, transitioning to the Holocene epoch, the current geological epoch, bringing sweeping changes to the climate, affecting flora and fauna. Dry, arid steppe lands transitioned to lush, humid forests while megafauna and small, rapidly breeding animals gave way to a broader mix of animals. Following the warming of the lands, the human lifestyle adapted to meet these changes. Hunting styles adjusted from group hunting of larger game and an often nomadic lifestyle, which had served us for millennia, to encounter hunting, trapping, fishing, and gathering. Limited textiles, ceramics, and farming, all too often associated only with the later Neolithic period, also emerged, as did microlith stone tools. We call this period between the end of the Last Glacial Period and the emergence of the later Neolithic period, the Mesolithic period, or the "middle stone age," in some locations and Epipalaeolithic in others.

The Neolithic had begun nearly 5,000 years before Ember's birth in the Fertile Crescent and Northeastern China. Yet, in 5500 BCE, most of Europe was inhabited by Mesolithic peoples. Mesolithic Europeans lived alongside the Neolithic people pouring into Europe from Anatolia and the Fertile Crescent. Their DNA can be found in much of modern Europeans, which indicates a genetic admixture – the interbreeding of Mesolithic and Neolithic peoples.

Analyzing DNA and skeletal remains, we now believe many Mesolithic peoples likely had dark skin, with blue eyes being reasonably common – though not exclusive. In addition, they generally stood taller than subsequent Neolithic people, perhaps owing to a diet richer in protein and what may have been an overall healthier lifestyle. They tended to live in small tribal groups, from single families to perhaps one hundred individuals.

Ember's people colloquially refer to them as "Forest People," given how many of their villages can be found deeper in the forests, in contrast to Ember's own Neolithic river-dwelling culture, whom the Mesolithic "Forest People" tend to refer to as "River Dwellers," or "Earth People," given their extensive farming and general proximity to rivers.

That night, Ember dreamed that she was a mink. Ember, the mink, ran along the riverbank faster than she could have as a mere human. Grass and small debris flew past her as she sped along. The world was so giant, and she, a mink, so small. On and on she ran, keeping watch for hungry owls. After a time, she found what looked like a safe place. After searching for signs of danger, she came to a stop and curled up around her soft bushy tail for a warm nap in the Sun. There, she slept and dreamed sweet dreams. The dream was quite pleasant until a poke to the stomach brought her around. She squeaked, as minks did when poked in their soft, furry tummies, then opened her eyes.

She lay against the fur pile beside a hut as the morning Sun warmed her face, suddenly not so furry. But, how could it be morning? She had only laid her head against the furs by the hut for a moment, then she would return to the woods and find a hiding place. Yet, the Sun was out. She was considering the light and the source of the poke, still half asleep, when she felt a second poke to her now human tummy from something hard, like a wooden pole.

Ember turned to see her surroundings and instead found twenty-one people standing around her, several with spears and bows. An older man holding a fishing spear, seemingly the one who had poked her, looked as though he would speak, but Ember didn't give him a chance. Instead, like the quick mink in her dream, she suddenly stood, turned, and threw herself back onto the pile of furs rolling over them, less gracefully than she hoped, and onto the other side where the people were not. Ember stared at the confused people for a split second with a blink, and then darted away. This was her preferred method of getting out of bad situations.

I should have taken the name runs-like-mink when I took on this silly quest, she mused. The people behind her screamed as she ran as fast as she could. Again, she was glad for her less pronounced body.

That girl last night definitely couldn't do this, she thought with a smile as she ran as fast as she could, arms pumping hard at her sides.

She ran through the woods until she was confident they couldn't see her, and then turned and ran back toward the camp, hoping this would throw off the mob of people pursuing her. Her radical change in direction, doubling back, seemed to be working as she noticed no pursuers near her. Likely, they were chasing her deeper into the forest, or so they thought. Off to her side, the path she had initially took, Ember could hear the people chasing her the wrong way. She would simply run through their now empty camp and flee the opposite way. She wouldn't be anyone's captive.

Ember burst into the camp, dodging poles, cordage, and other obstacles as she raced for the freedom of the river. Suddenly, she tripped on a stick left beside one of the huts, falling hard on her side. There was a sharp pain in her ankle and stars as she hit the ground. She rolled over and saw the mob of people emerging from the woods. They had figured out her trick, but she was still far enough ahead to make an escape.

Quickly, she rolled onto her knees and leaped to her feet. Ember let out a painful cry and fell back to her knees as a sharp pain radiated through her ankle. She must have injured her left ankle, the adrenaline masking the damage until she tried to stand. Ember briefly considered hopping, but she knew that would never work. Quickly, the men surrounded her staying just beyond knife reach. She sighed and accepted capture without any means of escape and twenty-one pursuers, most of whom were young and in good health. She sank to the ground and started to cry, more out of frustration than fear. So, she would be a prisoner again. Perhaps this was better than dying in the cold season to come. She was probably very far from her goal, for whatever that was worth. Feeling helpless and defeated, she lay on the ground sobbing and beating her fist into the dirt.

Why does everyone always want to capture me? she wondered.

The people who had surrounded her were at a loss for what to do next. Before them lay a young woman dressed like a man who looked at least part river dweller, wounded and sobbing. She didn't even look like she had stolen anything, their first suspicion. Finally, after a moment of group indecision, a woman came forward, pushing the others aside to kneel beside Ember. She began slowly stroking Ember's hair and spoke to her in a questioning, yet comforting tone. The petting, a bit odd for this grown woman to be doing, had a relaxing effect on her. Her mother, East, used to stroke her head to help her sleep when she was young. Unfortunately, she had become overwhelmed in her moment of panic and let her fear and frustration take control. She didn't know what to say to the woman, but she stopped crying and cautiously looked up.

She was still surrounded, but the men had lowered their weapons. They were starting to appreciate that this was a lone woman and not something more malevolent. However, they remained suspicious given the unlikelihood of a sole person wandering so far from a village. Ember was barely armed, not well clothed, and not painted in the striking ways river people often did before conflict. This meant that she was probably lost or perhaps she had run from her people, but there were no river people villages for many days in any direction, which made her appearance, confusing.

The eldest man approached and said something to the men. Reluctantly, most of them formed into groups of two and headed off in different directions. Ember guessed they were searching for the remainder of Ember's "group." Of course, they would come back empty-handed, but she understood their fears. She could be a decoy for a raiding group or worse.

The elder man leveled his gaze at the woman kneeling beside Ember. As they started talking, she realized that this was the same woman she had seen the night before with the man, by the river. Perhaps the previous night's foray had left her in an extra-compassionate state, for she seemed, to Ember's reckoning, to be convincing the man of her position, which appeared to be favorable toward Ember. The elder listened to her passionate plea and slowly, thoughtfully, nodded his head in reluctant agreement. Then, he turned his gaze to Ember and spoke slowly and carefully.

"Ertu auen?" he asked. She stared at him without understanding, wiping the tears from her eyes. Her ankle hurt more than she had thought it would as the adrenaline wore off. He thought for a moment, then spoke again, this time in an entirely different language, judging by the tone and cadence.

"Veetae sae?" he asked. The second language was smoother and more flowing than the more guttural language he first used. Ember shook her head with a look of confusion. The man smiled and thought once more before trying again.

"Do-you know my-words?" he asked, slowly and with a heavy accent. He had spoken the local language that southern traders often used with her people, though barely correctly. Ember knew this language as the traders from the South came to her village every other harvest, during the warm season, and stayed for perhaps a tenday or more. Ember had always been good at learning new languages and had learned that specific trade language, one of many, at an early age. The sounds were clear but not well strung. The language seemed to be made more for common understanding than ease of use or complex articulation. The cadence and structure of the trade language always bothered her, but at least, it was a language they both shared. Ember forced a smile, hoping the kindly-looking elder was indeed as he looked.

162

"I-understand," she answered. He observed her thoughtfully, eyes searching her face for truth, she supposed. It was the way of many elders to be skeptical, or perhaps simply being so helped one live long enough to be an elder.

"Are-you one, many?" he asked as best as he could.

"One, tired..." she said. Her vocabulary in this common trade language was limited to perhaps fifty out-of-practice words. The man gave her a broad smile and nodded.

"Rest. Soon, food, talk," he said. Ember noted the man's own unfamiliarity with the language, though she took his meaning. The woman, who had knelt beside Ember, introduced herself as, "Kis'tra" It seemed that she was to be Ember's advocate, at least for now. Ember was unsure what these seemingly friendly people had in store for her, but she was in no shape to do anything about it. Kis'tra escorted the ragged redhead to her small hut as the rest of their group watched, obviously eager to ask questions, yet oddly remaining silent.

Does she know the language too? Ember wondered. The walk was painful, but Ember was now sure that she had merely overstretched a muscle and nothing more severe. She would probably be back to walking in a few days, but she needed to rest for now. Kis'tra carefully helped her into the small hut, offering her a seat on a wooden stump that seemed to serve as an impromptu chair. The hut was small but cozy, with a simple wooden pole construction covered with reed and leather mats. There was a large bed of furs in the back and a single hearth.

"I-help," she said in a thick accent. That meant that she did know a little of the trading language of the South. It was easier to expand a language you already knew than learn another. Perhaps she could talk with Kis'tra and pick up some of her words, but where to begin?

I can't start with, "Hello Kis'tra, I saw you and a man rolling on the sand last night. Perhaps you could name your firstborn after me, or is this too soon?" The thought nearly made her laugh aloud, but the shooting pain in her ankle soon removed that prospect.

"Where Kis'tra-home?" Ember asked, as clearly and as best as her vocabulary would allow. She adjusted herself on the stump, rubbing her ankle to reduce the swelling.

"Far-north," she answered after a time, though it seemed that she may not have fully understood the words. Kis'tra's skin and complexion were much darker than Ember's people, and her eyes were a bright shade of blue, like a clear sky. Ember wondered from just how far north she came and why these people traveled this way at all. Most trades were to the South and East. Ember supposed that she was technically to the South of their tribe. They were definitely forest people, a common slang term for the people who lived in the lands beyond the rivers. They were said to be the first people, far older than river people.

"Do-you trade-south?" Ember asked, annoyed by the contracted words. She had no idea why there were not single words for "do" and "you," rather than a single word meaning "do you."

"Yes. North, [go] south. Trade. [Go] north, no [snow]," Kis'tra said, using her hands to pantomime the words for "go" and "snow," adding them to Ember's vocabulary. Ember understood, though it was rough. These people came south and stayed until the snow melted and then returned. That would mean they probably came every two harvests. This made sense as the traders from the South made the same cycles, as far as she knew.

Communication was slightly hampered by the lack of vocabulary and the very nature of the language. Trade languages were really a set of a few dozen single and double word pairs, commonly used by most of the region's peoples for the purposes of trade. The language was very inexact, and sentences were horribly constructed. Ember didn't even think the words came from the same base language but were really bits of other languages. She had always been able to hear the minor differences in languages, though she had only listened to a few others besides her own.

"Rest. You, I, talk. [Off]," Kis'tra said and pointed at Ember's ragged clothing. Before Ember could determine the final word, Kis'tra had bent over and produced a large fur. The fur was actually many rabbit pelts sewn together. She gestured to the reed mats and soft furs, which made a bed on the floor. Ember understood now. She would disrobe and sleep under the furs. Kis'tra initially sat a polished wooden dish of washing water in before Ember, but seeing that she was indeed clean from the previous day's swim, she put the bowl away.

The day was not yet warm, but it likely would be. Lying under furs with dirty clothing, or clothing at all, was an uncomfortable experience. Ember was somewhere between a captive and a guest, she figured, so she might as well accept the hospitality. The group had found a tired and ragged-looking Ember on a pile of furs sleeping, so Kis'tra probably figured she was exhausted and needed sleep. In truth, she was still tired, both physically and emotionally, from being alone for so long. With a smile, Kis'tra helped her out of her shirt.

Ember removed her tattered loincloth, then placed both dirty garments on the reed mat covered packed dirt floor near the door. Ember quickly wrapped herself in the fur and sat on the mats. Kis'tra sat on the stump-chair while Ember snuggled into the bundle of warm furs, feeling more relaxed than she had in a tenday. The two began speaking, learning words, and building their infrequently used skills in a language not native to either of them. For the rest of the day, the women talked, ate dried deer meat, and drank from water skins as they chatted. Ember felt her body relaxing for the first time in days. She was starting to finally feel safe.

Toward the evening, Kis'tra's lover, perhaps husband, Zhek, poked his head into the hut and said something in their language. Kis'tra replied in a warm tone harboring a twang of passion. He gave both women an awkward smile and bowed out quickly, slightly embarrassed. Ember and Kis'tra turned to each other and found themselves laughing. Ember was unsure what had been said, but Zhek's awkwardness at seeing the two women was profoundly funny for some reason she could not quantify. Men were brave and tough, until suddenly they weren't, which had always amused her.

"You, Me, Geve," Kis'tra said. Ember understood the first part but not the last word. They had been sharing words for much of the day, and this had been a frequent situation. Ember produced an exaggerated expression of confusion and replied to Kis'tra, "Geve?" Kis'tra lifted a small stone from the floor and pretended to eat it while repeating the word.

Geve must mean eat or food, Ember thought. She quickly repeated the word back to Kis'tra with a look of understanding while nodding her head.

It must be time for dinner! I wonder what these people eat? Fish for sure, she pondered as Kis'tra motioned her to stand and follow.

Ember slowly stood but nearly fell as her ankle gave way again. Kis'tra was there in an instant to catch her. Like other forest people, she was taller and slightly larger than Ember. Being half forest person on her father's side, Ember had always been tall among her people, yet Kis'tra stood half a head taller, and Zhek was a full head. Offhandedly, she wondered what their people were called, as "Forest People" was just a slang term. Kis'tra was quite strong and helped Ember sit on the wooden tree stump chair, a cheery smile the entire time for reassurance. It was nice to meet good people, she decided.

Kis'tra handed Ember a worn leather wrap with heavy fringe and a cord to secure it to her waist. Her soft doeskin shirt was just too dirty to wear, and her loincloth was barely holding together. Kis'tra placed her hand in a clay jar by the bed, producing soot and oil-covered fingers. She had obviously traded for the pot as forest people didn't typically possess the skills to make pottery. Such secrets were closely guarded by each tribe, though Ember was hardly any good with pottery. Most of the pots and figurines she had made had literally detonated during firing. East had explained that the restless redhead had not given the clay time to dry, resulting in the clay shattering in the fire.

Kis'tra drew horizontal streaks anew across her face, then dipped her fingers once more. She bent forward toward Ember with an inquisitive glance. Ember gave a nod, and Kis'tra started working. Ember nearly giggled at the strange, bug-eyed look Kis'tra presented as the tip of her tongue protruded from her mouth while she carefully worked to paint Ember's face. Family members often painted each other, making the experience otherwise quite expected.

"Eh-yeh!" she said in her native language, finishing. Ember suppressed another laugh given how close whatever Kis'tra had said sounded to "Aeeya," an obscenity she used so often. Her laughter suppressing face was finally painted, likely in black dots, like her shirt, if she guessed correctly. The rest of her body was still lightly stained purple-red with zigzagging patterns, not really traditional of her people. Nevertheless, she was painted and now wore a new leather wrap skirt with a lovely fringe. For the first time in a while, she felt presentable. Ember looked up at an approving Kis'tra and smiled. She supposed the word, or perhaps they were two words, Kis'tra had used moments ago signaled success or completion.

"Aeeya," Ember said, to which the woman nodded, obviously thinking Ember had repeated her similar sounding word. The rascally redhead giggled at her playful foolishness.

As Zhek left the hut, he stepped past a woman wearing a frown worthy of an elder and a stare so pensive that it should have hurt. Aya watched him passing by, lost in thought. She was less than friendly toward anyone who might interfere with her exploits. She had been manipulating several of the men on the journey so far, especially Ven'Gar, but with a new woman, she had suddenly lost her position as the center of attention. Her goals were not expressly malicious nor so petty as simple attention-seeking. However, that minor point was still an annoyance. She had long sought a position of importance among her people, an escape from what had been her meager life, so far. She knew her place was one of leadership, yet there was a problem. A missing item that grew between the legs and without, seemed to seal her fate.

Three methods existed for elevating social status: age, deed, and marriage. She was young and had at least twenty harvests to gain influence based on age, something she might not even live to see. Influence by deed was possible at any age, but she wasn't likely to do anything so special. Such heroes came only rarely, and the feats needed were often dangerous. Aya wasn't afraid of risk, but she wasn't stupid, either. Fighting a bear or similar was more likely to end with the bear returning to the other bears with tales of bravery and a full belly. Not to mention leaving her a dark reddish smear on the ground.

The final method was marriage, effectively position by proxy. Sadly, this and age were generally the only two available to women, and marriage was the only method if she wished for status before she became too old to enjoy it. If she found a man of worth, one likely to rise in prestige, she could join with him and at least speed her rise to recognition. It was laughably absurd that she couldn't rise without a man, extreme age, or the severed head of an enemy, but that had long been the way, handed down by the gods. Aya had a few words for those gods.

Women were not considered fully equal to men, so becoming elders and influential didn't come frequently. Gaining power through a man was not ideal, but it was her only realistic path. She resented that, and she resented the redhead. It wasn't that the newcomer had directly wronged her, but she was yet another obstacle. Worse, she had already captured the attention of the men, making her task all the more challenging. Nevertheless, Aya was willing to do what it took. She would be a flower in a field of grass for all to see. To that end, she had used her bright hazel eyes, long, honey-brown hair, and charm to their maximum.

"Is she coming, or have we decided to throw her to the wilds?" she asked with painfully apparent disdain. Zhek was beyond her control, given his obvious and oddly adorable love for Kis'tra. She wouldn't have even tried if she could. She liked Zhek and Kis'tra, though she envied their pure and unambitious love. Besides, her choice was made. Each flower bloomed only so long, and choices had to be made with what time she had. Zhek walked past, rolling his eyes, his thoughts suddenly broken by Aya's intrusive comment. She folded her arms and glared, still unsure of what she'd do.

Guess who's coming to dinner... Zhek thought with some mirth and a wry smile. Behind him, Aya glared, though her expression saddened.

CHAPTER TEN
A FAIR TRADE

Trade in specialty wares was actually quite commonplace in the Neolithic world. Artifacts from the far corners of Europe and Asia have been found all over the continent in many archaeological contexts, including burial sites. The supposition that people traded between the North and South quite regularly isn't a stretch. Less than 2000 years after Ember lived, a man would die in the Ötztal Alps while seemingly conducting long-distance trade. He was found crossing the mountains wearing clothing only slightly more advanced than what Ember's people wore, the famous Otzi the Iceman.

Ember and Kis'tra strode from the hut to the central fire where all the camp had cleaned and gathered for dinner. It seemed that other meals were eaten alone, but the last meal was shared. This was the way of many tribes, though Ember's people also ate breakfast communally, within the family. The group was just as she had surmised. Many were paired, like Kis'tra and Zhek, and all seemed to be from the same tribe, judging by their ethnicity and cultural similarity, aside from perhaps one woman who looked slightly different. Though Ember couldn't be sure as she was too far from the fire's light. Fortunately, Ember was greeted with a generally warm welcome. Apparently, having not stolen anything, even though she had the chance, had done much to earn the trust of these people.

As she sat by the fire, the old man who had first poked her with his spear reached over and handed her a reed basket with a few long strips of what looked and smelled like roasted beaver, as well as a lump of sour wild grain mash with salt and boiled beans. Ember's people grew beans and stored them, dried, through the cold season. She supposed that they dried beans and brought them in sacks, as she had seen no one growing anything.

The older man had light gray-blue eyes, which held a powerful spark of intelligence, though he said very little to the group. What hair he had left existed only on the back of his head and had turned a brownish-gray color. He wore an ornate leather shirt cut from a dozen or more smaller

169

bits of hide. The shirt had many beads in complex patterns sewn into it and several feathers adorning the arms. His legs were covered by long leather leggings with an extra-wide loincloth hanging from the center. He wore high-quality boots made from thick leather and double-wrapped. Ember appreciated the quality of his clothing, which spoke of his standing with his people.

The elder man introduced himself to Ember using the trade language. "I-Nor'Gar. I-lead," he said, indicating the camp with his hand. Nor'Gar spoke to the group and then to Ember in turn, perhaps translating their conversation. "You, Kis'tra, talk?" he asked, obviously frustrated with his own limited vocabulary. Kis'tra nodded. Nor'Gar spoke to her once more, obviously wishing for translation. Ember gave him a confused look, and Kis'tra explained.

"[Grow] Words, no [old]. Kis'tra, no [old]," she said, using her hands lifting to mean "grow" and an exaggerated hunching of her back to indicate, "old." Like her own language, gestures were used in place of some words. Ember was confused by the statement but semi-understood now that it was a joke. Nor'Gar had given the task of learning to speak with Ember to Kis'tra because she was younger. Perhaps the funniest parts had been lost in the translation. She could tell these people had a complex and full language, and they were obviously distressed by not being able to speak but a few words with her. She hoped she might stay with them for a while and perhaps learn some of their actual language, though she did not expect to become fluent anytime soon.

For the remainder of the evening and well into the early night, the group sat and talked as they ate. Kis'tra would translate between Ember and the group as needed. Both she and Ember were getting much better at handling the language.

"[He]-talk, [best] good food, Kaelu?" Kis'tra translated for a young man with dark, extra-curly hair and a humorous look about him.

What is my favorite food, huh... well I'll have to give that a moment's thought... before answering you with the words of a child of four harvests, she mused.

"Berries," she said in her own language, lacking the vocabulary to reply in the trade language, to which Kis'tra frowned.

"No-understand," Kis'tra said. Seeing the confusion, Ember pointed to a basket of berries sitting beside the fire. Nor'Gar quickly understood and stepped in with a translation and a smile.

"Oh! Marag, yes," Kis'tra said, using their word for berries, "Marag." At first, Ember didn't understand her, but Kis'tra made the hand motions of eating berries, and Ember thought she understood. She supposed this was going to be troublesome, as some key words were unknown to either group. She figured that she would start to understand more as time progressed. Until then, these odd and illogical sentences would continue to come up. The extra-curly-haired man shook his head and said something with a half-smile that seemed to immediately draw the ire of some of the women. Ember cocked an eyebrow and looked at Kis'tra, who had folded her arms across her chest with a smirk.

"Sv'en-talk, [women] eat [sweet]," she said, holding her hands to her chest, which Ember supposed meant woman, and then pointing to the berries and honey, which she suspected meant sweet. She continued, "Sv'en-talk, [men] eat [salt]," she concluded, using similar hand gestures. The curly-haired man, apparently named Sv'en, nodded in accord with her words, even though he probably didn't know if she was translating faithfully. He was the man she had seen by the river, whom she had incorrectly thought was named Sev'een. Though most of their jokes were lost on Ember, she had to laugh with these odd but humorous people. Their attempts at humor were often funnier than the jokes they told.

I love sweet and salty, so what does that make me, Ember mused.

"[Who] talk trade-words?" Ember asked Kis'tra and Nor'Gar, the rest of the group eating and listening.

"More, you!" spat a honey brown-haired woman in an angry tone on the other side of the fire. Ember glanced at her a moment, honestly unsure if the woman was angry or perhaps this was another joke. The woman's face spoke of irritation that had finally boiled over. But why?

Did she mean to say, "more than you?" Ember wondered. The woman, Ember had heard her called "Aya," had a lovely face given to occasional grimace. She had not spoken to her, yet Aya seemed almost angry at Ember out of seemingly nowhere. It was truly nonsensical, in her opinion. She disliked bullies and discordant people, yet there seemed like something much deeper going on. Unfortunately, she lacked the vocabulary to really ask, not to mention the social standing and familiarity.

It can't be anything I said since I can barely say anything, she mused with a chuckle.

Unfortunately, Aya seemed to react even more poorly to the laughter. She looked away in obvious disdain, leaving Ember entirely at a loss. The camp was quiet for a moment with a few rolled eyes and the sounds of eating. After a short moment, Nor'Gar told a joke, and the

171

talking resumed. Ember supposed she could ask Kis'tra for a better explanation that night, assuming she would stay in Kis'tra and Zhek's hut.

Towards the latter part of the meal, as night took hold of the camp, Nor'Gar passed around a waterskin full of some sort of fermented horror which tasted like death but left Ember feeling light, with a burning belly. She almost swooned as the liquid fire rolled down her throat and set her innards aflame. Nor'Gar nearly fell over laughing with the rest of the group at the sight of the rocked redhead trying to hold down the drink. It was harsher than the sacred brew she had drunk with Kanter and Blossom, but perhaps something she could come to like, given time.

Over the next few days, Ember and Kis'tra spent a long while working on their limited vocabularies and adding a few of Kis'tra's words into the mix. Once her ankle healed, Ember proved her worth to the people of the small group as she demonstrated her skills with fishing, quickly landing a catfish a third of her weight and in water, deeper than the other women would venture. She couldn't help but smile as she hauled the giant creature from the water.

After all, I am from the People of the Great River, she mused. As she worked, Ember learned the names of each member and a little about them. The only exception was Aya, who shunned her entirely. Kis'tra had been unwilling to fully explain the situation. Their people considered some discussions inherently private, or so it seemed. Ember was quite confused where Aya was concerned. Perhaps she would eventually figure her out. Ember didn't let it trouble her as life was far too short to worry over angry people, in her opinion.

Each night, the group would dine together on a feast of fresh meats, fish, long tubers and their leaves, lentils, and those tasty beans Ember loved. Some nights, berries and mussels were eaten, along with river amphibians, roasted with salt. Rarely did Nor-Gar pass around the nasty fermented beverage. She supposed this was due to the limited supply of the stuff, which had to be carefully made by hand from fermenting berries, grains, and honey.

On the fourth day since joining the group, Ember and Kis'tra strode through the forest, practicing their speech during the break most took during the midday when Ember discovered the source of the beans. Not far from the camp was a small meadow where the beans and some peas were grown. Standing in the field were two of the women, Ana, and Ena, along with Ena's husband, Borjk.

Ena and Ana were sisters, according to Kis'tra, though their matching oak brown hair in buns, just lighter than their dark skin, with matching blue eyes were a giveaway. Ena held a wooden tool with a roe deer antler lashed to the end. She was tilling the soil near the planted area while Ana and Borjk bent low, picking the beans and tubers. The work was hot, and Borjk had stripped entirely, his long honey brown hair tied into a braid. Sweat rolled down his back as he picked beans, placing them into a small reed basket. Beside him, Ana knelt, doing the same work just as hot, though she wore a leather wrap.

They stood in a roughly barren area that looked like it had been slashed and burned with a small, controlled fire. Ember's people had several large growing areas like this one, but much more extensive. Each season, several would be used while several would not be. Over time, they would cycle their planting, preventing over usage. These people planted a much leaner and less diverse crop, but that made sense to Ember as they were only here for about two seasons at the most, barely enough time to grow much. Ember wasn't sure why they dug up the soil before planting. Her people just plopped the seeds onto the dirt. Perhaps they would explain this technique to her later.

Ember watched as Borjk, Ana, and Ena worked hard on the crops, pausing in near unison to enjoy a cool breeze that happened by. The weather was growing cooler, but the work under the Sun was tough. All three had removed any jewelry they wore, which would only get in the way as they stooped to the ground. Ember caught her eyes lingering on Borjk a little too long and quickly turned them to the harvested crop before Ena noticed. She had not actually been "looking," but sizing up another woman's husband was not the best way to endear herself.

Seeing her apparent interest in their farming, the woman named Ana sat with Kis'tra and Ember for a short break to talk about how each of their tribes grew crops. As the Sun danced across the sky, Ember and Ana had a lengthy discussion, translated by Kis'tra, about farming techniques and secret tips. Ana was quite interested in agriculture and a likable person. She explained that their group ate the beans and dried plants they brought until these crops grew. The growth took nearly the entire time the group was camped. The beans would be harvested just before leaving to provide a food source for the remainder of the trip. Ena and Borjk listened to the entire discussion, tossing in their own points now and then. The more Ember spoke with the forest people, the more they seemed to open up. Though one thing caught her ear. If they harvested before leaving and they were harvesting now... She pushed that thought aside for the moment.

After they left the bean and pea field, Ember asked Kis'tra to return to her hut. She had been having odd feelings all day, and she was now very sure of what the cause might be. She had felt the first indications of her pains. Ember was a woman now, and for a few harvests, she had undergone the pains of being a woman. She was luckier than most women she knew, experiencing only a few days of very mild discomfort. Unfortunately, the best treatment was to remain indoors until the event was over. She thanked the gods she was not like her friend Fire Blossom, who would be stuck in her longhouse for five or six days of heavy bleeding.

Old lady Oakwood had told Blossom that her heavy pains were a great indication of blessed vitality or some silly thing. The pain seemed like a cruel "blessing," in Ember's opinion, though it reminded her of an ever-present fact. She could probably bear children, and her people's customs encouraged this as soon as she was ready. Ember had considered the idea many times before, and the horror of the old man trying to have his way with her had once more reminded her of this fact. Her body was a powerful instrument of creation but also a great liability. She barely felt like a woman, most of the time, and dwelling on fertility did little to help these feelings. Ember exhaled, pushing this too from her mind. She had accumulated several things to think about that night.

During the next three days, Ember remained in or near the hut. It just wasn't practical to do much while she bled. As it was, she wore a loincloth with dried grasses stuffed within to absorb her blood. It was fine in a hut or longhouse, but outdoor labor was sure to make the bleeding worse, and changing grass was not something she would enjoy doing in public, especially where men might watch. There was also the issue of headaches and other discomforts many women dealt with. Luckily, it seemed these people had social mores against women and men mixing during such times, though she still found the emphasis on her feminine aspects bothersome in a way she could not quite come to terms with.

While waiting out her pains, Ember spent much of her time humming or singing as she worked, something she had generally done since childhood. Unknown to her, Sv'en and several of the other men had taken to relaxing outside of Kis'tra's hut in an effort to listen to her beautiful songs. Kis'tra had noticed the amusing antics but neglected to tell Ember for fear it might lead to an awkward encounter. While some female voices annoyed Kis'tra, Ember's slightly deeper voice was somehow soothing, and she caught herself listening from time to time.

During her time off her feet, Ember worked on sewing furs into blankets for Kis'tra. Sewing was a difficult and very time-consuming task. However, her efforts would benefit the group, even if she wasn't fishing or working in the fields. She had considered helping Kis'tra with weaving clothing, something she had been doing each night. Ember knew how to twine nettle fibers without a loom, just as Kis'tra did, but she never had the attention span for such slow, lengthy work. At least she could sew, though only barely. Ember had many skill related failings, though she made up for them in other ways.

A sewing needle was made from a tiny sliver of bone carefully carved and ground into a straight, flat implement. A hole would be made at the end, often with a sharp, pointed stone tool. A very thin piece of leather thong, plant fiber, or sinew would be inserted. A hole was first placed in leather using a pointed bone piece as a punch, called an awl. Only then was the needle inserted. Forcing a needle through leather without first creating a hole was a quick way to break a needle. The furs were a vital trade item, and Kis'tra was keen on Ember making several blankets. Still, furs were not the primary reason the group was so far south. Rather, it was the yellow rocks. Ember still found this to be an odd reason for such a long trip.

The entire operation seemed to be mainly composed of gathering the yellow rocks, hunting for furs and bone, which they mainly had stopped due to the time required to tan the leather before they left, and support activities, such as fishing and farming. The yellow rocks were gathered from a small tributary stream that fed into the Great River. Since the start of the warm season, when the group had arrived, they had amassed six handfuls of the rocks. The yellow rocks were removed from the stream by hand gathering. Each thawing season, the rocks were washed down the stream anew.

According to Nor'Gar, the sacks of yellow rocks would trade for many obsidian pieces and several unique sharp tools made from a red and green rock that could be hammered, much like the yellow stones, into an extremely hard edge. Unfortunately, these special tools only came from the farthest southeastern lands and were very hard to find. The skins would be traded for many specialized wares, such as beads, dyes, and medicines.

Even though the yellow rocks and hides were their main trade wares, the group had more salt in their possession than Ember had expected, two full bags. This was because of a salt spring that flowed near their home, according to Sv'en, who liked stealing a pinch now and then. Salt springs were flows of subterranean water that burrowed through natural salt deposits, producing incredibly salty water flows. Salt was an important commodity and commonly traded. Ember's wandering thoughts were reigned in as Nor'Gar spoke again.

"Many trade, we-trade, salt, [ivory,] [figures]. We-go North, more," Nor'Gar said, his trade language skills coming back to him after a few harvests of non-use. He pointed to his ivory necklace and used his hands to indicate figures, not having trade words for them. As he finished, Ember pointed to a wooden carved religious figure he had referenced and spoke their word for figure, "Wen," much to Nor'Gar's surprise. Ember had been learning their language for many days with Kis'tra's help, and she was already able to speak some, at least simplistically.

"You talk ula yu'uana?" he asked, hoping she understood his native tongue, but sadly, she only knew the first two words.

"[Some] words," she said, using two fingers held closely together to indicate "some" or "small," causing the old man to chuckle. The words she had to imply with her hands, props, or entirely pantomime made speaking rather rough, but they served for the time being. Ember wondered if, given time, she might learn their real language. She had a natural gift for languages, yet a full language was so much more complex than a trade language. Instead of words with implied meanings, a complete language had complexity which imparted nuance, something the trade language could not.

With that, Ember and Nor'Gar sat chatting as Ember finished her pains. Oddly, the old man had ignored his people's rules concerning men mingling with those having their pains. It made Ember happy to have an additional friend, while Kis'tra was out working the fields. Talking, their day passed, the very young learning from the old and wise, as human of an act as could possibly be.

About a tenday passed as the first indications of the cold season began to arrive. Ember helped the forest people, for whom she still had not learned their name, while they seemed to avoid asking her anything of her past. Their rituals and social mores were complex, yet even the most chaotic of them had kept to their customs, and so would she. The odd prohibition of asking about someone's background seemed to lift during one particularly festive evening meal. Kis'tra had told her the night before that the time had come, apparently connected to the Moon phases, somehow. Ember had expected this, yet she was still uneasy when the conversation around the fire shifted toward her.

The change was easily noticeable as all eyes turned toward Ember and all side discussion ended. Unlike the many languages of sound, body language had a universal vocabulary. Ember sat upright and crossed her legs beneath herself, propping herself up, taller. She sat on the sandy ground with the other group members, all in a circle around a small fire. She was nervous as the moment of explanation settled upon her, and she found herself digging her toes into the soft ground, a habit her mother always scolded her for as a child.

"Dirty toes make dirty beds," East would say.

Until now, none of the group had asked her much about her past. She had learned from Kis'tra that this was a matter of respect and not for lack of interest. Perhaps now was time to quench their curiosity. With her ankle and feet now healed and her vitality returned, she was ready to speak. Sv'en, a younger man who gathered the yellow rocks, had shifted the discussion from expectations of their coming trade, a hot subject, to Ember. Kis'tra, who now spoke to Ember using the trading language vocabularies of both women and her own words here and there to fill in the gaps, translated for Ember, allowing her to speak with more complexity – and this was a story that very much held complexity.

As she began to speak, Kis'tra listened and then began to speak to the crowd. She paused the rattling redhead to ask a few questions of her own, ensuring she understood each part before she continued. As she did, the group listened in wonder. Nothing was so wonderful as a good story, though this one was hard to believe.

"Ember is from a village to the Southeast of our camp, perhaps a tenday or more. She was sent west on a quest by her gods to find the end of the world, where the Sun goes each night," Kis'tra spoke aloud in her native language. At that, the group nodded in understanding. Nor'Gar frowned, unsatisfied with the first part of the story, and asked a question. It seemed that when the moratorium on asking questions ended, nothing was out of bounds.

"Ember is young and alone. How did she travel so far?" the elder asked, drawing many nods from those gathered. Wolves and other creatures made solo travel dangerous for all but a well-seasoned hunter or a large group. Ember had obviously only just become a woman and was hardly seasoned. Kis'tra turned to Ember and repeated the question in the trade language. Ember nodded, then smiled at the group. She had expected this to come up.

"Naulos, deru meg'denn…" Ember spoke in her own language, meaning "boat, traveling the Great River." She held her right hand horizontal and flat over her moving arm to pantomime a boat on the river. Ember's green eyes flashed with delight as she began to impart the tale once more, with Kis'tra translating. While her passion for storytelling was evident, Ember was not a natural at it. Her erratic arm movements and excitement caused those who sat next to her to scoot away, though everyone listened with rapt attention.

"Ember was thrown from her boat by that same storm that blew down Tor'kal and Sv'en's hut two tendays or more ago. I am still amazed she lived, but you wouldn't believe what happened next," Kis'tra said to the group as the enraptured redhead, now standing and using her entire body as a prop, began to dig deep into the story. Despite it all, she failed to mention her short captivity with the men, finding the whole experience best forgotten. She wasn't quite ready to bring up her shame and fear for the crowd's amusement.

After a few more exchanges, the group seemed satisfied for the day, and the talk changed to more social matters. When Ember had finally sat back down, she noticed that Aya had gotten up and left sometime earlier, probably with her never-ending scowl. She ignored the tiresome woman and took a drink from her dish as the jokes and conversation returned. Ember was starting to feel that she might just be okay. Her problem now was the need to complete her journey and a lack of any real ideas about how to do that. Just then, a thought crossed her mind; one which might solve her western problems. It would have to wait until the next day, but there was one other thing she could take care of right now.

"Kis'tra, what you people name?" she asked, catching her friend's attention. She had a more extensive shared vocabulary with Kis'tra, making speech easier, though it was still rocky. For a moment, Kis'tra's bright blue eyes regarded her in confusion, then she smiled. She took a moment considering her words and how best to explain. In the end, she spoke the words in her native language, pointing to herself, trees, and other hand gestures until Ember understood.

"We People [of] [Dark] [Forest,]"

The People of the Dark Forest. Ember considered this as Kis'tra's attention was grabbed by Zhek. Why they had not told her until now and why they had waited to ask her questions, she might never fully understand, but it was nice to have a name for her new friends.

The next day, Ember approached Nor'Gar, hoping to chat once more, especially about the idea she had the night before. He sat by his hut, carefully working a piece of flint. He used a deerskin scrap to hold the flint against his knee while applying firm pressure with a deer antler point.

Flecks burst aside as the antler's force won the battle of stone vs. bone. He casually looked up with a smile as she approached. Ember brushed the dust from the front of her once again clean, soft leather shirt out of habit. It always had some debris about it. She wore her loincloth but no leggings, which made kneeling easier. Unfortunately, leggings tended to catch on the knees when one knelt, making them terrible for farming.

"Hal'ja," she spoke cheerfully in Nor'Gar's native tongue. He smiled and returned the "hello" greeting. He was one of the friendliest of the People of the Dark Forest and probably the best to speak to about the idea she had come upon the night before. She took a moment to consider how to explain herself while he patiently waited for her to continue in the reserved and polite way of his people. After a moment, she spoke, using both trade language and words she had learned from Kis'tra.

"Nor'Gar, I-need go-west, north," she said, slowly. The elder looked back, obviously surprised by her skills. She had only lived with them a handful of days, and yet she was already learning enough to speak, at least crudely.

"You-need, nast," Nor'Gar said plainly, using his people's word for boat, and using his hand to imitate a floating boat. He understood what she was really asking even before she could finish. For all his softspoken reserve, Nor'Gar might very well be the smartest of the group. He wasn't just generally a deep intellectual, but he seemed to carry that legendary wisdom of the elders, a quality which took both age and experience. Ember smiled and nodded, as Nor'Gar resumed his knapping as he continued.

"We-build, boat. Tor'kal, Sv'en know, boat-make. Ask. Tell Tor'kal, Sv'en, Nor'Gar-speak-build," he said. The language gap was impressive, but she understood his words well enough. Ember's heart leaped at the offer, so much more than she had expected. He had offered to have Tor'kal and Sv'en make a boat for her. But why? Sure, she had proven herself helpful in gathering resources and performing more work than some of the others. She had grown into an asset to the group in merely a tenday, but make a boat? She had only hoped for help with making one herself. Hearing his words and understanding them, Ember was dumbfounded by how easily Nor'Gar had offered to help.

How can he see my mind more plainly than I do? I wasn't even sure how to ask, and he said yes before I could, she wondered. Ember's sense of equality gnawed at her, and she felt that she must offer something in return for such a task. The creation of a boat was no small matter, as well as highly time-consuming. She thought for a moment, considering what might be a good trade as Nor'Gar stared at her curiously. Her flint pieces were of quality, but the pieces Nor'Gar was currently working were quality pieces, too. Surely her pieces would not do. Blossom's goddess pendant was for a local god, but she wouldn't have traded it anyway, and definitely not for the people of another land who undoubtedly had their own gods. She needed her obsidian dagger if she was to make it west. He continued to wait, seemingly finding her confusion amusing.

Wait! I know! she thought as she realized that she had overlooked an important item of trade. Ankle now quite healed, she stood and sprinted towards Kis'tra's hut, where she had been staying, turning just to give Nor'Gar a "please wait" gesture with her hands. He watched her scamper away and thought to himself, as he so often did in his older season.

Ah, the young, and an energetic one at that. I saw the same sign in the sky that brought you to us. I will aid you. The gods are involved, somehow. The falling star was red and green, burning brightly, just as you. Nor'Gar's memories returned to a cold, snowy night so long ago and an old memory from another time. He had said goodbye that night to his brother, a man who Ember reminded him so much of.

Ember did return, a moment later, with her original leather bag. She again knelt and produced from the bag a rabbit pelt with something large wrapped within. She beamed Nor'Gar a broad smile of anticipation and then spoke.

"Boat, trade!" Before he could speak, she produced the piece of solid water, a blue crystal twice the size of a fist and clear throughout. Nor'Gar stared at the raw gem for a short time, his mouth open in surprise. How had this young river woman obtained such a fantastic item? It was indeed a beautiful thing, if not entirely useless, at least in practical, worldly matters. Such items sometimes had utility in communing with the gods and other such magical properties, the reason many tribes kept such items as a focal point or sacred item. Nor'Gar was thoroughly shocked by the offer, but he raised his hand as if warding from the gem and made a gesture of "no."

"No. too... too-much, [he spent many moments trying to remember the words], we make, boat. For, Ember." The puzzled look on her face reminded him so much of his brother, though it was just a coincidence, he supposed. Yet the similarity was hard to shake. Deep from within, Nor'Gar wondered if spirits returned and lived once more in new bodies. It wasn't the way he had been taught, but those green eyes and hyperactive personality were so familiar, not to mention the red hair.

Ember replaced the gem in her bag and leaned forward, giving the old man a deep hug. Her eyes rimmed with tears as she squeezed for a short time. This would have been considered a bit too forward to his people, but to Ember's more relaxed customs, such a hug was quite acceptable. Besides songs and dances, river people were also huggers. Old Nor'Gar just sat there accepting the hug with a slight mist forming in his own eyes and shivers dancing up and down his spine as he recalled a private memory from long ago. Meanwhile, a different pair of eyes boiled in anger from behind a hut not far from where they embraced. Aya stared in disbelief. The rakish redhead had hugged High Hunter Nor'Gar... like she was his daughter or wife.

Build her a boat? We don't even know this person! she thought.

"You know that she will leave us when we finish the boat," Aya said as she leveled her gaze at a wary Ven'Gar. The pair stood alone in their small hut shortly afterward. Aya had worked hard to improve her life since she had become old enough to really understand how life worked. She had surrounded herself with mock innocents and carefully staged events since leaving Tornhemal, one of the People of Dark Forest villages. Each facet of her plan played off the last, weaving a delicate fabric of tiny nudges which would see her joined with a man, a utility, who would aid in her quick rise to prominence.

Aya's goals were not so much ruthless as they were opportunistic. She was determined to have a high place in her village and the regional villages, and this was her one chance. Women were generally equal among her people, except when it came to positions of leadership. Unfortunately, fate had not smiled on Aya, and she had learned at a young age that power came to those who took it. She had experienced this dark truth firsthand and would never let herself be in a position of powerlessness, again. A position of power would allow her to influence her village and perhaps all the regional villages if her delicate dance was executed perfectly. Unfortunately, the reckless redhead was the proverbial mouse in the wool for her plans.

Her mother had died during the birthing of what would have been her brother when Aya was young. Their family was of low standing within the tribe, outsiders really. Normally, an extended family provided the support for orphaned children. A family of dozens of extended members watched over each other, but not Aya. Her mother had come from another tribe beyond the Dark Forest. Her father had run off after leaving her mother with a child, and left the pair without a family. She was lucky to find a family who took her in, reluctantly, and not without cost… dark memories she would never fully escape.

Her mother had left her nothing, that is, nothing material. What she had left Aya were her looks, which she now used as a weapon sharper than obsidian to craft the men around her as a knapper worked flint. She carried a decent body weight, which her people considered the pentacle of beauty, unlike the rangy redhead's skinny frame. Such gifts were fleeting and shallow, but she had put them to good use, coupled with a sharp mind and the will to do whatever it took. If it was to be misogynist rules she had to play by, then she would exploit them to their fullest.

The tribe's trade groups tended to produce some of the greatest leaders of her people, such as the High Hunter Nor'Gar. They were also filled with young, single men from the collected villages of her regional people. She meant to become wife to the man who was most revered upon their return to Tornhemal. If power only came to men, then she would seize power through men. In an unfair system, she would be unfair. That was where Ven'Gar had come in.

Everything had been going well with the man until the redhead came. Ven'Gar was the most skilled hunter in the group and the most likely to take charge if something happened to Nor'Gar. Unfortunately, he was all too often caught looking at Ember as the little creature plucked one large fish from the deeper water after another. Ven'Gar was by far her best hope for a life of status. He was strong, well connected, easy to manipulate, and not too rough on the eyes. She would merely need to join with him and bear a child, and the deal would be sealed. She felt that she could even love the man, given time. That was hard enough without some new, exotic woman arriving and causing her problems.

Aya did not hate Ember, but she saw her as a threat to be removed. In all truth, she wished she could achieve status in her own right, though she supposed that, in a way, she was actually doing this. It wasn't fair, but she simply accepted this as the way of things, and she knew of no other way of being. Deep down, the rambunctious redhead represented someone she could never be – a woman carving her own path in the world by her own hands. Perhaps that was what hurt the most. Her thoughts were interrupted as Ven'Gar's deep voice filled the room.

"I hope she remains with us and perhaps returns to Tornhemal after we finish our trade," he said without noticing the evil looks he received from Aya in return.

How typical, she thought, *he doesn't even know when he is being foolish.* If only his thoughts were as deep as his voice, she lamented. Well, she would just have to figure out some way to discredit or remove Ember herself. If only the right opportunity would arise.

"She is helping us with our usage of the trade language, with Kis'tra's help. That will be useful when we arrive south. Now, Nor'Gar won't be the only one who can speak for us," he concluded.

Fool as you are, you have a point, Aya conceded. If something happened to the old man before then, perhaps Ven'Gar could assert some control and even return with some valuable trades. Aya supposed she was technically being too hard on the redhead, who had not actually spared Ven'Gar a single look, at least that she had caught, but chances were taken by fools, and she wasn't a fool. Right now, she needed to quickly remove the radiant redhead from Ven'Gar's mind, and she knew a simple trick which would do just that.

She would just have to work on adjusting him a bit. She manufactured a smile that seemed to satisfy Ven'Gar, who plainly couldn't see the venom in her eyes. She abruptly dropped her clothing to the floor, standing before Ven'Gar. He drank in her visage, all thoughts of Ember lost. Aya reflected upon her luck that at least she could still turn his head from the interloper, for now. He gazed upon her body as he would a doe for the hunt, like the hunter he was. She leered back at him with dangerously level eyes, like the wolf she was.

Too easy, she thought and almost laughed at the irony of it all. Unfortunately, poor Ven'Gar mistook the smile for interest.

CHAPTER ELEVEN
TO BUILD A BOAT

To Neolithic peoples, boats were useful and sophisticated tools. Boats allowed faster river travel than could be afforded by the raw, untamed land, having no paved roads or directional markers of any sophistication. The first "boats" were likely mere wooden logs a person would sit upon and float. This caused problems in the cold and didn't afford any protection for the legs, an issue in some lands.

Early boats, such as the boat Ember used, were dugout boats made from a single solid piece of wood. These simple craft were useful in navigating the inland waterways, lakes, and shallow streams, but they were hardly ocean-going. Creating a dugout boat was a time-consuming process that involved controlled burning and digging with specialized stone tools. Along with reed boats, stretched leather over a wooden frame, and boats made from bark, the dugout boat would remain a staple craft of prehistoric Europe for thousands of years, as well as a commonplace design among many other cultures outside of Europe.

The next day, Ember approached Tor'kal and Sv'en. She found the pair next to a nearby stream that fed into the river, kneeling at the muddy bank and working hard at extracting the yellow rocks. All around, a handful of the Dark Forest People waded in the knee-deep water extracting the heavy resource. Though she had seen them do this many times over the past few days, she had yet to really watch precisely how they did it. Upon closer inspection, their method was entirely unexpected. She had figured they would pick the yellow pieces from the sand in the streambed, yet that wasn't their approach at all.

As she watched, Tor'kal knelt in the water scooping a handful of the sandy bed. He placed his hand into the water and moved it back and forth, vigorously. The silt quickly disappeared as the water washed over it, leaving heavier pebbles and a single, tiny fleck of yellow. After a moment, the dark-haired and best friend of Sv'en extracted the yellow stone and placed it in a tiny pile at the shore. As he did, he turned, catching sight of Ember and nodding a greeting. Tor'kal was a tall man with dark, curly hair that hung nearly waist length. His dark, wet skin and lovely hair caught Ember's eyes, though she quickly turned her attention to Sv'en, lest she stare too long. Tor'kal was solemn and quiet, always carefully working on getting his job done and done well. He wore nothing, like most who worked in the water when the weather was warmer, though a small pile of leather clothing sat on the shore beside the yellow pile.

"Kaelu," Sv'en called, waving his hand, though it came out more like, "Kee-luh," than the proper, "Kay-loo." Ember waved back, glad for a distraction. Sv'en, by contrast, was always telling jokes and looking for fun, a human whirlwind. Sv'en was a little shorter than Tor'kal, with hair somehow darker. He wore leggings with a shorter apron and a reed smock as he knelt on the shore picking yellow rocks from a pile of material Ena had brought as she worked, not far down the stream. Ember approached, unsure of how to begin her discussion, especially given the language gap.

Sv'en returned to pulling at a tooth in his mouth and wearing an odd set of expressions. Tooth issues were always a concern, as a sore tooth could kill even a strong hunter. In fact, one of the most common causes of death was a sickness brought on by an aching tooth. The only known remedy was to pull the tooth from the mouth and hope the body healed. Ember hoped he was merely dislodging something caught in his teeth and nothing more sinister, as she had already come to know the goofy man as one of the nicer people she had met, though a bit naughty.

Both men were covered in mud and wet up to their knees. Near them worked Ena and Kat'ja, the latter having the only unexpected look of the group. Her eyes were narrow, and her facial structure was different in some unique but hard to pin down way. Her skin was a little lighter than the rest of the People of the Dark Forest, though darker than Ember's hair. Her hair was also different, being thicker, straighter, and darker.

Ember wondered why Kat'ja looked so different from the others. Had her mother or father come from some other place, much as Ember's father had? Perhaps she was like Kanter, from another tribe. Though she looked physically different from the others, her cultural aesthetic and her clothing were exactly the same as the others… piled on the shore. Ember noticed her full form as she stood in the water, her skin wet in the sunlight… Her interest was suddenly dashed when she noticed that she wasn't the only one with eyes. Suppressing a chuckle, she snapped her fingers and watched Sv'en's attention shift from Kat'ja to her. His slightly guilty look quickly changed to one of amusement. Ignoring his antics, Ember took a breath and addressed Tor'kal, whom she knew understood some of the trade language.

"Nor'Gar speak. Make boat for-Ember. Ember-need, boat, [go] west." After she was finished, Tor'kal gave her a short nod, then spoke to

Sv'en. It sounded to Ember, by their words, which she now understood a few of, and from their body language, that they would help her with the boat. She had expected more pushback, or maybe some skepticism, as a boat was no simple task. She wondered if Nor'Gar had already spoken to them, given how easily they understood her request and agreed to do it. If he had, Tor'kal and the others made no mention of it.

"Yellow Rock," Ember said in the Tornhemal language, gesturing to the stream and the hand panning operation they were engaged in. Tor'kal waved his hand dismissively, "Rock, day. Boat, night." Ember believed that she had understood the Tornhemal words for "rock" and "night," though they tended to sequence their words in a way that Ember still had trouble following. It sounded to her as though they would build the boat in the evening, after work. This would take much longer but not delay the panning.

Putting aside her worry over the order of work, Ember nodded in agreement, lacking a good way to express her thanks. Given the beaming smile from Sv'en and Tor'kal's return nod, it seemed they had understood. Ember held back a tear at the joy of knowing there were still good people in the world, people who would help her. Her capture and the devastated village had not entirely destroyed her belief in humanity, though it had not helped. Now, here she was, receiving help from genuinely caring people. With her spirits lifted, Ember approached the water, considering how to go about finding yellow rocks in this most peculiar of ways.

Seeing her apparent interest, Kat'ja waded over to show her how to hand pan. A raft spider and many water insects rushed away as Ember stepped into the cool water, considering removing her own garments as the friendly yet oddly unique-looking woman beckoned her forward. Beside her, Sv'en kept his head down, drawing no attention. However, Ember could almost feel his urge to sneak a peek at Kat'ja, whom she was now entirely sure Sv'en was interested in. Nearby, a turtle slipped into the water as a lazy frog croaked.

Well, you are looking for something precious in the stream, she mused, then caught herself before she blushed.

"Here," Kat'ja said in her own language, kneeling in the water. She took Ember's hands, dipping them into the silt. Kat'ja placed her hands in the muck as well, also scooping a large handful. Still submerged, she agitated the silt in her hand. The lighter silt drifted away with the current and Kat'ja's quick hand motions. Ember noted that larger stones would not be moved by the agitation. Memories of a certain proud bolder the mighty river could not move came to mind. Since the yellow rocks were heavy, this might mean they would stay in her hand, she supposed. Next, Kat'ja indicated that Ember should do the same, then began sifting through her own silt for yellow rocks.

Ember started poking the dirt and rocks with her finger, but Kat'ja laughed and stopped her.

"No, silly, don't use your hands yet. Put it in the water and let the stream do the work," she said in the Tornhemal language. Ember didn't understand the words but followed her motions. Kat'ja moved her hands around in a gentle, circular motion to indicate what to do. Ember followed suit, swirling the water in her hands. The remaining silt washed away in the water, leaving the heavier rocks behind. The yellow rocks were indeed quite heavy, and she quickly realized that her suspicions were correct and that they would remain in her hand. The actual process took a reasonable period of time for each handful of silt, yielding only a few tiny flecks of yellow rock per scoop, if she were lucky.

"Ember, good," Sv'en said in the trade language for Ember's benefit, to which Tor'kal nodded in agreement, though Ember was doubtful that she was. Even Ena wadded over to see how things were going. With smiles all around, Ember started her new job as a gold panner. She was off to an enthusiastic but slow start, losing several handfuls to the stream, but soon enough, she was panning with ease and good results. That first day of panning, the group found a few tiny pieces of the yellow rock and many tiny specs. Ember was worried that she had not done her part, but Sv'en assured her that this was actually a good day of panning.

That evening, Sv'en spent time by the central fire preparing the yellow rocks. Melting them was not impossible, but nearly so from an open fire without several people waving reed fans, charcoal, and far too much work. Instead, Sv'en settled for carefully cleaning the flecks and safely securing them in several pieces of leather before placing them in a pouch. Losing the precious yellow material would mean less trade, something sure to bring the wrath of the other traders down upon him.

Melting and crafting techniques belonged to people who lived much farther southeast than even Nor'Gar's group would journey. Between them lay many mountains and rivers. Few would make the journey over the mountains and never during the colder seasons. Ember could imagine herself lying dead on such a mountain, either killed by the cold or shot with an arrow in the back by a thief, an unsavory prospect. It was the people from beyond those mountains who would trade most dearly for the yellow rocks. The southern villages, where these rocks were headed, would, in turn, trade during the next warm season with traders over the mountains, from those distant lands known to traders as the "True South."

Ember had seen the simple pendants made for Kis'tra and Zhek from the yellow rocks, and she had to admit they held a particular appeal. It was the weight that really impressed her, she decided. The beautiful reflections in the light were also important, but that little tug of weight around the neck reminded the wearer of the significance of the pendant. Significance and memories were important to people, and Ember hoped these tiny speckles of yellow that she found would bring someone, somewhere, a little joy. Perhaps one day, she would find someone to love. Ember decided she would give them something made from the yellow rocks, though that was likely far in her future.

A typical adze

Over the next tenday, Ember and her newfound friends worked toward building a boat when they were not otherwise collecting yellow rocks, gathering hides, or doing their other chores. The boat had started as a single log which Sv'en had felled with a stone ax. The branches and bumps on the log were carefully removed with a sharpened stone hand ax and adze by Sv'en, leaving a rough but mostly bark-less piece of wood. The ax head was a sharp, worked stone with a groove in the middle allowing for an easy fit into a wooden handle with a carved hole to fit the stone. The handle and the head of a good hand ax could be kept for many harvests, being of significant value.

After the ax and adze removed the bark and limbs, the friends heaved the log back to camp, where it could be further worked with the assistance of three other men. The wood was as wide as Ember's hips with room on each side of about two or three fingers width of wooden hull and ran as long as two men. The finished boat would actually be large enough for perhaps two people, but Ember assumed she would load it with supplies.

During the first few nights of work, they dug grooves into the top of the log, Sv'en and Tor'kal taking turns showing Ember how the work was done. Now and then, Kat'ja and even Ena joined in to help. In the grooves, they placed hot embers from a fire. Next, they would blow on the embers, even adding burning tinder when needed, to cause small, controlled fires. The burning dug into the wood much more quickly than an ax or adze. After each burning, hand tools made of stone would be used to remove the charred wood. The process of digging out the center of the log with fire took much of the early night for eight days.

The friends worked diligently after each hard day of labor, fixated on this overt act of charity. Ember continued to help with the gathering, farming, and fishing, during the day, the least she could do. At night, while the men worked the inside of the boat, Ember and Kat'ja used sharp stone tools and rougher rocks on the outside hull. Slowly, they removed the tiny bits of remaining bark and bumps, smoothing the hull. Finally, after a tenday of work, the boat had an angled bow and a dugout center large enough to accommodate Ember and her belongings with room to spare.

During the many days of work, each of the Tornhemal traders came by to help and add their advice on boat building. After a few days, even Ven'Gar arrived to help with scraping the hull. His strong arms ground a rough stone against the wood, scraping it flat before Ember and Kat'ja smoothed it with sand and leather, followed by smooth stones. Unfortunately, Ven'Gar's help ended when Aya happened by and promptly dragged him off for tasks that required "his skills." Strangely, neither of them had returned to help. While the boat building operation functioned just fine without Aya, Ember wished Ven'Gar would return. He was a friendly sort, if not a little too reserved for her taste.

Ven'Gar aside, Ember found Tor'kal and Sv'en to be entertaining people, both being argumentative and strong-willed. The two men fought like a couple as they worked while Ember and Kat'ja laughed. Even Kis'tra lent a hand a few times when she was finished farming and fishing. Kis'tra was not very good with panning or boat building, her skills being weaving and leatherworking, but she was able to help with some of the finer details.

Offhandedly, Ember had wondered why all Tornhemal names were formed either from two sounds with a pause, such as Nor'Gar and Kis'tra, or a single sound, like Zhek or Ana? It didn't seem to follow gender or any other notable aspect of life. And why was the "Gar" sound strongly pronounced while the "tra" sound was soft? Her own people didn't typically break their names into distinct parts, favoring a continuous sound, like Kaelu or Aneha, which meant Ember and Blossom, respectively.

One thing she did like was their lack of gendered words. While some cultures had feminine or masculine words, the people of the Dark Forest had gender neutral words, aside from pronouns, like "he" or "she." Ember would prefer to have removed the pronouns, too, but she was unsure how feasible that was. She would have slapped anyone who tried to call her "he," but she was not that fond of "she," either. She supposed it was related to her lack of truly feeling like a woman. She had rejected most girl and womanly things growing up, but she had never considered until the last few days just how much "she" and "her" bothered her.

Besides her non-stop side thoughts, Ember and Kis'tra also continued to work together on their verbal skills each night after work on the boat was finished, given that they shared the same hut. As the nights rolled along, she worried about the intimate space shared with a young couple, but Kis'tra and Zhek tended to remain outdoors working or socializing, sometimes disappearing into the woods at night, and generally only using their bed for sleep. This left Ember with her own soft fur bed, some privacy, and time to recover from each long day of work.

Ember spent her nights dreaming of swimming in the warm waters by the bank of the Great River, but unfortunately, the warm season didn't last forever. The days were still mildly warm, but the nights were slowly becoming cooler and less friendly. There would be perhaps four tendays before she would need to find shelter for the cold season and only one or two tendays before she might find the air too cool to swim during all but the warmest of days.

With this in mind, Ember began to have misgivings about continuing her trip. She supposed she could ask to follow the people of the Dark Forest on their trade trip to the South, but what of the boat? The work already put into the small craft was staggering, but time was running out and a trip down the river during the cold season was hardly advisable. She had just become so entranced by the work that she had not even considered the weather. Could she travel with them, wait out the cold season, then perhaps return and find the boat once more? Ember's poor time management and the planning skills of a small tuber root had once more left her with a dilemma.

☼ ☼ ☼

Pak watched from the brush as the troublesome redhead and two other women returned to their camp while cheerfully singing some sort of working song. On a branch beside him, a mantis stalked an unaware grasshopper, its meal at hand. He had seen enough. These people had taken in the girl who had caused his group so much trouble, though he couldn't help feeling a sense of respect for her as she had taught that aggressive and bullying Rosif a lesson he would not soon forget. Pak had trouble reconciling his sense of duty to his people with his secret feelings of relief at her departure and that he now found her safe. She was a sort of enemy now, perhaps, and before she had been a mere woman, his group's property. That was how his people would see it, yet that didn't sit well with his morals. Life was much like the current sky: grey.

Would you resent being captured and tied to a tree? his inner voice nagged. Pak let go of his confused emotions and tried to make himself angry once more. He knew what Rosif had in mind, and he would need to clear his head. He thought of the suffering his group had endured recently due to this girl. Rosif had developed a fever soon after his emasculation, and Pak had spent many long days watching over first both sick men, then eventually, after Calpano recovered, just Rosif. All because of this girl... No, he scolded himself. She was a woman, and he was calling her a girl to minimize her. Yet, she had stood up to Rosif when Pak had been afraid to. He realized that she was braver than he was, an admission which carried a pang of guilt. Pak's emotions continued to dance about, warring between the ideals of his culture and his personal morality.

She had even stollen whatever item Rosif had taken from the dead elder, an item of potentially unlimited power if it was a focal point, as he suspected. In the end, Rosif had driven their group toward revenge, having lost part of his masculinity, the wonderous item, and possibly his sanity. He had partially recovered in a single tenday, at least enough to become obsessed with killing the girl who had wounded him in so many ways. In reality, he should still be resting, but he wouldn't take the time when his vengeance was close at hand. The group had now been in the wilds for nearly four tendays, a very long time, and desperately needed to return to their village. This would have to end one way or another.

As he watched, the reckless redhead tripped on a stump and nearly fell, being caught by the darkest haired woman of their group. The women excitedly chatted about what had just happened, giggling as they spoke.

Their humor infected Pak as he watched. Before he knew it, he smiled along with them as anyone would. As he smiled, his tortured thoughts returned to the task at hand. He shook his head and stopped watching the women. He had to follow the orders of his leader, but how could he?

Ahh! Why do choices have to be so complicated? Why am I the only one who seems to have trouble knowing what to do? he thought. Pak shook his head and tried to remind himself that this woman was an enemy. Yet, every time he saw her face, his reaction was not what one would expect from the sight of an enemy. He took a deep breath and forced the thoughts into the hole where he had forced his conscience. They simply conflicted with the male-dominated society he had been born into, a thought process as difficult to change as moving boulders.

He pulled back from the brush and silently walked toward the other two in his group, hidden near the river. Tracking the redhead had been easy enough. She had made a straight line down the river, moving north as the river turned. They found her camp and even her simple traps, which concerned Pak and Calpano. Traps meant that she was worried about them following her and clever enough to have set them. Rosif wasn't even slightly bothered by the traps. All he could feel was a burning need for vengeance, and so on they pursued.

The westerly moving river was winding more north than west, but soon it turned and flowed southwest. Calpano had meant to catch her with an end-around ambush, with the hunters moving southwest and cutting through the forest, intercepting the river after it turned south. Unfortunately for them, she had not continued down the river. After retracing their steps, the hunters finally found her among a group of forest people. She hadn't been so much sneaky as simply lucky.

This whole business is just messy, he thought. He hoped he could stay mad at the woman in light of Rosif's desires. But was it not her fault anyway? Was she not a thief? Pak found it hard to lie to himself as he returned to his group. He was careful to avoid a rabbit trap set in the same bush he was now leaving. *Why do I keep feeling like the bad guy?* he wondered.

Ↄ Ↄ Ↄ

Kat'ja, Kis'tra, and Ember spent the middle part of that same day forging in the woods nearby the camp. Not too far away, Sv'en watched the women as he carefully placed rabbit traps. His traps consisted of a leather thong with a loop that would hang from a low branch or a tiny stick. A slice of tuber would be placed where the rabbit would need to poke its head through the hole to obtain it. The hungry rabbit would find and nibble on the food, pulling the noose around its neck. It would bolt as fast as it could in fear once it felt the rope pull tightly. Once the trap caught it, the rabbit's own speed would secure the noose around its neck.

The rabbit would sometimes escape, but this took time. So a wily rabbit hunter needed to check their traps often. Ember always found rabbit traps a little cruel, but so was starvation. The group had taken to foraging and trapping recently as a side project to diversify their food supply in preparation to leave. Seeing a large bush not too far from him, slightly swaying, Sv'en smiled and thought of the rabbit presumably caught in his trap. He was a bit confused when he finally made it to the trap and found it unused.

That night at dinner, Ember and Kis'tra sat by the fire and ate roast legs of rabbit, thanks to many well-constructed rabbit traps. The rabbit meat was warm and oily, but a little salt and the crispy fire-kissed meat tasted like nothing else. Sv'en had caught several rabbits, and there had been enough to go around. Kis'tra had just finished licking her fingers clean when Aya approached and suddenly spoke, turning many heads. Ember wondered why she tended to just abruptly speak. She suspected that if the woman spoke her language, she'd have antagonized her much more.

Thank goodness for language barriers, she mused.

"Where you-go, now, Ember?" she asked roughly in the trade language. By her more complex use of word choices, it sounded like she had been learning. Ember was pretty sure the woman was smart, just a bit mean.

"West..." Ember said, thinking the whole encounter odd. She had already explained this to everyone two tendays ago and several times since then, though she was starting to wonder if following the People of the Dark Forest would be smarter.

"Cold, soon. You-go, soon?" Aya asked as if she were prompting Ember to leave that night. But, instead, she used a few of her own words, not having the vocabulary for them in the trade language and not really caring if this caused Ember a problem. Luckily, it didn't cause a problem as Ember had also been learning Aya's words.

"Soon. Boat soon done," Ember spoke in the People of the Dark Forest language, using her growing vocabulary. Several people nodded, impressed by Ember using their language.

"Good!" Aya said, turning and then leaving, obviously startled by Ember's growing skill. Ven'Gar stood and followed her as she did, pausing long enough to give Ember a confused shrug. Luckily, Aya didn't see the shrug. There was silence until they left, and then the camp broke into discussion and gossip while Ember sat there looking confused. Kis'tra, now the best with the trade language between the two and with their more extensive shared vocabulary made from their amalgamation of trade and Kis'tra's own language, tried to explain.

"Aya jealous of-you..." Ember waited patiently as Kis'tra tried to find the correct words. "Aya think, Ven'Gar like you. Aya-want own, leader." The wording was course and without depth, but Ember thought she understood the problem, but she didn't understand how it had happened. She had never pursued Ven'Gar in any way. A woman who believed another was trying to steal her lover was a dangerous foe, but Ember had done nothing of the sort. Sure, Ven'Gar had been friendly but had yet to make any gesture that seemed amorous. If anything, he was overly cautious, likely due to his lover's insecurities.

"Why?" she asked Kis'tra, hoping she would elaborate.

"Aya has her pains! They never end," Sv'en said in his native tongue, referring to the frequently painful cycles women endured. He spoke with great laughter, drawing frowns and smirks from the other women around the fire. His jokes were usually funny, but angering all the women at dinner was not likely to get much laughter, though oddly, Kat'ja seemed to be repressing a smile. Ember kept her face neutral as she doubted that they realized she had fully understood the joke. Her ability to understand their spoken language was greater than her ability to speak it, a common situation when learning languages.

Perhaps Ven'Gar had spoken to Aya about taking Ember as a second wife if Aya first wed him? Polygamy was a common practice among many tribes, though Ven'Gar had barely earned the right to take his first, let alone a second, wife. A second wife often required the first wife's permission, a tough sell in most cases, at least among Ember's own people's customs. It was a supposition at best. Perhaps he had even suggested an interest in Ember in some other way. Kis'tra doubted Aya would take well to any of that. She laughed and took another bite of meat. Neither would she. Kis'tra would slap Zhek in the head if he ever suggested such ideas. The friends discussed these and other suspicions throughout the evening, giggling away at their ludicrous musings. Regardless of their fun, the tension Aya had caused was partially Ember's fault insomuch as she had, at the least, come to their group.

That night, Ember slept lightly, her thoughts on the camp and the coming cold. She liked Nor'Gar, Zhek, Kis'tra, Sv'en, Ena, Tor'kal, Kat'ja, and the others, but she was worried that her presence had burdened their group overmuch, upsetting their tightly woven group dynamic merely with her arrival. Worse, she still had not chosen what to do about the coming cold, and it was not that far away.

The next day, she awoke to find Kis'tra holding Zhek, as they did every morning, before leaving each other for the day. As she performed her regular stretches, Ember thought about how they cared for each other and wondered if such deep emotions were part of what caused Aya to become so angered. Love was a powerful emotion, perhaps more so than even hate. Yet, she remained puzzled about what she might do to fix the problem between herself and Aya. Unfortunately, she had no rituals, guidance, or songs for this sort of thing.

After breakfast, several women gathered at the river to fish early in the morning when the fish were easy to find. Aya was among them, yet she made a point not to look Ember's way. Ember considered explaining that she didn't want Ven'Gar, but that was out of the question. Her vocabulary was too poor to explain the details. If she said she didn't want Ven'Gar, she might imply that he wasn't worth chasing. If she failed to convince Aya, the already angry woman might become even more fervent in her territorial displays. Ember couldn't care a bit if Aya took all the men in the group for her personal harem and became the matron of five tribes. She just wanted to finish the "will of the gods," whatever that might be, and return to her people. If only she could speak to these people in her native tongue, it would clear up a lot.

As the day wound on, Ember, Kis'tra, Ena, and Kat'ja all ventured off into the woods to forage for food once more. The foraging required farther trips each day due to resource exhaustion. In a traditional village, the gathering would be regulated by area and season to keep food stocks in good order. This was why people tended to grow as much food as they could. Unfortunately, forest people were not known for their farming, commonly making only small gardens. In fact, she was a little surprised that these people farmed so much. Was it typical of The Dark Forest People, or just the one village of Tornhemal, she wondered?

Cultivation was both easier and harder than gathering, at the same time. The easy part was the more predictable food supply and the obvious location of the food. The hard part was bending over all day in the Sun. Ember often helped gather wheat and barely from her village's fields, and her back still hurt remembering it. Perhaps if they raised animals, life would become easier. She had heard of a tribe to the East who raised wild pigs to eat. That would not do for this mobile group, but perhaps it would for her tribe. Her mind wandered during these long working periods. Daydreaming helped keep the mind going.

Each of the women stood in their own area digging tubers from the dirt, or picking leafy greens and berries from the bushes, what few remained. Kat'ja had even found some fallen early nuts and filled her reed basket. The birds had obviously picked the forest nearly clean, though a few nuts and fruits could still be found. In fact, she could hear the birds' mocking calls as she worked. Oddly, the birds that day were making some unusual calls, but this was a different place, she supposed.

Perhaps birds sounded different wherever you go, Ember pondered as she approached a likely place for a tuber, a now recessed flower stem protruding from the ground. She remembered a specific bird call she had heard each morning from her bed when she was a child, an owl if she recalled. On occasion, she had heard a similar call since then, but only rarely. Such sounds provided Ember with a reassuring rush of memories, as did familiar smells and tastes. Life was a field of memories, each a flower to be seen and smelled.

Ember knelt and dug the tuber from the dirt with a sharp stick. She placed the dirty little white, elongated tuber in her basket. With a sigh, she stood, adjusting her leggings and brushing off her leather skirt before moving to the next tuber. Her attention was suddenly caught by the rustle of a welcome sight. Before her was a sour berry bush with a few remaining berries. She had probably startled a rabbit causing the sound. Lucky for her, too, as she would likely not have noticed the bush, otherwise.

It was her best find in days and a perfect gift for the friends she had made. She would fill her basket, and her mouth, with loads of the sour but tasty morsels. She rushed over and pulled her leggings a little up as she knelt before the bush. As she started to work, she noticed something poke through the bush, something sharp and flint-colored.

Pak watched the women fan out and carefully moved ahead of them, trying to guess where they would go. Hunting animals was difficult, but he found that hunting humans was turning out to be even more complex. Finding the sour berry bush had been a boon. He knew the mischievous woman would most likely see the bait and try to harvest berries from such a large bush. Anyone would. Quickly, he moved behind the biggest berry bush and signaled Calpano with a bird call. Calpano made a bird call in response. Rosif was also close but unable to provide anything but an angry growl, so he kept quiet.

The three men now converged on the troublesome woman. They had been watching the camp for a day now and waiting for her to separate from the group. She was not really alone now, but Rosif couldn't wait any longer, and her company appeared to only be a few young women. Even Pak admitted that this was probably the best chance they would get. As the redhead knelt before the bush and began picking berries, Pak's breath quickened. He slowly placed the arrow through the bush, wanting to ease the startling as best he could. If he scared her too badly and too fast, she might scream and summon men.

As the arrow emerged, she looked up and cocked an eyebrow at the sharp flint head. Suddenly, she realized what she was looking at, her pupils dilating with fear. So far, everything had been going well until she looked up, her bright emerald eyes matching his. She was terrified, and the look hit Pak like an arrow. At barely an arm's length, he faced off with his "enemy," yet all he saw was the woman he had harmed, a woman he and his group had enslaved. He looked into her eyes and saw fear but also, the reflection of his own shame.

ↄ ↄ ↄ

Ember nearly screamed as the arrow moved through the bush, slowly, and then up as its owner stood. The fear from the arrow stayed her tongue as she came to realize who the bowman was. The man, barely a man by his youthful features, was about Ember's age and about her height. He looked as he had when they had first met, about three tendays ago. He still wore his leather boots, leggings, loincloth, and long shirt; a tuft of dark hair covering his head. When his bright blue eyes leveled with hers, fear rolled through her body, dancing up and down her spine. The man slowly stepped from behind the bush keeping his stare level with her. Watching the sharp, transverse flint arrowhead and the drawn bow filled Ember with panic. The need to lower herself toward the ground in fear came upon her, an instinct so deep she didn't even consider it as she slowly crouched, holding her hands out as though warding him back.

Cowering was a natural and submissive instinct most humans possessed, and Ember could not yet resist it, though growing anger deep within her was starting to push aside such primal dictates. She wanted to run, but she knew she couldn't outrun this hunter, especially with his bow drawn. Her body warred between the urge to submit and live, or to fight or run, but maybe die. Finally, the man opened his mouth and issued a single sound.

"Shh," he whispered, emphasizing his bow with his eyes. The message was clear – *don't speak if you wish to live*, but would she be allowed to live, anyway? Her thoughts were answered when the man called Calpano stepped into sight from behind another tree and leveled a deadly stare at her. Tears welled in her eyes and rolled down her cheeks. Suddenly, the older man stepped into view. His expression was the opposite of hers, a nearly manic glee at what was to come. His gaze held a promise, a guarantee that she wouldn't just die but that she would feel such pain first. The fire of her anger instantly blew out as a fresh gust of fear blew over her.

Rosif, though she didn't know his name, was as large as she remembered, but now he wore an open apron over his wounded groin. His previous loincloth was too tight for the excruciating injury she had given him, an injury which had left him debilitated and barely able to urinate. His look told Ember her fate before he said anything. She would not just die. No, this man meant to hurt her in as many terrible ways as he could. Her only saving grace was his inability to do anything ghastlier because of the injury she had given him. He'd never do that again.

The men were closing in, and the youngest hunter stood not the length of a man from her, his arrow keeping her stilled. Seeing Rosif filled her with such terror that she dropped back to her knees. Tears fell freely, and she held her arms close to her chest in horror. He had terrorized her for days, constantly reminding her that she wasn't in control. She had not realized how badly that had affected her, not until now. She tried to stand but found her legs too weak, and so she cowered. She struggled hard against her fear attempting to master it as another tear rolled down her cheek. Again, she wasn't in control.

The younger man watched her with a curiously confusing look. He seemed almost attached to her emotions the way his expression appeared to waver in tune with hers. The blonde-haired man, Calpano if she remembered, whom she had made ill with the poisoned food, kept an eye out for the other women, who were not so far away. At the same time, the ever-maniacal Rosif stepped forward with a visible limp. Calpano had thought this revenge a poor idea and merely wanted it done and finished, as soon as possible.

Ember watched in panic as Rosif advanced. She fought to rekindle her anger, the same emotion she had used to escape, fanning it, forcing it to the surface as she cried and whimpered in fear. She would need anger if she was to survive this, but it was so hard because she was terrified. The monster came to tower over her like the darkest night. She wanted to cry out, yet she knew help would not arrive in time.

"Please... I didn't mean..." she started to plead out of desperation but stopped as she remembered that the men didn't understand her. Besides, she had intended to cut him. He had come for her, and she had cut him quite willingly. She had savored every moment of his pain and meant it all. It had satisfied her and brought a sense of triumph, a feeling of control, the flame of a warrior. Her anger flared in response to her momentary weakness, like a fire responding to wind. She stared at Rosif head-on, her resolve building as her fear became overshadowed by a new emotion. Terror was a powerful force, but so was hate. Her body twitched in uncontrolled panic, yet the fire of anger was finally building into an inferno. She had to kill or be killed, but could she do what was needed? Would she be the rabbit or a fox.

You deserved it too, she thought, anger creeping in, slowly starting to outmatch fear and trauma. His sneering face wrought the fire of her anger even hotter, like a reed fan to flame. He could likely see her expression changing from fear to naked hate, but the look of perverse pleasure in Rosif's eyes told her that he didn't care. He suddenly reached forward and grabbed Ember by the hair, and pulled her entirely to her feet. She let loose a horrific scream from the sudden pain and violence.

The youngest hunter grabbed Rosif's arm and pulled, trying to keep him from yanking Ember's hair so violently. He seemed confused, torn between his allegiance to his group and his mercy toward her. She barely noticed, pain shooting through her like a bolt of lightning. The pain fueled the hate. Rosif threw the young man's arm aside with a sneer and spoke to him in their language as he reached forward and pulled Ember's obsidian blade from her side.

Pak grabbed at Rosif's arm, his empathy taking hold. Rosif glared at him angrily, a mixture of glee and abject hatred in his eyes.

"Let me go before I kill you too! The little beast needs to die. But I'm not doing it fast, no... She will suffer like I did... like we all did!" Rosif spat, and with that, he yanked her hair again, producing another scream. Rosif paused for a moment feeling an odd wave of heat passing over his body. They had started a few days after the wound and had left him feeling hot even in the cooling air. He shrugged off the feeling, returning to the only task which mattered.

Ↄ Ↄ Ↄ

The brush parted as Kis'tra and Kat'ja appeared, summoned by the screams. A moment later, Ena rushed from the woods with a circular flint knife in hand. The three women had heard Ember and had come to help. Now they stood a short distance away, a bit wary of advancing as two of the hunters before them leveled bows their way, the third holding Ember by the hair. Their small stone knives were made for cutting and not for warfare. Worse, each of the men out-massed them as much as two to one, and they were armed with bows.

Rosif laughed at Ember, wagging his finger, mockingly scolding her.

"No, you won't get away this time. Perhaps we will take these women to make up for our lost time," he said while licking his lips, though Ember didn't understand him. This time, Calpano spoke up.

"We have no need for women. She has wronged us, not these women. You will not harm them. Take her. We will leave before their men come." Pak thought this sound advice, but he couldn't speak as his mind was racing through thoughts he simply couldn't quantify. He understood Rosif's anger, but his heart ached each time the woman's hair was pulled. Seeing the terror in her eyes caused him to choke back his own tears. He felt a lump growing in his throat, a gnawing empathy for her that didn't make sense. He knew deep down that he was in the wrong, but how could he stop now? How could he defy Rosif?

Pak kept evaluating the events that had occurred and trying to find her fault in them. She could have killed him while he slept, but she had merely wanted to leave. Rosif wanted revenge for the wound and the fallen sky, a rare item she had stolen, but did he really care about Rosif's revenge? Had Rosif not antagonized and threatened her for days, even trying to rape her? Now that he thought about it, Pak realized that Rosif had not acted sane once in a tenday or more. Pak's morals started to weigh heavily. Lying to oneself was all too easy, but seeing the truth through a lifetime of conditioning was far more difficult, as was overcoming the instinct to follow the group.

○ ○ ○

Rosif pointed at the three women and gave Pak and Calpano a nod to capture them. Calpano shook his head and yelled something at Rosif, which Ember didn't understand, but a moment later, Rosif replied with something hateful. He pulled Ember's hair, producing another pain-laden yelp from her, and started dragging her by the hair, making to leave before men came. *So, this was it,* she thought. She would either do something now or be a captive again.

No! She would not be a captive. She would rather die! But she would hurt this one first. It was frightening to attack such a large man, like facing a bear. He was enormous and could hurt her badly if she did, but what if she didn't? She was becoming stronger and thinking clearer as her anger burned the indecision away. She was unarmed, yet an idea formed as the man dragged her away toward some hideous fate. Behind her, she heard her friends screaming for help and menacing the men, probably trying to delay them until more people came to help.

Ember stumbled behind the large man, being led by her long hair. Rosif held the hair at the center and not near the roots. She had enough room to maneuver with such long hair, at least a little. Not daring the think, lest her resolve break, Ember stepped forward, planted her left foot onto the ground right behind Rosif, and kicked her right foot between his legs with all her might. Her feet were not very strong or very large, but quite pointy, and her target was decent sized. Her foot made contact about the moment her hair pulled tight; the slack having run out. She was suddenly yanked forward, stumbling to her knees with a scream.

Just then, her hair fell slack. Glancing up, she saw Rosif fall to his knees holding himself as tears welled in his eyes. Blood ran freely down his legs from a freshly opened wound. Whatever wound he had been dealt by her blade the night she had run, her kick had reopened it and caused the man absurd levels of pain. Ember had no idea what it felt like to be kicked between the legs as a man, but she suspected it was their greatest weakness and one of the only vulnerable places on a man's body.

Ember stumbled backward, standing as fast as she could, and started to back away when Rosif's whimpers suddenly changed. To her confusion, it sounded like he had begun to laugh, a crazed sort of laughter. Both hunters looked upon him fearfully as he slowly stood and rounded on Ember. Blood rolled down his legs as he smiled. His crazed expression told her all she needed to know. He had been pushed too far for mere pain. He would likely kill her here and now, finally pushed beyond even the need to drag her away. Rosif wasted no words pulling free an obsidian dagger – her dagger – and came at her.

Ember shrieked and fell backward, tripping in her quick motion to back away from the massive man. He was on her instantly, arm plunging downward with the dagger, an unstoppable force of pure fury and rage. He collapsed upon her with the dagger in his hand and a scream from his lips… and then he stopped moving. The force of the man landing on her blew the wind from Ember's lungs, and blackness and stars filled her vision as Rosif landed with all his mighty weight. He was easily twice her mass, and he had been plunging like a mighty tree falling.

A few moments later, she opened her eyes, unsure why she was alive and why her murderer was stilled. The great monster stared back at her in bewilderment, yet his eyes slowly lost focus. She had seen such a look before, as death was no stranger to her people, yet she wasn't sure if his spirit had passed. It was as though he were still there, watching her as his spirit fought to free itself. Ember had no idea what had happened, yet she felt no wounds. The man who had tried to kill her lay upon her in the throes of death. Tears replaced adrenalin as Ember's emotions began to break beneath the enormity of what had happened.

"I… am… in… control…" she heard herself whisper into his dying face as the last of his spirit seemed to leave. His eyes slowly dilated, though she knew they would constrict by the next morning. Everyone had seen death many times as the seasons claimed family member after family member. But at least he was dead, somehow. Had he slipped and fallen on the blade? Unfortunately, the two men were still alive and probably prepared to avenge their leader.

Ember rolled the large man off her, a difficult task as he had nearly crushed her with his massive form, and crawled away, grasping at her obsidian dagger, more confused than ever. The blade lay free and couldn't have been what killed him. As she stood, the culprit became apparent, for Rosif had an arrow shaft protruding from the base of his skull. It had severed his spine and killed him almost instantly. Ember looked up to see the youngest hunter standing with a pained look in his eyes. In his hands, a loosed bow awaited a new arrow. He had killed his leader. Ember stood there breathing hard and entirely confused. Around them, her startled friends stood with their foraging knives, ready to fight if need be.

Ember's obsidian dagger

The sound of men from the camp could be heard through the woods. They were coming to discover what had befallen the screaming women. The younger man looked at Ember, and she could see the pain in his eyes. This man, this monster of a man, had apparently lost his mind, and the young hunter had done what needed to be done, but at what cost? She knew nothing of his relationship with the old man, but the shocked look on Calpano's face told her of the enormity of this event. She had been right when she had first guessed that he was not in agreement with her capture. She didn't forgive him, nor did his final good deed fix what he had done, yet his disposition toward her had changed into something else; not a friend, no, but not entirely an enemy. Ember touched her chest and spoke, her voice still wavering.

"Kaelu," she said. He gave her a weak, guilty nod.

"Pak," he replied. He and Calpano turned and moved off into the thick woods, disappearing quickly. Pak turned only once more to regard those deep green eyes. He would remember them for the rest of his life.

Perhaps we will meet again, brave Kaelu. I'm sorry... he thought.

CHAPTER TWELVE

TRADERS

Ember had made some interesting changes, becoming more like a hunter and warrior in some respects. The idea of a warrior or hunter woman is not actually a new concept. Warrior women have existed throughout (pre)history and are documented in recorded history. Though regrettably, little mention of them is often made. Many cultures have featured proud warrior women, such as the Scythians, Picts, early Iranians, general Celtic Peoples, and a host of other groups. Sometimes they were unique individuals who rose above their cultural gender roles, while other times, their respective cultures allowed women to regularly attain such posts.

Warriors were probably not very common in the early Neolithic period of Europe, given the overall lack of evidence for significant warfare, such as fortified dwellings, at the beginning of the period. However, it is likely that warriors did exist in some fashion. The role of tribal defense was probably the job of everyone, though primarily men. However, it is probable that women aided in the day-to-day hunting and the defense of a people when conflict arose. Though no body of evidence of this exists, the possibility may be inferred from the general existence of such practices within the descendants of the same Neolithic peoples, in later times, and the proven martial ability of women, such as Pantea Arteshbod of the Achaemenid Empire or Boudica of the Iceni.

That night, the attack was all the talk of dinner. No one addressed her directly as speaking to her about it before she had indicated that she was ready to talk was improper to the Dark Forest People. They spoke in their own language, among themselves, speculation on their foreign tongues. She couldn't fully understand them, but she knew what they spoke of by their tones and the few words she understood. Kis'tra assured her that it wasn't as much about her as she thought, but all she could feel were eyes watching her. They wanted to know what had convinced three men to track her down and try and murder her.

After the men had arrived following the screams, led by Ven'Gar, Ember had convinced them not to follow the hunters. They had found her holding her dagger and standing over the body of a very large and dead man. The men were taken aback by the scene. A woman, a single young woman, had apparently defeated or driven off three hunters. Their leader lay dead at her feet, and none of the group had been harmed, aside from Ember. The women who had been present tried to explain what had happened, but the men seemed too wrapped up in their initial impression to listen. To be fair, Ember was the only one covered in blood.

Ember had also tried to explain that the man named Pak had killed the vile man, but Ven'Gar and the other men were apparently too impressed by her calm explanations and escape. While they seemed to accept that she had not actually killed the man, having no bow, that did little to hamper their excitement over her apparent victory. The scene had also confirmed her earlier story of a daring escape from the men, which she had eventually told after she had become more comfortable with the people of Tornhemal. Vengeance was her right alone, and she had forfeited that right, asking Ven'Gar to let the men go. She wanted no more death.

What had amazed the men even more, was Ember's insistence that she take a moment to sing a death song for the fallen man. She hated him, but she was not sure she was comfortable with his violent death. Singing the death song would assure her that his spirit might find some sort of calm in the afterlife. She supposed she was doing this more for tradition and the appeasement of the local spirits than for the violent man, for whom she held nothing but contempt. After she had finished the long, mournful song, the men had carried the body away.

Before the men buried Rosif's body, they had severed the hands and feet to render the spirit less deadly if it came calling after death. Spirits of the dead were a troubling thought, especially if that spirit belonged to the nameless brute who had attacked their women. Luckily, if it came back to life or some other vile act, it would be less trouble without hands and feet, or any of his other missing parts. This bothered her less as taking the body parts of a fallen enemy was commonplace, and something warriors from many tribes were nearly expected to do.

The attack was not the only thing that troubled Ember. After so many days with the people of Tornhemal, she knew it was time to decide what she would do about the coming cold. She had come to a hard but necessary decision as she sat by the fire eating. The camp had already begun preparations to leave for the South and would soon depart. But, more importantly, the boat was ready and had already proven river-worthy when Ember had used it two days before in the shallows of the river as a test.

Well, I guess I might as well get this over with, she thought.

Ember put down her food and stood, waiting for everyone to notice and become silent, observing the customs of their group. Even Kis'tra was curious at the abrupt interlude, pausing her discussion with Zhek to listen. Most immediately expected her to present a short "good-bye" speech if such could be had with her small, shared vocabulary. She had been hinting that she would leave for days, and the boat's construction was a direct indicator. Ember looked at each member, avoiding Aya's icy stare, and finally settled her gaze upon Nor'Gar. She smiled and began.

"Ember, go-west, when no-snow. It soon, cold. Ember, go with, Tornhemal-people, south? Ember, go-north, go-west when warm?" She had asked to journey with the group all the way to the South, where they traded and remained during the cold season, and why not? The weather might hold out, but what would she find when she arrived? The entire journey was based on a "sign," for whatever that was worth, and she honestly didn't know what to expect. Most likely, she would find some other tribe and be forced to join them out of necessity. In truth, she was starting to consider remaining with the people of Tornhemal instead of finishing her journey. Perhaps the cold season would give her time to come to terms with these thoughts, but she needed a clear path for now.

Ember stared at Nor'Gar, but her mind was elsewhere, and Nor'Gar could see it in her young eyes. She reminded him of his younger brother, who had left so long ago, never to return. He had that same look of wonder and the need for adventure. He had left their village when he was a mere sixteen harvests and had never returned. Nor'Gar wondered if he had found a life someplace, some reason which kept him from returning. His brother also bore green eyes and red hair, though darker than Ember. Nor'Gar wondered, and not for the first time, if red hair and green eyes, so rare among his people, were some sort of mark. Perhaps an indicator that the gods had some interest in them.

He quickly shrugged the idea aside. Ember wasn't "chosen" or otherwise special because of some cosmic will. The gods didn't control people in that way. Instead, they granted natural talent and let each person succeed by their own merits. Still, the striking features were hard to ignore. Even among river people, such coloring was uncommon. The fact that her darker skin implied that she was at least half forest people in heritage was another enigma.

It was entirely possible that a powerful fox spirit had imparted part of themselves into the girl at birth, perhaps to experience the world as a mortal. He had wondered the same about his wayward brother so long ago. Or maybe, he thought with mirth, he was entirely too old and saw spirits and coincidence where there was none. Of course, helping her wouldn't bring back his lost brother, but something about it felt like the right thing to do. Perhaps he would let her join them, for the memory of his brother, Winterborn of Tornhemal. Besides, Ember had been a great help around the camp, and the rest of the group liked her, with the exception of Aya, of course.

"Come with us south and help our trade. You have been of great help, and you have the heart of a warrior. We will return to this camp before the warm winds blow again, and your boat will be waiting for you," he said, glancing to Kis'tra to convey his message. There were general gasps among the people. No woman had ever been called a hunter, let alone a warrior. Ember felt her emotions blaze at being so accepted by these people, but she held her eyes firm with a deep breath. She didn't know what to make of being called a warrior. Was he joking? She was a woman, not that she ever felt like one, and couldn't be a warrior, at least among her people or any other people she had heard of or met.

Kis'tra finished the message, and Ember was filled with hope. The people of Tornhemal really liked her, and would even preserve her boat, somehow, until she returned. She was overcome with joy, as well as relief as Nor'Gar's proclamation had resolved several major questions, all at once. Ember beamed a smile at the gathered traders, who laughed and smiled back her way. However, the mood was interrupted when Aya, having seen how Nor'Gar was so enthralled by Ember, suddenly stood and stalked away to her hut.

Nor'Gar closed his eyes as she left and hoped he might be able to do something about that problem.

Ah, to be so young and so stupid, he thought with genuine envy and a chuckle. He'd trade all his wisdom for youth, and yet wisdom was so highly prized. It seemed a person could have one or the other, but never both.

"What-of, boat?" Ember asked, almost apologetically, to Nor'Gar.

"Boat fine!" butted in Sv'en, "Birds, squirrels, no use," he said, using his native words for the animals. His ability to tell a joke, even with a fifty-word vocabulary of a partly foreign language, was quite impressive as the laughter around the fire told. Ember was unsure what the resolution would be, but it seemed like Sv'en had some idea of what to do. With that, it was settled. Ember the "Warrior" would journey south and return in the warm season by this same route, so she wouldn't become lost.

Traveling on land was too dangerous alone, another reason she would return with the group. She would then continue her journey via boat.

That night there was much food and dancing as each person mentally prepared for the trip. Ember sat with Kis'tra by the fire, thinking as she watched people dance. There was much to consider, like being a woman and being a warrior. In most tribes she knew, men were dominant, and roles were separated by gender, no exceptions.

Am I now Ember, the Warrior? she thought. A warrior? Was he joking? He had not performed any of the rituals normally associated with becoming a warrior, yet he was an elder. Among most people she knew, elders held the power to proclaim someone a warrior, or strip them of such a power.

She created a mental image of herself wearing full warrior regalia of colorful body paints, feathers and sporting a massive spear. The thought made her giggle until the image of Rosif returned... the cost of being a warrior. She thought again of Rosif's handless and footless body being hauled away to a nearby valley, stripped, and quickly painted with ash. He was buried that same day in a very shallow grave without any weapons or tools of his trade, whatever that had been. To do so worried Ember considerably as spirits wouldn't look favorably on people who sent them off with nothing. Sv'en and Tor'kal had insisted that this be done with dishonorable enemies.

Enemies... which must make me a warrior. Only a warrior would walk around with "enemies" doing battle, she thought. That night, Ember thought of Pak, the only one of the hunters she knew for sure by name, and how "evil" he really was. In reality, Ember was starting to see that evil was less defined and more a point of view. Pak could just as easily have killed her. He had spared her, yet he had also participated in her capture. In fact, though she was not entirely sure, she still believed he was likely the one who had shot her with the stun arrow. At least it wasn't a poisoned arrow, she grimaced.

The fight had left her filled with potent thoughts, dark memories, and many nights crying herself to sleep over the violation. Still, she had not been entirely helpless in the end. She had nearly killed the one probably called Calpano and stood her ground against the mighty one, twice. Knowing that she could stand before such a man and maybe even win did more to calm her trauma than anything else. That night, she sang and danced around the fire with her new friends as they prepared to leave. Her thoughts were still dark, but she felt she had grown, at least a little.

The following day, the group pulled down their huts and prepared to leave. Disposable wares, such as the reed mats, were dispersed on the growing plots to aid them as they decomposed. Everyone knew plants liked decaying material, but no one knew why. Poles and specially shaped rocks, too heavy to carry, were placed in stockpiles as sheltered as possible to await their return. Not much pottery was left, for the people of Tornhemal were not potters. Instead, they used wooden bowls, baskets, and a few pots traded for. What few ceramics they had were treated tenderly.

Ember's people, and most other tribes to the East, created beautiful pottery rich with vivid details. Her tribe created clayware with beautiful designs incised into them. Hers was a culture of linear decorated pottery, though her own tribe added plenty of dots around the rims of the pots, much like the black paint dots Ember wore under her eyes. The people of Tornhemal didn't wear much body coloring, though she wasn't sure if their greater culture, the People of the Dark Forest, were also so inclined. By contrast, Ember had recently coated herself in a vibrant red color made from berries, with zigzagging lines. It wouldn't do to be seen unpainted.

As she worked to prepare for leaving, she thought about the predicament the women faced when confronted by the men with bows. The women had merely carried simple flint blades, suitable for cutting plants. While ready to cut even the mightiest plant, none of the women had any real defensive tools. They had been totally at the mercy of the attackers, though they had bravely faced the men all the same. If Ember were indeed a warrior, should she not learn to use a war club, the most common weapon, or at least a bow? All the animals of the world had natural "weapons." Even the tiny stag beetle she watched climbing the tree she leaned against had a weapon if one considered its mandibles. She had fired a bow before, and most of the women used bows to shoot fish or very small game. But a light game bow was much different from the heavy bows men used to kill deer and each other on occasion.

She grimaced at the thought, but the world was as it was, and she had to either learn to defend herself or find herself at the mercy of men. She decided at that moment to ask one of the men of Tornhemal to instruct her in archery. She was always quite impulsive and quick to make decisions, something her mother had constantly fussed at her for. As the thought occurred, she caught sight of Tor'kal carrying furs toward a larger pile of trade wares to be packed. She took a deep breath and approached the hunter.

"Tor'kal. Help." Tor'kal heard the statement and turned to see the reluctant redhead approaching. She was smiling and seemed slightly shy, though nothing appeared to be significantly wrong despite her words. He paused, curious to hear what she might want. This would be the first time she had spoken to him fully alone, and he was pleased that his slightly more annoying friend, Sv'en, was nowhere around. He patiently waited while she considered what to say and how to say it. Above all, Tor'kal was a patient man.

"I-want know [bow.] You-show?" she asked almost apologetically, using her arms to pantomime a bow. Nor'Gar had referred to her as a warrior, so he supposed her request made sense. The bow was considered a man's weapon, as well as the spear and war club. While he had never before met a woman who would face an enemy head-to-head nearly three times her size, before him stood such a woman. He had come to respect her and believed that she might truly be capable as a warrior. In the village where he had grown up, men and women had specific jobs, and these tasks rarely ever mixed. It was simply the way of things.

On the one side, he found the idea of a female warrior bizarre, while on the other, he also found it inspiring. He had always planned to marry a traditional woman and lead a traditional life, the way of his ancestors. Still, he wondered what it would be like to be married to such a strong woman, a deadly warrior. He realized that his introspective thoughts were drawing confused stares from this particular woman, so he simply nodded his head in reply. Most people did not consider him talkative, but Tor'kal's "words" were plentiful, though mostly heard from within. Finally, he turned and walked away, needing to find Sv'en and ask if he had a spare bow, leaving Ember quite confused.

Was that a yes? If someone asked him to marry, would he just grunt? she wondered, her confusion changing to amusement.

Before the mid-day meal, the entire camp, now twenty-two "traders," stood ready to leave. Ember was impressed by how fast these semi-nomadic people could become mobile. Each person now made their way around the campsite, looking for anything unfinished or potentially left behind. Leaving something behind was a common human trait, especially for Ember, and always a pain. Most people owned few personal possessions, and those who did generally kept them in their huts. Borjk had assured Ember that back at Tornhemal, their small village half the size of Ember's, each person had left their best possessions.

First-meal was the last meal to be eaten around the dowsed central fire. Immediately afterward, the group stood and lifted their belongings

211

for the trip. The meal had been eaten much earlier than usual, so walking could be more fruitful the first day. Each person carried their possessions, clothing, building materials, and trade wares. They had a long way to go, and they had amassed plenty of hides and furs to trade, requiring everyone to carry at least some wares.

Ember stood wearing her leather leggings, knee-length leather loincloth, and the sturdy leather boots Kis'tra had given her, along with her doeskin shirt. Around her waist, a woven leather belt held her lower garments up, courtesy of Ena, to which she had also affixed her dagger and her pouch. Around her neck, she now wore Blossom's goddess pendant on a leather thong. On her back, she held a leather bag with a single strap passing over her left shoulder and down to her right hip. The bag contained several bundles of dried meat and enough beans, tuber leaves, and tubers to last several people a tenday. Attached to the side of the pack were a dozen wooden poles used for setting up racks and spits, and ten roles of leather thong. Most importantly, a small bow and a quiver of twelve arrows were attached to the large bag, given to her by Sv'en and Tor'kal. They had found her sudden need to learn to fight both amusing and a little inspiring.

"Ember warrior need-weapon," Tor'kal had said with Sv'en nodding profusely. She could never tell if they were serious. She was not skilled with a bow, a man's weapon, but she would need to know how to use one when she again journeyed alone. Before the morning meal, Tor'kal and Sv'en handed her the bow, one of Sv'en's, and prompted her to try it. She had found stringing it, the act of fastening the bowstring, the hardest part. A bow left strung would soon lose its reflexive ability, and tilling a new bow, the act of making a bow reflexive, was a long and involved process. Ember could barely flex the bow enough to place the string loop around the nock of the bow, the name of the end piece.

After finally stringing the bow, she found drawing it much easier than she had expected. Tor'kal had explained that her bow was lighter than most bows. This meant it was less powerful, but Ember could use it without her arms shaking with strain. She then attempted to fire a few arrows at a pile of used mats to be left behind. Sv'en stood behind her and expertly helped her hold and fire the bow correctly. Ember found that the bow came very quickly to her, intuition being one of her stronger qualities. Her aim was a little off, and she was very new, having shot only a few arrows from the bow, yet the weapon felt good in her hands, like an extension of her body.

"She's a natural," Sv'en had said using his own words, though she understood him reasonably well. She had accepted the compliment, though she doubted they had expected her to understand it. If there was something she was actually a natural at, she suspected that it was languages. She hoped that would come in handy wherever they were headed as she owed the people of Tornhemal so much.

Ember's boat was flipped upside down and left covered with brush to prevent anyone from finding it. With luck, animals would not get into the boat, and it would remain hidden until she returned, though it would require some drying in the Sun before use. Ember hoped that she would finally know what she wanted for herself when she next saw the boat. Until then, she would need to become acquainted with trading and archery.

Boats, wolves, bows and arrows, trading, warrior stuff... well, I guess I am a proper man now. Now I just need a wife, she mused.

The group set forth carrying a cargo of nearly one hundred furs and skins of different sizes. Most were small but of high quality. There were mink, fox, and beaver, as well as five small handful-sized bags of the yellow rocks and various odds and ends of value. In addition, Ana had crafted nearly two-hundred colorful bone beads, and Sv'en had made little animal toys from antlers. The party was sure to return with a generous bounty after a cold season of trade with one of the larger villages to the South.

Two hunters were sent forward and one to the rear to act as fore and rear guards as they traveled. They only carried about half of their usual load, alternating with the other men each day. Ambushes and attacks on traders were not common, but neither were village massacres, and Ember had seen one of those. She welcomed the protection, knowing that hunters were far ahead, leaving signs in the dirt to tell the party what was ahead. It made for an uneventful yet safe travel.

The first five days of walking were a dull march through thick forests and hard lands, though at least it was safe, and the eighteen people immediately around her provided ample chatter to keep Ember occupied. She had never actually ventured so far from the river and had not realized how "thick" the world of trees really was. The climb out of the river valley had taken the entire first day, yet the trees just continued, it seemed, forever beyond.

Nor'Gar had explained that if the trip were straight on level ground, like the riverbed, the whole journey would have taken a little over a tenday, walking from sunup until sundown. With the hard lands and brush, it would take perhaps twice that long, walking all day. It would be cold before they arrived. Luckily for the group, yet unfortunately for her, everyone, except Ember, had cold gear. She would require such items made for her on the way, and with Kis'tra's help, she would do just that each night as they rested.

CHAPTER THIRTEEN

Modern convenience is all too often taken for granted. For example, Ember and her friends would have to walk perhaps 350 miles (560 km) from southern Germany to central France. Today, such a trip would require several hours of driving or possibly fourteen days of hard walking on paved roads. In Ember's time, the same journey would probably have taken the group twenty or more days traveling at an average speed of about 3 km/h. This rate may seem slow, but paths would need to be hacked through the wilderness without roads, and every kilometer would be many times more trouble to walk than on a flat, paved road.

Besides the reduced walking speed associated with hiking through the open wilderness, the travel time was also increased for families with children or the elderly. Everyone in Nor'Gar's group was young and in good physical shape. Nor'Gar was still in proper condition, despite his age, but he would probably not undertake many more such trips. The general fitness of the group and having lived their entire lives in what modern people might term "the wilds," aided Nor'Gar's band of traders in their trip south at a reasonably fast pace.

Six days into the journey, a dreaded event occurred. Ember had lost track of the last time she had dealt with her pains, but it always seemed to reappear about the time she forgot how long it had been. That morning, she had awoken to a splitting headache and a rumble in her lower abdomen, the omens of pain. After a quick trot away from the group to a private tree and then the local stream, Ember knew she would have to make preparations. It had been more than two tendays, she guessed, since the last time she had experienced her pains. As she walked around the makeshift camp holding her head, she was approached by a concerned Kis'tra.

"What, wrong. Ember head, hurt?" Kis'tra asked. Ember blew a sigh and a knowing look while rubbing her hand across her lower stomach. Kis'tra suddenly developed the most peculiar expression.

"Baby?" she asked, one hand covering her mouth in shock. For a moment, Ember stared at her in confusion, but before she could respond to the absurd question, Kis'tra took her into a deep and friendly embrace of excitement. Ember quickly swatted her away and dragged her aside before she could say something others might hear and spread through the camp. Luckily, Aya was not listening from some hiding place this time, as she was clearly visible on the other side of camp helping secure their belongings.

"No baby... blood," Ember said, using their still small vocabulary. For a second, Kis'tra looked confused, then her expression turned to humor.

Oh, now she understands, Ember thought as she rolled her eyes. Kis'tra gave Ember an offhanded smile and waved a hand, summoning her to follow. Kis'tra knew just how to take care of these problems. Ember wondered just who she had expected the father of her "mystery" love child to have been, somewhat amused.

Kis'tra led Ember away from the main body of people and behind a large tree. She shuffled through her backpack, producing two long and wide leather strips, perhaps mink, she supposed. Ember knew what to do at this point. Most of the women in her tribe used such wide loincloths in conjunction with long, dry grasses to keep their bleeding under control. Often, women simply kept themselves within longhouses during this time as movement could be painful or, at the least uncomfortable. Ember was fortunate to not have as bad of problems as many in her tribe, but the prospect of walking with the group was not comforting.

She immediately felt guilty for worrying over her own problems when she caught sight of E'lyse and Gar'ath. E'lyse and her husband Gar'ath were more "free-spirited" than even Kis'tra and Zhek. E'lyse was already showing signs of a coming child. How could she complain about something most women dealt with every few tendays when E'lyse was walking with a child on the way? Poor Gar'ath had taken to carrying all her load and his own so she could concentrate only on keeping the unborn baby safe. She had become with-child somewhere along the journey to the warm season camp, at least eighteen tendays ago, and she had braved the most dangerous early part of pregnancy during the hot season while sitting and cooking. At the time, such was possible, but now she was forced to walk, baby or no. Ember's sympathy lasted until the first cramp.

If I could just get "knocked up," by my mystery love-child's father, I could at least get rid of this headache, she mused. Ember rarely thought about having a child, but she knew it was a likely outcome. Most women would find a man, and soon afterward, a child would be born. There were many fears associated with pregnancy. Sometimes, a woman would catch a sweating sickness and die, or simply die during childbirth. All too often, a child was born already dead. Many women who survived to bear a child would die within the first few tendays from illness, and children often didn't make it through their first year. In Ember's opinion, the act of childbirth seemed like a deadly pursuit.

As if that was not enough, there was the pain. Ember had watched many women giving birth, and the pain they experienced seemed incredible, at least it sounded so. Even when she didn't watch, she could hear the screaming throughout her village. Childbirth was never secret. *Why must we all find a man and squeeze out children?* she wondered, though a bit rhetorically. The regimental nature of this system seemed absurd to her. Also, she wondered, and not for the first time, why the men got their share of the joy with none of the pain? She had seen plenty of enthusiastic men enjoying their all too short moments of bliss without worry over the pain to come.

Ember sat beside the tree, stuffing her loincloth with dried grass and fuming over childbirth and menstruation as a gentle rain fell periodically, yet never enough to break too far through the forest canopy. After a time, Kis'tra returned with willow bark powder to ease Ember's head. It was a helpful pain killer, though too much caused undesirable side effects, such as stomach pains.

The next few days brought pain and suffering that only Kis'tra could appreciate as the friends walked, staying towards the back. Ember was forced to make "special" stops several times a day to change the loincloth and clean herself. This was a task much easier for her than for other women. She had always thanked the gods for this little special reprieve she enjoyed. Unfortunately, her stomach continued to bother her, and she felt a bit bloated. She was glad when Zhek quickly got the hint and left them alone when walking.

During the nights, the group slept under the stars in calm but cooling weather. It had not rained but twice during the trip, which was quite abnormally dry, but not unappreciated as no one liked walking while wet. Nor'Gar had explained to Ember that the weather became warmer as one journeyed south. He wove tales of strange places far south where the days were always hot and the cold season never seemed to fully arrive. Unfortunately for Ember, the group would not be heading that far south. Still, she wondered what it would be like to travel so far and see such warm lands where one could swim during all seasons.

Ember and Kis'tra set to work constructing cold-weather clothing with thoughts of the coming cold. Each night, the two women worked to make a pair of dark rabbit fur mittens and a matching dark rabbit fur hat.

The hat was an impressive creation, though Ember's people did have something like it, a simple folded leather cap, but this hat was far more impressive. The hat was sort of a cone shape, with the bottom folded upon itself, making a band of thick fur around the forehead. Ember found the hat quite warm and stylish too. She had been worried about using some of the furs, but Tor'kal had shown her a full sack of the yellow rocks she had personally found. They would easily trade for the same value as fifty of the pelts, though she still had trouble accepting that, given that she had always been told by traders that the rocks were worth very little.

A little less than two tendays after leaving the camp, the group had already walked a considerable distance. The weather still held most days, but Ember had to wear a deer hide draped over her like a smock with armholes on several occasions, as well as a hastily woven grass cape when it rained. The weather was becoming cold and forcing her to bundle tightly, but she couldn't deny that her new garb was quite fanciful. She had even spent a few moments during a break admiring herself in a pool of muddy water. It wasn't the best reflection, but her mind filled in the hard-to-see spots.

Her red hair was now tied in a ponytail, the excess bits poking from her pointy, bowl-shaped dark rabbit fur hat. She wore deer leather leggings just reaching her leather and nettle fiber cord boots, stuffed with grass, and a roe deer leather loincloth held in place by a woven waist cord. Her upper body was warmed by her doeskin shirt protected by an old but well-made deer hide coat. Her hands sported a pair of dark rabbit fur mittens, which matched her cap. With a grass cape against the rain, Ember felt well dressed for whatever the South had to throw at her.

Ember was geared for cold weather travel as long as it didn't rain too hard. Footwear was created especially for wet weather and had to be worn in place of regular boots if anything was worn at all. Often, feet would be exposed to the rain and footwear hidden safe from the water, but only for a short time. After a short while, if the rain didn't subside, the group would find shelter and camp. Feet could be warmed by a fire, but wet footwear could be damaged, and walking in water-logged footwear, or even barefoot for an extended period, was a sure way to become sick or even develop foot ailments.

Ember had seen a man from her own tribe named Southern Breeze, who had made a long journey with a felled deer during the cold season with improper boots. When he returned, he became very ill and spent many days by a fire recovering. His feet were bright red with dark patches and smelled odd. Southern Breeze had recovered though his feet had been badly injured, and he walked with a limp. Ember remembered hearing the story's details from his daughter, Cool Winds, while the two girls played by the river. Ember pushed such dark thoughts from her mind as she continued the march.

Each night, Sv'en or Tor'kal would instruct Ember on how to fire her bow, much to the amusement of many of the group. She was much better with the bow than either of the men had expected, taking to it almost immediately. This pleased Ember greatly as she had been terrible with making fires, scraping hides, gathering with a net return, and many other chores. It was nice to have two skills she could honestly say she was really good at, the other being languages.

The operation was simple enough: you merely nocked an arrow, fitting the bowstring into the notched bit of wood at the back end of the shaft behind the feather fletching. Then, the bow would be drawn and gently lifted towards the target. When Ember had calmed her breath and felt the target was within aim, she simply let loose the bowstring. Ember was somewhat bothered by how easily the weapon could be wielded. The act of shooting something was so simple – so casual. She thought of Pak pointing his bow at her and how easily he could have fired. The thought brought a chill down her spine.

As the group traveled, the large, thick trees Ember used for practice began to diminish. This was probably for the best as arrows required constant maintenance, especially after hitting a tree. Typically, Ember used what Sv'en called "play arrows." The play arrows had a thick and heavy bit of wood shaped like a stone arrowhead tied to the tip instead of an actual arrowhead. The wood tip mostly simulated a typical composite microlith arrowhead. The arrow could be fired many times before becoming too damaged to use. A good stone arrowhead might easily fracture into bits if shot at a tree, and they were simply too valuable for flippant use. Perhaps she would trade for some better arrows when they made it wherever they were headed.

Ember had noticed the change in the landscape from dark forests to vast rolling hills and smaller trees. She had expected some greater demarcation between the North and the South, but really the "South" was just a continuation of the "North," as far as she could tell. The only real difference was the lack of her beloved Great River and the slight changes in the thickness of the foliage.

As the group hiked to the top of a small hill, a man in the distance came into view, waving at them from beside a large wooden pole. When the group approached, they recognized the man as Al'Gar, one of the hunters sent forward to scout. Those few who had made this trip before understood what he had found, but Nor'Gar paused to explain for those who didn't know. Such informational breaks were few and far between, but everyone's feet appreciated them. After a moment, everyone gathered around him with eager expressions.

"That is the marker for traders coming south or heading north. It means that we are intersecting a trade route. While we are in the Mighty Valley, we cannot become easily lost, but once this valley ends, which way should we go? This valley narrows to a small opening, so the marker has been placed where it will most likely be found. The answer is provided for us by other travelers. We can walk towards the landmark carved on the pole to find the next point. Traders have used these for countless generations."

Kis'tra listened and then translated for Ember's sake, even though Ember actually understood most of what he had said, for she had been working on expanding her vocabulary in these people's strange guttural language. In many ways, their language actually had similarities to her own, if not a touch thicker. She had only recently started to notice the same patterns in their speech. The people of Tornhemal had a native language very different from the trade language, which was really a mix of words from other languages blended into a workable admixture. Many action words were combined in ways Ember disliked. Nor'Gar had explained that the words had come from the far South with the traders and were not like those of the river people, such as Ember's or the Eastern river peoples; there was another great river farther to the East than the Great River.

When the group had met up with Al'Gar, each person took a moment to examine the pole. It had rotted at the base and would probably need replacing soon. The day was coming to an end, so Nor'Gar informed the group that they would be staying here tonight and replacing the post. It was every traveler's responsibility to keep the markers working, and the wooden markers tended to rot away quickly enough. The grounds near the marker had the look of having been used for this purpose often. The ground was smoothed, and the fire pit holes were well worn. Tor'kal set to work with felling a small tree nearby and limbing it to make a new pole. Unfortunately, these markers only lasted a few seasons at best, but the next few groups passing would find their way using a fresh tree and a little work.

It was dark when Sv'en set to work carving the landmark into the new pole, about the size of a man. The landmark was a low mountain peak far off in the distance. A line-shaped like a snake pointed the way in case the weather prevented seeing the mountain. Nor'Gar explained that the South had a large expanse of these mountains, which separated the "True South" from the colder south.

The True South was a journey across perilous peaks of ice and snow into lands of warmth and Sun. It was said that a tribe in the True South could live with never-ending supplies of food and ever-warm seasons. Perpetual warm days sounded great to Ember. She had spent the long cold march dreaming of running free through long green grass wearing nothing but a smile and a blanket of warm wind and sun. She would love to spend her days jumping into cool waters and swimming until her heart was content. But, unfortunately, the trip to the True South sounded much more deadly and cold than what she had to deal with now.

The following day, the group quickly packed up and resumed their journey, finally leaving the valley they had spent at least five days within. Proceeding out of the valley, the group saw villages along a small river, which flowed halfway between their camp of the previous night and the mountain, which was too far to be seen in any detail. Ember could see people in the small villages working and carrying on their daily tasks much as she would have been if she had not started this journey. Several times, she saw a local waving back at Nor'Gar's group.

"Ember, you-will like South. Men, Women, dance. Many colors, shells, feathers." Nor'Gar said, interrupting Ember's watchful activities. He was getting better with his trade tongue. She responded using words from both languages, allowing a greater vocabulary and the ability to speak without as many of the strange, conjoined words the trade language used.

"I-like South because, people of-Tornhemal, are here." Nor'Gar took the compliment with a smile as Aya simmered not far behind. Aya watched the disgusting display of wanton ingratiation with contempt. She normally would not have cared if the ruthless redhead gained favor with the elder by any means, but her current efforts were distracting Nor'Gar from teaching Ven'Gar the ways of the trader. If he didn't pick up enough skills and impress the elders, he wouldn't become the next leader of the critical trading trips. She fell back to Ven'Gar's side and grabbed at his hand.

"She has become quite a friend of Nor'Gar, don't you think?" she said, shooting him a coy glance while masking her anger.

"It would seem. It's like she was his long-lost daughter – like the daughter he never had," Ven'Gar remarked. "His wife died long ago in childbirth. Perhaps that has something to do with it," he pondered aloud. Aya frowned, wanting to suggest something more sinister, but unsure how far to take this. She needed to seed his mind with doubts and resentment, but that was a delicate affair. If she pushed too strongly, he might react negatively. If she were too subtle, he wouldn't react at all. With an angry mental sigh, she began casting her seeds of doubt.

"I think they look more like lovers. She's quite pretty and I bet he has noticed. Late at night when everyone sleeps, I bet she does more than compliment him. I would bet that he..." Aya was interrupted as Ven'Gar suddenly grabbed her by the shoulder and whipped her around so fast that she almost collapsed.

"You Will Never Speak That Way About Our Leader! You may say what you wish about anyone else, but never about High Hunter Nor'Gar!" he spat, leveling a dangerous glare at Aya. Her chest heaved as anger and a little shock danced through her body at the sudden act. She was not afraid of Ven'Gar and knew he would never harm her, but she had to balance her manipulations and his anger at her suggestions. One poorly chosen statement, like the one she had just made, and she could lose her chance at the position she desired.

Aya's chest heaved with a quick burst of fury when suddenly she realized that Ven'Gar was looking down at her with an odd sort of superior moral authority and from a full head taller. Aya wondered why she had just thought that, but she quickly dismissed the notion. Her chest resumed its regular patterns, though she felt infuriated and a little afraid, perhaps merely frightened by the sudden events. Aya backed away and fell back to the end of the group to stew. She burned like a crackling fire, too lost in her immediate anger to plot, but later she would get back to doing just that.

CHAPTER FOURTEEN
THE SOUTH

By 5500 B.C.E., Europe was experiencing an influx of people from the East and South. Most of these new cultures, labeled cultures by their distinctive pottery and artifacts and not necessarily by the modern usage of the word "culture," were centered near rivers or lakes. As Ember travels south, she will leave the territory of her own culture, the Linear Pottery Culture, and enter regions dominated by Mesolithic people and a few of the early Cardium Ware culture villages in France, another Neolithic group entering Southern Europe.

It is a common mistake to assume that the change from Mesolithic to Neolithic happened suddenly or that changes were homogeneous within a geographical area. Like all new things, time is required for adaptation and assimilation. Not only did new advancements likely progress slowly and asymmetrically, but some likely spread, died out, and then again expanded before finally becoming accepted. The ancient tribes of Mesolithic Europe slowly adapted or died out, yet they lasted several thousand years beyond this point.

After a single day following the river in an easterly direction, the group caught sight of their first indications of a village. Borjk had returned from scouting with word of animal traps to the South, which meant they were entering the lands of a tribe and were probably not far from a village. The direct signs of a village along the small riverbanks were the final indication that the group was on the correct path. Women could be seen smoking fish by the river while children played a game with little wooden spears and some kind of target. Ember smiled to see that life continued as normal everywhere she went. She was starting to wonder just how big the world really was and if it just went on the same way, forever.

After so many long tendays of walking and riding in her boat, she continued to meet people much like herself. They looked a little different, dressed somewhat differently, and even spoke distinct languages. Still, the basic trials of life seemed to permeate all people she encountered. Across the river's bank sat a small girl picking the last few flowers of the season. She had long brown hair set in several braids and a broad smile, her face entirely painted in yellow ochre, which she flashed at Ember, who smiled back. Ember recalled being just like that young girl, playing all day and watching traveler's pass. Now, the roles were reversed.

Well, I'd have been playing with a frog, more than likely, she thought.

The group continued east, following the small river. The first village they had encountered turned out to be relatively small. Though Nor'Gar, Kis'tra, and Ven'Gar traded a few pelts for some quality arrowheads, a few woolen textiles, and a quality ceramic pot. The group had left soon afterward upon hearing rumors of a larger village nearby. In fact, a quality fox pelt had been traded to an elder woman who had provided the exact course to travel. Finding a large village wasn't usually too difficult, and Nor'Gar had assured everyone that he had never failed to do so. Yet, the trade had made the task much easier.

Toward the afternoon, the forward scout, Sv'en in this case, excitedly returned to report that he had found the village. Just beyond the next bend in the river, in fact. According to Sv'en, it was a large village, perhaps three hundred people or more, and by all appearances, a trade village. A few villages in the South obtained a considerable portion of their wares from trade. Daring people would brave the passes through the mountains or along the coastal waters and bring goods to and from the True South every warm season. In reality, such towns still provided many of their food and wares internally, but they were cultural and material showrooms for others in the area. The interest in serving as a cultural clearinghouse for ideas and goods was a new one. Only a few lucky villages were afforded the convenience of a ready food supply, the placement between differing cultures, and the pure luck of their design to serve in this capacity.

Ember and Kis'tra shared a look as Sv'en excitedly explained what he had seen. This would be the first large village Ember had encountered, and only the third proper village since leaving her own. Ember had never seen another village like her own, and the prospect of experiencing a nearly parallel world was exciting. Kis'tra seemed more worried, as her people didn't live in large villages. The people of Tornhemal were a small village connected to a dozen similar, yet tiny villages, forming The People of the Dark Forest culture. For her, this was more of a visit to a foreign people who lived and even looked very different from her people. Ember and the group headed toward the village and, hopefully, cold season quarter.

As they rounded the river bend, the village came into view. Ember was taken aback by the sheer size of the construction. The village was set within a depression against a series of small hills. A vast range of mountains erupted from the clouds to the Southwest like some distant god staring down at the world. Ember had never seen anything like the scene, yet there they were. In the fields not far from the edge of the village, a group of children ran about playing, the beauty of the vast mountains lost upon them as they chased each other around without a care. This was their home, where they grew up, after all.

Around the outside of the village ran a palisade of pointed wooden poles, with small piles of used shells discarded against the palisade in some places, called middens. The palisade surrounded the entire village affording a small degree of security, though Ember couldn't imagine who would be brave enough to attack such a large village. Each of the poles had been painted, their tips white with chalky paint made from clay. Interestingly, entire sections of the massive palisade were different in size, age, and construction.

Inside the palisade, the houses were long and wooden, much like the longhouses Ember grew up in, with roofs of mud and branches coated in the same white clay which painted the palisade walls. Each stood twice the height of a man and four times as wide or more. In all, they were probably no larger inside than a longhouse, but they were strange and exotic to Ember. Many houses sported colorful designs on their walls, but most looked to be washed away. A few showed signs of fresh paint, however. Red and white checkerboard patterns wrapped around walls, with a significant number of variations in the size of coloring of the squares.

The center of the village had a long path made of dirt and caked mud, obviously the main passage through the village. Along its sides, large drying racks and other wooden constructs lined the path of what purpose Ember couldn't deduce. At the far edge of the village, wooden pens held goats and pigs. These people were apparently breeding and keeping animals to, perhaps, eat? Ember knew of some tribes who kept animals for food, but this was still an infrequent practice. Those who did benefited from food even when hunting and farming were difficult, as well as wool for weaving and various animal parts used for a variety of utilities.

In the center of the largest mass of houses, she saw what looked like an extra-large hut, but she couldn't get a good look due to trees blocking her line of sight. The enormity of the village held Ember in a state of awe. There had to be at least 200 or 300 people, more than double the size of

Ember's tribe. Ember had never seen so many people in one place. For a moment, she stood there trying to imagine what it would be like to live near 300 people.

Not far to the west of the village sat several large fields where crops would grow during the warmer seasons. The fields were largely deserted now, but Ember could see several workers tirelessly removing debris before the snows fell and in preparation for the coming warm season. As she looked, she caught sight of a woman carrying a heavy rock from the field. This was a common task as rocks got in the way of planting and needed to be carried off. It was nearly as arduous a task as weeding, which caused Ember's back to ache even remembering.

The worker looked different from the lighter-skinned villagers, most of whom had a complexion similar to hers. The woman had skin darker than the traders of Tornhemal with long brown hair, hanging loose, unlike her peers. She wore a leather skirt, though it was of poor quality and quite worn, her feet bare. By her estimation, she was taller than those she worked with, standing at least a few fingers taller than Ember. Her skin was painted with black paint in swirl patterns, unlike any of the locals. Ember guessed that the exotic farmer was about the same age, or perhaps a little older than her.

The woman paused and glanced their way as they passed, obviously curious about the newcomers. Ember came to a stop, Kis'tra nearly running into her as she caught the unusual woman's glance. The brunette's large, hazel eyes held an odd species of sadness so profound that Ember could almost feel it at a distance, at least empathetically. Her eyes were beautiful to Ember, so she stared, all consideration of modesty forgotten. They held each other's gaze for a brief moment, then the mystery woman looked away and returned to lugging her large rock out of the field. Ember took a moment to breathe, all thoughts of trade momentarily on hold. She decided to ask about the brown-haired woman when she got the chance, though first, she'd need to learn at least a little of the local language.

Behind her, Kis'tra stared, at first confused but quickly realizing what was happening. She smiled at the confirmation of one of her suspicions. This explained why Ember acted slightly differently from the other women, though not untoward. Many of the men had lightly flirted with her, yet the radiant redhead had mostly ignored their attempts, seeming to not even realize. The most amusing part of this was how absurd the realization made Aya's obvious jealousy and protection of her prize, Ven'Gar. Though less common, those of different sexual orientations from heterosexuals were not uncommon nor a cause for concern.

When they approached the walls, hunters from the village emerged from wherever hunters lingered. They stepped boldly forward carrying war clubs and spears. Warclubs were not hunting weapons, nor were the heavy spears they carried the kind one used to hunt. These men were not hunters, Ember realized, but warriors. She had been called a warrior by an elder, but she still wasn't sure how serious the claim had been. The warriors wore beaded leather leggings with leather shirts, much like Ember's, and long loincloths. Their feet were snuggly garbed in rough, ankle-high wrapped shoes, and their faces were painted with light ocher. The men wore their hair tied in buns with one or more hair sticks holding the buns together.

The warriors approached the group, which slowed to a stop while Nor'Gar came forward with his right arm raised in a gesture of friendship. Nor'Gar spoke to the warriors in what sounded like the trade language, though she couldn't make out the words as they were spoken quietly. After a few nervous moments, made more so by the appearance of several more warriors with bows and a few hunters, the warriors nodded and came forward to inspect the group. They stalked past, inspecting each person slowly and with care, as warriors did. One of the warriors stepped past Ember, pausing to eye her red hair and bright green eyes, to which he issued a smile and winked his eye. She was not entirely sure of what that meant, but she had a feeling it was some form of compliment. The attention was a strange mix of amusing, annoying, and embarrassing.

After a short time, the warriors returned to Nor'Gar. An elder had already approached him from the village and started speaking while the warriors satisfied themselves with the group's "true" intentions. Sated, they nodded to the elder, who smiled and cast his arms wide open in greeting. Ember supposed this was both a requirement with so much trade, as well as a bit of a show. There were theatric elements, though memories of the destroyed village continued to remind her of the severe underlying nature of the warriors, grandiose or not.

"Welcome, Welcome!" he spoke in the trade language and ushered her group into the village. The elder wore a woven wool robe, open in the front. His waist was clothed in a leather wrap with ample beadwork, and his feet were kept warm by a set of sturdy leather boots, each intricately painted. The elder had little remaining hair, a common affliction of men. Yet, by the conventions of Ember's people, his facial hair was extremely long, falling more than two hand lengths down his chest. The facial hair and bald head gave the man a sort of wild look, which intrigued Ember. He was a stark contrast to the well-manicured people of Tornhemal or even her own tribe.

The group followed the main path through the village toward the center. On each side, houses were placed a short distance apart. Many villagers sat outside working on various crafts and chores. They looked different than Ember had expected. Their skin tone was slightly lighter than hers and much lighter than those of Tornhemal, though they were quite tanned from the Sun. The predominant hair and eye coloring were darker than hers, tending towards deep browns and even black. Most people had curly or wavy hair, which the men tended to bind into a bun with crisscrossed sticks to hold their hair in place.

Women tended to tie their hair into dual buns, one of each side of their head, with a significant portion of the hair remaining loose and flowing down their backs. Ember was impressed to see many men and women with colorful beads in their hair and quite complex facial and body paints. Dark red, likely from berries, and ocher were the two most common face and body paints, though none wore black swirls like the dark-skinned woman in the field had. She looked nothing like anyone else she saw, a beautiful enigma.

The villagers wore mostly leather clothing like Ember's people in the cold season, but they also wore some exquisitely woven bark or plant fiber jackets, wool, and even linen clothing. A little flax grew in the North, but it was usually imported by southern traders. The fiber was bothersome to obtain, requiring the freshly dug plants to be placed into a pond, dew drenched field, or a stream and allowed to rot. Afterward, women used large, rounded rocks and wooden bats to remove the unwanted outer parts of the plant, releasing the fibers. Wooden combs were used to further extract the fibers from the woody bits. The clean fibers would then be spun into thread, a lengthy process.

Ember watched as a woman strode by, quite close. She bore hazel eyes and wavy long honey-colored hair set in twin side buns with a long portion flowing to just below her waist. Her hair was decorated with white beads and little blue feathers. Her skin was coated with red ochre in thatched lines for decoration. She wore a long, woven bark fiber wrap skirt and sandals, her baby held tightly as it nursed. The baby was wrapped in a soft leather blanket, though the midday was still warm. The woman wore a cloak over her back of woven plant fiber with a quality Ember had never seen. The fibers had been braided and carefully twined into a corded panel rather than her people's simple weaving methods. On her back, she carried a bundle of sticks she was obviously gathering. She smiled as she passed and gave the group a nod, which Ember enthusiastically returned.

Not far to her right, she saw a group of women sitting on leather mats beside a building, talking among themselves while obviously watching the new group. Among them, one older woman sat weaving a basket, her skin wrinkled with time and sun. Her body was dyed entirely red, her breasts hanging to her protruding navel, a sign of wisdom and prominence among women. Ember doubted she would ever have breasts that hung so low. Even after going through the pains of growing them, they were still smaller than most women in her tribe. The elder also had a protruding navel, unlike Ember's slightly indented navel, the former being widely regarded among river people as a sign of blessing from the spirits.

Beside her, a middle-aged woman knelt, seemingly taking a break from grinding wheat, her child in her arms happily suckling milk. The nursing mother seemed quite content as she sat back, listening to what was likely her extended family chatting. Ember had never felt comfortable in such settings, yet she could see why they held appeal for most. As she watched, the mother glanced an approving look her way, causing Ember to smile, a common reaction she had when a pretty face turned her way.

Such beautiful people and a fantastic place, she thought, entirely wrapped up in the excitement. Her hopes for celebration that night rose with each passing moment. Traders would likely be a good enough excuse. Besides, everyone would be too busy looking over the wares and the new people to worry about work. Generally speaking, any excuse for a celebration was used among her own people. The reasons were not really as important as a chance to celebrate. She hoped that same mentality permeated this giant trading village.

Nor'Gar and the group were ushered by the elder and two of the warriors to a set of four large buildings which looked as though they were often used by guests, bearing no family markings common for large buildings. Beside the buildings sat a large courtyard with an even larger building within. The large building seemed to be the most significant. It was painted with different imagery of animals and anthropomorphic figures from the other buildings. Ember wondered what went on in such a unique building. Before she could get a closer look, the group was motioned to enter their buildings.

Once inside, the elder explained that their group could remain in the village during the cold season. However, they would be asked to aid in general maintenance of the village in return for food and lodging. Nor'Gar handed the elder a small leather sack, no doubt containing something of value, and gave the man a hearty slap on the back. The elder looked a little rattled by the slap but nodded and left the group before the forest people could cause him more trouble. Ember and Kis'tra laughed at the confused look on his face at having been slapped. She supposed that life in a large village made such men unused to the ways of more rustic men like High Hunter Nor'Gar. But to be fair, Nor'Gar could barely hide a smile, which told Ember that he was not entirely unaware of his faux pas.

After the elder had left, the group quickly began to spread out. Ember examined the building, which was much larger than she had realized, once inside. The floors were packed dirt with a central hearth, much like her longhouse. Along the roofs, holes were propped open by poles to allow air in and smoke out, also common among her people's dwellings. If the stories she had heard had been true, forest people lived in small hut-like dwellings, which might have explained why Kis'tra and Zhek looked so shocked by the large building, their eyes wide and mouths slightly ajar.

As the travelers began to split between the dwellings, a man who looked much different from the people of the village stepped from one of the buildings, looking slightly confused. He quickly smiled and nodded to Nor'Gar, seeming to recognize the trade group for what it was, only a moment later. He was shorter than the locals with darker, tanned skin, which had seen a fair amount of sun. His hair was dark and curly, unlike the wavy and straight hair of Ember or Kis'tra's people. He had a more prominent nose and thicker eyebrows than Ember, as well. After the man and Nor'Gar had stepped aside to talk, Kis'tra explained that the man was probably from the True South, likely a merchant from over the mountains. Ember and Kis'tra's vocabularies in the amalgamated Trade-Tornhemal language were now quite large, and, at least between themselves, they could communicate quite well.

"Do-people, look different, wherever you-go?" Ember asked.

"I-do not know," Kis'tra replied, noticeably looking at the foreign man with more than a bit of interest, "but-it seems so." Ember repressed a knowing smile, not wishing her friend to realize her wandering eyes had been caught. She had little doubt Kis'tra would remain faithful to Zhek, given how deep their love ran. Still, it was amusing to catch her friend having a look. Ember was quite sure no one would so easily catch her peeking.

While the people of Tornhemal split into smaller groups of five or six people to share the houses, Ember and Kis'tra spoke at length about other colors and looks people might have from different places. It was idle chatter, the best kind, but there was little to do, at least until the evening.

Within the house that Ember, Kis'tra, Zhek, Ena, and Borjk finally settled upon a short time later, sat the dark-haired man from the True South as well as another such man and woman. All three had dark hair, tanned skin, and the same rich, strong features. Their clothing was similar to the people of the trading tribe, other than the colorful designs on their clothing, made with dyes of red, purple, and blue. Ember was taken aback by the rare and beautiful colors of their woven clothing and longed to journey to the True South. What wonders might await her if she did? But also, what dangers? The mountain passes were dangerous, and the trip could prove quite deadly, as many had learned.

Ember began laying out mats and furs to construct sleeping areas, pushing such thoughts from her mind. They would be living here for as much as nine tendays if Nor'Gar was to be believed. While that time would pass quickly with all the side work the host tribe would require of their visitors, it would still be a lengthy stay. To that end, Ember quickly scouted a comfy spot near the door so she could slip out at night without bothering anyone. Waking people when one needed to relieve oneself on a cold night was not the best way to make friends. With a bed picked out and assembled, Ember set her attention upon the new faces in the building.

It was not long before she had struck up a basic dialogue with the woman from the True South, named Napana. She, her husband, and his brother had traveled from a place called Yarehk, many dozens of tendays to the Southeast. Napana spoke some of the local trade language Ember had learned, though her thick accent made her difficult to understand. The place she had come from, Yarehk, had been called a "Mekdu," which Kis'tra had explained meant a vast village, a proto-city.

Ember had trouble with the notion of a "city," apparently a village so vast that its population exceeded ten times her own village, or more. As she listened, the woman described structures made from mudbrick and heavy wooden beams built upon one another and using ladders for access. There was even a wall, though that portion of the proto-city was no longer inhabited. Ember could spend all night listening to the oddly accented woman describe the wondrous place from which she came, though Ember suspected that Napana's deep brown eyes and constant blushing might also have something to do with it.

"Tell-more city," Ember asked, quite interested.

"Yarehk, Nara'kit, Isut'na, Tessar?" she asked.

"There are more 'cities' in the world?" Ember asked, forgetting to speak in the trade language, so excited by the prospect.

One day, I must journey to the True South if I don't die on the way west, first, she thought with a chuckle. Kis'tra sat back laughing as she watched the two women discussing cities, her own eyes wandering to Antor, the husband of Napana. She had never met anyone so easily excited by tales of distant lands, as the rambunctious redhead seemed to have the flame of adventure burning within, and she suspected it would not be long before the restless redhead ventured off on her own. Deep down, Kis'tra wished that she too could venture into the unknown, but her life did not seem to fit such adventure. She had a baby on the way and responsibilities when she returned to her village. Luckily, she had found someone she loved and who loved her deeply, a treasure beyond all trades. However, that didn't mean she couldn't look around now and then, as long as her eyes were the limit of her interests. Ember certainly was. She smiled to herself and sat back to listen.

That night, there was no trading or celebration, which took Ember by surprise. Apparently, the village customs dictated that travelers would be given a few nights to acclimate before any such events. This was the opposite custom of her people and difficult for Ember to understand. Still, these people were also accustomed to much greater numbers of travelers than her tribe. Perhaps the number and frequency of travelers made this practice of some importance. Either way, she figured that she would spend those first few days exploring the large and beautiful village. Meeting new people was always fun, and maybe she could even learn the name of the village, which she had oddly not been told.

Over the next few days, Ember and Kis'tra ventured around the village, observing the people and scoping out potential trades for later. The people of the village, called Nes, as they learned, were inviting enough and even offered Ember and Kis'tra occasional treats, such as cooked meat on a stick or a reed wrapped, salted tuber. The village was also bustling, with people working all day and children running about lost in the joy of play. Soon enough, her group would be among the many working to repair the palisade, clear the fields for planting in the thawing season, or any number of random chores. But, for now, they walked about observing and learning.

Nes was essentially a few dozen buildings, a handful of fields, and reminded Ember of her own village, though much larger. Each of the houses contained at least one complete, extended family, by Ember's reckoning, perhaps twenty to forty individuals. Most houses were single floored, but Ember noted that a few had smaller caverns dug beneath them or smaller hut-like structures built on top of their roofs, specially supported with heavy logs. She couldn't begin to guess what any of these special constructions were for, but they were numerous.

After a while, the friends came upon a burned building with a makeshift wooden fence surrounding it. On the ground beside the ruins lay long extinguished torches. Torches were used for light or to ward off animals. They were only carefully used within a village as they could set homes alight, a dangerous event. When a hut or longhouse burned, there was a risk of secondary fires forming from the primary fire. A burning longhouse usually couldn't be saved, but careful management of the fire could save the rest of a village.

Who would use a torch to burn down a house in a village, Ember wondered? This seemed quite odd indeed. There was one way to get answers: ask. Before Kis'tra could stop her, Ember approached a warrior, one of about five who seemed to be very good at merely walking around in a constant state of "toughness," and inquired about the house.

"Hello. House, fire?" she asked, using simple trade words and hoping the overly tough man understood her. Both women gave each other pensive glances, unsure of how the question would be received. Of course, Kis'tra wouldn't have asked, but Ember was far too curious of a person to let this go. The warrior gave her an inquisitive look before answering, seeming to size her up, as warriors did. His eyes indicated that he found her lacking, though his gaze also lingered, drawing her ire.

"Sickness. Fire," he muttered in the trade language. Then, after giving Ember another odd look, he wandered off to protect a less talkative area. Neither woman was satisfied with the strange and featureless answer, though the language barrier was probably a significant factor. Further inquiries would be required. By the end of the day, the two friends had spoken to many, including a man who could fluently speak the trade language and had learned that a group had come to the village from the extreme Northwest a harvest before. The group had been three men and two women. They had been traders of exotic dyes and beads.

Not long after arriving, they had become ill from an evil spirit and had been confined to the now burned building. Several who came into contact with them also died. However, one older man had suggested that the issue had resulted from preserved fish they had brought, and many had eaten. Ember could not imagine how preserved fish could cause one to become weak, have giant lumps form under their skin, and even cough up blood, the description of the sickness. She had heard of river fish going bad and making people ill, but never like that. Bad fish usually attracted rodents or made someone ill and vomit.

Apparently, the High Priest of the village had used his magic to bless a woman, his assistant, and then sent her to care for the people. Sadly, she had also taken ill and died. Even stranger, whatever evil spirit had killed them, it had spared a single woman. She seemed to have been immune to the sickness and not become ill. After a cleansing ritual and a waiting period had passed, she was freed. The building had been burned to remove the evil spirits, just to be safe. No one knew what the sickness was, but these things happened from time to time. What bothered people more was why it had spared one woman.

The only survivor from the trade group had been accepted, barely, into the tribe and now worked the fields as a widow. She was quite young and had only been joined with her now-dead husband for perhaps a season or two. Ember and Kis'tra found the story quite sad, yet not as uncommon as one might hope. The woman was obviously not well thought of, and it was rumored that she had somehow cheated their god of death and brought bad luck. No one would say more, but Ember got the feeling that something else had happened. She decided that she would eventually have to meet this woman, whoever she was. Most interesting of all, she was from the far Northwest, the place where Ember was "fated" to go. Perhaps she could provide some insight on what Ember could expect to find?

On the fourth day in the village, the elder came again and informed the group that the time for celebrations had come. The day was chilly but warmer than any other had been, and the elders felt that a celebration should occur before a day of trading. Ember had not seen the darker skinned woman with black swirl paint since her first day and hoped that she might encounter her at the celebration. The chance to ask her about the West, as well as speak to her in person, added a bit of spice to the coming festivities and an escape from the monotony of the past few days.

That evening, Ember and her friends excitedly prepared for the celebration. They painted their skin with the black soot and the horizontal streaks of the Tornhemal people. Each adorned their hair with feathers and a few beads. The three traders from the True South wore colorful woven clothing featuring horizontal stripes of color. Their necks sported colorful and heavily beaded necklaces. Each painted their face a deep red, using ochre paint. Ember and the woman from the True South named Napana helped each other paint, as painting one's back and face was difficult. Besides paint, Ember wore her loincloth, deer antler pendant, and her owl and black feather, expecting the dance area to be well warmed by fire. Around her shoulders, she wrapped an old bear fur left behind in the communal building, though it had an oddly musty smell.

As it turned out, the tribe had created five massive fires in the courtyard outside of the large, decorated building. Huge fires burned at the four corners of the court, while a large fire burned in the middle. The result was an area relatively warm, regardless of the chilled wind, and plenty of light. Around the fire, many costumed dancers moved to the beat of hide drums, sound sticks, deer hoof rattles, and bird bone flutes as song filled the night. Off to the side, a group of elders hurriedly entered the main building wearing the most serious of expressions, though Ember and company paid them no mind.

Most of the local tribe people wore ocher paints, necklaces with ample beads, and feathers hanging from their belts and necks, their upper bodies bare but for paint and bead. Men and women alike wore skirts of leather and textile, each intricately adorned with beads. At least two hundred people had gathered for dancing and food, representing much of the tribe. Near the dancing area, food was prepared, and much merrymaking was at hand. Ember and Kis'tra danced into the group while drums were beaten, singing was heard, and the night was young. Festivals were one of the most important activities for any tribe, and any possible reason to have one was often enough.

As she danced and spun, Ember could not help but eye the beautiful costumes and decorations people wore. By far, the most impressive was the flax string skirt worn by Napana, the True Southerner. The light garment danced in the wind as she spun and sang, her hands raised in the air. Ember was a bit mesmerized by Napana's beautiful dancing, so exotic and yet vital. She held her arms wide like a bird and slowly circled her husband, Antor. While she did, he held his hands to his head like the horns of an aurochs and stalked her menacingly. As their dancing became more intense, many paused to watch. Was this some sort of True South ritual, Ember wondered? *I must get her to teach me how she dances!*

After a moment, Antor rushed toward Napana, trying to poke her with his "horn" fingers, though she danced skillfully aside, slapping his backside for the effort. This continued for a while as the gathered festival-goers danced and watched. Then, suddenly, Napana reached out, grabbing him by the "horn," and simply led him away, obviously wishing a different sort of dance. Ember was sad to see her leave, but there was a reason dance and fertility were linked. Although to be fair, they were hardly the first couple to part ways with the celebration. At least a dozen others had run off as the dance had moved them toward primal yet natural urges.

After a while, the dancing and the music slowed, and a path was made before the front of the large building. Once silence had engulfed the tribe, the wood frame door opened, and a tall man, whose body was painted intricately in rich black lines from head to toe, emerged. He wore a long, beaded loincloth of wool cloth and a fine wool panel cloak that hung to his knees. In his hand, he held a staff with complex designs carved into the upper third and the body of an extremely heavy-set woman with exaggerated features at the top. Ember needed no explanation to recognize a head religious figure when she saw one, though Nor'Gar seemed bothered by his proximity.

"He is priest Duruth. He speaks for the gods of this land. I advise you to avoid him. Never make eye contact or approach him. He holds great power, and whatever he decides may not favor you." Nor'Gar, not far from Kis'tra and Ember, whispered this to his people in his native tongue. Ember understood most of what he had said, though Kis'tra translated it for her, anyway. At this point, she could understand most Tornhemal speech unless the topic became overly detailed.

Ember frowned at the statement. A man who speaks for the gods? In Ember's tribe, it was usually the job of a woman, Morning Dew, to interpret the gods' will, and rarely a man. Ember reflexively rubbed her hands on Blossom's goddess necklace as Duruth stepped forward and theatrically observed the entire spectacle. He looked serious as he pronounced something in his language to the people. He stepped forward a few more paces and continued speaking. Nor'Gar translated as best as he could, using the trade language for Ember's sake, in a hushed voice.

"He-say, gods angry, more-dance." Suddenly, Nor'Gar looked shocked, "He-say, another-man, dead, today! He, just-learn. He-say, gods kill-man, gods-angry. Man, no [wound.] Man, name Aris," he finished, using a hand signal for "wound." Quickly, Nor'Gar restated the same message in his native language, which Ember honestly understood better at this point, followed by a few shocked sounds from those gathered. Oddly, the people of Nes seemed much less appalled than her own group. Their expressions were fearful, yet more resigned.

Beside Ember, a man from the tribe breathed something hateful under his breath, causing her to cast him a curious glance. The older man

236

looked a bit disheveled with curly brown hair and a simple leather wrap wound around his waist, and worn leather shoes, so much like many others. At first, she thought he was outraged by the idea that someone was found dead, just as other people around him were muttering in disbelief, but his expression was more menacing. He almost looked like he was hatefully glaring at Duruth. While this seemed quite odd, Ember was the outsider, and she could not deny that there might simply be more complex elements at work than she realized.

After the pronouncement, the dance became much less fun, instead taking on a more religious demeanor. Outsiders were restricted from dancing near the fire, given the critical religious elements now in play. These people had apparently experienced recent and unexplained deaths and were appealing to their gods for help. With the death announced, the festival had become an important ritual event. Perhaps the oddest part of it to Ember was that the high priest seemed under the impression that the gods were killing the people.

What gods are these who take lives at random? But... don't people die all the time? Is that not also the will of the gods? These scenarios were the same, and yet entirely different. Ember was quite confused by her own thoughts as the night wound on. In her tribe, the goddess of the snow and ice was known to kill people at random, as well as the god and goddess of fertility, but this sounded more like murder to her. Many stories spoke of people struck down by the gods and spirits. However, the gods usually used the natural world or sickness. Finding a person free of wound or the mark of sickness, yet dead, just wasn't a common occurrence, but was it truly a god?

Toward the end of the event, priest Duruth stood and held high his hands to silence the crowd. Once everyone had stopped, he motioned, and a woman was brought into view. She stood with her head bowed forward, her hair obscuring her face. Her skin had been covered with black soot and her hair in white clay powder. As she passed by Ember, she could be heard sobbing as she was led by several elder women. Ember glanced around and found that the events, as they unfolded, were obvious to those from the tribe and apparently expected. Ember and Kis'tra each had little idea what was going on, so they simply watched. The sobbing woman wore a simple leather skirt and no decorations. Ember supposed that she might be the widow of the slain man, but this was just a guess.

An elder woman slowly escorted the clay and ash-covered woman around the main fire, the opposite way everyone had been dancing, which held significance, Ember suspected. Toward the end of the first orbit, the woman began to wail a mournful song or perhaps appeal to the gods. She was not sure, but the words sounded nearly like a song. She sang the mournful words off-key and between fits of sobbing. Her words were foreign to Ember, but she could feel the woman's pain. Memories of the slain people at the raided village returned to her, and she became moved to tears. There was something about watching such grief, hearing the all too human sounds of pain and loss, which impacted nearly anyone, transcending culture, and language.

After a short time, the woman gave in to her emotions and was helped away from the festivities. Afterward, Duruth spoke to his people briefly and with a tone of finality, then simply turned and walked back to the central building. Everyone appeared moved by the display. Ember supposed she had just witnessed some sort of death ritual, though she couldn't imagine something like this occurring in her tribe. She wanted to help, to find out why this had happened, and to prevent another death, but she was a stranger, barely even a woman by age. *But you are also a warrior, and warriors protect the people, right?*

The next day, the trading started in earnest. Wares were laid out on mats and hides for inspection. Men and women stood around making deals and talking about the quality of wares. The mood had improved a little, but a woman could be heard crying every now and then in a dwelling not far away. Ember had quickly confirmed that she was the wife of the now-dead man thanks to the loose lips of many a villager. The trading area was in the open area near the large building the priest had come from and just adjacent to both the dwellings her traders inhabited and the smaller one with the crying woman.

Ember had watched many older women enter the structure, seemingly to console her. Oddly, the building wasn't decorated like the other buildings, which bore distinctive markings, likely indicating specific families. Ember moved closer to the trading area to take her mind off the death and sadness, though she couldn't quite get it out of her mind, nor her suspicion that the deaths weren't divine. Kis'tra was sitting with Zhek and four others, striking deals on quality deer and rabbit pelts as Ember approached. Kis'tra wore dark rabbit mittens as she showed the dark rabbit pelts she had to trade. Ember recognized them as her mittens, made by Kis'tra during their long march south, and sat down beside her.

"What do I need to-trade for my-mittens," she asked? Kis'tra laughed and held out a hand to point at a large bundle of flax fiber thread she had already traded. There was probably enough for a full wrap skirt or more.

"I-charge high price! Good furs," she said with a wink. Next to the group, Sv'en sat with a collection of deer antler toys. He had carved the little figures from the smooth antlers of red deer. A little girl was holding an antler-carved doll with a tiny leather skirt and rich coloring while using her most potent expression of pleading to obtain the doll. Her soon defeated mother offered a quality piece of obsidian to which Sv'en gave a slight bow and a smile. He quickly snatched the obsidian and gave the tiny girl a rub on the head.

Ember was pretty sure he would make a great father, if only he could settle down and find the right companion. Behind them, Nor'Gar paced back and forth, watching the trading, and ensuring everything was swapping for the right trades. The group traded as one, not individually. As a result, their entire tribe could benefit from their trades when they returned. After a short time, he walked up to Ember and gave her a pat on the back.

"We-do better. Good-trades." With that, he hurried off to help with an exchange of the precious yellow rocks that had just started. Ember shrugged at Kis'tra, and they both exchanged a laugh. The entire experience was surreal and much more impressive than the simple trading which occurred in her small tribe. The hustle and bustle of activity filled Ember with excitement and growing anticipation for each major trade. It was almost addictive just watching. Offhandedly, she wondered if perhaps she might become a trader as a means to adventure and see the world, but her thoughts vanished, as usual, the moment another trade stole her attention.

She stood and ventured around to see what was happening. As she strode about the trading area, she couldn't help but notice a man from Nes, a local, staring at her. He looked like an average fellow with a pointed leather hat and simple, robust leather clothing. She thought she had seen him before but was unsure. He gave her a wink and walked away quite suddenly. The encounter left her a bit confused and a little creeped out, but she soon forgot when E'lyse stepped from the crowd to reveal a beaver skin bag with a durable strap she had traded for. It was the perfect baby holder.

"[Hold]-baby," she said, using her hands to indicate holding a child. The meaning was simple, and E'lyse was a friendly person, though she had difficulty using the trade language. This had been an ongoing problem with several people in their group. Ember wished that she could speak with people more readily and freely. She was learning the Tornhemal language quite quickly and decided to try her luck.

"Good trade, E'lyse!" she said in the Tornhemal language bringing a shocked smile to the woman's face.

"You speak our language!" she said, luckily using words Ember knew. She tried to reply, but she was cut off by the sound of a man calling E'lyse's name.

"E'lyse! Come, you need to see this," spoke an enthusiastic man from behind Ember. Gar'ath, her similarly enthusiastic husband, emerged from the crowd, having just completed a trade of furs, and the happy couple left with E'lyse waving farewell. Ember stood there for a moment, feeling a sudden longing for someone to care for, a person to emerge from the crowd and call upon her, and then the thought passed as screaming children caught her attention. A companion probably meant eventual sex, and sex resulted in those... babies. As she turned to watch the playing children rush by, her eyes fell upon an unexpected sight.

Before her stood the woman from the field, who dressed and looked so different from the others. She was standing just a few lengths of a man away and watching the trading. Up close, it seemed that she was nearly a head taller than Ember with rich brown skin, darker even than the people of Tornhemal and significantly darker than Ember or the people of Nes. Her gorgeous, long brown hair was wavy, unkempt, and sported several small braids of varying lengths and no discernable pattern. She wore a simple leather wrap skirt and a large, worn fur wrap to keep warm. Whoever this woman was, she was quite unique.

Ember's eyes slowly rose, examining the beautiful forest woman in detail. All thoughts of being noticed were lost as her attention became hyper-focused. The woman's arms and legs were well defined, likely owing to long days laboring in the wheat fields of Nes. Her bare feet and lack of the many layers of clothing commonly worn in the cold spoke of a woman more accustomed to the chill. However, she might have had little else to wear, given the generally poor quality of what she had worn. Her breasts, legs, and arms, protruding from the fur wrap, were painted in dark swirl patterns, so unlike any of the aesthetics of Nes. Ember drank in the details, slowly rising to her exotic face... until their eyes met.

"Aeeya..." she whispered at having so thoroughly been caught looking. The profane expression was as natural as breathing, something she realized she had stopped doing for the last few moments. Soft hazel met bright green as their eyes locked, yet didn't sway. Ember expected a confused or even angry reaction, and yet there was none – just simple curiosity.

"Dhue eshe wehnose..." Ember whispered under her breath, then turned away as embarrassment overwhelmed her. Who was this mystery woman who lived among the people of Nes? She looked like a forest person, though a little darker, and she was the only one of her kind Ember had seen. Then it hit her: was this the survivor? Was she the woman who the evil spirit had spared? She looked young, around Ember's age, but she could have been joined. Moreover, hadn't she and Kis'tra spoken of how those from other lands looked different? She had never been to the far West, and this woman looked like no other woman she had ever seen. *In more ways than one,* she mused.

Flustered and blushing deeply enough to feel the warmth from her own skin, Ember decided to turn and look once more. As she did, her heart sank as the woman was gone. For a moment, she looked about, hoping her distinctively dark brown skin would make her easy to find, and yet she was gone. After a moment, Ember turned with a sigh, hoping to return to the trade. She could hunt down the mystery woman later. *Aeeya... Meg'wehnose.*

◯ ◯ ◯

The woman with brown skin and hazel eyes stood beside a pile of baskets, rubbing a bruise on her arm. She worked whatever menial jobs were available, the common lot of someone without a family or standing, not to mention heavily disfavored by most. That morning, she had bruised her arm while carrying items for trade in exchange for some wheat, barely a day's portion, from one of the major clans. She wasn't forced to work, yet hunger and the need for a roof over her head were a well-known encouragement.

She had finished her last task and had decided to look at what was being traded. She owned nothing, so she could only look, yet there was still joy in seeing beautiful things. Her meager clothing had been cast-offs from others as her original clothing had been burned with the building when... She quickly banished those memories. At least the Goddess of the Moon had seen fit to spare her body from the horrors she had seen, yet to what end? Was it enough to merely draw breath? Could she spend the rest of her life living in Nes, barely tolerated? Would she be forced to give in to some man in exchange for food?

At least her dark thoughts had melted for the moment when she had caught one of the traders openly regarding her. The rustic redhead was quite unique in appearance, though she had the look of a river dweller.

241

She wasn't a fan of being so plainly observed, especially at length and shamelessly. Yet, those green eyes held no hidden agenda, no deviance, nor prurience. Instead, there was purity, a sort of innocence and curiosity. Far from a wolf staring at a meal, the radiant redhead had gazed upon her more like someone admiring a beautiful flower. A tingle danced down her spine as she recalled the fresh memory. She hadn't felt joy in a long time, yet her body fluttered with emotion. Perhaps the most important and unlikely part of all, the redhead had not been a man.

Brigdha smiled.

CHAPTER FIFTEEN
THE COLD SEASON

The village of Nes is located in what is now eastern France. They were an early member of the Cardium Pottery Culture, spanning much of southern Europe at about the same time as Ember's Linear Pottery Culture to the North. The Cardium Pottery Culture of 5500 would be more populous to the southeast of France, along the southern coast, yet Nes is close enough to the discovered sites that its placement is plausible. Of course, Cardium Pottery Culture sites were usually smaller than Nes, though larger settlements may have existed.

While observing the Nes, Ember would have seen many remarkable advances, including large-scale dedicated farming operations, domestication of animals, a primitive well, and a budding textile market. Their pottery would even differ from Ember's, featuring little patterns made by the imprinting of shells against the surface of ceramics. However, while Nes may be slightly more advanced than Ember's village, so too are the problems they face. Nes has crime, murder, plague, and many other ailments of large groups of people living closely together, not suffered as heavily by Ember's river people.

With much of the trading completed during the first day of trade, the group returned to their dwellings to await the end of the cold season. Some sporadic trading occurred afterward but never anything like the first day. It was expected that each group member would help the trading village in any way they could in exchange for being housed and fed. The influx of labor allowed for repairs and work, which would usually have waited until the warm season. This extra effort resulted in increased time for work during the warm season focused on food and growth instead of repairs. Such labor helped the tribe immensely and more than made up for feeding the traders.

As the days became shorter and the nights became colder, the tribe of Nes remained indoors more to keep warm. The slightly squarish longhouses turned out to be quite efficient at retaining heat and warming everyone with their large central hearths, though Ember worried about not having a backup hearth. Their walls were made of large poles with a

243

lattice of thin sticks between them, and mud caked in the holes between, quite similar to the construction of the longhouses Ember grew up in.

Each day, the teams would harvest firewood or fresh meat while others would clean and cook the food and tend to the hearths. Ember and Kis'tra had taken to helping E'lyse with her coming child, as one did. E'lyse and Gar'ath had moved into Kis'tra and Ember's dwelling to make the job of caring for her easier. The room was getting cramped, but the more people in the room, the warmer it became. E'lyse had taken to removing her skirt and lying under a deer hide blanket. She was also urinating quite often, with little result for each try. At this point, she was better off staying in the longhouse. Gar'ath kept to his work while Ember and Kis'tra took turns watching E'lyse and performing odd jobs where they could. All thoughts of the deaths, speaking with the woman from the far Northwest, and the mystery of the gods of this land were pushed aside by more demanding work.

Unfortunately, whoever or whatever had been the cause of the deaths hadn't lost interest. It had been a full seven tendays when death again stuck the tribe. On a chilly evening, a mere three days past the shortest day of the seasons, Duruth called an assembly of the entire tribe before him in the courtyard. Great fires were lit against the cold, and to light the area, as the Moon was a mere waxing crescent and didn't provide enough light. Nor'Gar again translated in hushed tones for his group, though many had picked up a little of the local language.

"Daker of the Kiku was found dead near the woods. He was collecting firewood and didn't return. Several hunters searched the area and found his body not long ago," Nor'Gar continued to translate as several people exclaimed in shock. "There was a bump on the back of his head, but his skull wasn't cracked, and it did not seem enough to have killed him."

Perhaps he just fell and hit his head, then died from the cold, Ember supposed, now understanding the Tornhemal language well enough to fully grasp what was said. With all the ice and snow on the ground, it had to be possible. There had not been a death since before the trading day, and now, three moons later, death returned? Accidents also happened, and Ember couldn't help but suspect this was just such an accident. Yet, the murmuring around her from the locals suggested that her dismissal was not shared. Her attention returned to Nor'Gar as he continued his translation of Duruth's words.

"I cannot rule out the chance that this was the anger of the Gods! I can only think of one way we may have angered them so, but I am not sure yet. That is all," Nor'Gar translated.

Descriptive fellow, Ember thought with a frown. Duruth turned and walked back into the large building with several of the elders. The general muttering increased as the tribe's gossipers ignited like pine tar in a fire at the news, both what was said and what was implied. A name kept being mentioned, "bree-gh-da." Ember had made a few inquiries since she had seen the hazel eyed woman so many days before at the trading day, yet she had not seen her since that last warm day, quite an accomplishment, even in a large tribe. Brigdha was the name of the woman from the far Northwest who had lost her husband to the sickness.

Many she had asked about the exotic brunette had said that she had cheated death. Worse, many more seemed to think that she had brought the wrath of the gods upon the tribe. One man had even claimed he saw her out walking in the forest the night of the previous death. Luckily for Brigdha, she was not at the gathering. Instead, she had taken refuge in what Ember had learned was called the "Widows' Hut," a building which had once belonged to a now defunct clan. Several others without a clan lived in the small building and were generally regarded as outcasts. The idea of outcasts within a village was entirely alien to Ember, but Nes was so much larger than her village.

As Ember and Kis'tra returned to the trader buildings, they passed the Widows' Hut, where yelling could be heard. Ember couldn't make out much of the language, but she clearly heard the words for "killer," "gods," and the name Brigdha. The wife of the man who had died the day before the main trading day, many tendays before, had been from another tribe and had no place to go after his death. At least in the short term, she had moved into the Widows' Hut, which could provide the support she needed until another family took her in. Unfortunately, the screaming woman sounded like that very widow, though Ember could be mistaken. Could she be taking out her anger on this Brigdha woman? Ember hoped not.

That night, Ember found herself back in the village of the Great River People lying in her bed. She awoke and stood in what felt like the warmth of the warm season, her favorite season. She casually strode through the longhouse, passing her many family members as she approached the main doorway. Opening the door, Ember was greeted by the pale light of the Moon, so much larger than she had ever seen it.

Oddly, it hung just above the trees right outside of her longhouse, though she always remembered it rising and setting to either side.

Her thoughts were dashed as a soft hand touched her bare shoulder. Ember turned to find a woman in the darkness, her body garbed in the moonlight with a gentle smile upon her exotic face. Her naked body was painted entirely in striking black swirls so dark they contrasted her otherwise brown skin. She was beautiful, like the spirit of the Moon. But, as she watched, the woman's smile slowly faded to fear and sadness. Before she could ask why, the beautiful stranger began to scream. Her cries of terror filled the night.

Ember leapt from her bed, pulling her obsidian dagger free and rolling in a crouch, ready to fight an unseen enemy, her brain still trapped between the real world and the dream world. She quickly realized two things: firstly, E'lyse had yelled and might perhaps be starting labor, and was also the source of the screaming. Secondly, she was crouching with a dagger in hand, covered in sweat, and everyone was staring at her. E'lyse's shocked expression grounded Ember in the moment as the pregnant woman spoke.

"Too much has happened to you," E'lyse breathed between labored gasps as she lay with a stunned look. A rabid redheaded warrior was not what she needed to see just as she went into labor. Ember put her father's overly large dagger away, carefully slipped into her leather skirt, and kicked her deer hide bed covers out of the way. She decided not to even try to explain what had happened, realizing it was both too personal and complex. Besides, if E'lyse entered labor, all would be forgotten, no matter how it turned out.

When she moved to E'lyse's side, it became evident that labor had set in. The mat beneath E'lyse's bed was wet as the water of the gods had come, a blessing of the spirits given to all who bore children. It wouldn't be long now, hopefully. Some of the others from the group came to the hut now carrying water to heat by the hearth as well as soft leather and dry grass. The entire night and into the morning, E'lyse lay moaning and sweating heavily. Just beside her, Gar'ath constantly fretted, handing her water to drink from a clay cup and a clay dish with some soft food to eat. He looked more of a wreck than his pained wife.

E'lyse understood why, though she didn't broach the subject. She was resigned to whatever happened, life or death, and nothing would prevent the results. She supposed that she had at least a four in five chance of surviving the birth, and a good chance of surviving recovery. She was going to have at least one baby, whether it lived or not, or die trying.

Gar'ath, on the other hand, felt the need to somehow influence events. He couldn't just allow nature to take its course, yet he had to. E'lyse felt sympathy for Gar'ath's feelings of helplessness, so contrary to his way of being. But unfortunately, her sympathy ended upon the next wave of pain.

Later in the day, E'lyse's painful cramp-like pains became more regular and with growing frequency. The time had finally, mercifully, come. Several of the women tried to convince Gar'ath to either leave the building or, at least, remain out of arm's reach of E'lyse, but he simply would not listen to their suggestions, remaining beside his beloved wife. With her head in his lap, he stroked her long, dark hair as she pushed and pushed, her screams filling the longhouse. Any thought of speaking in the trade language was gone as she rambled on in her native tongue. Ember knew enough of the language now, and what she said sounded less than pleasant.

With the crazed look of someone forcing something large through something much smaller, E'lyse pushed, again and again, bringing the baby into the world through sheer will. This was a dangerous fact of life. The woman, the child, or both could die during childbirth and often did. A woman having her first birth was in the worst danger, such as E'lyse. If she and the baby lived through delivery and the first tenday, both were probably going to be okay. One could not be too careful until the first complete harvest had passed, for a baby was a fragile being indeed. If she successfully bore a child, any babies she might later have would probably come more easily and with less danger. Much as men faced life and death when they hunted in the wilds or defended their village, so too did women. In fact, a woman had faced at least one chance of death for each person alive in the world.

After a painful but relatively short birthing made smoother by Ember's calm and soothing songs, E'lyse lay with her newborn baby boy, Vander, happily feeding on his first meal, as much as an infant would. In fact, instead of suckling, many infants initially just licked or fell asleep, but that was natural. It would be a day or two before E'lyse's milk flow fully activated. Until then, baby Vander would make do as babies did. Gar'ath had suggested several other names, but E'lyse reminded him who had gone through the pains of birthing the child. She scolded him, speaking in her native tongue. All notice of Ember, and especially her odd waking behavior, was lost in her motherly bliss.

"It hurt me, but it only felt good for you, Gar," she whispered, perhaps half-jokingly.

"You didn't seem too hurt by the occasion," Gar'ath replied with a smile. Before he could say more, Kis'tra tapped him on the shoulder and pointed down. The floor was covered in blood, gore, and the placenta, as Ember and the others quickly cleaned up while keeping the new mother warm. Gar'ath quickly conceded the point. Ember decided not to point out the vicious fingernail marks dug deeply into Gar'ath's legs. They had told him to stay out of arm's reach of E'lyse, but he didn't seem to notice.

Beside the sleeping mother and baby, a small reed basket sat with the placenta inside. No one knew what the placenta was or why it was connected to the baby, but it was considered essential to keep it protected until it left the mother shortly after and detached a few days after birth. Such mysteries always fascinated Ember. For a long time, she sat staring at the baby and the odd tube coming from its stomach. Nearby, Gar'ath knelt praying to the gods and giving thanks that his beloved wife and child had lived, no small feat, indeed.

Ember sighed, a deep relief at the outcome. E'lyse had perhaps a two in five chance of death counting the birth and the next tenday. She lay back and played with the wooden goddess figurine pendant as she considered children. She was expected to find a man and do what was needed to make a child. The act wasn't without pleasure, for sure. Kis'tra made it seem like the greatest of after-hours pursuits, and yet it came with such a risk. There was a chance of a child for each connection, and with it, a significant risk of death. Was it worth such a risk for a bit of fun? The men seemed to think so, but they also had the least risk. And yet, so many women willingly took the risk, not just for tradition, but for pure joy and pleasure.

Glancing over, she saw mother and baby bonding, her loving husband watching over them both. Perhaps it was not so much about the brief moments of pleasure and more about the long-term joys? Creating a child and feeling such a deep love seemed to Ember like something worth risking a life for. If she would risk her life to save a child, wasn't that the same as risking a life to make a child? There was something illogical in her thinking, but she couldn't quite figure it out. So instead, she lay back, considering her other dilemma: the exotic brunette.

The next day, Ember made her way to the Widows' Hut to find and speak with the woman named Brigdha, or perhaps Breeda? She wasn't sure what she hoped to find, but her curiosity was simply more than she could handle, especially given the boredom of the cold season. She had a strange feeling that she was being driven by something more than just simple curiosity, though she wasn't quite able to pin down what it was.

Her emotions and thoughts had been a bit chaotic of late, though confronting their sources was certainly one way to sort things out. Ember was never one to do anything lightly.

As she approached the building, she found a warrior standing before the door. The concept of guarding something really wasn't a thing among her people. The closest analogy was someone standing watch over a field to protect the workers from animals or chase away birds. Still, it didn't take too long to figure out what the man was doing as he stood there brightly painted and holding a spear meant for hunting men. He noted Ember's apparent destination and addressed her plainly and in a curt fashion.

"Stop! Why, you-come?" he spoke in broken trade language.

"I come to see the woman, Brigdha," she said, using the Nes language she had learned over the past 70 days. To this, the warrior flashed an immediate frown, both at her request and her ability to speak his language.

"No. No one sees Breeg-da. Duruth's orders," he spat. For a moment, she stood there, unsure of what to do. Worse, that was perhaps the fifth different pronunciation of the brunette's name she had heard, and she still had no idea how it was properly spoken. Forcing her way past the man was always a possibility, but she had no way of being sure how he would respond. His spear was large and menacing, and while it was meant for hunting men, she suspected it would work just as well on a woman. As she took his measure, the man cocked an eyebrow, obviously noting her intentions. He stood stoically, almost daring her to try. Ember was amazed that anyone could be so bored as to look for a fight just to give themselves purpose.

I should have come long before now, she thought. She wasn't entirely sure of the politics that surrounded the hazel-eyed brunette. Still, she suspected if she waited a few days, things might calm down, and she might try again. That, or one of the guards might slip up and leave the door open for her to wander in. Flashing a grimace at the warrior, she turned and left for the traders' buildings to help E'lyse. She would wait for the right moment to make her move.

"Stupid guard with your stupid spear. I bet no one likes you," she muttered as she wandered away.

Over the next few days, E'lyse and the baby continued their bonding, and life went on. After a day or two, E'lyse's milk began to flow fully. It was the second day since she had given birth when a local woman had stopped by with a child whose mother had fallen ill and asked E'lyse to feed the infant along with her own. This sort of communal feeding was commonplace and kept children alive as there was no other food source for a child so young aside from sheep or goat milk, which came with its own problems. Given that she could not work having just given birth, E'lyse quickly agreed to care for the second child, also providing her with a task to justify Nes feeding and housing her. This was how people lived – looking out for each other.

Several days passed without incident as the cold season slowly passed. Ember stopped by the Widows' Hut many times, yet it remained guarded. She had considered sneaking in at night when perhaps the guard might not be present, but she had discovered only a few days before that indeed the guard remained, even at night. At first, this simply annoyed her, until she began to consider why the tribe might be guarding the brunette. She didn't understand whether they feared someone doing something to Brigdha or perhaps the brunette herself doing something to them. Her days of wonder ended at the news of another incident.

The first and the second deaths since their arrival had been considered by many to be potential accidents, isolated tragedies. But even the most fervent naysayers gave in upon this next death. This time the victim was a woman named Caladis. She had apparently relieved herself in the woods the previous evening and had been returning to the village when she was killed. Her head showed a similar bump, but not enough to have caused death, but enough to arouse suspicion. Of course, it was entirely possible that she could have fallen, hit her head, and simply died of exposure. But many clues suggested that this wasn't what happened. Besides, how many people of Nes could die the same way in a single cold season?

Firstly, her eyes were open. If she had been unconscious from a fall as she died, her eyes would have been closed. When people died while conscious, like someone being murdered, their eyes tended to remain open. Secondly, the blood was pooled in the front of her body, causing it to darken. If she had died slowly by freezing, it would not have pooled so quickly, as her body temperature would have been lower before her heart stopped, and the darkening would have been much less pronounced. The people of Nes didn't understand the science behind this, but they had observed enough dead animals while hunting to have a general understanding of how bodies reacted to death. If a person died abruptly, the blood would be warmer when the heart stopped, causing a greater degree of darkening to the skin below the body, which is what had been observed.

There hadn't been a set of tracks from anyone but the woman, but a gentle snowfall that night would have obscured them, especially if someone had actively tried to hide them. Furthermore, she had died so close to the tree line that she would have been able to cry out had she been conscious and injured, which meant that nothing added up unless her death was a murder. So, the question became, who, how, and why? The most likely cause was an evil spirit, of course, but there was usually a reason for spirits to attack, which left the entire tribe frightened and searching for answers. It was only a matter of time until people were summoned to the courtyard at the center of the tribe.

There were many calls for something to be done to cleanse the tribe of the wrongs against the gods and spirits. She had heard such sentiment for many days, but now what had started as a simple spark had become a roaring fire. Out of the conflagration of raw emotion fueled by fear of the unknown came cries for punishment and sacrifice. But, above all, one name stood out.

"Breeg-da!"

As the traders from Tornhemal joined the rest of the villagers arguing over what was to be done, cries for the death of Brigdha filled the air as people desperately sought something they could do, some act they could take against an unknown foe. Priest Duruth stood before the gathered people, the group of elders at his side. While Ember wasn't close enough to hear them in detail and wouldn't have fully understood them even if she had been, it was apparent from their mannerisms that they were arguing with the rest of the villagers over what to do. At first, she thought the calls for vengeance would abate as order and reason took hold, but then she heard the scream.

A group of villagers stepped forward all but dragging the hazel-eyed brunette across the courtyard toward the priest. She was barefoot in the snow, blood dripping from her knee where she had obviously tripped and scraped it. The scream Ember had heard had likely been hers only moments before. The men dragged her through the village until they stood before the priest and elders. Brigdha was thrown to her knees, though this time, she only offered a simple moan. For a brief moment, Duruth gazed dispassionately at the woman at his feet, then held his arms aloft to silence the crowd.

"Be silent! The gods have again shown us their anger! We can no longer wait to see what they want. We must act to protect ourselves. Over this past cold season, the elders and I have thought on this matter, and I believe we have concluded unanimously. We believe it very likely that Breeg-da is the reason for the anger of the gods and spirits," he announced as the elders nodded approvingly. All around, there were screams of anger as more than one person brandished a weapon. Before anyone could act, the priest threw his hands out wide once more, indicating that people should wait and listen.

"Hold! You must not be angry at this woman, this Breeg-da. It was not her choice to escape death. Any of you would have done so in her place! It is possible to anger the spirits by no deed of malice, but by simple defiance of their will, even in ignorance. In her own way, she is also a victim, but as much as it pains me to say, her choice to live must be corrected," he concluded. As he spoke, many nodded in agreement, though Ember could tell that not all believed she was simply an unfortunate victim. Villages were really collections of extended families. Almost everyone knew one of the dead reasonably well, which made emotions soar. Poor Brigdha cried on her knees in fear, understanding where these events were headed yet having absolutely no way to control them. Ember found herself caught in the moment, a lump forming in her throat over the fate of the poor woman. She knew that resigned look of helplessness and it hurt her to see it.

"This is not right," she said to Kis'tra, Sv'en, and a few others from the group who stood nearby. "They will kill her." The others said nothing, but their looks seemed in accord with her own.

Duruth continued (translated by Nor'Gar).

"It is the determination of the Elders that Breeg-da, the widow, will be given to the gods in three days' time. She will now be taken and prepared for the offering. We can only hope that her sacrifice will appease the gods or whatever spirits she has offended." Duruth finished his speech with a look of regretful necessity. Ember stood, unable to move as the enormity of what was to come sank in. Brigdha was to be killed, and for what? Nothing about this seemed like spirits or the will of gods to her. Spirits didn't sneak up on you in the woods. They killed you in front of your friends and family without care, from illness. As for gods, their anger usually manifested in a bad harvest or something similar. This smelled human. It also smelled disgustingly wrong.

A warrior fights to save the lives of those who cannot protect themselves. She fights for what is right, no matter what... If I am a warrior, then that is what I must do, she thought, a tear in her eye and a lump in her throat. The brunette was to be murdered, and something about this pained Ember deeply. She had been a victim, her will entirely usurped by powerful men. No one had rescued her – no hero had arrived to save her. Ember had never been one to back away, and she was no coward. This woman could not help herself, so Ember would become her hero. The question now was not whether she would do anything… but what she would do.

CHAPTER SIXTEEN

THE RIGHT CHOICE

Ritual sacrifice has been part of humanity, probably for as long as there have been humans. The reasons vary, but the root is likely a product of our sentience. Being sentient means that humans comprehend their own lives and mortality. Death is one of the greatest fears of human beings and, as such, probably amounted to the ultimate "gift" to appease a deity, spirit, or even another human. Interestingly, human sacrifice is not always unwilling. Many examples of ritual sacrifice have been documented as having "willing" participants.

It is easy to look at the people of Nes as acting abhorrent or immoral, but from their perspective, the gods were very real, and failure to appease them could mean the death of scores from famine or disease. Without knowledge of diseases, how might they have looked upon Brig'dha being spared an illness which killed everyone else who came into contact with her longhouse? Perhaps Ember will do something about this before another falls to the "will of the gods."

Ember watched as the majority of people left, including the traders from Tornhemal, her friends. The elders and the priest stepped into their communal building to prepare the sacrificial woman. Brigdha knelt in the snow where she had been cast, tears flowing freely. She was surrounded by over three hundred villagers and yet entirely alone. She was a foreigner, an outcast, and now a scapegoat, and soon she would be no more than a nameless woman lost in the dusts of time, forgotten.

Ember's heart ached for the poor woman. She couldn't stand for this. She would have to do something, but what? She briefly considered trading the chunk of hard water for Brigdha's life. Unfortunately, she knew that wouldn't work. The frightened people of Nes needed to feel like they had done something to stop an unseen enemy and would likely just take the precious blue item from her and murder Brigdha anyway.

Ember caught up with the rest of the group, who had gathered in another of the guest buildings, leaving E'lyse and her baby alone with the travelers from the True South. The last thing she needed was stress when nursing two children. When Ember stepped in, her eyes told anyone who looked upon her what she had planned. Kis'tra, Ena, and Kat'ja had seen that look before when Ember had confronted the large man in the forest. She had fought him, and she had put her life on the line to save them. Nor'Gar quickly shut the leather flap door and motioned for everyone to quiet.

"Borjk, stand by the door and keep watch. We want privacy. What these 'earth people' want is vile," the High Hunter said, using a slang term for those like Ember's people who farmed larger fields and lived in the newer ways. Pausing to let his words sink in, he continued, "Gods can take life, I know this better than many," he said, referring to his wife, dead from childbirth long ago, one of so many taken by time and chance. Around the room, many nodded or muttered in agreement. To Ember's shock, even Aya seemed disgusted by the prospect of human sacrifice.

"Gods can smite with lightning, storms, the might of nature! What god hits someone over the head? Each victim had a bump on their head. A man or woman is killing these people. We must leave before we are a part of this evil. In three days, the woman will die, and we must be gone before then or become tainted by this crime," he spoke with finality. Many began to murmur agreement. Their trades had been very good, and the worst of the cold season had indeed passed. It was a bit early to leave but manageable.

"kedh, apu'Breegdah?" Ember spat in her own language, drawing confused stares from the gathered forest people. She was so upset that she had forgotten the language barrier. Then, taking a moment to breathe and blow the long red hair from her face, she spoke again in the Tornhemal language.

"What of Brigdha?" she asked, laying her objection before them almost like an accusation.

"We cannot let her die," Tor'kal added, most uncharacteristically, as silent as he usually was. All around, there were nods of agreement, though a few seemed hesitant. Of course, they were no warband or hunter group, and such a martial decision needed to be unanimous. Ember watched as those around her began to argue and debate. She thought fast, trying to think of an argument that would sway them. If they disagreed, she would try to save the wayward brunette on her own, though she had a terrible feeling how that would end.

"How would we stop them?" Nor'Gar asked as much as pleaded, searching for an answer. How could perhaps twenty traders free a woman from a village of three hundred? The task was daunting.

"We cannot all fight, and there are more than ten of them for each of us," Kat'ja spoke in fear.

"We could try and trade for her?" Ana added. Ember looked around frantically, watching expressions change from outrage to desperation, some settling on resignation. She had formed a basic plan involving a small group sneaking in at night to rescue poor Brigdha, but it wasn't going to work if she couldn't get enough support. Unfortunately, fear was beginning to sway the group just as the momentum had been growing. Even Aya, who had so uncharacteristically seemed interested, was now wavering. Ember frowned, wishing to ignore the grouchy Aya. She seemed to care more about her own status and Ven'Gar's than anyone else.

"We could die if we try and fight them," Zhek added to much agreement.

"Fight them? I'm too old for war. No, we cannot fight them. If anything is to be done, it must be another way," Nor'Gar spoke with finality. Ember's anger began to spike as fear and doubt began to take hold among the group. Then suddenly, Aya spoke.

"Ven'Gar can do it," she said, causing the discussion to pause. All eyes met with the honey-braided woman with sharp hazel eyes and pursed lips. Ember consciously closed her mouth, her anger suddenly on hold as she awaited the typically adversarial woman who had suddenly spoken up at just the right time. Even Ven'Gar shot her a confused look, not entirely sure what he was supposed to do. Aya dug her hands into her hips and regarded the rest of the group with mild disdain. Discordant though she was, the woman wasn't one to back down.

Not only would this daring rescue boost Ven'Gar's position, and by extension, hers, but she also had a soft place in her heart for the woman. She had been an outcast as a child, yet no one had stood up for her. She would never admit it aloud, but the larger part of her reason for rescuing this Brigdha woman had to do with her own past. If that meant working with the rakish redhead, then so be it.

"Nor'Gar is far too old for a fight, and we are too few to fight. However, suppose we were to sneak in at night and rescue her. In that case, I'm sure Ven'Gar would take the lead," she said, pushing up against Ven'Gar in a not too subtle gesture informing him that her suggestion to everyone else was more like a commandment to him. Ember hoped her shock didn't show. Not only had Aya taken a stand, but she had proposed essentially the same plan Ember was going to suggest, though with her prized Ven'Gar as the leader.

"Will we just walk through their entryway?" Zhek asked a bit incredulously. Aya ignored him and continued speaking as though he had not just raised a valid point. In fact, Nes was surrounded by a wooden palisade. Ember had never considered it an effective defense until now. This was a part she had not yet worked out, but by the confident look on her face, it seemed that the ever-grouchy Aya had.

"You of all people should know how we will get in. You and Kis'tra sneaked out of an unfinished part of the wall to 'enjoy the night' when we first got here, if I recall." As she spoke, looks of recollection and slight embarrassment overcame both Zhek and Kis'tra. In fact, they had slipped away quite often but had switched to sneaking behind a building where food was stored after the snows fell. *Leave it to Aya to know where everyone was and keep tabs on all rivals*, Ember thought, rolling her eyes.

"Aya is right! We will sneak into the main building and sneak her out after we have seemed to leave. We can use this unfinished part of the wall if Kis'tra can show us where it is. Ven'Gar should lead," Ember added, giving Aya a neutral nod and hoping she didn't anger the ambitious woman too much. The plan sounded a little less convincing when she heard it spoken aloud, but she stood behind it. Setting up Ven'Gar for a courageous act of bravery would do nothing but help his status among his people, which would likely bring Aya to her side. It was a delicate dance, but Aya had actually started it. Most of the group simply stared back at her confused, perhaps waiting for more detail, but Sv'en dove in before anyone could object.

"We could probably sneak in and get her out in two days. After that, she could hide in the woods for the night and await our departure."

Ven'Gar frowned, "No, that would seem too obvious. She could also die in the woods if left alone for a night. That is no place for a woman." He stopped when he realized that Ember and Aya were independently glaring at him for different reasons.

"I don't know why I even speak sometimes," he said, throwing his hands up, a touch exasperated. Ember and Aya both laughed, then caught sight of each other and promptly stopped. Brushing the laughter aside, Ember suggested a modification to the plan.

"What if we leave early the day before she is to be killed and come back to get her that night? Maybe a small group?" There was a murmur of agreement around the room. Nor'Gar smiled as it looked like the group was putting things together, his eyes finally settling on Aya and then Ember.

"You have the cunning of a fox, and Aya has the tenacity of a badger. Yes, these are good ideas. There are other tribes south, and we can avoid this one for a few harvests. They will forget in time, and once the killer is caught..." the High Hunter spoke as a cunning smile began to replace his earlier doubt.

"Are you sure it isn't the spirits?" Aya interjected, cutting him off. Nor'Gar frowned as he spoke, "I've lived a long time, and I have seen the work of gods and those of men. Just as I can tell a wolf's prints from a fox, I can tell this. This was the work of a man." Aya nodded after a moment, though she still seemed apprehensive.

"Or perhaps a woman?" she added, drawing a smile and nod from the High Hunter. Ember was glad to see her coming around. It had only taken most of the cold season to finally convince her that she wasn't trying to steal her Ven'Gar. Then, rolling her eyes in exasperation, Ember turned to the group, already deep in discussion. The remainder of the night was spent discussing the details of the rescue. Nor'Gar sat back and watched as Ember took a crucial role in the planning.

If my brother had been born a woman, you'd be his spitting image, he mused. But, unfortunately, he would never know what happened to Winterborn of the Dark Forest People, though he liked to think his wayward brother had found whatever had driven him off into the wilds almost twenty full harvests before.

The next day, the entire group was in a state of high alert with both their plan in the works and the danger of an unknown killer. Most of the tribe, as well as Nor'Gar's group, walked in groups of two or more wherever they went, and no one wanted to go out at night. It had been ten tendays since the group had arrived, and the general mood of the tribe was dower. The deaths had unnerved people, made worse by the announcement by the priest that Brigdha had angered the gods by cheating death. Ember didn't believe this one bit as she had already learned how completely random the gods' wills could be.

Unfortunately, the general consensus among the people tended to affect the "conclusions" Duruth "came" to when he gave his speeches explaining the mood of the gods and spirits. As a result, he made populist and often rash choices. Ember and her friends would make the right choice. Ember wondered if the actual will of the gods could even be known by any person. Perhaps the deeds of a brave person were their true will. If so, she concluded that these priests and holy people merely existed to help people become comfortable with their own decisions. Either way, gods and spirits aside, Ember had a will of her own.

The early morning of the second day after the meeting, only one day before the sacrifice, the group from Tornhemal had finished preparing to leave. The ground had a sprinkle of light snow, and the days and nights were cold, but the cold season had been decently manageable. Therefore, it was probably safe to journey a full two tendays earlier than usual. The group would move slower with the cold, but everyone was ready to leave. Even E'lyse would be able to keep up the pace, having given birth many days before. Her thankfully healthy son, Vander, was wrapped in a large beaver skin bag with a leather strap looped around her neck. Vander was further warmed by several of the rabbit furs which had not traded. E'lyse's kept her open vest pushed into the bag, just under the furs. This would keep both of them warm and allow Vander to feed as needed along the way.

Nor'Gar had kept his tone neutral when the elder, and spokesmen of the tribe, had come to him asking why the group was leaving early. He had informed the man that his people looked poorly on human sacrifice and could not attend. He wished their tribe the best of luck and that he would be on his way. Within a short time, the people of Tornhemal had said goodbye to any friends they had made and the people from the True South who were not planning on leaving in such cold. And then they were off, all twenty-three in total, counting Vander, back toward the camp a full two tendays or more away to the Northeast.

The final night before the sacrifice, Brigdha lay on a worn leather mat near the back of the large communal building listening to an elder woman chanting. Her hands and feet were bound with bark fiber cordage. Over the last two days, the Elders had performed a series of cleansing rituals to prepare her for the gods. Her hair had been washed, and her body cleaned, washing away the magically protective paints she usually wore. She had been stripped and coated with scented oils by the elder women. She now wore a simple woven wool wrap skirt of fine quality. It was of better quality than anything she had ever owned, yet she couldn't care the less.

Brigdha was terrified. She had not been an adult but a few harvests, and yet here she lay being prepared for sacrifice. This was not the way it was supposed to happen. Her husband, companion, and friend Mohdan had died in her arms from the sickness. She had hoped it would take her as she watched him die, but somehow, she had been spared. Now she would be killed by these frightened people to appease their gods. Her mind raced through fear after fear as her anxiety rose. This was her last night, and soon it would be the morning of her final day. It wasn't made any better by the nonstop chanting of the elder, which drilled its way into her skull like an itch she couldn't scratch.

She couldn't even perform basic warding spells or properly invoke spirits or her gods with that cursed noise. If she were less stressed, she could probably have ignored the older woman, but the stress has inflamed her senses. Though autism would not be understood for many millennia, Brigdha felt its effects as the sound grated on her every nerve, all but choking the life from her. She wondered how much longer it would be until she simply welcomed death as a release from the sound.

Her greatest worry was that her spirit would become lost if it were given to another god. If she died and was offered to the gods and spirits of another land, how could she be with her family in the afterlife? Would the Moon Goddess take her in her arms and deliver her spirit from these vile people? That particular fear worried her more than any thoughts of death. That was the nature of blood rituals, one of the reasons her people banned them. Controlling and enslaving spirits was a perversion of nature and an offense to the gods.

Her anxiety-fueled terror was briefly interrupted when Duruth entered the building and came to kneel beside her. He smiled with an expression of sympathy. She would have bitten his face off if he would just move a little closer, but the wise priest kept his distance. Taking her head softly in his hands, he looked at her tear-streaked face with a deep sadness. She couldn't tell if it was real or a mock emotion, but in the end, it didn't matter.

"I do not want this, but if it is the will of the gods, then it must be. Will you take food your last night?" Food? The vile son of a wild boar would kill her because he needed someone to blame for murders he couldn't solve, and here he was asking about food? At least he had interrupted the damned old woman. Her constant chanting was nearly enough to make anyone welcome death. She gave a sarcastic chuckle which turned into a sob. No one would save her, and she would be killed for no reason. How could she worry over food now? She would spit in his face if she were not so profoundly depressed. After a moment, Duruth merely stood and walked away, accompanied by the sounds of hundreds of bone beads adorning his woven wrap.

As he left, he heard the elder resuming her chanting. It was critical to keep any malicious spirits away from the sacrifice lest they taint her spirit before properly offering it. Duruth felt sad for her, but he knew in his heart that he was doing the will of the gods. The streak through the sky last warm season had signaled the attention of the gods of the sky. They had sent signs when they required people to do their will. Unfortunately, it had taken him until now to realize that will. He felt sad for those who had died before he understood the messages, but he had done the best he could to interpret what little information he had.

Stepping outside, Duruth was comforted by the light of a full moon. He stepped over to the sacrificial area, a large wooden frame where a person was tied, arms and legs spread, and their neck opened with a knife. The structure was set so that the individual would lie at about a 45-degree angle with their head pointed mostly down. At the bottom was a large clay pot that would catch the blood for the primary ritual, afterward. He could almost see the frightened woman on the frame, and the thought pained him. She would be cold as her blood left and filled with fear, yet she had done nothing more than upset the natural order.

He would risk the ire of the gods and give her herbs to make her calm, he decided then. While sacrifices were usually unclothed, he would allow her to be covered in furs, keeping her warm as her blood ran, a significant concession. He supposed that these acts shouldn't anger the gods much as they seemed only displeased that she had escaped death, not for any deed which warranted pain or suffering. She wouldn't know what was happening nor experience great discomfort, and would slip away without much pain. It was the best he could do.

At that moment, he heard a rustle in the bushes not far from the palisade, near the unfinished section. Most of the tribe would be asleep by now, leaving much of the village deserted. Duruth wondered who or what had rustled the bushes, though he supposed it might be a pair of lovers. It was a bit cold to abandon a warm building for a bush. Still, he had forbade people being out alone until the sacrifice. As he approached to see who was brave enough to disobey his direct command, the whole world suddenly exploded in light, and stars filled his eyes.

The club had been aimed at his head and was already swinging to hit when Duruth started moving. His abrupt and sudden motion forward had taken the man swinging the club by surprise, and the end of the club had only clipped his head. Truly, luck was with the priest at that moment. He stumbled forward and fell onto one knee. His head swam with confusion as he looked behind and saw a man, a farmer from one of the outer parts of the tribe, stalking forward with a club in one hand and a rabbit fur in the other.

Ɔ Ɔ Ɔ

As the Dark Forest People of Tornhemal left the lands of Nes, two scouts remained some distance behind the group to ensure no one followed. The goal was to get everyone who wasn't involved in the rescue as far away from the village as possible. If they succeeded and returned with Brigdha, they would likely be followed for quite a distance by a group of particularly unhappy former customers. The rescue team could probably move fast enough to avoid them, but E'lyse and her child, as well as Nor'Gar, would have trouble with such a pace. Giving them half a day's head start had been decided to be the best strategy.

After heavy debate, the rescue team had been selected two nights before: Sv'en, Tor'kal, Ven'Gar, Ember, and Aya, who refused to let Ven'Gar run off with Ember where she couldn't watch. Nor'Gar had tried to argue with the women, but Ember had reminded him that he had called her a warrior, and she had survived wolf attacks, obsessed hunters, and the Great River. Aya had just ignored him, unphased by the mighty hunter. He had finally conceded, realizing that there was no way he could win against both Ember and Aya, who ironically made for a formidable pair when collectively arguing against a common foe. Nor'Gar opted out, due to his age, entrusting the leadership of the rescue to Ven'Gar, which delighted Aya.

When the Sun had reached its zenith, the group had found itself far along a small brook where they had stopped for a quick rest, and so the team could prepare. Ember had coated her face in soot with large white clay spots crossing her face, like an exaggerated version of her usual face paint. If it had been warmer, she would have painted her entire body the same. She wore her long doeskin shirt and loincloth, along with her leggings and leather boots with grass insulation. She wore her obsidian blade at her waist, while across her back was strapped a quiver with twelve forest people style arrows and the light hunting bow she had been given, her feathers secured in her fiery red hair.

Off to her right, she caught sight of a lynx high upon a rock outcropping. The cat was hard to see with its light fur and spots. Ember flashed it a smile, approving of the predator's "choice" in body décor. A lynx was a good omen for a hunter, but she was unsure if that also applied to a warrior. The lynx suddenly vanished, as lynx did, in the deep forest. To her left, she caught sight of Aya chanting softly as she painted her face with ash. Beside her, Ven'Gar did the same, though their chants sounded slightly different. Forest people were said to be magical, and they were definitely more likely to chant rituals than Ember's people. Yet, even her people would ask the gods and spirits for help before a task like this.

Ember stood before the group dressed as a warrior, her face and body painted and a weapon across her back. She was no man, but who said that a warrior had to be a man? She felt powerful like something had been awakened within, a sense of adventure mixed with fear and exhilaration. There was a feeling of immortality and idealism guiding her toward danger. Such sentiments had led many young warriors to their deaths. Ember had nearly died four times since leaving her home, which reduced her immortal feelings of youth a bit, but if she died, at least she could tell the gods she had made the right choice.

The world went black once more as he was kicked in the stomach by the attacker. Duruth felt a sickening ache through his abdomen as he doubled over. Peerth? Was that his name? The man came to stand beside the priest, though he spared Duruth another kick, at least for a moment. Where were the warriors? They were nowhere near the longhouse, and at least one should have been here. If he survived this, he would need to start assigning more of them at night to guard. It was odd what the mind thought of in such a dire situation. It was the sort of disassociation his consciousness needed, perhaps to objectify what was happening. Or maybe, just because he had been kicked too hard.

"Well, everyone's asleep for the big day tomorrow, Duruth... man of the gods," the attacker spoke with obvious disdain. "My wife would be there, but... she died. Remember when the sickness took her? Do you remember? I doubt you do. But I remember you, Duruth," the man spoke with eerie calm, a calm that was merely the eye of some great storm of hate. The incensed man towered over the priest, his very silence following those eerie words spelling the promise of what was to come.

"Who... Peerth? What are you talking about? What is this?" Duruth asked, his head throbbing in pain. His mind spun, still quite jarred from the blunt trauma he had received. Vaguely, memories of a woman associated with Peerth began to return, but it was hard to think. All Duruth wanted to do was let go and embrace sleep. Unfortunately, he knew it was a slumber from which he would never awaken if he did.

"Yes, it is Peerth. I am surprised you even know my name. I harvest the food you eat. Since the start of the world, my family has lived on this land, yet I don't think you have ever spoken to me. You ordered some of the women to look over those traders, the sick ones. You said your magic would protect them. You said the signs showed that they would recover. You sent her into that blighted place, and she fell ill. Do you remember?" Peerth babbled on. Suddenly the priest understood what was happening. His addled mind was slower than usual, but the pieces had finally fit into place as his vision began to solidify.

"You are the killer? You did this because your wife died?" Duruth asked as neutrally as he could, hoping he might keep the man babbling until a warrior came. Anyone as upset as Peerth might welcome the chance to spill their grievances and hopefully buy him a little time. Unfortunately, he couldn't scream for help as the younger, stronger man would likely kill him with a single impact to the head with whatever it was he had first used, and this time he would not miss.

"No!" Peerth spoke, his voice wavering on the edge of screaming. Behind him, the nonstop chanting from the elder in the main longhouse drowned the man's voice enough that likely no one would hear.

"I am not a killer. I am the hand of the gods! It came to me as I watched her die from the sickness. I watched your medicines fail and the elders dancing for nothing. Elders… dried chaff to be winnowed. The gods gave us the tools to perform their will. They gave us strong arms and hands. The reason they're angry is that we listen to people like you. I guess that means I'm just as guilty in a way. I should have realized this so long ago, but how do you give up what you have always known, even if it's a lie? How do you see what is true?" he said, lifting the club.

You're beyond reason! You have lost your mind, Duruth thought, though little good any realization would do him at this point. These were not the words of a man longing for any sort of mutual resolution. These were the words of a man who had been pushed beyond any normal reasoning, though he suspected that more might be involved than simply the death of his wife. While Peerth seemed to think the priest had never paid him much mind, it was hard not to know anyone in a village of only 300 people. Peerth had always been violent and had been involved in many altercations. Duruth suspected that the death of his wife might have simply been the final tug that snapped the wool, or so the saying went.

"You hit people with the club to knock them down and then smother them with that fur? Is that how you kill without leaving marks?" Duruth asked, still stalling for time. Though it sounded strange when he said it like that, the technique had allowed for many deaths to occur before the manner of death was determined. If he had outright bludgeoned his victims, it would have been much more noticeable. Instead, the lesser wound was easily mistaken for the injury sustained when somebody simply fell.

People always felt that they had "reasons" for their actions, often a supposed injustice. People whom society would consider "bad" typically considered themselves on the side of justice, wronged, and deserving of some sort of recompense. Life was not entirely so black and white, at least in the subjective. Perhaps he would try and make this one complain about his injustice until help came. He was sure he had heard a person in the bushes near the palisade. The memory of the bushes had only just returned as his mind continued to clear. Though he wondered why help had not already arrived.

ɔ ɔ ɔ

While the dark of night had come, the Moon still bathed the world in its soft, revealing light. This was a problem for the rescue party, yet there had also been no time to wait for a better day to rescue Brigdha. This was one of the reasons they had painted themselves dark in ash. There had been a cultural and religious component, as one always painted themselves for the occasion. Ember's own people considered unpainted skin to be indecent, and a warrior's paint also served as a sort of magical protection against harm. The Dark Forest People of Tornhemal didn't have quite the same strict viewpoint, but they also considered painting for the occasion if the event was important enough.

Quietly, Sv'en, Ven'Gar, Tor'kal, Ember, and Aya crept toward the large snow-topped berry bushes just beside the missing section of the palisade, not one quarter of the way across the village from the main longhouse. They hardly provided much cover, but given their painted bodies and the darkness, at least as dark as it was, they would probably give them enough cover. No one was visible, not even someone relieving themselves. In a village this large, that was a stroke of luck and a sure sign of the favor of the gods, though luck could change as fast as the wind.

Ven'Gar turned to the women as if to ask them to wait, but their determined looks stayed his tongue. Aya was not someone to be pandered to, and Ember had already faced down a hunter in single combat, something he had not done and was glad that he had not had to do. He shook his head and moved off towards the palisade, taking the lead. When the group arrived, they saw no warriors, and with luck still on their side, no one at all. The young leader looked back at the small group of rescuers, placing his finger to his lips. It wouldn't do to be caught this deep in a foreign village.

"They are probably sleeping to ensure they are ready for their sacrifice tomorrow," Sv'en said. Rituals were often held early in the morning or late in the evening. If this one was to be held early, it would certainly explain why no one had stayed up late.

"Or, too afraid to be out," Aya added. Everyone nodded in dark agreement. *Just let that killer bump into us. I'll carve a toy out of his face,* Sv'en mused to himself, quite bored, and stuck in the back of the group. Beside him, Tor'kal merely waited, quiet as ever yet determined to prevent injustice. Beside Ven'Gar, Aya knelt, her expression intense yet hard to read. Everyone knew she was ambitious, yet her genuine interest in saving a stranger had puzzled the group. It wasn't just that she wished to share in the glory of Ven'Gar's leadership. Instead, she seemed to have taken the situation quite personally.

While Aya's motivations remained a mystery to anyone who had not grown up feeling utterly isolated as she had, Ember's motivation was much plainer. The radical redhead was simply the kind of person who could not sit back and watch misfortune consume the innocent. The group had realized her motivation as soon as she had entered the longhouse, only moments after hearing of Brigdha's fate.

She had made it very clear that if her friends did not help her save an innocent woman from what was obviously a string of unrelated murders, she would take it upon herself. As luck would have it, the people of Tornhemal detested human sacrifice on a cultural level. Moreover, they were a group of young, adventure-hungry traders who had already chosen to leave their village for a chance to experience something different. It was the perfect combination of youth and altruism, but it was also a recipe for disorder if Ven'Gar didn't keep a hold of the group. These were not seasoned hunters. Worse, nearly half of the party were women, an idea Ven'Gar could barely wrap his mind around.

Unfortunately, that fiery spark of altruism which drove the reckless redhead took hold. Ven'Gar cursed beneath his breath as Ember leapt from the brushes and made her way house by house all the way to the communal longhouse in one quick journey. The rest of the group simply watched her leave, unsure of what to do other than simply follow. Ven'Gar had been about to propose a plan of action, but he had obviously taken too long. Even in the brief time they had known her, it had been evident that Ember had a short attention span and more impulsivity than a red squirrel. She was more like a fox than a wolf.

"Well, we don't want to be the last ones there, right?" Aya said, cutting off Ven'Gar before he could speak. She abruptly stood and began making her way toward the large longhouse using approximately the same route Ember had taken, both women leaving the men behind. Sv'en, Tor'kal, and Ven'Gar exchanged a look.

"We will tell no one of this part of the rescue," Ven'Gar grumbled, to which the other two men nodded in agreement. A moment later, they stood and began following the same path the women had taken.

The large, communal longhouse sat close to the palisade on the Eastern side of the village, abutting a hill, which afforded safety. This required the group to traverse much of the village, a significant but unavoidable risk. Glancing behind, Ember quickly realized that she had rushed forward too soon. She had honestly expected to be immediately followed, and yet here she stood alone. She knew that she should wait for the others to approach, but there was always the possibility they might have encountered someone and be simply unable to follow. Time was of the essence, and the longer they remained, the higher the chance that someone would notice them. Now was not the time to wait.

Ember pulled out her large obsidian dagger and poked a tiny hole in the mud and straw wall between two large poles at the back of the building to take a peek. Lying on a leather mat in the back corner of the longhouse was Brigdha. The room was dimly lit by the central hearth, yeah flooded by the sound of an elder woman endlessly chanting some sort of ritual song. Her eyes misted as a lump formed in her throat at the sight. It had not been that long since she had been bound to a tree awaiting violation and death.

I bet you think that everyone has forgotten you... that there's no hope. I am your hope, a fox in the night come to rescue you, and I have a blade for anyone who stands in my way, she thought as she blinked to clear her eyes. She wanted to burst in right then, but she knew the rescue would be a team effort. She took a deep breath and waited for the right moment as the first member of her group arrived. Unexpectedly, that first person was none other than Aya. Her honey braids had been tied extra tightly, though one was slightly loose. Her face wore black streaks of soot, at odds with her lighter leather long shirt and similar clothing to Ember. She glanced at Ember for a moment with what might almost have passed for a smile, though she quickly regained her defiant composure.

"Let's do this," she mumbled, then quickly advanced to the edge of the longhouse to keep watch as the rest of the group began to arrive. She was pretty sure Ember was not going to make a move on Ven'Gar, but she was not sure the same could be said for him or that she entirely trusted Ember. Suddenly, she heard a muffled sound, like someone hitting something, followed by an odd sputtering sound from around the corner. Turning her head to listen, she thought she could hear the sounds of a person speaking, though she could not make out the words. Behind her, she could hear the rest of her people as they gathered at the back of the longhouse. Reporting what she had just heard would have been the safest choice, but curiosity was ever so tempting. Aya leaned around the edge of the longhouse, hoping to catch a glimpse of who was speaking.

Before her knelt a man who looked very much like the priest named Duruth. Behind him stood another man with a wooden club. It was hard to be sure, but it seemed as though the standing man had just hit the kneeling man with the club. As she watched, the two men exchanged words. Was it her imagination, or did the man with the club have the same build as Ven'Gar? The front of the longhouse blocked the Moon's light from his face, but even his voice sounded like her lover. He had only been just arriving at the back of the longhouse when she had crept around the corner. The timing didn't make any sense, but Ven'Gar was fast. If that wasn't her lover with the evil priest conquered at his feet, who else could it be?

If she was standing beside him at the very moment the rest of the group caught up, the deed would become linked with them both. Not only would the tale of the brave rescue include Ven'Gar standing over the defeated priest, but her name would also be sung along with his. It was a prize too glamorous to be ignored and certainly something to be acted upon quickly before pesky things like reason, logic, or random redheads caught up. Aya rushed around the corner to join with her lover before the rest of the group advanced.

At least that rash redhead didn't beat me to it, she mused.

"You will not live long enough for help to come, Duruth," Peerth said in a matter-of-fact tone as he slowly stepped forward with his club. He knew the priest was stalling, waiting for help to arrive. But it wouldn't be fast enough. If a warrior appeared or someone screamed, he would simply swing the killing blow. In fact, it was taking nearly all his self-control to keep from ending the man's life. He knew he was being foolish taking the time to speak. Duruth would learn the truth when he was in the gods' hands, yet he couldn't help himself. Something simply had to be said. Some feelings couldn't be held forever. And then something very strange happened.

Suddenly a foreign woman came rushing from behind the longhouse aiming directly for both men, a most unexpected event. Duruth saw her approaching and tried to cry out for her to seek help, but he was still very dizzy, and he was having trouble keeping conscious. Peerth stood before the priest, absolutely caught off guard by the strange soot painted woman rushing toward him with the most bizarre expression of enthusiastic delight.

A...w...k...w...a...r...d... he thought. This was bizarre and definitely not in his plans, but he was open to change. If the gods wished to send him such willing sacrifices, how could he help but oblige? He lifted his club, ready for another victim. As the woman approached, both men now recognized her as one of the forest people from Tornhemal. Her presence made absolutely no sense, yet there she was.

"The gods send me more work, I see," Peerth said, causing the woman to slide to a halt nearly at arm's reach. Peerth was still bathed in shadow, but she was now close enough to see the difference in his form as well as his voice. She stood in sudden terror, so shocked at rushing into the face of what could only be the killer.

She knows, Peerth thought. *She knows what I am. She has been sent to me as another sacrifice. This must be a new task! I understand you and I am your hand!* He stepped forward with his club, passing Duruth, who was still too stunned to stand. *I'll kill her, and then I will kill you. Don't worry, tonight I will paint the world in blood!*

ɔ ɔ ɔ

Aya froze in her tracks as fear washed over her. She had thought the man before her was her lover, the evil priest at his feet. Yet it had been some random man from Nes. Worse, the club in his hand and the wild look in his eyes told the story all too clearly. This was the actual killer; it had to be. Just as Nor'Gar and Ember had predicted, it was a man, not a god. He stalked forward, a club in one hand and a rabbit fur in the other. Aya stood there gripped with fear. The man approached and lifted his club. His sheer size and intensity held her still, even before he reached her. She was too terrified to turn and run as death itself approached.

"Aya, drop!" yelled Ember from behind in her unmistakable accent. For once in her self-absorbed life, Aya listened. The sound of someone she knew reached out to her like a hand in the darkness. It wasn't an action that made sense, but it was an action she could perform. Aya dropped quickly into a crouch, unable to do anything more than follow commands, her scheming and bravado reduced to shear obedience in the moment.

When she fell, Peerth's eyes followed her in confusion, then began to rise as he noticed movement in his peripheral vision. In less than a heartbeat, he started to focus on the person behind Aya, a woman painted for battle and wearing an angry expression. As Peerth's eyes focused, they began tracking an object approaching him at high speed. His brain determined that the new woman had thrown something and that he should move, but a moment too late. A hand-sized rock slammed into his face breaking his front teeth and sending blood spewing from his mouth. Peerth stumbled backward, clutching his ruined mouth, right into the waiting arms of Sv'en, who had just come up behind him.

"Hello! Don't fall yet!" Sv'en said and quickly put a flint dagger across Peerth's neck, opening it to the cold night air.

"Okay, now you can fall!" Sv'en pushed Peerth towards the frightened Aya and stood there with a victorious look and a blood-soaked blade. Peerth came to a stop just before the crouching woman, blood pouring from his mouth and neck, looking at everyone now gathering around him. Forest people, a group of five of them. He slowly dropped to his knees and then to the ground. *I was the hand of the gods... I was the...* and his world went forever black.

Duruth watched the scene before him and waited for his turn to die. There could be no doubt that they had come for Brigdha. She was a forest person, like them. He doubted they were from the same place as Brigdha's original group, who had come from far to the West, over the Greatest River. He knew the group from Tornhemal came from farther north. Perhaps they simply felt a kinship? Either way, they had killed Peerth only to replace him. Exactly how many people wanted to kill him, and why had they all picked this night? Duruth nearly chuckled at the irony.

Suddenly, a leather boot strung with nettle fiber and stuffed with dried grass landed beside his face. He rolled over and looked up, his head still spinning, to find a fiery redhead, a river dweller by her look, looking down at him with an enormous obsidian blade in one hand and a merciless look in her eyes. Barely the length of a man away stood another man with dark, curly hair, a strange, playful smile on his face, and a flint carving knife in his hand. He decided to keep his mouth closed and hope that the redhead was more rational than the man she had just defeated. And then, she spoke.

"Man… not gods," she said, indicating the dead man. "Your life for Breegda's life? Will you trade?" Duruth understood the woman, though her words were heavily accented and not so well spoken. This young woman, hardly old enough to be joined, would trade his life for the sacrifice's life. He had no doubt she would kill him, and he was far too weak to escape with a head wound, chased by a dexterous person thirty harvests younger than him. Besides, even if he escaped her blade, her friends would finish what she started. He sighed as he realized he had only one choice.

These people from up north drove a hard bargain, but he now saw that Brigdha's life was not meant to be forfeit. This had been staged by the gods for some reason, perhaps a test? He would have time to uncover that later if he agreed, or he could ask them for the answer right now if he refused. A life for a life seemed quite adequate to the defeated priest. He nodded and said, "Good trade," forcing a weak smile. The redhead towered over Duruth, her face and body painted in the way of a warrior, dagger in hand and bow at her back, her hair blowing in the wind. For a brief moment, Duruth thought he felt something, like a presence. Was this woman more than she seemed?

"Ehg ne'kerord dhue…" she said in her river people language, then stepped over the prone priest toward the longhouse door.

☽ ☾ ☽

Brigdha lay bound and without hope. She had considered biting her tongue and killing herself, but she couldn't bring herself to do it. The pain would be great, and she was too frightened. Her life had been a series of unfortunate events culminating at this dark point. She had never known her father, reportedly being a trader from a distant tribe, and her mother had died when she was young. Even her marriage to her now deceased husband, Mohdan, had been arranged and not born of love. Robbed of family, friends, and love, the only thing she had left was her beliefs. Above, the light of the Moon filtered through the hole in the roof used to vent smoke.

Before she had left on her ill-fated trading trip, she had sought to become a priestess. She had studied the Moon and even had a knack for reading portents. But in the end, what did the gods matter? If they were worth any of this, she would have been freed. She sat back, wondering what death would be like. Would she be absorbed and consumed by some evil god of a foreign land, or would she return to the gods of her own land? Perhaps she would disappear into nothingness, and the world would continue along without her. She mumbled yet another prayer to the Moon Goddess, though she was nearly out of the emotional strength to do much more.

Her thoughts were interrupted when the old woman watching over her suddenly coughed and choked, sounding startled. She had been chanting loudly for a long time, and Brigdha was glad that she had stopped. Offhandedly, she hoped the elder had choked and died. She and her fellow elders had been chanting non-stop for three days. It was enough to make her nearly welcome death as a release from the song. She could barely move, her hands bound, and her head hung low in shame and sorrow.

Suddenly, she heard the sounds of people entering the longhouse and the elder responding excitedly, though not in a positive fashion. Whoever had come had done so in the middle of the night, and their very presence had alarmed the elder. Had a mob grown tired of waiting and come to kill her this very night? At least she would be free of the singing, and a mob wouldn't have the divine power to sacrifice her properly to the evil god, so she might actually have a chance of making her way to the Moon Goddess.

"Taseh geneh!" she heard a low, yet feminine voice speak with an accent and language she had never before heard. Brigdha looked up, whipping her neck to drive the hairs from her face enough that she could see who had come for her. As she lifted her head, the scene before her was sudden and frightening. Her tear-soaked eyes had trouble focusing, and her hair still covered part of her face. Several people were entering the room, one of them standing before the elder.

In her blurry vision, she made out one single figure coming straight at her with what looked like a knife. So this was it – she was going to die now. She had not expected her executioner to be one of the younger women who treated her so badly, but the person approaching was obviously no man. She closed her eyes and held her neck up, hoping it would be quick and clean, an end to the pain that had become her life.

Suddenly, her hands were free. She opened her eyes in surprise, caught entirely off guard by the strange turn of events. For a moment, she thought she saw a fox spirit baring its teeth before her, but she quickly blinked her eyes and looked again. Instead, a radiant redhead was smiling back at her. Brigdha was stunned. She hadn't expected anything could

273

distract her from impending death, but the emerald eyes gazing down upon her filled her with hope, and so much more. It was like the blood had returned to the corpse of her empty life.

"Kehp aeis, Breegdah!" the redhead said in her thick accent, almost playfully. The redhead seemed much more disturbed by what she had found than she showed, her smile plainly forced. Though Brigdha didn't understand the words, the intent was plain. These people, and this woman, in particular, had come to rescue her. There would be time for questions later. For now, there was only time for salvation. Weak as she was, Brigdha wrapped her arms around the woman, her hero, and felt the woman's strength lifting her from her fate, raising her anew.

With strong arms and a gasp of exertion, the redhead lifted Brigdha to her feet. Her legs stung from a loss of blood from being bound, though they would quickly recover. Brigdha held the redhead tightly as she felt the blood returning, and her strength with it. Then, as delicately as a child pulling a petal from a flower, the redhead removed the strands of hair from Brigdha's face with her free hand as she supported the freed woman with the other. Even beneath the warpaint, she could see that it was the redhead she had met during the trading day. The shock, the beauty, and the relief were all too much for her.

Brigdha wept.

Sv'en stood beside the old woman wagging his finger in her face and holding a bloody dagger. She had finally stopped chanting when a knife was put to her throat.

"Maybe I am also a shaman. You want to meet the gods? I can show you how, or you can be quiet. shhh..." the toymaker said with a smile.

CHAPTER SEVENTEEN
THE GREATEST RIVER

Yersinia pestis bacteria is responsible for one of the most feared diseases of history: The Plague. While it is often thought that the plague was introduced to Europe from elsewhere, evidence of Yersinia pestis has been isolated in the teeth from graves in Europe as far back as approximately 4500 years ago. If this was the infection that killed Brig'dha's husband, and everyone else in the house, then Brig'dha is extremely lucky to have survived. Bubonic plague, spread by infected fleas, could have easily destroyed the entire village of Nes. Interestingly, their choice to burn the building likely saved their entire tribe, though they had no knowledge of this.

The next morning, the rescue party caught up with the people of Tornhemal. They had walked the entire night and so quickly that their pace was barely sustainable. However, Brigdha turned out to be in decent physical shape and capable of walking after being given a short time for her legs to recover. Luckily, it didn't seem that any permanent damage had been done, though she would still have marks around her wrists and ankles for many days to come.

As soon as they caught up with the group, everyone stopped for a quick break to ensure everything had gone well before continuing. They were nearly a half-day walk from Nes, using a less than direct route. Nor'Gar had found pursuit unlikely, given the nature of the people of Nes. He had explained that they would likely call a meeting to determine the proper action, and those deliberations could last for a few days before action. This was the way of some larger villages.

Ember was not wholly convinced, given how intently people had sought Brigdha's death. She had been followed many days' journey and ambushed by similarly incensed men, and she had little trust that Duruth would keep his word. He had an entire village seeking vengeance and closure that he would have to control. Given what had happened, he would probably try and focus peoples' anger toward someone else, lest they turn on him, and Ember was certainly a possible focal point. She had taken their sacrifice. Worse, the dead man represented a failure in their beliefs and leadership.

As everyone sat and took a quick break, there was little discussion of the rescue. Brigdha was present, and no one was harmed, which was what really mattered. Food was passed around, and water poured. Brigdha sat beside a tree wearing her sacrificial woolen skirt and a cloak of sewn rabbit furs Ember had stolen from the longhouse. Her feet were covered in simple leather shoes, pieces of leather cut to form a protective shell around the feet and sewn tightly with nettle cord. They were hardly proper footwear for the cold, but the elder Ember had liberated them from needed them less than barefoot Brigdha had.

Brigdha slowly ate a mixture of dried bread, ironically procured from Nes, as she drank water from a water carrier made from a goat's bladder. She had eaten almost nothing for three days which meant that she desperately needed food to keep marching, yet her body wasn't ready for anything but the simplest bread and water. By the evening, she would probably be ready for something more robust, such as salted meat.

As they ate, Brigdha said nothing and kept her head down. Ember could plainly see that it was a mixture of exhaustion and rattled nerves. Brigdha didn't seem frightened of the group, though that made sense. Any group willing to risk their lives to rescue someone was unlikely to immediately harm them. Ember felt terrible for the brunette and hoped she would perk up after getting some food in her. She, of all people, had some understanding of how Brigdha must feel. She had experienced captivity, the constant threat of violence, and the trauma that paired with such things. It wasn't something someone forgot after they were merely given food and a short rest.

Ember and the rest of the group quickly ate their food and prepared to journey once more. Unexpectedly, Aya stood and walked from her lover towards Brigdha and Ember. She came to stand before the redhead, initially saying nothing. Ember peered up in full expectation of some mean comment, her mouth full of food, but Aya held a serious and thoughtful expression. The two women simply stared at each other for a short time. Aya examined her enemy's face for a long, awkward moment and then nodded her head once. Her words seemed forced but sounded genuine.

"Thank you," she said. Then, quickly, she stepped away, blushing deeply. She needed to be alone after all but having admitted her own failings. The redhead had saved her when she could have just as easily let her die. She had never been anything but adversarial to the river woman, and Ember had never once made a move toward her lover. She had also helped position Ven'Gar, and by extension, Aya, for an act of bravery sure to win them both status, precisely what she had wanted. She had even saved an outcast from a tribe who had never respected her, something Aya understood all too well. It was all her pride would let her say, but she couldn't live with herself if she hadn't.

Kis'tra and Ember glanced at each other with stunned looks. Ember had nearly choked on the unleavened wheat bread she was eating. They were unsure what had overcome Aya, but she suspected it was shock from her near-death experience. Ember's own mindset had also changed in only a few moons' time. The primary catalyst had been multiple near-death experiences mixed with a complete change in her environment and the sudden need to be empowered and take control of her life. It was amazing what nearly dying could do to the living.

Beside them, Sv'en stared at the scene with total interest as he chewed his food. He had always found life amusing, but the strange ways people interacted with one another was the most amusing part of all. Carving toys was one of his specialties, yet what really interested him was simply observing the people around him. Humans were fascinating creatures if one took the time to observe. He chuckled under his breath as he watched Aya finally maturing. He suspected she might even make a good elder someday once she stopped acting so childish.

The little badger finally relaxed. Ha! he thought with a laugh. After the small meal and a moment to relax, the group resumed their travels north. No one spoke to Brigdha about her experience out of respect for her privacy and to give her time to come to terms with the horror which had almost consumed her. She was weary and mentally exhausted, but her body was strong, and her will rejuvenated. It would probably be some time before her mind began to heal, but as she set out after nearly three days with barely any food and only a small meal in her stomach, Ember wasn't the only one impressed at her vitality.

The gods made forest people strong, Ember thought with a laugh, though she caught herself looking a little too often and scolded herself. Brigdha needed time to heal, not someone pestering her. Of course, she reminded herself that she was half forest person, as well. Besides, the beautiful brunette would likely have her eyes set on a man soon enough. Ember fancied all types of people, though she found women to be the most beautiful of all. Sadly, that was a desire far too uncommon to hope for, given how few people she had encountered in her short life. She sighed, wishing it were not so.

⊃ ⊃ ⊃

Brigdha stood and stretched, her legs still hurting from three days lying on a hard floor. Yet even in pain, there was elation. Oddly, the two most prominent thoughts on her mind were her freedom from ever having to listen to the elders' chants again and those emerald eyes which had risen at the dawn of her freedom. Few were ever given such a direct and expedient reprieve from fate, but there was nothing quite so wonderful as a hand reaching into the water to save one from drowning in the sorrows of life. The redhead was the most prominent savior on her mind, and yet she wasn't the only one.

She was supplied with spare, warm clothing from anyone with extra gear, to her amazement. One by one, people came by, dropping off spare clothing while she sat there, too stunned to even thank them. She was not so good with thankyou's, anyway, having always found verbal communication quite stressful. She had endured life so long among people who loathed her very existence that such a life had begun to seem quite natural, like a storm that would not pass. She had escaped with a simple rabbit fur blanket and old worn leather shoes the redhead had liberated from the finally silenced elder and her sacrificial woolen skirt. Yet, she now wore a strange mix of clothing, but she was, at least, warm.

Before they left to continue walking, she had obtained an old beaver-skin cap from an amusing man named Sv'en, brown furry mittens from an exotic looking woman named Kat'ja, thick leather leggings and a short goatskin loincloth from a woman named Ena, and a long leather shirt and warm dried grass stuffed leather boots from the group's leader, a man named Nor'Gar. Forest people came from small villages where everyone knew each other quite well and tended to look out for one another, sharing everything as needed. Yet such a gesture from people she didn't even know brought tears to her eyes. As she wiped them, the memory of those emerald eyes returned to banish negative thoughts before they could form.

The weather was calmer than usual for this time of the seasons. The ground had a light coating of snow, but nothing too thick. The wind blew only a little, and the Sun provided a bit of warmth to Brigdha's skin. The warming Sun would set soon and was only in the sky for a short time each day, though this length of time was growing. Due to the light snow and calmer weather, the group made good time through the temperate wilds as they traveled towards the Great River, at least two tendays or more to the Northeast. The distance between the group and the village of Nes slowly grew, and with it, her relief.

Duruth stood before the tribe that morning, helped by a younger man. He wore the wounds and the bloody clothing of the previous night, a personal choice intended to convey a point. All around, people stood in astonishment at what had happened. There were many gasps and looks of shock from the bewildered people of Nes. Apparently, a climactic battle had occurred between their spiritual leader and either the gods or some evil spirits while the rest of them had slept. Everyone fell silent as Duruth cleared his throat.

"Last night, as I finished performing my rituals, I stepped out of the ritual longhouse for some air. As I took in the night, I saw good man Peerth struck down by the Gods themselves!" There were gasps from the villagers as he continued to theatrically describe the smiting in detail. Behind him, one of the elder women wore an angry smirk, but she had been told in no uncertain terms that if she spoke, she might be found to be "possessed." So, she kept her mouth shut and watched the show as Duruth continued, though not without intense eye-rolling.

"...and so, I checked and saw that he had been killed! I knew what had to be done, so I immediately entered the longhouse and killed the woman right then and there. Had I waited, someone else might very well have died this morning!" With luck, the people were buying his outlandish story. He had dragged the man into the longhouse where he would "examine" the body and have it buried before anyone could see the less than spiritual wounds. He hoped the people would accept his story, though only time would tell.

Peerth would receive a proper burial, which he might not have deserved, but then again, Duruth had a hand in his wife's death, if only by chance. It was all quite sordid. Mostly, he hoped that the will of the Gods had actually been settled. There was no way to be sure, but those green eyes continued haunting his memories. Had she been a woman with a fox spirit possessing her? Duruth shook the memory from his mind and concentrated on the storytelling. His back hurt, and he had a headache worse than death.

☽ ☽ ☽

The third day into the trip, the group arrived at a sheltered area between a thick forest and a steep hill. The wind was broken by the natural barriers, providing some shelter. This made it a good place for a camp.

They stopped early in the day after having moved farther than usual in the past few days. Most of the group made open-air camps around a central fire. In contrast, Ember and Kis'tra made a temporary lean-to hut against a large rock using the poles Ember carried. The women placed mats over and below to ensure a comfortable sleep. Fires were quickly ignited, and many removed their boots and let their feet warm by the fire. Keeping both feet and footwear dry was an extremely critical goal for any traveler. Failure to keep your feet dry could result in a multitude of terrible illnesses.

Before doing anything else, Ember took a few moments to stretch and just breathe. Humming a song under her breath, she flexed and bent each muscle, something she did every day. Afterward, she quickly crawled into the hut and removed her boots. She took Kis'tra's boots and placed them beside her own, just close enough to dry by the fire but not too close, so the leather wasn't damaged. Then, she quickly sang a short prayer to the fire spirits to clean the boots of any negative spirits they might have picked up from the ground. She knew that such prayer could be of great importance when ensuring feet stayed warm and dry.

After a few moments of warmth, Ember quickly expanded her lean-to with additional poles and hides from Gar'ath and invited E'lyse, her baby, and husband inside. E'lyse was in a generally acceptable state, given the rapid hiking with a baby. Gar'ath had carried her load as well as his own while she cared for the baby, as was expected. Luckily, breastfeeding the baby provided all the nutrition it needed for the first few seasons. E'lyse placed water in a clay pot by the fire to warm so she could clean little Vander, who had developed a most unsettling odor. Ember watched the general gore being removed from the bottom parts of the baby with a rapidly growing nausea.

I cannot imagine having one of those. They are only deceptively cute, she thought.

Needing fresh air after witnessing such gore, she left the lean-to and set out to find the woman named Brigdha. She found the brunette by herself on the other side of the large fire where most people had set up camp. She seemed lonely and lost in her own thoughts, likely worsened by the Tornhemal practice of not inquiring about somebody's life story for at least a certain period. It was probably a reasonably good practice, but sometimes people needed to speak, so she would do her best. She had wondered about Brigdha since she had first seen the out-of-place woman laboring in a field all those moons before.

Noticing the redhead, Brigdha looked up, her eyes filled with caution, then quickly looked away. She had been saved, but no one had said much of anything to her in three days. She didn't know her place with these strange people, and no one seemed willing to provide much information. Of course, she disliked interaction with most people, especially people she didn't really know. There was a certain peace and calm in not understanding nor being expected to understand her rescuers' language. Her lack of eye contact had also been expected, making her less-than-common interaction methods socially acceptable, at least for a time.

As Ember looked, she noted a space beside the brunette where she could sit. The brunette's body language was hard to read, but while it spoke of apprehension, it did not outright reject interaction. One could learn a lot from body language if one took the time to look. Given how little the brunette said, which had really been nothing, she supposed that learning to read her body language was looking more and more like a valid way to communicate with her.

Ember examined Brigdha in greater detail. She was nearly a hand taller than Ember, owing to her forest people heritage. Her long brown hair was wavey and cut at different lengths, being quite unkempt and poofy. The large mass of hair held a series of randomly placed braids of differing lengths. Her eyes were lovely hazel orbs, seemingly larger than most eyes Ember had seen. However, this was probably somewhat of an optical illusion. Her lips were thin yet well placed on her soft, brown skin, giving her a striking appearance, though she looked similar to the people of Tornhemal.

She had removed her leggings and shirt, wearing her rabbit fur cloak and loincloth as she soaked up the fire's warmth and let her main clothes dry. Through the cloak, Ember could see strong arms and legs, muscular and defined from a life of hard work. Brigdha was larger than her and probably stronger, yet her mannerisms conveyed what could only be described as softness. It was a juxtaposition that stood out to Ember, captivating her in the moment as she noticed it.

As Ember approached, she slowed, watching Brigdha as she gently worked to patch one of her boots. Her gentle movements belied her physical strength, seemingly delicate to a degree that stood out to Ember. As she watched, the brunette carefully laced a piece of thread through a tear in the leather of the boot, pulling it ever so gently through the hole she had made with a bone awl. Next, she placed the thread between her lips and carefully punctured a new hole in the leather. Why was she watching this, Ember wondered, yet here she stood, all thoughts of her original quest suddenly forgotten. After a moment, Ember looked up and realized, much to her embarrassment, that pair of beautiful hazel eyes were regarding her right back. She had been caught looking, once again.

"Uh... Hello?" Ember said, her skin color beginning to match her hair. Luckily, Ember was darker skinned than most of her people, and blushes were a bit easier to conceal. She had no idea what language or languages Brigdha spoke, but she had to start someplace. To her surprise, she was greeted by large, hazel eyes and what seemed almost like the beginnings of a smile. Brigdha's smile was as slight and delicate as the first embers of a fire. If one blew too hard, the fire would never grow and burn out before it could. Ember took a deep breath, forcing herself to step forward and sit beside the brunette, as standing there staring dumbfounded would do little to help the situation.

"My name is Kaelu," she said, speaking in the language of Nes. She was not proficient with it but hoped the brunette spoke it. Oddly, the shy woman said nothing in return. She wondered if it was possible that the brunette had not learned much of the Nes language? But had she not lived with them for at least a full harvest? Could she simply not wish to speak? Some people were terrible at learning new languages. Her friend Blossom had never even been able to pick up the trade language, the opposite of Ember. It seemed unreasonable, but there was one way to find out.

"Name, Kaelu," she spoke in trade tongue. For a moment, Brigdha said nothing, merely taking the thread from her lips and twisting it between her nimble forefinger and thumb, then threading it through the new hole and pulling it ever so delicately until the stitch was tight. Ember caught herself watching and mentally shook her head to keep focused. How could watching someone sew be making her so...

"Name, Brig-dha," she replied with a thick accent after a moment, returning Ember to the moment. Her words were crude, but she had spoken them. This meant that she probably had a reasonably limited trade language vocabulary. Had she been using a limited understanding of the trade language to speak with the people of Nes for over a full harvest? This, too, seemed unreasonable, yet it was the only thing that made sense. If they were going to be together for a few days more, Ember would try and learn some of Brigdha's language or teach Brigdha her own. But first, she was curious where the brunette was from. That was something she could likely explain, even with the language gap.

"Breegdha, where you-from?" she asked, using her hands to gesture the words, as Tor'kal and Sv'en, only a short distance away, stared at her

282

in taboo-induced horror. It was too early to bother Brigdha with such questions, as the people of Tornhemal judged things. Yet Ember wasn't bound by the rules of etiquette of the people of Tornhemal. Brigdha looked at Ember for a moment as if thinking about how to answer. She had stopped sewing, and her mood already seemed to perk up.

"Kr'thal, Greatest River, [boat]. [20] day, north, west, Great River," Brigdha said, using her hands to indicate a boat and numbers. Ember frowned, unsure what "Kr'thal" had meant.

"No-speak, Kr'thal" she said, hoping the brunette would elaborate. Brigdha thought about it for a moment, absent-mindedly fidgeting with the string in her hands as she did. After a time, she waved her hand around, perhaps indicating the land. Then, she tapped the dark earthy soil before her and said, "Ethale." Ember supposed that she was referring to the world or perhaps the immediate surroundings, "Ethale," and using the ground to indicate this. Brigdha next placed two fingers on the ground and pantomimed walking. Suddenly, her other hand blocked the walking hand. "Kra," she said. She reiterated this display a few times until Ember suddenly understood.

If Ethale means world and Kra means end, then Kr'thal means the end of the world... Aeeya!

"Breegdha, you-from Kra Ethale?" Ember asked, pointing toward the West. To this, Brigdha nodded, seemingly pleased that Ember had so quickly understood her.

Ember was taken aback. Her suspicions had been correct. Here was a woman from possibly where she was supposed to travel. Could this be the task at the end of the world? Was this Brigdha somehow connected to her quest? In the many days since she had originally left, she had begun to consider the possibility Morning Dew had lost her mind, and yet, here sat a woman from the far West. She had to know more, but the language gap made things difficult. Ember needed to know for sure, so she pressed using a mixture of the trade language, hand gestures, and the Nes language, though she supposed Brigdha knew very little of that, hoping she was clearer.

"What is at end-of-world?" she asked, curious why the brunette knew the specific and probably uncommon trade words. Brigdha had probably had to explain where she was from before, which made a likely reason for why she knew them. Ember knew enough Nes language to generally understand what was said, but her vocabulary to speak it was still limited. She had mostly learned what she had needed to speak to the warrior guards, but not much else. Brigdha thought about her question for a little while and then slowly explained. For some reason, speaking to the excited redhead seem to be lifting her spirits, quite at odds with her normal anxiety over speaking to people.

"Great River ends. Great River become Greatest River. Very wide and deep," Brigdha said as she drew a line in the sand, indicating it to be the Great River. She drew the shore of the lands with wavy lines to show the Greatest River. Ember sat wide-eyed. If what she drew was correct, the Greatest River was hundreds of times as wide as the Great River. It appeared that the Great River actually became the Greatest River. More specifically, it seemed like the Great River suddenly became hundreds of times as broad and was then called the Greatest River. It was an odd distinction and something she filed away to consider later.

Brigdha drew a small shape, like an island in the river, not far from the river's mouth.

"Inn'bry'th," she said, pointing to the island. Then, pointing to herself, she said, "Isen'bryn." If Ember understood, she was from a tribe called the Isen'bryn from a land called Inn'bry'th, an island on the edge of the world to the West, in the Greatest River. Ember sat absolutely still, completely stunned by what she had heard. She was hardly a priestess and not exactly the most devout individual. Yet even she couldn't deny a sign this specific. The spirits had all but delivered the final piece of her quest into her hands.

Brigdha would need a boat to make it back to where she came from, a land far to the West where the Sun set. Ember just happened to have such a boat. If she could convince Brigdha to allow her to help her return to her homeland, that had to be the way to complete her quest. This had to be the will of the spirits. *If it's more mysterious than this, you can do it yourselves,* she thought as adrenaline flooded her veins at the thought that her quest might finally come to an end. Her thoughts were interrupted when the brunette spoke once more. It seemed that both women only knew parts of the Nes and trade languages, which complicated communications.

"Name not 'Brigdha.' Name Brig'dha," she said, stressing a slight pause between the first and the second part of her name. Ember had been so lost in her thoughts that it took her a moment to realize what Brig'dha was saying.

"Brig'dha," the brunette repeated.

"Breeg-da," Ember replied, elongating the "e" sound due to her river people accent. Brig'dha smiled, ignoring the accented part and simply pleased to hear her name mostly correct. For a moment, Ember lost all thought of the end of her journey as she gazed into those large hazel eyes. With a mental shake, she restored her concentration, but she still had more questions to ask.

"You go to Inn'bry'th, Breeg'dha?" Ember asked, using the correct pronunciation of her name, mostly. Brig'dha fidgeted with the shoe for a moment, unsure how to put her thoughts into words. The question was simple, but its implications were far reaching. She knew others spoke plainly, and without much effort, but for her, answers were always so complicated and taxing. Finally, after sorting through a few answers and calming herself, she spoke.

"No Inn'bry'th. No [boat]" Brig'dha said, sighing with finality. She was many days east of the Greatest River with no idea how to get there and no boat. Regardless of what she wanted, it seemed that her only reasonable course of action was to remain with her rescuers. Whether she fit in or not, it would be an upgrade from where she had just been. As she looked up, Brig'dha was confused at the beaming smile lighting the green-eyed woman's face. It was an intoxicating look of enthusiasm that spoke of a woman with a plan.

Suddenly, Ember placed her hands excitedly on Brig'dha's shoulders, all but blasting her wide grin into the brunette's face. Brig'dha sat wide-eyed, looking into Ember's deep emerald eyes and unsure of what might happen next. She hated being touched, normally. Yet, the random redhead's touch bothered her so much less. Her heart began to race as her breathing became shallow and quick, a flutter dancing through her body at the expectation. Then, just as she expected something entirely different, Ember began to speak excitedly.

"Kaelu and Breeg'dha walk Great River, to west, to Greatest River. Kaelu and Breeg'dha take-boat to Inn'bry'th together," Ember said, joining her hand and Brig'dha's hand to symbolize togetherness. Brig'dha searched Ember's face as if looking for truth. The sudden sadness of her failed expectations from a moment before evaporated as her mind struggled to understand the words and hand gestures. She had lived with the Nes for over a full harvest, yet her skill with their language was barely existent. She was a little better with the trade language, but only a little. Unless she had misunderstood entirely, the radiant redhead had just offered to escort her home. She had also taken Brig'dha's hand in her own, something the brunette had difficulty ignoring.

"You, Me, boat to Inn'bry'th?" Brig'dha asked, using hand signals to ensure understanding.

"Yes! I have a boat," Ember replied mixing words from the trade and Nes languages. Brig'dha sat there a bit confused, but the slightest smile crept upon her face. It had been so long since she had smiled that she didn't even remember what it felt like. Somehow, this chaotic woman could bring a smile to her face where no one else had in such a long time. She felt a flutter running through her body as she gazed into those rich, emerald eyes, a flutter with more than one cause. Then, realizing that she had stared too long, Brig'dha quickly returned to her sewing, simply nodding her agreement.

Over those many days, Ember, Kis'tra, and the rest of the Dark Forest People of Tornhemal had come to learn much more about Brig'dha, with Ember serving as her interpreter. The group's social mores against questioning people too soon eventually wore off, and the conversation did much to help Ember learn Brig'dha's language. It also seemed that Brig'dha was perfectly willing to answer questions, though she didn't say very much at any given time. Ember was starting to suspect that her silence was a personality trait rather than trauma from Nes or a language barrier.

Ember and Brig'dha spent those many long days of walking discussing their respective homelands. Ember seemed to have a knack for learning new languages and quickly began to pick up the language of the Isen'bryn. It sounded more guttural than her own but not significantly more complex. As it turned out, Brig'dha wasn't so good with languages, unfortunately. While she learned a few Tornhemal words and a few of Ember's most basic words, the pair spent most of their time teaching Ember the Isen'bryn language.

Brig'dha's people, the Isen'bryn, lived on the coast of the large island known as Inn'bry'th. There were many forest people tribes on the island, perhaps hundreds, though no tribes like Ember's people. She had left with her husband to seek dye and other rare items from the South not long after she and her husband had joined. Their journey had been a success, and their trade group had done well until they had become sick. Brig'dha had begged the Moon Goddess to save them and even the Sun god to save Mohdan. Following his death, she had cursed the Sun God, vowing to follow only the Moon. Her explanation had switched from calm to quite distraught as she explained her blasphemy and resulting vow.

As a result, Ember and the group at large had not broached those topics as they were none of their business and would likely be a source of pain for the already emotionally healing woman. Ember had been a bit disappointed when she had learned that Brig'dha had a husband, dead or not. It was the way of most women, and there was no fault in it. Ember had met so many wonderful women who would go on to find men to love. She would remain a friend to so many, close and yet always and forever at arm's length. Though she wished deep down that it had not been the same with Brig'dha.

Beyond questions of her past, Ember had many questions concerning the Greatest River. How wide was it? How deep was it? The answers she got back had been unsatisfactory. If Brig'dha were to be believed, the river was perhaps as deep as a mountain and wider than the eye could see. This seemed impossible, yet the brunette was adamant. Switching to other topics, Ember had even asked about Kanter's talking fish or bear people, to which both women laughed.

One of the most interesting things Brig'dha spoke of was the large stones erected on a hill near her village. The stones, according to Brig'dha, were as tall as a man and took entire seasons to erect. Every solstice and equinox, as her people understood them, the village elders would gather to perform rituals on the hill. The tribe would adorn themselves with paints and feathers, dancing for the entire night. Brig'dha told of how much she enjoyed the food, the rituals, and the beautiful body art. Each family tried to outperform the next in complexity and coloring. Thick black paints would be applied to the body in intricate patterns and swirls. The swirl pattern on Brig'dha's body was fashioned after some of these shapes.

As the group spent the next two tendays walking northeast, the friends talked and became closer, Brig'dha, Kis'tra, Sv'en, Ven'Gar, Tor'kal, Ena, Kat'ja, Ana, E'lyse, and even shy Eva. Aya kept her distance but gone from her face was the petulant anger. Instead, it had been replaced with some sort of respect. Ember would never be close friends with Aya, but she had won over the woman, a feat that she considered much more impressive than simply having defeated her with hateful words or the conquest of Ven'Gar, a man whom she respected, yet had absolutely no interest in.

Ember had missed this sort of close bond which she had shared with her friends in her village. It was nice to be around people she could speak to and laugh with. Ember was only saddened when she considered how soon she might give it all up for her chance to travel to the end of the world. It was the nature of life to love and lose, just as a flower bloomed and then wilted. Being natural didn't make it any easier, but at least it provided an explanation, a reason for why things were the way they were.

Perhaps the biggest problem was Brig'dha herself. Every time she saw those beautiful hazel eyes, a sense of sadness filled her as she remembered Brig'dha's tearful memories of her departed husband. She considered it quite strange how something that never was and never could be could feel like such a great loss. At least when she finally made it to the mysterious island at the end of the world, she could then look for someone to join with. Of course, it would be expected within a season or two, given her age. But would she find a woman to love or be forced to find a man?

Ember's thoughts were halted as she stepped over the edge of a rise only to be confronted by the mighty expanse of the Great River winding before her. Three tendays and three more days after leaving Nes, they had finally returned to the river. She stopped and slowly sank to her knees with a strange sense of accomplishment, though there was also loss. As if she understood Ember's thoughts, Kis'tra stepped forward and placed her hand upon her shoulder, stopping to gaze at the river. It marked a bittersweet moment for them all.

Ember would be leaving them soon, and the thought was enough to bring a tear to Kis'tra's eyes. Together, they gazed at the river, both knowing what it meant. The river seemed to be both Ember's salvation and the source of her greatest sorrows. It represented, above all, change. Change was like a mighty forest fire that burned away the old and beautiful trees she had come to love, yet would replace them with something beautiful and new from the ashes. Ember quickly dried her eyes before her friends took notice. It wouldn't do to upset any of them. Wiping his own eyes before anyone noticed, Sv'en stepped forward, having caught Ember's silent tears, and turned to address those nearby.

"She's probably crying because she can't swim until the warm waters come. Everyone knows she's part fish," he said with a chuckle. Several people laughed while others frowned, worried that his comment might upset Ember if she fully understood it. Beside him, Brig'dha merely stood watching the river without enough vocabulary to really understand what had been said outside of a few words.

"Don't be so crude. She has a destiny far to the West and will be leaving us soon. I believe she cries because we are her friends. I respect her for this," said Tor'kal, most unexpectedly. Many simply stood nodding their heads in agreement while also impressed that the man had said as much as he had in a single sentence, his first all day. Unseen to the group, Ember smiled, having understood what was said and appreciating the joke to cheer her up. *I will remember you, my dear friends,* she thought.

Over the next few days, the group maneuvered along the river to the warm season camp. Using landmarks and a keen sense of direction born from a lifetime of navigating the wilderness, Nor'Gar had intercepted the river only a short distance east of their camp. The accuracy of his journey was one of the most impressive feats of navigation Ember had ever seen. All the while, Ven'Gar had asked questions and memorized landmarks, perhaps hoping that he could take the next group on the journey. The young learned from the old. It was the way of things.

There was less talk as they approached the camp. Instead, everyone felt a deep sadness looming over what was to come. The group would spend perhaps three or four nights at the camp before continuing north to their lands, two or three tendays away. The rest would do E'lyse well, for she was quite tired from walking. Breastfeeding took much out of a person who was already expending energy hiking at the same time. She had to drink water often, and she ate significantly more food than anyone else, though she had lost some of her weight during the three tendays of walking with a baby who drank much of it away.

When the camp was located, the group entered and quickly moved about securing the area and checking on the status of the materials left behind. The rocks, being rocks, were in great shape, but most of the disposable mats and material had rotted into the growing area and would help produce better crops next season. In just a season, the camp had been overtaken by animals. Tracks from deer and smaller animals could be found everywhere. At least not much plant life had grown due to the cold season. Nor'Gar had explained that after a warm season unattended, the camp would become entirely overgrown by plants and small seedlings.

That night, the group sat around the hearth with a raging fire talking about the results of the full harvest's trip. They had many large bundles of woven flax, many exotic spices, pigments, beads, toys, spiritual items, and even seeds had been obtained. They would be in great shape once they returned. Unfortunately, they would have to say goodbye to their greatest find of all, a good friend, the warrior Ember. A lot had changed since the group had left Tornhemal. Vander was born of E'lyse, and now Kat'ja, Sv'en's lover, was showing what might be early signs of a child on the way. Sv'en had explained that she was just a hardy eater, though this comment had earned him a slap from Kat'ja. Even Aya had achieved her greatest hope, becoming the lover of Ven'Gar, a likely future leader of these long trips and assuredly on the quick path to becoming an elder.

As the night drew long, Ember slept under a starry sky to the light of a waning Moon. The wet season was about to start, but the night was dry and warm enough to sleep under the stars without being uncomfortable. She watched the stars as they slowly crossed the sky. Every now and then, she saw a streak of light pass by. As she slowly drifted to sleep, Ember considered how her life had changed and what was to come. She had made friends and grown so much since she left home, yet she felt like so much still lay ahead. She was a warrior, perhaps, a trader, a rescuer, and sort of a woman – maybe? That last part still felt odd. Perhaps most importantly, she was now a friend to Brig'dha, a woman she had just met and saved. If only there could be more between them... her eyelids lost their battle, and the restful redhead slipped into sleep.

On the last night before leaving, Ember sat beside Nor'Gar, warming himself by the main fire. For a time, the two just sat and watched the stars. She had not said a proper goodbye to High Hunter Nor'Gar and was having trouble bringing herself to do just that. After a short while, Nor'Gar started speaking. He did so comfortably using his native language, as Ember could now understand him reasonably well.

"This may have been my final trip south," he said with a half-smile. She turned to eye him inquisitively.

"What do you mean? You are mighty High Hunter Nor'Gar. You will have many chances to make this journey in coming harvests," she asked, more like a pronouncement than a question. He chuckled, finding her enthusiasm refreshing, yet his wisdom carried too much perspective to ignore the truth of his age.

"Ember, I grow old," he said. As soon as he had said it, he smiled and reassured the suddenly worried Ember.

"I won't be leaving any time soon, but my body cannot stand long days of walking anymore. It is time for younger men and women to take my place. Perhaps Ven'Gar. I think Aya may have finally relaxed a little," he said with another chuckle. Ember started to say something, but Nor'Gar cut her off with an extended hand followed by a smile.

"Do not worry for me, young one. This final journey has been my greatest and worthy to be my last. We traded well, made good friends, and saved a life. It's time for me to end my travels on that good trade. And you – I'm sure you will find whatever the gods wish of you, to the West." At that, Ember frowned.

"How can you be so sure that I'll make it?" she asked, perhaps more from her own self-doubt than valid skepticism. She had come a long way in such a short time, yet she was still so very young. The old man smiled, but remained silent for a short time before replying. When he did, he spoke more gravely, in the way of an elder. This would be his advice to her, a proclamation for her to consider.

"You have the heart of a warrior and the spirit of a fox. I've only seen one person like you before. My brother, a man lost to me long ago. Do not cry over leaving. Instead, rejoice in the chance to see the world. I see it in your eyes, that need to know what is beyond the next hill. You only live once in this world. I started trading long ago as I would rather have died living my life to the fullest, than wither away in regret," he said with a chuckle, "Now go and find out, Ember the Warrior," he said with finality. For a short time, they sat there in silence as Ember wiped fresh tears.

His words had moved her, not just as an elder, but for some unexplainable feeling of kinship to the man, as though he were a grandfather or uncle. Besides, to be called a warrior by an esteemed elder of a tribe was no small matter. Among her own people, to be declared as such by one of the official elders carried the weight of the people – it was official. To be a warrior was no small matter, either. He had also said that she possessed the spirit of a fox. All these proclamations would need to be considered in detail, but for right now, the only thing Ember could do was sit back and look at the stars as she fought to keep her composure.

After a short time, others came to the fire for a group social event. They enjoyed each other's company throughout the early part of the night, as they often did. The fire was always the place for people to sit and talk to one another. Ember was full of mixed emotions welling deep within. She opted to merely listen to the others speaking as the night progressed. She had dealt with such loss once before, and her heart ached each time. Even the sight of her new friend Brig'dha sitting on the other side of the fire did little to quell her feelings.

While she sat around the fire with the rest of her friends from Tornhemal, she breathlessly sang a mournful song of loss. Before she had realized it, her voice had become loud enough for several people to hear. At first, Ember was embarrassed, but Tor'kal encouragingly waved his hands. Ember looked to Nor'Gar and Kis'tra, finding approving glances. Then, she slowly began to sing a more cheerful song, aloud and for the entire group to hear. After a short time, Ember's words filled the forest and brought a tear to Nor'Gar's eye. Her people were singers and dancers by nature, and her song was uplifting and welcome. Even Brig'dha seemed enthralled by Ember's voice, perhaps more so than anyone else, though she kept her expression neutral. Ember enjoyed her final night with her friends, enthralled in song and dance.

The following day, Ember and Brig'dha left to a non-stop outpouring of emotion. In truth, Ember wanted to get the travel underway before she broke under the weight of so much emotion. It was one thing to leave on a journey when the possibility of return was reasonably high. But no matter how much she spoke to the contrary, Ember had a nagging feeling that she would never see any of them again. They would live out their lives remembering her as she would them, and yet their paths would never cross.

Sv'en and his toys, silent Tor'kal, her good friend Kis'tra, who was already showing signs of a child on the way, and Kis'tra's husband Zhek, not to mention all the others. Oddly, she was even going to miss Aya, who had somehow grown to respect her for reasons that still made no sense to Ember. Perhaps none hurt so profoundly as knowing that she would never sit with Nor'Gar again. There was something odd about the man that felt like home whenever she was in his presence, as though he were some long-lost uncle she had never known. It was silly, but she knew it would hurt.

She had said her final farewells and set back in the boat as Sv'en gave it a push with his foot sending them deep into the river and away from the Dark Forest People of Tornhemal, forever.

Was the short-lived beauty of a flower worth watching it wilt, she wondered?

CHAPTER EIGHTEEN
THE SPOILS

Hollywood would have you think that an arrow wound nearly instantly kills an enemy and that death was a quick and tidy affair. In reality, arrow wounds were some of the most painful and deadly of the ancient world. Arrow wounds typically found their way into the upper body and upper extremities, sometimes passing through entirely but often ricocheting or embedding within bone. In contrast, arrows that found the abdomen or chest would become so deeply lodged that removal was often fatal. Blood and bodily fluid mixed with the sinew holding the heads to the shafts, causing the heads to dislodge and remain stuck within the victim. Death from a dislodged head could take hours, days, or longer, leaving the victim in agony. Worse, historically, arrow wounds were rarely singular, with victims commonly receiving many. In short, the bow and arrow was a fearsome weapon: both deadly and debilitating.

Ember found herself back where she had started, drifting down the Great River in a small boat. The difference, this time, was her new friend Brig'dha, sitting just behind her, and a greater sense of purpose. Since that fateful sunny day nearly twenty-three tendays ago, she had traveled as a trader, been huntress and hunted, captive and captor, and now, perhaps, even a warrior. More importantly, Brig'dha had given her the purpose in her quest she had sought for nearly a full harvest. If life was about change, then indeed she had lived. She draped her hand into the cold river water as the boat drifted down the Great River feeling the raw power of its mighty current.

Sometimes, she wondered if quests and tasks were more about a person finding reasons to match their beliefs and less about "destiny," but she couldn't be sure. Too many events of late had been hard to quantify outside of fate, and her mind had trouble accepting the idea of not knowing why something happened. She had found that she truly enjoyed adventure, despite the sorrow and terror it occasionally evoked. It was partially her sense of wonder that helped drive her towards her goal. She let out a small laugh as her mind wandered.

Behind her, Brig'dha stared at the rapt redhead's long hair blowing in the wind as she laughed at some secret thought. Brig'dha really didn't know what was so funny, but she supposed that Ember had some deeper insight than she. Ember seemed relaxed and even carefree in the face of events that frightened Brig'dha to even consider. The night she had been rescued, the reckless redhead had, by all accounts, broken the face of the man for whose crimes she was to have been killed. It was even said that she had fought a mighty warrior from some other land and killed him with a single arrow. Ember always seemed to know what to do and quickly took the lead. For Brig'dha, this was relaxing as she often had plenty of trouble determining how to interact with most people.

Of course, that Sv'en fellow had told her the warrior story, and he had seemed a little too flamboyant in his telling. Besides, her understanding of the trade language had made even understanding the toymaker quite difficult. Ember had denied that she had killed the man, instead saying it was one of the dead man's own group who had done him in. Still, she couldn't deny that Ember had been the one to free her. Even the men of Tornhemal had called her "Kor'gha e'Kaelu'e," which meant Ember the Warrior, in Ember's own language, which she assumed they used out of respect. She wondered how they had learned Ember's words, though she suspected someone like Sv'en had probably annoyed the river woman into telling him. That thought almost brought a smile.

Ember was her savior, quite friendly, brave, and beautiful, in her own way. Brig'dha's people preferred women to wear a little more bodyweight, and Ember was built like a stick, though a muscular stick, to be fair. Brig'dha couldn't help but note Ember's well-defined arms as they hung over the side of the boat. Unfortunately, eyes would likely be her only experience as few women shared Brig'dha's tastes. She had never been attracted to men, which was a problem in a small tribe where no one else shared her way of being. It was natural and common enough for people of the same sex or gender to love each other, but there simply weren't enough people in her tribe to find a match. In the end, she had settled for Mohdan. Sweet, kind, Mohdan.

He had truly loved her and done everything he could to please her, yet he had never realized how she felt. She had given in and provided him the illusion of a loving wife. It had been difficult, especially when they were intimate, but she had seen no alternative. At least he had been gentle and kind, if not wholly unobservant. As the last member of her family, one of several small clans of her tribe, she had needed a place to go, a family to belong to. Yet, in the end, she had been left alone. Always alone.

The women of Nes had mainly shunned her, which had done nothing to help her find a companion. But, in the end, having a friend like Ember was at least something. Brig'dha sighed and pushed such thoughts from her mind. She had seen Ember looking at the man named Zhek when his back was turned, a sure sign of her oh-so-common interests. She turned her head to watch the scenery as she held the steering pole, not wishing to watch the carefree redhead, who represented something she could never have. Since she couldn't get Ember from her mind, she instead considered the stories from her past and how they fit the warrior woman before her.

There were odd similarities between Ember and a legend from her own tribe of a goddess named Brid'da, for whom Brig'dha was named. In the stories, the young goddess tracked and killed the vile beast Gho'taig, a shadow beast who could only exist in the dark of night. The beast had been unleashed by the god of snakes by accident. Gho'taig terrorized the First People, those whom the gods had made from river mud. For three new moons, Gho'taig had come in the night and taken children for his dinner. The First People were terrified with so many missing children and no means to fight such a creature.

Brid'da, daughter of the Moon Goddess and Sun God, was a mighty huntress, famed for her skills with the bow and her bravery. Though less told, she was also renowned for her crafting and healing abilities. During the next new moon, the mighty huntress found Gho'taig and slew him with an arrow of fire and freed the children. Then, to ensure that beasts like Gho'taig could never harm the First People again, she taught them the secret of fire. It was a story taught to children, yet it came to mind as Ember's long, red hair blew into sight, even as Brig'dha watched deer on the shore. She sighed once more, unable to keep her mind off the redhead.

Brid'da was known to have long red hair and was often depicted with blue or green eyes. Though she knew Ember was no goddess, she wondered if perhaps someone like Ember had been the basis of the story. It seemed entirely possible, as gods and spirits had actually walked among the mortal realms. Of course, she had often wondered how many stories were simply created to explain the world in an entertaining and memorable way. So, it remained an open question, one she could ponder on the long ride down the river.

The women spent the long day keeping the boat steady as they traveled the Great River. The water provided ample time, and the gentle sway and pleasant slopping sound helped relax both women into thinking over their lives and where they were going. Ember would occasionally sing a song as the two drifted, something she did merely out of habit. Brig'dha truly enjoyed her songs, though there was a tease to the sound, which brought with it sorrow. Ember's alto voice had a slightly rough timbre, which she found oddly pleasant, though most women she knew preferred a deep male voice. Her own voice was much higher-pitched and had always bothered her.

In the forward third of their small boat, Ember slowly drifted into another song, this one about rabbits which she had learned as a child. Beside her, Brig'dha's booted feet wiggled ever so slightly, acutely reminding her of the brunette's presence, as though she could forget. She forced her mind aside as dwelling upon her friend would only lead down paths she could never walk. Instead, she considered what she would do after she found the end of the world. Perhaps she could return to her tribe and see how Yellow Flowers was coming with her task, a beaded skirt or some such domestic chore. How would she put it?

Hello Flowers, I have beaten a man to the ground, twice, saved a life, journeyed to the end of the world, and seen the sights, so how's your dress coming? The prospect was delightfully petty, producing another giggle, though she would never actually be so mean to her former rival. Something about wolves chasing her and men trying to kill her had put such pettiness into perspective. Perhaps she could return to the people of Tornhemal or even organize such a trade group from her own people. There were many possibilities, though she still had a task to complete first. Most of all, she was starting to wonder if she really wanted to return to her people.

Ember laughed aloud once more. Reflection could be its own reward. Most women wouldn't be afforded the right to discuss such things, but if she could return as experienced as a hunter and with a piece of warm ice, she might very well find a voice among her people. She was still not sure what the blue rock was, but it was nearly twice the size of her hand and would emphasize her position, should she suggest a trading group to her people. She sat back in the boat and smiled at the thought. Behind her, Brig'dha sat, helping her steer the little craft down the river. She was still at a loss over what Ember found so amusing.

The introspection suddenly ended when a poorly anticipated change in the river's flow caused a splash of icy water to cover both women. The low ride of the boat was a constant worry and simply the result of two women in a boat really built for one. Luckily, Sv'en had given Ember two precious clay pots to scoop water out if needed. She hoped that another storm would not arrive, given just how low the boat sat in the water. Unfortunately, the pottery had to be traded for as the people of Tornhemal had not learned the techniques for making it, which made a water scooping pot a precious item.

The snow on the shores was melting, and the warm Sun was starting to win over the cold nights. The result was the Great River flowing faster and filling higher than usual. This also had the effect of causing their boat to move much faster than expected. At this rate, they could hope to travel many days of walking with each day on the river.

The women spent much of the first day keeping the boat steady as they sped down the river, taking occasional breaks in the smoother parts to daydream. After their first day, the changes were already apparent. The river here was twice the width of her home banks, and the flatlands were becoming coastal inlands, with greater numbers of reeds and scrub bushes than they had seen before. Ember was unsure how much farther they would have to travel, but Brig'dha seemed to believe they were getting close to the Greatest River.

The Sun was setting when Brig'dha and Ember steered their little boat into an inlet for the night. They pulled the boat ashore and placed a hide covering over the top to keep water and animals out. Ember unrolled two deer skins and placed them down to sleep upon, then got to work making a fire with her new fire-bow, a gift from Zhek, and some dry wood.

My hands thank you greatly, fire-bow, she mused. Brig'dha removed some deer meat from the traveling pack and then scouted the immediate area to find some other food if it could be locally had. That night, they ate local tubers, early greens, and dried deer meat. The local plants were still mostly unavailable due to the recently ended cold season but given a few tendays, they would sprout. Unfortunately, that meant fish, game, and a few odds and ends that could be gathered during their journey. It wasn't the most nutritious, but it would at least be filling.

As the night rolled in, Ember regarded Brig'dha, hoping for some conversation. The brunette still seemed timid from her ordeal, though that made sense, given what she had endured. It had taken Ember many days to even begin to recover from what had happened to her. In truth, she wasn't entirely sure if she would ever completely recover. Brig'dha mostly sat before their small fire staring at the stars and only occasionally smiling back, though it seemed a bit forced. Ember wondered how much of Brig'dha's reactions were from her experiences and how much was simply her nature. Some people were naturally more introspective than others. But perhaps she was wrong to think her shyness abnormal. She recalled how Tor'kal and Zhek rarely said anything while Sv'en talked enough for both.

She may have always been this way, and that's alright, she thought. Ember was certainly not timid anymore, so she would lead their party. But first, she would slowly drag Brig'dha into a conversation about boats and how she felt about traveling by water. It wasn't easy, but eventually, the soft-spoken brunette was indeed lured into speaking. The conversation flowed naturally, using a mixture of trade language and the small vocabulary of words from Brig'dha's own language, which Ember had quickly and skillfully learned, not to mention plenty of hand gestures.

As the two women sat on the ground watching the stars, their conversation changed again to talk of Brig'dha's homeland. She explained that her people lived in small, round huts often built into the sides of hills or with dirt mounded over them. They erected stones to honor their gods and loved a good festival. Ember listened to her talk about her people until Brig'dha drifted to sleep under the light of a thin and waning crescent Moon. For a while, she watched Brig'dha as she slept, then closed her eyes and joined her under thick furs for the night.

The next two days on the water brought even more radical changes to the land. The scenery became flat, and the river broadened as it approached what Brig'dha had called the "edge of the world." Each night, Ember and Brig'dha would camp under the stars, and a little rain, as they plowed down the river at nearly four times the average speed of land travelers. At night, Ember would hunt small game with her bow, though she still had a lot to learn about hunting. Being good at hitting a target did little to prepare her for actual hunting where the animals moved.

On the fifth day's otherwise slow travel, the calm was interrupted when Brig'dha pointed out smoke coming from near the water. As they drifted past, they saw a small river people village. The village featured small huts standing upon poles above the ground. This sort of design was common enough and found wherever people lived on an active flood plain. Flooding was very inconvenient but provided rich soil for planting crops.

As Ember squinted to make out the details, she oddly saw perhaps fifty people standing by the water's edge, their shocked expressions ranging from anger to pain and grief. Ember saw women wailing to the sky and men weeping in anguish. The source of their pain seemed to be four pyres burning beside the water. This was a funeral, something Ember had quickly recognized. Normally a single person would die and require a pyre and a ceremony, but not four. Of course, accidents happened, and sometimes several people could be wounded or even die, but something struck Ember as odd about how the people acted. They looked nearly as angry as they did pained. Additionally, several of the men looked wounded, obviously being helped by others to stand. It only took her a moment to realize what had likely befallen these people. Memories of the ruined village flooded her mind as her curiosity turned to shock.

These people may have been attacked! Ember concluded. As they drifted by, one old man looked up at Ember and Brig'dha and yelled a warning in the trade language, though only two words made sense, the others being unknown as the trade language changed with distance.

"Yen-em, ut ware! Raiders!" Ember waved, indicating that she understood. In fact, she very well understood, for she had seen such a scene once before. Memories of that horrible massacre continued to dance through her mind, but this time, outrage and anger replaced her fear and sadness. Raiders had taken her father's life and murdered so many in that dead village. Ember hated injustice, bullies, and she seemed to have a special hatred for raiders and those who would harm the innocent.

"They have been raided," she said matter-of-factly.

"Other near tribe?" Brig'dha asked.

"I do not know. Probably. Happens. No one die, normally," she added. Offhandedly, she wondered how many words Brig'dha had actually understood, though obviously enough to grasp what she was saying.

Generally, raids were more bluster than violence. A small group of raiders would emerge from the trees and rush into a village, taking what they could grab and warding off attacks with their dangerous weapons and bluster. Sometimes, things went wrong. Ember felt terrible for the people as they floated away. If only she could have helped them, she thought. But, of course, that was an irrational thought as one woman with a bow would hardly have made much of a difference against the group of raiders.

Ember lay back in the boat as the day passed, considering what she had seen then wondering why such awful things happened to good people. All it took was a short distance trek from a village, and all the humanity and common decency seemed to quickly disappear. She had experienced this before, and no one had stood up to defend her. The young man named Pak had nearly done so on several occasions, or so she suspected, but in the end, she had been forced to free herself. She wished that more people would make the right choice.

☼ ☼ ☼

On the sixth day of their journey, Ember was becoming excited. She had found the end of the river, judging by the way the river had widened with sandy banks and lots of inlets. Old Nor'Gar had described the world's end in this way, with only the never-ending Greatest River awaiting discovery. Perhaps she would come across the Greatest River this very day. Brig'dha was also excited and of the same mind as both adventurers saw the end of their journey at hand. Excitement tingled down their spines as they watched the world change before their eyes.

Ember was thinking about what a never-ending expanse of water would look like when her attention was suddenly caught by movement a ways from the river along the bank. Many trails found their way along the shores of the river, and travelers could sometimes be seen. Looking more closely where she had seen movement, Ember quickly spotted what looked like eight people walking along the ridge of a small hill not far from the riverbank. Perhaps others were also on the same journey as she? The thought was exciting and tickled her mind to consider.

At first, she thought to wave at the mystery group and even possibly come ashore to talk and see what might be offered in trade, or, at least, to warn them of the raiders. The people were traveling the same direction as she, following the river, but they were probably locals and would know the land quite well. Still, the prospect of trading for something better to eat than their iron rations was too tempting to ignore. Ember took a quick look over her shoulder, and Brig'dha nodded, obviously of the same mind, though a bit more timid.

The women began to steer their little boat toward the land, quite a distance from the wide point in the river where they had sailed. Ember was considering what she might ask the people when suddenly one of the smaller figures, they were still too far away to get a good view, fell forward awkwardly... too awkwardly. It looked like a woman or a girl, and she had not used her hands to stop herself as she fell hard to the ground. Ember had experienced that before, firsthand, when she had been bound by Rosif. It was an odd sight to behold, most unnatural as everyone put their hands out to stop themselves unless those hands were bound.

While she watched, some of the smaller figures stopped, but they were shoved forward by the larger figures. The truth of the scene took Ember in a gasp. These women were prizes. Spoils of some raid. It had to be. Her thoughts were confirmed when one of the larger figures roughly lifted the fallen person and shook them before thrusting them forward.

Her blood instantly boiled. She had quite probably, though unintentionally, caught up with the raiding party from the village they had passed the day before. As Ember stared, Brig'dha said what she was thinking.

"Raiders, from near village. Evil!" Her wording was not quite adequate to say more, but it was enough for Ember, who simply nodded. Brig'dha continued to mutter other curses in her native tongue. Apparently, Brig'dha's people were none too fond of raiders either, a point which made Ember feel even better about her choice to travel to meet them and help Brig'dha return home. A proper hatred of raiders was a sign of a good person, in her opinion.

Women taken in raids were common enough, but somehow Ember couldn't let it go. These men, if it had been them, had killed at least four other people. The world was full of both good and evil. What separated the good from the evil was compassion and empathy, two emotions that now burned in Ember's chest. The tribe they had passed not a single day before came to mind. Both women remembered watching the devastated people weep for those they loved. The whole story unfolded in Ember's mind. These women had been working a little way from the village when they had been snatched just as she had almost been by the hunter Pak.

The four dead were either women who resisted or men close enough to come to their aid. Ember had to admit that she didn't know if her beliefs were true. Either way, she also knew that before her were a group of what looked like men roughly escorting a group of either younger women or possibly older children, and apparently against their will. These men would probably take them back to their tribe or worse. What hope did they have? Did they even know if their loved one's lived? When she was bound and captive, no one came to help her. Now, she had a chance to do the right thing, to make the right choice. Ember the Warrior had to act.

"We have to do something, Brig'dha!" Ember said in her native tongue, drawing a confused sound from Brig'dha.

"We-must help," she said to Brig'dha, this time in the trade language and using Brig'dha's word for "we." She twisted backward to stare the brunette square in the face, a tricky maneuver in the small boat. Brig'dha remembered that stoic look from the night of her rescue. She was frightened, but how could she say no to Ember's request? More oddly, she wondered how the otherwise lighthearted and almost childlike redhead could suddenly switch to become so deadly serious. She supposed that everyone had their triggers, though she had never met someone with such a stochastic thought train.

"Yes. What we-do?" Brig'dha asked, truly interested in helping but having no idea how two women could face a group of armed men. The notion was absurd on its face, like a pair of rabbits facing down a pack of wolves. Though, as she gazed into those emerald eyes, it began to feel more like one rabbit and perhaps a fox, yet they were still contemplating facing down a pack of wolves.

"Head down!" Ember whispered. Quickly they ducked to make themselves as small as possible and hoped they had not been seen, but on the rapids as far from the men as they were, Ember doubted they had. The trail the men now followed steered them away from the river, though it was easy enough to see that the path again returned farther up ahead. The boat moved many times faster than the war party and quickly had a significant lead on the raiders, who continued along with no indication that they had noticed the little boat.

Quickly, they maneuvered the boat into a sheltered inlet, a good walk from where the men were last seen. A group of tarpans, wild horses, quickly scattered from the inlet as the boat slammed into the shore. Brig'dha noted one light brown, stocky horse with quite a mane, its body covered in little dark spots. Her original people often ate such horses, though she had never seen them as far south as Nes. Noting the spots upon the robust redhead's face, she took that as a good omen that the spirits of the land backed their actions. Yet, omens wouldn't save them from arrows. She hoped Ember had the luck to match her boldness.

They were ahead of the raiders, and Ember hoped to lay a quick ambush. With great haste, the women pulled their little boat ashore. The reckless redhead removed her bow and hastily strung it, slinging it over her shoulder afterward to carry. She also grabbed her bag of black pigment, made from oil and charred bone, and the small sticks she used for her cooking and drying frames, a plan forming in her mind as she worked. Rosif and his men never encountered her traps, so she thought, and she never got to see if they had worked. This would be a good chance to find out.

Ember laughed to herself, despite her seething anger mixed with a healthy dose of fear and anxiety over the absurdity of what she had planned. She wouldn't have taken on something like this when first she had left her people. *And you shouldn't, now,* the part of her brain responsible for self-preservation said, but she ignored it. She was young and afraid then. Now here she was, still young and frightened, acting as a great warrior, or more like a fool, taking on five men. She knew Brig'dha would be of little help, but her willingness to endanger herself regardless of the odds gave Ember the strength of heart she needed. They would make a stand for what was right. Ember had journeyed for many long days and had nearly died many times, and for what? If this wasn't a cause worth dying for, what was? These women could very well have been her friends, perhaps Kis'tra or Eva. Even one such as Aya didn't deserve this.

Aya just deserves a good slap and a cold bath, she mused.

A large hill stood between her and the coming men. Between the hill and the river was a small grouping of trees and shrubs. They would make their stand there. Ember had a very short while to wait before the men came, and she would need to act fast. If they turned out to be something other than what she had expected, she could stay hidden, and they would pass her trap. In the sandy dirt near the trees, the women quickly dug pits a hand length across and deep. Then, using the small cooking sticks, Ember and Brig'dha sharpened their ends to make deadly spikes. This only took a few quick slices from the razor-sharp obsidian dagger.

Ember's palms were sweating, and her heart was starting to race as she wondered if she would finish before the men arrived. Quickly, she used one of the sharp steaks to punch holes in the dirt, in which Brig'dha then plopped a sharpened stake, point up. Their mutual anxiety spiked through the roof as the women covered the stick traps with grass and reeds. A foot would find those stick spike traps, placed an arm apart, with horrific results, she hoped. Next, Ember laid six of her twelve arrows on the ground, five lengths of a man behind the traps by a large bush. She could nearly feel her heart beating in her ears as the time ran out fast. She fought to ignore her better judgment pleading with her not to get involved in such a foolish rescue.

While Ember stood with her arms outstretched, pointing at various landmarks and reciting some plan to herself, Brig'dha quickly started moving a large stone behind the bush at Ember's request. She didn't really understand what Ember had in mind, but she couldn't argue with the woman who had saved her from a village of sacrifice-crazed people. She had gone from farming and trading to navigating the Great River with this warrior woman in such a short time. Her entire life had changed so radically over the last two full harvests that very little seemed real anymore. Yet, strangely, the only thing which gave her any hope and brought any peace to her mind was Ember. Even if it cost her very life, she would follow her into battle and beyond.

Ember noticed the stone being moved by Brig'dha and quickly helped her finish placing it behind the bushes. She would fall back to this point if need be. Seeing the confusion in Brig'dha's eyes, Ember quickly explained the plan, hoping to calm the terrified brunette, as well as herself.

"I-will meet-men. I-will talk. If raiders..." Ember used her hands to quickly gesture as she explained her plan in the trade and Isen'bryn tongues to Brig'dha, for they had little time remaining, "...I-will hide, here, shoot. You-hide, tree... If I die... Run," she said, awkwardly, too anxious to remember much of her newly learned vocabulary. Ember barely appreciated the significance of her last words, but she was still young enough that her sense of mortality had not fully matured. She was more aware of death and the narrow line people walked between life and death than most her age having nearly died several times. Yet, that youthful feeling of immortality clung to her like a warm cloak. It wasn't much, but she knew that if she thought about it too deeply, they would simply get back in the boat and flee.

Beside her, Brig'dha stood in sheer terror, her mind entirely filled with the fear of what was to come. Ember dipped her hand into her small leather pouch of black pigment and removed a glob of the paint. She turned to face the wide-eyed brunette. Brig'dha stood in silence, stunned as Ember began to paint swirls on her skin, mimicking the designs she had first seen Brig'dha wear so many moons before. Ember began to softly sing a song of luck as she stood a hand's length away, tracing black lines across the brunette's face in preparation for battle. This was what a wife did for her husband, and suddenly Brig'dha realized that she had momentarily forgotten that she was about to die, and worse, that she was being touched.

Moments before, time had been racing as they had worked frantically to prepare their ambush. Now, as those emerald eyes stared back at her and delicate fingers worked to apply paint, time seemed to have stopped. Brig'dha remembered to breathe, though she recalled very little else. Wearing her boots, leggings, loincloth, woolen skirt, and leather shirt, the random redhead had only Brig'dha's face to paint. However, she still took a moment ensuring the swirls were right before she handed the paint to Brig'dha and bid her do the same in return.

The Sun was warm despite the cool season, so Ember had left her long leather shirt back at the boat along with their coats and mittens. The redhead wore nettle cordage boots with dried grass stuffed within for warmth, a pair of leather leggings, a long leather loincloth, and her goddess pendant. In her hair, she sported a pair of feathers, one black and one tawny. A heavy obsidian blade in a leather sheath hung from her hip, and a light hunting bow crossed her chest, held by the bowstring, its quiver at her back.

Brig'dha had painted a series of black dots horizontally beneath her eyes, just as she had seen Ember apply herself, as well as black stripes around her arms and legs. The sight of Ember so thoroughly dressed as a warrior nearly took Brig'dha's breath away. She was indeed striking, beautiful yet dangerous in appearance, like an obsidian arrowhead, or given her long red hair, a fox. As she stepped back to examine what she had done, Ember finished her song and gave Brig'dha a wink.

Brig'dha returned a fearful look, her chest heaving with anticipation, and trotted off behind a tree, her flint knife in hand. She would have much rather stayed for a second or perhaps third look at the beautiful warrior, but the men were already overdue, and it was almost time for her to go get herself killed for a noble cause like the fool that she was. Of course, the entire idea was absurd, but she owed Ember her life, so she would follow the foxy woman's plans, even if it was the last thing she did. Besides, even if the men killed her, she was at least free from that dreadful song of the elders of Nes. That, alone, was worth a life debt, in her opinion.

Ember glanced at the brunette hiding behind a tree as the sounds of the men approaching finally appeared. Brig'dha looked like she might cry, her face awash with anxiety and fear. Ember wasn't sure if Brig'dha would hold together if she were killed, but she had to hope for the best. She still could not believe that she was about to do this. One full harvest before when she had left on this foolish trip, she certainly wouldn't have. She was still young, but she had already experienced more life and death struggles than most of the women in her tribe ever would, aside from perhaps childbirth.

The men were now close enough to see movement up ahead through the trees. As the time of the encounter approached, Ember took stock of herself. She was fit and sound, and all her wounds had long since healed, but still, each of those men was physically her better. If it came down to a brawl, she would surely die. Any man could easily deliver a punch that would outright destroy a typical woman. Her plan involved keeping the men at a standoff distance and exchanging arrow fire. She had been practicing and felt that she could outshoot them if they were close enough, but she'd never survive if they got within arm's reach. Even in her youthful misjudgment of her own abilities, Ember wasn't quite that deluded.

Thank you for the lessons, Sv'en. May you and Kat'ja have a hundred funny children, she thought with a wavering smile. With this in mind, she nocked an arrow and held another in the same hand she held the bow, parallel, for easy access. She gave Brig'dha one last smile for good luck. *This doesn't even feel real... almost like some sort of dream,* she thought as she breathed deeply in anticipation.

As the men approached, Ember knelt on the ground low behind a bush, watching. She slowly traced a circular Moon shape on the ground, quietly chanting a prayer to her gods. Her fear felt like a drowning cold and sinking feeling, and she was finding it hard to keep from shaking. Deep down, she had the urge to simply abandon her plan and flee with Brig'dha, but she had to keep it together. If she didn't save those women, who would? No one had come for her, and she couldn't bear to let others experience such fear as she had.

Her spike traps, a personal favorite, were down the path a little farther. She had moved ahead, hoping to get a better look at the men before retreating back to the ambush site. The women had done an excellent job masking the small, sharp spikes, and she hoped she would remember the way through the deadly traps when the time came. One wrong move, and she would find herself impaled through the foot and at the mercy of the men, who wouldn't take long to figure out who had left the spikes in the ground for them.

As Ember waited, the first man crested the hilltop. Like most of the men from the forest people tribes, he had dark brown hair and a generally broad face, with dark skin like Brig'dha or the people of Tornhemal, and deep, blue eyes. He wore a leather shirt and a beaded necklace with leather leggings and a deer hide loincloth. His feet were garbed in heavy leather boots, and a quiver, unstrung bow, and gear clung to his back. Ember had hoped he would look evil, a monster to hate. But, instead, he looked like any other man she had seen. For a moment, she wondered if he could be like Pak, a reluctant participant, but no, he would have his chance just as the others.

The other people came now into view. In total, there were three men in the front and two men in the back, each similarly dressed and each armed with unstrung bows and a mix of war clubs, spears, and various blunt weapons. Between the five men walked three women bound from behind. All three wore leather skirts and leather shirts for the cold, with simple leather and cordage shoes. They looked like they had been captured while foraging, given their outfits, though it was hard to say.

Each woman's red-rimmed eyes held a defeated look, like a woman who had given up. There was no escape, and they knew it. Their lives as they had been were over, and they had accepted their fates. Ember was tired of fate and injustice. She would see to it that this didn't come to pass, for she knew just what sort of fear these women now faced. The oldest woman was just a bit older looking than Ember, and the youngest was barely old enough to even be a woman.

"This will not be," she whispered as she slipped away from the bushes and moved off towards the ambush point, creeping as silently as she could. She hoped that she had not been heard, as one wrong move and the entire trap would be exposed.

The men were talking and laughing as they journeyed, obviously pleased with their raid. They carried themselves like big strong men should, but they looked none too old for such swagger. They were obviously recently come of age and in need of a trophy to secure their places among their people. Such raids were more common among river people, but even forest people seemed to feel the urge for such violence, a feature of humanity Ember could do without. Ember would give each of them a handmade arrowhead of the finest quality as a trophy to show the gods in the afterlife. She breathed deeply as her fear danced along her spine. This was it...

Ember stood from behind a bush and approached with a hip-swaying feminine walk to stand before the men, blocking their path. She hoped the extra feminine demeanor would throw them off and make them less likely to fire before hearing what she had to say. It was the main reason she had left her shirt back at the boat. Of course, her uncovered body wouldn't come as a shock or even be that appealing in a culture where nudity was commonplace. Still, such a clear reminder that she was a woman might just lower their guard when the time came. *What good are prejudices if you can't use them against the bigot?* she thought, trying to calm her nerves with a joke, but it fell short under such anxiety.

The entire group came to an abrupt stop. The man in the front had to consciously close his open mouth. In his midst stood a young woman, barely a woman, holding a nocked bow as though she knew how to use it and with a determined, though fearful, look about her. Her body was painted for battle like a man, yet she was quite obviously not a man. The most intimidating feature about her was her waist-length red hair blowing in the wind and bright green piercing eyes. They gave her a surreal look, like some sort of fox.

"Stop! Do you understand me?" she asked as forcefully as she could in her native tongue. The lead man looked at her incredulously and cocked an eyebrow.

"Do-You, understand?" she asked again, but in the trade language. The man listened and then turned to his party with a laugh.

"I guess she has come to return the women? Maybe this is some sort of joke, or maybe she's here to entertain us?" he said to his party in his native language. Ember didn't know what he had said, but she could guess, given his tones. Then, turning back to Ember, he spoke in the trade language.

"Girl. We five, we take-three. Calm," he replied with a laugh. He gestured to the women behind him and turned to laugh with his fellow raiders. Ember's blood boiled at how casually he spoke of the women they had taken and the deaths they had caused. Did he think this was a joke? Did he find this humorous? "We take-three," as though that was a fair trade? Ember would try once more. She desperately wanted to end this peacefully, even if she had to trade or beg for the women, but she needed the man to know that she would go all the way. She lifted the bow toward the man and gave him a deadly look, though she could barely hold it as her true inner fears were fighting with her to run.

"Free women, or-die," she said, slowly pulling back on the arrow. The leader returned his attention to Ember with a half-humorous look of disbelief. He was being threatened by a woman with a bow, and barely a woman at that. Behind him, the other men laughed, finding the situation so absurd that they hadn't even been angered. The leader stepped back from the front and stood beside one of the women. This was indeed a story to tell later to a disbelieving audience. With that, he reached forward and placed his hand against the face of the first woman who cringed at his touch.

"Free?" he asked, starting to laugh. His hand began reaching into her leather long shirt for a place he should not have tried to touch. Far from intimidated, he was going to grope her right in front of Ember, stripping this poor woman's remaining dignity simply to mock the rancorous redhead. The captive closed her wet, swollen eyes, preparing for what was probably going to be another of many violations. Ember's eyes twitched as something snapped within her, a line that had finally been crossed.

"I show-you what..." he began to say, tauntingly. He stopped abruptly and with a sudden gasp. The appearance of a shaft protruding from his chest told his disbelieving eyes that he wouldn't finish the touch. Both Ember and the man stared at each other in shock. She had fired her arrow cleanly and so abruptly that everyone had been taken by surprise. The man tried to grab the captive as he sank to his knees, but she stood firm and stared him down with supreme vindication. The thin stone arrowhead had slid neatly between his ribs and shredded his left bronchus, destroying his left lung and burring itself deep within. He let go and began gasping for air as his lungs quickly filled with blood.

He tore the arrow from his chest with great strength, but the arrowhead remained in his body, detaching from the shaft as it was designed to do. The other four men could only stare in shock as their leader coughed up his lifeblood, falling to his side and going into shuttering convulsions, his eyes never breaking contact with the captive. Her tears fell as she watched, yet they were not shed for him. Instead, they were tears of vengeance from the overwhelming emotion of watching a man who had hurt her dying so gratifyingly at her feet. The captive spit upon him, but her mouth was far too dry for anything but token spittle.

Suddenly, the shock of the moment was over, and the men tore their bows from their backs, backing away and stringing them as fast as possible. She had purposefully stood far enough back that none could charge her without the risk of being shot, so they had stepped back more willing to use their bows. She was counting on them believing her aim would be poor from a distance. If they had rushed her, she might have gotten another with an arrow, but they would quickly have killed her. Behind the tree, Brig'dha stared with her mouth open in shock. The redhead had struck down the enemy raider and was now nocking another arrow.

Ember yelled to the women in the trade language, "Down!" The three women dropped to the ground as quickly as they could. She used the moment to nock her free arrow and dashed for the trees, running through her small maze of traps hoping to draw the men from the women to keep them clear from the arrow fire. She loosed her second arrow in a blind twisting shot as she stepped between traps. The arrow shot wide, missing the men, but the one who had nocked and drew his bow misfired while ducking from the wild shot. The men had strung their bows faster than she had expected, but it had still bought her time to flee.

She ran behind a tree and pulled her body tightly against the cool bark. Her chest pounded as she quickly selected an arrow from her quiver. For some reason, she noted the fletching was made from a brownish feather. Ember's mind was trying to detach itself from the events unfolding, her nerve nearly lost as fear screamed at her from all directions to flee. As she did so, she heard and felt an arrow as it thudded into the tree just behind her head, exploding as the flint arrowhead blew apart from the force of the impact. The sudden thud brought her back into focus.

"Goddess, be with me," she said to herself as she summoned the courage to return fire. She looked across at Brig'dha, who was behind a nearby tree holding her small flint knife and wearing an expression of utter fear and exhilaration. Ember gave her a weary smile and moved sideways to stand in the open where she might take aim. She knew she would be a larger target, but one clear shot was worth the risk. In an even exchange of arrows, she hoped that she was a better shot. Sv'en had said she was a natural, and now she was going to find out the hard way.

One man was making a run for her when she took a bead on a second man firing. Ember wanted to duck, but she remembered kicking the wolves in the face, and the memory brought forth a short burst of inner strength. She stood her ground, ensuring her aim was perfect. She took a deep breath focusing on her target, and then let the wind gently escape her lips as she exhaled, relaxing her grip upon the bowstring. Both Ember and a man fired at once. The man's arrow flew past Ember's face, just missing her. Her arrow flew true and buried itself deep into the man's throat. He gasped and gurgled, falling to the ground, all thoughts of fighting lost in his own torturous pain. She now caught sight of the women, who had thankfully dropped to the ground and were cowering in fear.

Good, she thought, *keep out of the fight.* An arrow flew past Ember without harm, then suddenly, another arrow dug into her arm. The arrowhead bit into her soft skin as the shaft suddenly twisted sideways from its own momentum, cutting her flesh open. Blood rolled down her arm, yet she felt no pain in the moment. Ember dropped to the ground and crawled behind the bushes she had scoped out earlier as a refuge if things got out of hand. Things were certainly getting out of hand.

Behind the bush, her extra arrows lay ready to go. The three remaining men fired at her as she continued to return fire. The man who had been rushing at her had apparently had second thoughts after seeing his companion shot through the neck. Though the men were momentarily at bay, Ember realized she had a forming problem. She had lost the pace of the fight and was quickly being flanked. Worse, she only had a few arrows left. She had selected that very bush for just such a situation, and now was the time to use it. Lifting her body above the bushes, fully exposed, she took aim. She knew she would be an easy target firing from above the bush on her knees, but the men were not coming toward the traps, and she had to do something. Just as she took aim, one of the men fired his bow, and an arrow flew into the bush right where Ember's midsection lay.

Ember let loose a horrified scream and fell backward, her bow falling away from view. She wailed and started crawling away from the bushes on her side with an arrow protruding from her stomach, seemingly buried deeply. Blood dripped down the arrow as she cried and squealed, dragging herself as she crawled away, obviously in far too much agony to fight. Behind a tree, Brig'dha stared in horror, unsure of what to do next. She knew what Ember had planned, but she couldn't entirely be sure of what had happened. She closed her eyes and prayed to her Moon Goddess as she placed her own knife against her neck, knowing full well what she would do if the redhead died.

The victorious men came forward, quickly dropping their bows and unsheathing their daggers and warclubs. A deep wound to the lower stomach could leave this crazed woman in agony for a day before she died, but their urge to finish her by hand was overpowering. She had killed two of them, men they had grown up with and knew as friends. They would cut this beast-of-a-woman's throat after they made her last moments as painful as possible, then take her scalp as a trophy. A pack of wolves was always stronger than a little red fox. Unfortunately for these wolves, the fox was more cunning.

In his haste to finish the woman, the first man stepped directly onto a spike trap. He fell forward in a tripping motion as his foot was suddenly held fast by a hand-length spike protruding from the upper part of his boot. He screamed louder than the wounded woman he had sought as he tumbled to the ground with the awful snapping sound of his ankle fracturing under his own weight. The other two men looked back, hearing such a horrible sound from behind. For one of the men, this was a big mistake. He stepped onto another upturned spike that failed to puncture his boot but tripped him, sending the man sprawling forward. He landed face-first onto another trap, a wooden spike entering his eye socket and proceeding deep into what had been his childhood memories. He was dead before his body stopped moving.

The last man stopped, realizing that the fight had suddenly turned against him. He turned to see the wounded girl, who was suddenly standing and not so wounded. She stood with her recovered bow in her hand and released the arrow she had held against her side. The arrow fell to the ground with a soft clatter. She had held it tightly against her waist to give the illusion of an arrow poking through her. The blood had come from her cut arm. She had not expected the added blood for effect, but her body had produced plenty of it from her sliced arm, and she hadn't wanted it to go to waste.

The arrow in the bush had been close, but the rock Brig'dha had placed within had stopped it, as Ember had hoped it would when she had chosen that bush as an ambush site. Initially, she had hoped to use the bush with its hidden armor as a place to fire from, her wounded ploy being impromptu. Slowly, she nocked her arrow as Brig'dha audibly sighed from nearby. The man looked around in terror, suddenly realizing that he stood in a small field of unseen traps, and worse, he had brought a flint dagger to a bow and arrow fight.

Ember stood at a standoff distance with a razor-sharp arrow and a vicious, if not somewhat forced, smile. Behind the tree, Brig'dha breathed a second yet equally deep sigh of relief. When Ember had proposed her plan, including the last part where she might use the armored bush for cover, it had seemed a long shot at best. Now, the ground was covered with blood and dead or dying raiders. Brig'dha could not believe that Ember stood before so many fallen foes, and apparently, the only actual injury she had was a cut across her arm from a close call with an arrow. It was surreal.

"No-clothes," Ember said. The man stared back at her with genuine confusion, unsure of what to do. The rabid redhead stared back, her gaze as bitter as unripe fruit.

"No-clothes," she said once more, wiggling her bow for emphasis. Brig'dha actually looked confused as well, unsure why Ember would wish the man to undress. Sensing his confusion, she pulled the bowstring tighter to show her dangerous intent. This would be her last warning, and the man understood, words or not.

"No-clothes, or die," she said. Ember waited as the man pulled off his clothes until he stood before her just as frightened as the women he had enslaved. Ember had decided to spare him if possible. Enough lives had been lost, and no more would be unless no other way could be found. She repressed nausea flooding her body as adrenalin wore off. He would have to return to his tribe and explain this whole mess, which might be worse than death. She could hear the stories now. *We were attacked by fifty warriors!* he would likely claim.

"Go! Go! Run!" she yelled, holding her bow taut. The man retreated carefully, looking from the deadly spiked ground to the arrow-wielding redheaded woman and her promise of death. He held his hands out at her in fear, as though warding himself from her while backing away, then suddenly took off in a run as he cleared the traps, he hoped. Ember fired her nocked arrow just past him to keep him running.

That one won't come back for revenge any time soon, she thought grimly. Ironically, she would have been ill-equipped for a fight if he had tried, for she was actually nearly out of arrows.

Ember carefully nocked her last arrow and stepped towards the freed women. The scene before her was quite intense. A man lay on the ground face down in a pool of gore, occasionally quivering. Near him sat a man holding his booted foot and whimpering in anguish, his ankle twisted at an unnatural angle. Brig'dha had come out from her hiding place and now stood by the wounded man with her knife at the ready. Not far from the women lay a stilled man with an arrow in his throat, and next to the women, a man lay holding an arrow, blood staining his chest. He was either dead or soon would be. She couldn't tell if his subtle jerking motions were the last of his life or the shakes a body experienced after death as the spirit left, like a snake shedding its skin.

They had done it… they had actually freed the women, defeated the raiders, and lived. It made no sense. She kept looking from fallen raider to fallen raider as though expecting to find one missing, one more enemy to leap from the brush and kill her, yet none came. Ember glanced at her muscular arm, blood dripping from a nasty cut. She barely felt like a woman, normally, and now this? A warrior? Her people had a 3rd gender, a wergene, but these were people born male who lived as women. While those born female living as men were spoken of in a few stories, they had no special name. Moreover, Ember didn't feel like a man, either. Her introspection ended as the adrenalin faded.

Ember suddenly felt a cold shudder throughout her body when she approached the women and stumbled forward to her hands and knees. The enormity of what had happened filled her like a sickening and cold liquid. Ember vomited all over the ground as the adrenaline left. Her pain started to become noticeable, though the wound wasn't bleeding as much. Her left arm had a slice the length of her finger across it. The cut was not deep, but it would need to be cleaned and possibly burned before it became warm and sore. Her body had other random aches and pains as well, but the nausea only lasted a short moment. Ember was unsure of how she should feel. Pain, sadness, the thrill of victory, shame, all these emotions danced through her mind.

She slowly stood and staggered over to the women who were still cowering and crying, quite shocked by the violence of their rescue.

"Good, now. Stand. You walk home?" Ember asked, using the basic trade language and hoping her 'you walk, home' came out as the question it was. She removed her dagger and cut their bindings, her hands trembling as nausea came in waves. Each woman wore plenty of clothing, and they were in generally good condition, at least physically. The oldest woman, not more than a few seasons older than Ember, shook her head up and down, meaning to indicate, "yes."

"Home, [two] [days] walk?" Ember asked, pointing the way of the previous village and using her hands to depict "two" and "days." The oldest woman nodded yes once more. Ember smiled and handed the lead woman the knife from the dead man at her feet. She removed the dried meat from one of her pouches and handed it to the woman as well. It was plenty of meat for a single meal for the three. She gave each one of them a smile and motioned them to leave. She would spare them the horror of cleaning up after the battle. As the three women stood, unsure of what to do, Ember stepped toward them again and gave each a reassuring pat on the shoulder.

"Go. Go-home. Good. Many babies!" she said, unsure if they understood. She gave them a broad smile, and slowly they began to leave. The youngest woman, nearly a girl really, looked back at Ember and spoke in the trade language for the first time.

"Name?" she asked. Unfortunately, the word was so badly accented Ember barely understood.

"Kaelu, Breeg'dha," she replied, using her hands to gesture. The woman looked back at her for a long moment, then turned as her own tears fell and joined the other two women. Ember watched them go beyond the rise and toward their home. She was sure they would make it with only two days' journey ahead.

"Many babies?" Brig'dha asked, her own hands shaking from fear. Ember shrugged and forced a smile. It was all she could think of in the moment. Then, a yelp caught their attention, causing Brig'dha to scream. The wounded man was trying to free his broken, punctured foot from the spike. The stick was as thick as two of her fingers and would leave a massive hole when it was removed. Worse, from the angle of his leg, it appeared that his ankle was broken. Ember wasn't sure he would live if he pulled it out. On the other hand, if he left the spike in his foot, he would die of the sweats and redness in a few days. Either way, he was likely going to die a terrible death.

Ignoring him, Ember slowly approached Brig'dha, tears flowing as she fully realized that they had won. Before the startled brunette could react, Ember stepped forward and wrapped her arms around the woman crushing her in a teary hug. For a moment, Brig'dha stood there with her arms out wide, unsure of what to do, but when she realized that Ember wasn't going to let go anytime soon, she slowly wrapped her arms around the woman. Her cold hands touched Ember's warm, smooth back, and suddenly, in the middle of this field of death, there was nowhere that she would rather be. For a while, they held each other and cried. Honestly, Brig'dha couldn't believe they had survived and freed the women.

Finally, after a short time, Ember released her, and the two stepped apart. For a moment, Ember stared at the brunette with the oddest expression and then suddenly burst into uncontrollable laughter. At first, Brig'dha couldn't imagine what could possibly be funny in this field of carnage until Ember pointed at her shirt. Brig'dha looked down and realized that Ember's painted and bloody chest had imprinted a distinctly feminine shape on her shirt. A moment later, both women were laughing until they fell to the ground releasing all their stress in laughter and tears.

A short time later, the two women had pulled each of the dead by the legs to the gully near the wounded man. There, they stripped the weapons and valuables from the men and left each of them face down in the dirt. She should feel some pity, but the memories of the anguished look on the faces of the tribe she had passed and the dead in the ruined village she had once seen thwarted most of her sympathy. These men were in need of a lesson, and she had taught it. She was a warrior, was she not?

On the men, Ember found four flint daggers, twenty good flint arrows, and enough leather thong to string a full hut. They placed all these items in their cramped boat and removed the spikes from the ground to prevent others from being hurt. Before they left, Ember returned to the wounded man. No matter how little remorse she could feel for the men she had killed, she could not keep those feelings for the wounded man.

He had this terrible habit of looking at her with pained, frightened eyes as though he understood just how bad his fate would be. She felt that she had done the right thing. In fact, his wound resulted from charging at her with a knife, ready to kill her as she apparently bled to death from her supposed arrow wound. Yet, no matter how she rationalized it, she still felt sympathy for him. She approached and knelt beside the wounded man, Brig'dha standing close by with her knife at the ready. The brunette was far less forgiving of violent men, it seemed.

"I-am sorry," she said and placed some dried meat, a few of her sharpened sticks, and some dry brush by the man. If he wanted, he could try and make a fire to close the wound in his foot when and if he removed the spike. He would likely die alone in the wilds with a ruined foot, but that wasn't Ember's problem. He chose his path, quite literally, with a dagger in his hand, ready to kill a wounded woman. Perhaps he might come to some resolution with the Gods or perhaps not. Ember and Brig'dha simply walked away from the man and slowly boarded their boat, leaving him to his fate.

CHAPTER NINETEEN
THE END OF THE WORLD

Sexual orientation among humans appears to be a gradient, with significantly more variation than is commonly depicted in the media. Survey after survey paints the picture of human sexuality as more complex than simply heterosexual or homosexual. Brig'dha grew up in a society where homosexuality wasn't necessarily problematic. Yet, she ended up paired with a man due to her family, politics, social pressures, and her difficulty expressing her feelings, a side effect of her autism. Conversely, Ember wasn't exposed to such pressures and experimented freely. She quickly learned that she was attracted to all genders, what might be termed pansexual in modern terms. However, she heavily favored the feminine form. Sadly, our young adventurers have come to some poor conclusions which stand in the way of what could be. Unfortunately, such miscommunication is all too common, even today.

Ember and Brig'dha were silent as they drifted through the vast expanse of the Great River as it began to open into the Greatest River. During the eighth day past the attack, they had finally come upon wetlands. These were areas where the water expanded beyond the river resulting in beautiful marshes, grassy fields of water, mud, reeds, and innumerable animals. By the end of the day, they had come to a large, open area connecting several waterways. Off the side of the boat was a series of small inlets with reeds along their banks. Putting to shore here would be much more complicated than the much narrower and faster parts of the Great River Ember was used to.

As the boat sailed along the now smooth, wide waterway, the women came upon the broadest part of the river Ember had ever seen. More impressive than the shallow waterways and wetlands was the open expanse of water before them. In fact, the waterway opened in each direction, revealing an endless expanse of water. It suddenly occurred to Ember that before them lay the end of the world. It had to be. This was it, a scene so expansive and so breathtaking that it defied reality, exactly as Brig'dha had described.

Ember stared at the expanse, unable to fully take it in. To her left, she noted that the land continued for quite some distance, perhaps a full day's walk. To the right, the land simply ended in no more than a short walking distance. She nearly fell out of the boat while trying to stand, causing Brig'dha to burst into laughter. The water from the Greatest River stretched as far as the eye could see, like the skies above, yet wet. This made the Great River seem but a mere stream by comparison. As the water expanded, the wetlands faded, and a sandy shore could be seen. The women quickly maneuvered the boat to the left-hand shore, toward the beach.

Removing her footwear, Ember leapt from the boat as its shallow keel scraped the ground. The water was so much colder than she expected, causing her to gasp. Worse, the undercurrent was nearly as unexpected as the temperature. As she stood in knee-deep water, she could feel a strange suction, as though the Greatest River was pulling her away from land. While being sucked into the Great River was annoying, the prospect of being dragged into the abyss of the Greatest River was suddenly frightening, and Ember's nerves had only just started to calm after her fight a few days before.

"Aeeya!" Ember screamed in panic as she raced forward toward the land, pulling the boat along. Brig'dha dug her oar into the ground and pushed, forcing the boat forward. Together, the women pulled the boat onto the pebbles that formed the start of a beach. Only after her feet felt the pebbly shore did Ember relax. She had never felt a pull like that before. Sure, the Great River tugged you sideways, but never toward the center from the very shore. The ruffled redhead shivered for a moment, then breathed a sigh of relief.

After securing the boat, Ember simply stood and took in the view of the Greatest River as Brig'dha fetched the supplies for camp. Before her was an eternity of water. The water stretched the width of the world and traveled to the horizon. The Sun was low on that horizon, making the scene ever so beautiful, like a distant campfire playing with the clouds. Ember stood and watched the gray-blue water with whitecaps forming and waves crashing. She did not even realize that she was shivering from her wet legs and a light breeze.

A tear fell, and then another as she took in the enormity of the world. She had done it – journeyed to the end of the world. Even if she died right now, she had still completed her quest, at least at its most basic level. Brig'dha passed by carrying a role of furs for camp. Suddenly, Ember's mind and victory were both at odds. She quickly rolled the facts around in her mind:

Nothing is beyond the End of the World.
Brig'dha's island is beyond where I am.
Therefore, I am not at the end of the world.
Aeeya!

The syllogism was simple, yet its implications threw water on her fires of victory. She slowly sank to her knees as she realized that she still had a little farther to travel. Before her lay the enormity of The Greatest River, later named the North Sea, a vast and unforgiving expanse. Brig'dha's people navigated this waterway, and her stories of vast storms and epic waves suddenly sounded more accurate than when she had heard them, days before. Waves larger than a tree and darkness that could swallow entire boats. Ember took a deep breath, held it, and then released.

Just a bit more work to do...

Needing to get their minds off the coming trip, Ember and Brig'dha spent part of the evening exploring the beach. The pebbles came in all shapes and sizes and were washed smooth by the never-ending splashes from the Greatest River. The sound was relaxing and the smell from the water was unlike anything Ember had ever experienced. It was salty, with a strange decaying fish-like smell which was oddly pleasant. Their evening was filled with joyous exploration as they relaxed, stretched their legs, and set up camp.

Driftwood could be found scattered along the beach in plentiful quantity, making a fire an easy task. The early thawing season Sun and a not-so-wet, wet season had dried much of it, creating a significant fuel supply, which meant warmth and protection the entire night. As they sat by the fire eating deer meat from cooking sticks, the conversation shifted from the mundane discussion of food to the final trip to Inn'bry'th and the dangers of crossing such a massive river. Luckily, over the past half moon, Ember had been learning Brig'dha's language faster than either would have thought possible, supplemented by the trade language as needed, the words of Nes, mostly forgotten.

"You-see 'Bigworld' from Inn'bry'th, sometimes. Travel Greatest River is-danger. Water comes, water goes. We-must flee-from Sun, eat, and follow-Sun. Will-take a day if we are fast. Water-move [each way]." As Ember listened, she realized that Brig'dha was speaking as though the current of the Greatest River changed, which made no sense to her. In the morning, they would have the Sun at their backs. After eating a mid-day meal, they would follow the Sun. Ember wondered what would happen if they failed to reach Inn'bry'th by night.

The other main problem, as Ember saw it, was the boat. The boat rode too low, especially packed with so many supplies. They would need to dump much of the food and water and bring as little as possible, not a good choice before a trip into the unknown. Additionally, they would need to use the small pots provided to remove water as it filled the little boat while trying to fight against such massive waves in a boat riding a hand's length above the water.

The trip was going to require lots of work and hard rowing. The oars Sv'en had made were much wider at the ends than her original oar had been and would allow the women to move as they wished unless some unknown current carried them away into eternity. But for how long could they row? These were all grave problems to overcome, and Ember was unsure if she was up to the challenge. As if seeing the contemplation on Ember's face, Brig'dha continued, slowly and using her hands to aid the words. Ember almost forgot her woes as she watched the hazel-eyed woman waving her hands about.

"Isen'bryn make big-boat. Three more-big than Ember boat," she said, indicating that her people used a boat at least three times the size of their small dugout boat. Ember's people made larger boats than their little dugout, yet Brig'dha spoke of something much larger. Her hazel eyes flashed in excitement as she indicated a massive craft with her hands.

"Boat is more-deep. Big danger. Some die if storm." Ember didn't like what she was hearing, but if this was the fate of the gods, then perhaps she could pray for a good crossing. The Gods had been a mixture of helpful and not, so far. If this was their will, a moment given to them might make a difference. She winked at Brig'dha, causing the brunette to pause just as she was starting a new sentence. The random redhead stood and walked toward the sandy shore by the water. Brig'dha merely watched her, a bit bemused. Above Ember, the Moon hung, split between darkness and light, a neutral omen. She closed her eyes and stepped one foot after the other from the warm, safe fire toward the cold, dark water. There was symbolism in every movement, as was always the case when dance and song took on the elements of magic and ritual.

Ember stopped with a gasp as the first ice-cold waves tickled her bare feet and opened her eyes to see the darkness at the edge of oblivion. Somewhere in that eternity was an island they meant to reach. She lifted her head toward the Moon, raising her arms wide, and began to sing a ritual song of good luck. Such songs and dances were the way of her people, and she had to hope her gods would hear her. If they turned their backs now, they were certainly done for.

"Goddess of the winds, God of the fields, Goddess of the Moon and skies, God of the Sun, Goddess of rivers, Goddess of the soil, hear my words. Watch over us and deliver us from death. Spare us with your mercy and guide us to your goals..." she began to chant in her own language. Her voice was low and rich, carrying out across the water to the place where gods lived, she hoped. Then, there was a second voice. A soprano as soft as a flower petal emerged from behind, singing entirely different words in a foreign language, yet there was no conflict. Ember raised her voice, not in competition but in joy over the harmony. Behind her, Brig'dha raised her voice to the stars as she sang her prayers to the moon goddess she worshiped.

As the Moon slowly crossed the sky, the women sang together. Ember slowly danced, being from a culture of singers and dancers, while Brig'dha merely sang and watched. Her people were not dancers and so different from river people in so many ways, yet their songs flowed like the mighty river. They had two different cultures, languages, and came from different worlds, yet they were also fast becoming a harmony, a sense of purpose made manifest in their will to reach the West despite the dangers which lay ahead. Most of all, they were companions, united by fate.

The next morning, Ember awoke to the rising Sun and the sweet call of returning birds. The thawing season was in full swing, and within perhaps nine tendays, the warm season would return. She had no idea if she would live long enough to welcome the warm winds, but she had to hope for the best. Until then, she had one primary goal, the Greatest River. A quick whiff of her skin reminded her of perhaps a minor, yet more immediate goal: a bath. After a stretch, Ember headed toward the Greatest River, leaving a line of clothes behind.

Brig'dha awoke a moment later with a yawn and a lengthy stretch. She had slept beside the radiating redhead, the pair sharing body heat under the stars as they slept. It had been warm, both from the shared heat and the fire. Most of all, the intimate proximity had been so calming and welcome that she had fallen to sleep in moments and slept deeply, without the nightmares she had experienced of late. That part was a bit odd, as she had always disliked being touched, yet Ember seemed to be the only person whose touch was welcome.

Unfortunately, the cool air reminded her that the fire needed constant maintenance. She whispered a spell to the spirits of the fire and rubbed a bit of ash over her fingers as a quick ward against burns. Magic was the way of her people and a part of everyday life. That bit of spellcraft done, she quickly sat up to coax the fire back from the ashes. Unfortunately, the flames were gone, and the embers weren't very warm. That was when she caught sight of Ember leaping naked into the icy waters of the Greatest River. The fire's embers were not the only ones to go cold, it seemed.

Does that girl think she's a fish? That water will be very cold! Brig'dha thought with worry as she stared, dumbfounded by the arctic antics. Her own people would warm water in carved stone pots or baskets lined with pine tar, then wash within a warm hut by a fire. Water heated by fire was the only way to bathe, as far as Brig'dha was concerned. As she fumbled with the fire bow to relight the makeshift-hearth, that had fully died, Brig'dha watched Ember wobbling around in the cold water. She shook her head. It was absurd to see anyone playing in such cold water, yet the redhead seemed to have a near obsession with cleanliness.

What makes her do the strange things she does? Surely the gods possess her, Brig'dha wondered with a bit of mirth, though she continued to watch the redhead closely and with particular interest as she rotated the fire bow to rekindle the flames. As she watched, the redhead splashed about in the water, scrubbing her skin and rinsing her hair as she made loud, almost startling sounds from the cold. At one point, she made a squealing sound as she splashed salty water over her arrow wound, which had still not fully healed. Ember's body was strong, her muscles even more visible as water played with the light against her skin. Brig'dha noted this with more than a passing interest.

The smoldering around the fire bow grew into a small flame as Brig'dha watched. The warrior woman was powerful and cunning yet as playful as a pine marten… or, maybe, a fox. Brig'dha tried to imagine fox ears, and a tail sprouting from the warrior and found the task quite easy. Then, with a loud squeal against the cold, Ember emerged from the icy water and sprinted back to the fire, gathering her clothes as she did. *She even sounds like a fox,* she mused, recalling the high-pitched yipping sounds the bushy-tailed animals so often made.

Suddenly, Brig'dha felt pain as fire licked her fingers, causing her to drop the fire bow into the flame. Finally paying attention to the fire, she realized that what had simply been the smoldering wood she had worked hard to ignite had become a decent fire while she was paying attention to the wrong ember. Unfortunately, the fire bow had become its victim and mockingly burned as the bemused brunette took a deep, steadying breath. She quickly turned away from the playful redhead needing to find something else to do.

She is totally bizarre, Brig'dha thought, and yet she found herself smiling, despite the loss of the valuable tool.

By the time Ember had returned to the camp, Brig'dha had quite a fire going. Oddly, Brig'dha sat before the fire, looking both confused and embarrassed, though Ember couldn't imagine why. Ember quickly huddled by the fire wrapped in a deerskin for a short while until she was thoroughly dried. She took time to place her hair before the fire close enough to dry but far enough not to be damaged. She usually did not clean her hair each day due to the cold, but today she had dove entirely into the water. As she dried, she licked her lips, tasting salt, another oddity of the Greatest River.

Her people traded well for salt, a precious commodity required for cooking and sustaining life. Had they known they could travel to someplace like this and get all the salt they wanted, it would throw the entire trade network on its head, though she supposed this might actually be where the traders were coming from. There was also the odd problem of how one would get the salt out of the water. Ember sat before the fire, drying her hair and considering salt as Brig'dha recovered from whatever confusion had overtaken her that morning.

By midday, the pair had decided to wait a few more days until they had fully rested. Their gear needed mending, they also needed a new fire bow, and they needed to ensure they were well fed, given how little food they could bring. A few days of relaxing by fire never hurt anyone, Ember had reasoned, and the Moon would be full when they left. If the trip took longer than a day, the Moon could be a life-or-death necessity in the black of night. To be caught in the Greatest River during a dark night meant not knowing which direction they were going. Just as one could become quickly disoriented underwater, so too could they become disoriented on the water.

The big problem with the Moon was determining if it would rise for the night and how bright it would be. The elders of Ember's tribe could tell precisely when the Moon would be full using a wooden block with grooves cut into it. Ember was hardly an elder, but she figured she could watch the Moon for a few days and see what it did, then predict what was to come. The Moon changed each day and night, but always by predictable amounts.

The second important task was to eat. The faster and harder they rowed, the quicker the trip would be finished. They would have little space for extra food, needing most of their space for freshwater. Ember took eating very seriously, stuffing her face with as much of the dried provisions as possible. One warmer day, she even braved the shallow inlets where the Great River emptied into the Greatest River, spearing several large fish while Brig'dha tiptoed through the shallows gathering shellfish. Overall, their bellies were kept full, and their bodies were warmed.

ɔ ɔ ɔ

A full seven days after they had arrived at the edge of the Greatest River, Ember and Brig'dha awoke just as the Sun broke the horizon to start their journey. This was the day of crossing, chosen due to the clear weather and Ember's expectation that the Moon would be full and visible much of the night. Having long been interested in the religion of her people, Brig'dha was actually much better at determining the phases of the Moon than Ember, though the reckless redhead had never asked her opinion on the subject. She smiled to herself, realizing that Ember was correct, though she neglected to mention it.

Ember had created a set of awfully poor-quality clay pots from clay not too far from the mouth of the Great River. She had dried them over the course of four days by the fire, causing three of the ten pots to break, and fired the remaining seven. Unfortunately, only four survived, the others cracking due to moisture within the clay. Brig'dha had watched, her own people having no real notion of how to make ceramics and trading for what few they had. Though the pots Ember had made were tragically bad, one of them slightly cracked and the others terribly malformed, they would suffice to hold water for the trip. Oddly, the resourceful redhead had stood proudly before her monstrous creations, seemingly pleased.

The weather had been a little dreary the past few days, but the night before, the weather had cleared. All signs pointed to this being the day, and the women would not let such a day pass. If they didn't set out in the next tenday, they would be forced to wait for many more tendays, if not entire moons, for another chance. Besides, good weather was rare on the edge of the Greatest River, and so far, the day looked clear and calm.

After a quick wash and some food, Ember and Brig'dha stood by their little boat, now missing much of its supplies. The boat had been painted with what Brig'dha had explained were magical pictograms, using a mixture of fish oil and black soot from the fire. They needed all the luck they could get, and painting and blessing the boat had been an easy way to add just such luck, assuming the gods took note. The triple swirl patterns were stunning like those Brig'dha wore on her body. Unfortunately, they attracted birds a little more than Ember would have liked.

As a final touch, they had used the last of the red ocher paint given to them by Eva and Kat'ja as a parting gift and painted their bodies for luck. Ember had covered herself from head to toe in fingertip-sized dots while Brig'dha had chosen swirls around her knees, elbows, stomach, and cheeks. Both women had dressed as warmly as they could, which hid most of their paints, but Ember had assured Brig'dha that the gods could still see the sacred markings. Again, this was something Brig'dha already knew, having worked to learn her people's spiritual ways since she was young, but she said nothing and merely smiled.

It wasn't really Ember's fault, she supposed. The rambunctious redhead was always talking, enough for both of them. To be fair, Brig'dha rarely said anything. It wasn't that Ember talked over her or didn't give her a chance to speak, either. In fact, Ember would often pause, awaiting some response before eventually jabbering on. Brig'dha wasn't a very assertive person, and she didn't really feel the need to speak most of the time, so she let Ember constantly tell her things she already knew. In truth, she liked hearing Ember speak with her thick river people accent. Besides, the redhead's confidence wasn't exactly her worst attribute, in Brig'dha's totally biased opinion.

Before leaving, they checked their clothing, ensured the oars were tied to the boat, at Ember's request, and stretched their bodies. Finally, they stood before the Greatest River, the entirety of the world at their backs and their chosen fate writhing before them. Brig'dha slowly turned to give her companion a reassuring smile. Instead, the random redhead stepped forward, wrapping her arms around the bashful brunette, squeezing her into a deep embrace. For a while, they held one another as the world held its breath. Then, before Brig'dha could realize how much it meant, it was over. Ember stepped back, a smile and a blush lighting her face with the glee of a child and the grin of a fox. Brig'dha nearly giggled as a strange series of emotions danced down her spine.

"Ready?" Ember asked, effectively changing the subject before Brig'dha could become too wrapped up in the moment. Ember wasn't interested in friendship the way she was and taunting herself before such a critical journey would only bring sorrow, loss, and the dangers of inattentiveness. She paused for a moment taking a deep breath and steadying herself before she replied, then forced a smile and nodded.

"Yes." With that, both women removed their footwear and lower garments, tossing them in the boat where they would stay dry. Starting the journey with soaking boots and clothes was a sure path to sickness, and naked skin could be dried much more quickly than leather and cordage. With one final look back toward dry land, they grasped the heavy dugout and began pushing it into the waves. Quickly, they discovered that launching a boat into the Greatest River was nothing at all like launching a boat on the Great River.

The water buffeted the little craft as they fought to keep it straight in the waves. The water had risen quite quickly to their waists when Ember gave the signal to get aboard the boat. Ember quickly hauled herself into the boat, using the waves to help push her over the side. She paused for a moment to catch her breath before realizing that Brig'dha had not made it. While larger than Ember, Brig'dha wasn't actually that strong and couldn't quite lift herself. Worse, she was at risk of swamping the boat as she struggled, her body growing numb in the cold water.

Bracing her legs against the side of the boat, Ember wrapped her arms around Brig'dha's upper body and leaned back with all her might. Brig'dha flopped into the boat, nearly causing it to capsize, but within a few moments, she was in place at the stern of the craft. For a moment, they stared at one another in shock, a smile lighting Ember's face as Brig'dha shook from fear and cold. The next moment, the boat nearly capsized a second time as a wave hit far too perpendicular to the keel.

"Oars!" Ember called, grabbing her oar and biting deep into the water with its flattened end. Behind her, Brig'dha did the same, though a bit slower. The boat bounced through the water slamming hard into water and rocking nearly out of control as they fought to escape the breaking waves by the shore for the, ironically safer, deeper waters. After what felt like a short eternity, both women fought against unseen currents, waves, and a low riding slow boat not designed for such travel. Finally, the boat began to calm along with the water as the shore drifted farther away.

Lashing the oar to the side of the boat, Ember took a breath and carefully turned to learn the toll the breakers had taken. The boat was half full of water and riding very low, but most of their limited provisions had made it. Both women carefully scooped most of the water from the boat, using their hands for the last little bits. They had lashed the limited supplies to the back and front of the boat using their two large deer hides to protect the dried goods. Their water had been placed in Ember's crude pots with leather wrappings secured around their necks to keep the water from splashing out. Some water had been lost, but most of their meager supply was still in the jars.

As soon as the boat was dry and everything was checked and secured, they began drying themselves using the deer hides and then

donning their dry clothing. Neither had complete replacements for all their clothing, but what they could replace, they did. Wet clothing was laid out where the weak thawing season sunlight might dry it. Staying dry was yet another critical survival strategy. This was hampered by the need to nearly submerge themselves in water simply to start their journey, yet it couldn't be helped.

Ember had argued that a small fire could be safely lit in the boat's center to provide needed heat and light, but Brig'dha had explained how poorly boats and fires mixed. Additionally, all the extra wood would lower the already low riding boat. Ember had conceded the point after more careful thought. In the end, the women had decided to use body heat and their collection of furs, hides, and clothing to stay warm. It wasn't going to be much, but this trip was only supposed to last one day, they hoped.

CHAPTER TWENTY
A NEW WORLD

The Rhine–Meuse–Scheldt river delta is a section of wetlands and tributaries that effectively form the Rhine River's mouth, which opens into the North Sea. The danger inherent in the trip Ember and Brig'dha now face cannot be understated. The waters of the North Sea are cold and unforgiving. Unlike the Rhine, the sea could swallow entire ships with ease, and no one existed to aid those lost at sea. Luckily, the frigid winter winds would have mostly ceased by the time the women arrived at the coastline. At this point, they are approximately 32km (20 miles) south of the present-day city of Rotterdam in the Netherlands. It should be noted that 7,500 years ago, the coastline, water depth, and general orientation of the coast would not be quite the same as today.

The North Atlantic Archipelago (i.e., British Isles) was connected to mainland Europe only a few hundred years before our story. The landmass of Doggerland that connected the North Atlantic Archipelago to continental Europe had only fully disappeared beneath the waves a few hundred years earlier. Perhaps the shallower waters of the North Sea and the English Channel will afford Ember and Brig'dha better fortunes.

Ember grunted as she launched a small piece of wood into the air watching it hit the water with a splash. Unfortunately, they didn't have a lot of spare wood, but she was determined to figure out how the currents moved in the vastness of the Greatest River. The day was already past the midpoint, and they had been rowing South by Southwest without truly gaining much distance from the land. Ember had initially believed they could simply row away from the land and eventually reach their goal, but it seemed that navigating the open waters was significantly more complex than she had anticipated.

"Aeeya!" she grumbled as the piece of wood bobbed along the low waves keeping about the same distance from the boat as time passed. Ember considered this for a moment, as well as everything else she had seen. The only explanation that made sense was that the boat and the wood were both being dragged along by the water at the same rate, as their position relative to the land was obviously changing. At best, she was reasonably convinced that the water was flowing Southwest, though it was difficult to tell, and once she could no longer reference the land, it would become much harder.

"Mohdan say west, south, then west," Brig'dha said, remembering something her late husband had said about how to navigate back to their homeland. Ember heard but said nothing, both annoyed by the confusing nature of the currents as well as the reminder that the beautiful brunette had wed a man. She had nothing against men or the women who chose their company, but her former love implied a particular sort of unavailability which stood at odds with Ember's interests. She quickly scolded herself for such selfish thoughts and brushed them aside. Brig'dha was her friend, and she had stood beside the reckless redhead even at the risk of her own life.

Ember knelt at the bow of the tiny craft watching the water splash across the prow. She had to think of something different, and considering the unknown depths of the Greatest River was the first thing to come to mind. She couldn't see a bottom, though that didn't mean anything. Even in the Great River, the bottom was often obscured by silt and other impurities. It wasn't long before the curious explorer had tied a stone scraper to some of their nettle fiber cord, of which they carried about five lengths of a man's height. Ember couldn't imagine the water would be deeper than that, but there was only one way to be sure. Behind her, she heard Brig'dha chittering with amusement. Ignoring her naysayer, the recalcitrant redhead tossed the stone in the water.

To her surprise, she quickly ran entirely out of cord, holding onto just the very end wrapped around her finger. Yet, there was no indication that the rock had hit bottom. She tugged a few times but didn't feel anything impacting, which would have been apparent in the abrupt slack of the string. Ember turned a wide-eyed gaze at the bemused brunette. Brig'dha smiled, suppressing a giggle at Ember's antics. She had no idea how deep the water was, though she had always been led to believe that it was extremely deep, perhaps as deep as a mountain. There was no way to be sure, but people in her village who had swum in the deepest parts had claimed the bottom could not be seen. Brig'dha suppressed a shudder at the thought.

"Well, if we sink, we are really going to sink," Ember observed to herself, as Brig'dha wouldn't have understood her words. After extracting the cord and neatly wrapping it to dry, she lay back and began fidgeting with some of the dried rations and one of the water pots. It was about time for their midday meal. It wouldn't be particularly filling as they were so limited in their supplies, but at least they would have something. Rowing on an empty stomach was no way to cross the water, in Ember's opinion.

As the night rolled in, both women paused their efforts at rowing, unable to continue due to the darkness. The Moon would rise shortly after the Sun set, but for a short period, there would be only darkness. Ember gazed out across the eternity of the end of the world and saw nothing but a void gazing back at her. A light cloud cover had blocked out what little light the stars provided, leaving absolutely no light sources. Forests could be dark at night, but nothing had prepared her for quite how dark the open water was. It wasn't long before Ember realized that she was breathing hard, her body reacting to the fear of the void. The air was cold, and the sound of water could be heard in all directions, but nothing could be seen.

Ember held tightly to the side of the boat, her heart beginning to race as she looked in every direction, only occasionally catching the tiniest motes of unknown light. Perhaps some of the stars occasionally shown their way through the thin clouds, or perhaps spirits were swarming their boat like wolves surrounding a victim. Ember tried to calm herself, remembering the beautiful orange glow which had lit the sky as the Sun had set, but every time she opened her eyes, there was simply nothing. Her heart began to beat so hard that she could feel it in her ears. She was about to cry out when suddenly she heard the beautiful sound of singing slicing through the darkness like an obsidian blade.

Behind her, Brig'dha began a slow, melodic song, her words far too accented for Ember to easily pick out. What little she could understand brought to mind some sort of chant, perhaps asking the spirits for help or at least reprieve. Ember quickly focused upon the words, letting nothing more pass through her mind than the beautiful sound of singing. The words were delicate, slightly guttural, and yet beautiful, nonetheless. The tone changed very little, significantly more monotonal than her own people's songs. Ember reached for the music with her mind, holding onto it like a rope thrown at a drowning person. She would ask Brig'dha if her people sang such songs for just such situations or if this was something unique to her. But for right now, all she could do was listen.

After what felt like far too long, the soft light glow of the Moon's light began to drift across the Southeastern horizon bringing with it a much-needed reprieve from the void. Brig'dha ended her beautiful song as the light began to ward whatever darkness had surrounded them. She had been frightened by the darkness just as Ember's rapid breathing belied the redhead's own fear. One of the jobs of a priestess was to banish darkness and evil. Though Brig'dha had never achieved her goal of becoming a priestess of the Moon, that didn't mean she didn't have the capacity for such a basic skill. She grinned as the pale light of the Moon bathed the small boat in its merciful luminosity. But most of all, she smiled as she caught sight of two wide, green eyes gazing back at her.

A short time later, Brig'dha lay on her back, resting against the pile of supplies and furs behind her. Her legs, longer than Ember's, rested at the redhead's sides. There wasn't enough space for both women to lie down to sleep without her legs spreading around Ember. If Ember wished to sleep, she would have to curl her legs, not having room to stretch them. Moreover, she would have to lean back into Brig'dha's lap using the brunette as a headrest. For now, Ember gently rowed as Brig'dha lay back, trying to rest. It wasn't particularly easy, but she needed her strength if they were going to row hard the next day. Unfortunately, her mind wouldn't succumb so easily to sleep.

There had been something on her mind, a particular question that had been nagging at her ever since they had rescued the women. It was a moral question, something she had never expected to face. In truth, Brig'dha had not killed any of the men in any direct sort of fashion, but she had helped set the traps, and she had left the man with the ruined foot to die. Ember's skill with her language had been growing steadily, yet she wasn't sure how easily she could ask what was on her mind given Ember's limited vocabulary. Regardless, they were floating in a sea of eternity with a low chance of survival and absolutely bored out of their minds. If there was ever a time to ask a deep philosophical question, this seemed like that time.

"Were we right to kill those men?" she asked in her native tongue, speaking each word slowly and carefully for the redhead. Ember had already proven herself to be an accomplished linguist, but no one could learn a language within a few tendays. Even so, she suspected Ember would understand at least enough to generally comprehend the question. For a short time, Ember sat there gently stroking the water with her oar. After a moment, she lifted the wooden implement, placing it across her lap, then began to reply.

"Yes. Men bad. We save woman," she said, then returned to rowing. Ember had avoided the language of Nes, which Brig'dha and Ember shared more words in, yet reminded the Brunette of darker times. Her language was crude, and she seemed to have forgotten what Brig'dha had explained to her about pluralization, but they didn't need accuracy. While Brig'dha said very little, she was very thoughtful and tended to spend a lot of time considering what somebody had said. Ember had answered the question ontologically, but Brig'dha was looking for something deeper.

"What if the men have families?" she asked, digging a bit deeper toward the ramifications, the greater impact of what they had done. She could almost imagine a confused look on Ember's face, though perhaps she merely inferred it from how the random redhead stopped mid-row.

"Hine?" Ember asked, not having recognized the Isen'bryn word for "family." Brig'dha considered for a moment before replying.

"Hine means a woman, man, and children," she said, trying her best to explain the word family. She wished that she hadn't had to use the most common form of a family as a description. She had always envisioned a family with a very different configuration, though there had been no one in her tribe to grant her such a wish. She doubted Ember would even notice, given that the redhead would likely find herself a husband and bear many children. It was the typical way of things. Brig'dha sighed as she pushed aside what could not be. Thankfully, Ember replied, breaking the silence.

"Sad families," Ember said, using the plural form of family, though she probably should have said, "Hino." She was learning so fast, but even after she learned to speak the basic language, it would be quite some time before she picked up the nuance of pluralization and other such language mechanics. Ember continued, "but man make bad choice. Sad for woman families." Brig'dha considered this, realizing the redhead was probably correct. There was really no good outcome. Doing the least harm seemed to be the most moral choice, and when one had to choose between two harms, one chose the more guilty party to suffer harm than the innocent.

It wasn't that Brig'dha didn't already realize the answer, but she wanted to hear it from someone else. It was a validation that she wasn't guilty of what had happened, though it was hard to ignore a nagging feeling that she had played some part in something immoral. Even now, that man might still be lying on the ground, half emaciated and dying from the sweats. Had wolves come for him in the night, or had he simply slit his own throat? In the end, he had chosen the risk of battle, and that choice had been his. Dying during the rescue of the women wasn't so much different than dying during the raid. Brig'dha laid back, considering her thoughts as the water lapped against the side of the boat, slowly rocking her to sleep.

Only good people questioned if their choices were wrong. Evil people were always sure they were correct, Ember supposed as she considered the curious brunette.

Ember awoke to light rain at dawn break. The gentle pattering of water was hardly a threat to the boat and provided replacement water. Brig'dha had already laid both scooping bowls out to catch what could be caught. She had even taken one large piece of leather, one of their two hides, and placed it such that water falling upon the leather would roll into one of the clay pots. Such water would have a nasty taste, but it would also provide a free drink without touching the rest of their dwindling supplies. Ember opened her mouth to catch the droplets. She felt confident as the boat gently glided across the water.

The second day passed much as the first, with both women taking turns rowing. The only significant change had been the loss of sight of the mainland. While it was something both women had expected, there was something meaningful about finally being alone on the edge of the world. Using the Sun, Ember had generally kept the boat oriented in what she believed was the right direction, though it wasn't easy to tell. For all she knew, the Sun acted differently deep in the West. All of her measurements could be completely wrong, and she feared that they were.

She sat back in the boat watching the calm waves lapping against the low riding sides of the dugout, her hand lazily hanging in the water, feeling its cold, wetness. They had been lucky with the weather so far, but it was uncommon for the Greatest River to remain calm for more than a few days. Not far away, she noticed a small sliver of wood she had flicked into the water not long before. She was nearly out of test pieces, but she was already beginning to get a feel for how the flow of water functioned. It wasn't like a river at all. She had only known two styles of water flow in her life. Rivers, creeks, and other forms of stream tended to flow at varying rates from one direction to the other. Ponds, lakes, and other such static bodies of water tended to remain still, at least for the most part.

The idea of a vast river that flowed north to south and then south to north at varying times made absolutely no sense to Ember. But what she observed and what made sense were often two completely different things. How did insects and birds fly, but when she waved her arms, she could not? Why did most rocks sink in water, yet a trader had once brought a strange gray rock which had floated? Why did most of the stars move uniformly across the sky, yet there were a few odd stars which seemed to defy this stellar flow? Such stars appeared to follow the regular stars, only to slowly shift their position every night. The world was full of mysteries Ember couldn't explain, but that didn't mean there were no explanations. The Greatest River appeared to have a bidirectional flow related to the time of day.

How this affected them was a critical issue. If her assumptions were correct, instead of rowing in what they believed was the island's direction, a smarter idea might be to row diagonally in between the direction of the flow in the direction they wish to go. If the water was flowing north and they wanted to go west, perhaps they should row northwest. When the direction of the flow changed, they would row southwest. Doing this might use the current to aid them instead of wasting energy fighting against the natural direction of the water. Unfortunately, if she were wrong, they would be wasting energy rowing north and south when they needed to go west. Which was the correct choice?

That was when the monster touched her hand.

"Aeeya! Kehd eshe!" Ember felt a smooth object brush against her hand, evoking a primal reaction of fear. She quickly yanked her fingers from the icy water and leaned over the side. Feeling a fish brush against you, and on rare occasions, even ram into your leg, was completely normal within a typical river, but what sort of creatures inhabited the Greatest River? The object had felt at least the length of a human body, given how much had passed under her fingers before she removed them. Now, as she looked over the edge, she saw nothing but the blackness of the water.

"What?" Brig'dha called from behind, alerted by Ember's exclamation. Brig'dha hadn't learned much of Ember's language, but she knew what "aeeya" meant. It was effectively a swear word and one Ember used quite often. As the bewildered brunette began looking about for the source of the disturbance, she caught sight of something large on the opposite side of the craft. She had seen this creature before and heard many tales, though she had never seen one this close. Brig'dha swallowed in fear as she realized just how helpless they were.

Fear seized her when Ember looked over the edge as a giant form became visible just beneath the water. Whatever the creature was, it was at least as wide as she stood tall and at least five times as long, with a short dorsal fin towards its back. The monstrous creature glided by effortlessly despite its impossible size. Most strangely, its fluke, the fins that defined its tail, ran horizontal, unlike a fish's vertical fins. Ember wheeled around to tell Brig'dha, but her words died in her throat as she caught sight of the bedazzled brunette. Ember quickly turned her head following Brig'dha's line of sight, and then she too realized the enormity of their situation.

All around them, at least five of the massive creatures swam. Every now and then, the very tops of their backs would breach the surface for only a moment before sinking beneath the waves. Ember couldn't help but remember tossing wheat bread pieces at a school of fish when she was young. Large fish had swarmed the bread, buffeting it all over the place until one of them had finally swallowed it. They were insignificant in size compared to these creatures and entirely at their mercy. Just then, one of the creatures abruptly surfaced, releasing a massive burst of water and breath into the air, reaching high above their little boat and drenching both women.

"What this?" Ember managed to say in Brig'dha's language. Could these creatures be air-breathing, she wondered as a second behemoth surfaced and seemed to release its breath before diving once more. Ember had done such things when swimming so many times, but never to such dramatic effect. She had also never seen fish breathe air unless the water was so muddy and stagnant that they could not seem to breathe the water. But this water was dark and clear, and shouldn't have been a problem to breathe in, or so she supposed.

"They are called Ussa, a giant fish. They are a good omen, but they can kill you if you anger them. They usually swim alone," Brig'dha said. Ussa was her people's word for whale, though it described any type of whale, including the current pod of minke whales, as they would one day come to be known. Ember looked back at the creatures in absolute awe. She couldn't imagine anything so giant living in the world, and yet these creatures glided effortlessly through the water. Behind her, she began to hear Brig'dha chanting some sort of religious prayer. The words were mostly too accented to pick out, though she thought she heard the words for moon and whale, the latter having just been learned. She supposed Brig'dha was singing to the whales, probably asking them to leave them in peace.

This river has some really big fish, she thought.

"Ask usse help Inn'bry'th," Ember suggested, switching ussa to usse, the way her people pluralized words that ended in 'a.' She wasn't sure if that was how it worked with Brig'dha's language, but the brunette seemed to understand. Unfortunately, she quickly shook her head in disagreement.

"It is not safe to ask them for help without a proper offering. If they become offended, they may kill us," Brig'dha said, speaking slowly for Ember to understand. In fact, Ember only understood five words, but it was enough to understand what the brunette had said. Ember frowned, not liking the answer.

"Usse... um, Usse bad no help..." she began to say, then realized she simply didn't have the vocabulary to say what she meant. So she spoke in her own language needing to get the words out even though she knew Brig'dha wouldn't understand.

"These usse are greedy with their knowledge. I would help someone if I were in their place. Typical fish," she mumbled. Brig'dha cocked an eyebrow as though she had perhaps inferred some of Ember's meaning, at least from the redhead's tone.

"We need to row toward the West for the rest of the day and the night," Brig'dha said, speaking slowly, and with a change of subject. Ember understood some of the words, but she disagreed. Beside them, another ussa spouted water. This was the first time Brig'dha had made a proclamation on their strategy. Still, it didn't seem that she had taken into account the movement of the water. Although to be fair, Ember hadn't explained it though she had been thinking about it in detail for well over a day.

"Water move north. Water move south. We move north, west. We move south, west," Ember explained in broken Isen'bryn, using her hands to vigorously describe what she meant and how traveling at an angle might actually use less energy. Brig'dha watched and then laid her oar across her lap as she shook her head in disagreement. She held her left hand before her and said, "Inn'bry'th," clearly indicating that her left hand meant to represent the island. Then, using her right hand, she drew a zigzag line toward the island and said, "Much longer. We will grow tired and die." She then returned her right hand to the starting location below the left. She brought both hands together, indicating a straight path.

"If we travel straight, we might make it. When you sew a straight line, you use less thread than a zigzag," she explained, using her hands to emphasize the meaning of zigzag as she knew there was no chance Ember understood that word. She waited a moment for the redhead to process what she had said, given how many new words she had used. Unfortunately, they had struck a disagreement. Ember shook her head, growing frustrated both at Brig'dha's lack of understanding of the problem and her own inability to explain it.

"We move. Water move. Water, change south, north," she said, waving her hands about trying to explain the problem. The math that would describe the problem Ember was intuitively recognizing wouldn't be invented for another 5000 years. Describing the complex trigonometry was both beyond her limited vocabulary and her own conceptual ability. It wasn't that she truly understood the principles. It was more of an intuitive understanding. Just as a child knew how to throw a rock in a high arc and hit a target but couldn't explain the physics behind how it worked.

"If we do not go straight, we will die. We are low on food and water, and there is no land!" Brig'dha said, growing agitated. Rarely did the bashful brunette become argumentative, but an empty stomach, one small pot of water, whales, and the never-ending expanse surrounding them were beginning to have an effect. Ember held her hands up and started trying to explain the angles once more, but she stumbled over her own words. It wasn't that she was just missing the word for one concept or another, but large portions of the sentence. She became more and more frustrated as she tried to explain, failing at such a rudimentary level due to something so simple as basic language.

"No, we must go straight," Brig'dha interjected, interrupting Ember as she had just begun to form a complex sentence. Exhaustion, hunger, and a massive frustration over her inability to express herself suddenly came to a head. Ember slammed her hand against the side of the boat in an uncommon outburst of anger and frustration.

"Aeeya! I can't explain anything to you, and it's going to get us killed! We both have to agree over what to do if we are going to make it, but I can't even tell you what I mean. A child still suckling its mother's breast could speak better than I can. We have almost no water or food, and we don't have enough strength and supplies to try both ways. We either do yours or mine, and if we choose wrong, we are going to die!" Ember blasted in her own language, unable to hold back her frustration. As she looked up, Brig'dha began to tear up in frustration as well as having been yelled at. Ember hadn't actually yelled at Brig'dha, but the brunette had no idea what had been said and had probably mistaken Ember's frustration for something more direct.

They were both exhausted, and what had seemed like a good idea for a one-day trip was starting to turn into their inevitable doom. Brig'dha wiped her eyes, upset and frightened, while Ember hung her head in her own embarrassment. She hadn't actually attacked Brig'dha, but she could guess how it must have seemed to the other woman.

"I can't even tell you I'm sorry..." she mumbled under her breath. They sat there in silence for the rest of the evening as the ussa slowly departed for wherever giant creatures went in the Greatest River. In fact, there wasn't much to say, and there was no feeling of an imminent agreement. Both women realized they should probably be rowing, yet they felt their spirits dampened by the argument.

The Moon appeared in the Southeast later that night, a while after the last reddish glow of the setting Sun disappeared below the horizon. The Moon would rise later each night for some time, eventually rising during the day as it slowly waned. No one knew why this happened, but it was reasonably predictable if you paid attention. Ember had never had to spend this much time observing the Moon, something elders typically did. But as she watched, she caught sight of the bleak brunette as she too watched the glowing orb in silence. As far as Ember could tell, Brig'dha had initially intended to become some sort of religious person, perhaps a priestess or similar, among her people. It seemed that the Moon Goddess was her primary focal point. It occurred to her that she had probably missed a good opportunity to have learned what she needed to know about the Moon cycles by simply asking Brig'dha instead of trying to do it herself.

Brig'dha was normally a quiet woman, content in her own knowledge and without the need to tell the world what she knew. She was smart, and she was kind, yet silent and shy. Perhaps they could have become more in another life, but unfortunately, her previous marriage had indicated her interests. Regardless, she had the makings of a great friend, and their mutual silence pained Ember. As time passed, it began to not matter who had said what and who was at fault. In fact, it had simply been a misunderstanding – a mere inability to communicate. Ember considered for a moment that most conflict might just be an inability to communicate. Humans seemed to be better than the other animals at communication, at least in a complex fashion, yet humans were also violent and petty. Overcoming such basic instincts was difficult, but it was also the only way for people to survive in a hostile world. And so, Ember would try her best to overcome them.

Reaching into her bag, she extracted the last two pieces of dried deer meat. They had actually been part of her meal that morning, which she had saved. Of course, both pieces together wouldn't offer much sustenance. They had brought so little food with them to keep the boat as light as possible as it rode so low in the water. With a soft, barely audible sigh, Ember slowly lay back, placing her head in Brig'dha's lap. She doubted Brig'dha would welcome such a direct interaction when she might still be angry but turning around in the small boat would likely capsize them.

"Eat?" she said, having at least one simple thing she could communicate with her limited vocabulary. Above her and upside down from her perspective, the befuddled brunette frowned in return. For a moment, Ember felt compelled to lift back up into a sitting position, but someone had to be nice first. Ember smiled a forced and silly look. For the moment, Brig'dha continued frowning. She had mistaken Ember's words and believed that the redhead had yelled at her in frustration, something which had upset her. Brig'dha owed the redhead her life, and deeply she cared for Ember more than she could ever express, given Ember's lack of interest in women, as far as she could tell. But there was something about being angry in the moment that compelled one to hold their ground and maintain dangerous levels of frowning.

Suddenly, Ember's face began to change, taking on an extra silly look. Brig'dha's eyebrows furrowed as she tried to ignore the silly face. She should just turn away, but how could one look away from such a person as Ember? Ember's eyes began to cross as her tongue poked out, and then a strange childlike sound came from her mouth. Brig'dha's jaw twitched as her muscles fought against the smile of defeat. The argument no longer mattered as much as not being the first to give in. Yet, there the redhead sat in her lap, savagely bombarding her with one silly face after another.

"I Uuuuuuussssaaaaaa!" Ember said, puffing her face as she declared herself to be a whale. She looked absolutely nothing like a whale, and yet it was the final blow. Brig'dha surrendered to the onslaught and burst into laughter, unable to hold back against such magnitude of inane silliness. After a moment, she accepted the proffered meat. She wasn't sure where Ember had gotten it, but she figured it was something the redhead had saved. Besides, if she asked, she might feel guilty and refuse to eat it. This was surely a peace offering, and above all, Brig'dha valued peace. If the redhead had simply held out a short time longer, she would have been the one to give in. As it was, Brig'dha had already come close to the longest she could hold a grudge against someone she cared for. The whole thing was silly, and yet human social dynamics never seem to make much sense.

A short time later, Brig'dha lay back with Ember's head in her lap, having eaten their tiny meal and consumed half of the remaining pot of water. They kept a small amount for the next day, but that was the end. Above them, the stars covered the sky in a sea of beauty beyond anything which existed on dry land. About three hands distance above the horizon, a bright star with a slightly orange glow lay to the Southwest. It was one of the strange stars which appeared at any given night to follow the others but secretly traveled at a slightly different rate. The star would one day be known as the planet Saturn, though it was merely an enigma for now.

Near it hung the constellations of the Great Spindle and the Rabbit. Not far from them stood the Deer, out dancing through the night because the Huntress was hidden beneath the horizon and would be for most of the season.

"Do you think we will make it?" Brig'dha asked after a time. Her warm hand rested on Ember's shoulder, a gentle presence, yet nothing in the world was more noticeable to Ember at the moment.

"I no say," Ember said, indicating that she wasn't sure. If they did make it, she resolved to fully learn Brig'dha's language so she could stop speaking like a toddler. The matter of whose strategy to follow had still not been worked out, but Ember was tired of arguing, and she felt guilty for not having asked Brig'dha's opinion over the Moon, something she should have done. If the gods truly cared and had wished for her to come this way, then perhaps they would aid her, whichever choice she made. Though she was sure her diagonal route was best, she decided to place her trust in her new friend. In fact, it was the soft, warm feel of Brig'dha's hand upon her shoulder which had reminded Ember what was truly important in life, and it wasn't just winning arguments.

"We go [straight,]" Ember said, using her hand to indicate a straight line. For a moment, Brig'dha said nothing, having been caught off guard by the non sequitur statement. Then, after a moment, she recovered and began to protest.

"Oh, no. We can try your way. It's just..." she began to say, but Ember cut her off. If they both let their empathy guide them to the point of ridiculous placation, they would remain indecisive, and that would also be their death. Ember looked up at the beautiful brunette, her head silhouetted by the nearly full moon, and shook her head.

"No. We go Breeg'dha," she said, indicating they would use the brunette's plan. Ember smiled reassuringly, hoping to convey that she was entirely on board though she still truly believed her diagonal course was their best chance. Brig'dha gazed down, watching the moonlight reflecting off the redhead's green eyes, though they failed to show color in the lowlight of nightfall. She could see the indecision and the plainly obvious concession for what it was. As much as she had cared for Mohdan, the man had been stubborn and would never have backed down from his position. That was typical of many men she had met, though Brig'dha had known plenty of stubborn women. It seemed like a simple concession, but she knew the redhead believed that their very lives hung upon who was correct.

This meant that Ember had just willingly chosen what she believed was the most likely course to her death to restore harmony to their friendship and show her trust and Brig'dha. While many might not have realized the significance of such an act, the enormity of it hit Brig'dha like an icy breeze. A wave of emotion danced through her body as a lump formed in her throat. Her eyes began to water as she considered how much it meant to her that someone had finally listened and respected her judgment. Yet, there was resentment and sadness as well, as she considered how many times she had simply been dismissed by her former husband, the People of Nes, and so many others over her short life. Worse, this one instance of validation could cost them their lives.

People equated her calm, quiet, and reasonably passive demeanor for weakness or even incompetence. But it wasn't true. A flower hidden behind trees and bushes bloomed just as beautifully as one prominently placed for all to see. And while that may be true, Ember had been the first in a long time to simply treat her with respect. Brig'dha wondered deep down if her feelings were genuine, or merely the product of the need to cling to someone, anyone who showed her basic respect. It was too early to be sure, and she hoped it wasn't the latter, as that was unfortunately so common. They would choose when the Sun once more rose, a final choice. Finally, with a sigh, she lay back and watched the stars, letting the dark waters of the Greatest River rock them both to sleep.

"Breeg'dha!" The bewildered brunette awoke to the sound of her name called just above the howl of the wind. As she opened her eyes, she immediately realized that everything that seemed calm was no more. The first thing she noticed was the clouds above. They were darker than night, and the texture of the wool of sheep kept by river people. They grew significantly darker toward the South. As she sat up and looked, massive curtains of water could be seen on the Southwestern horizon. It was an enormous storm, and by the look of it, they had both slept through the very beginning. Brig'dha shook her head, trying to get her bearings as adrenaline worked to remove the sleep from her mind. All around, the wind was picking up, and what had been a relatively calm Greatest River had already turned into large waves beginning to splash over the edge of their small boat.

"Breeg'dha!" she heard her name once more as her mind finally stepped into the present. Looking around, she realized that her oar had slipped overboard. At first, panic flooded her veins, overpowering the previous panic, until she discovered the cord Ember had insisted be tied to the oar had held. She grasped the nettle fiber cordage and tugged the oar from the frothy water. She quickly tapped Ember on the back, signaling that she was awake and helping. The wind was so loud it was becoming difficult to hear. Brig'dha stabbed the tip into the churning water and began rowing as hard as she could. She had seen storms like this before as her people lived on the edge of the Greatest River. She had seen waves as tall as a tree and knew what they were in store for. Unfortunately, this wasn't something one usually survived.

Ember fought to keep the boat from turning sideways against the waves as they would surely capsize, but what had been such calming waves that had put her to sleep the night before were suddenly as tall as she stood and seemed to be growing. Wave after wave slammed across the bow flooding the boat with water. Dugout boats were made of wood and wouldn't really sink, but if they became too full of water, they would lower to just under the surface. Sitting on a log just beneath the surface of the water was probably better than openly swimming, but it wasn't much better, and they would quickly freeze to death in the icy waters. Ember knew what they needed to do, though to do so was committing them to an act they couldn't undo. They would need to toss all their precious supplies overboard, which would lighten the boat just a little. It wouldn't do much, but it might gain them just a short moment, perhaps enough for the gods to get off their lazy butts and do something.

"Brig'dha, throw the supplies overboard!" she screamed, forgetting to use Brig'dha's language, though she probably couldn't have said it anyway, having no idea which words to use for supplies, overboard, or throw, for that matter. Squeezing the oar between her legs to keep it secure, Ember grabbed the supplies and began tossing them. She even tossed their water bailing pot as it would probably be washed overboard anyway, and they wouldn't have the free hands to use it.

As Ember shoveled a leather hide overboard, she noticed the clouds before them towering higher than the rest, looking almost white and puffy at the top amidst the dark clouds of the storm. She wondered why those clouds were different, but right now wasn't the time to consider the nature of clouds. Instead, she grabbed everything not bound to her body and tossed it overboard, watching the boat finally starting to rise in the water, just a little.

Behind her, Brig'dha understood Ember's intent within moments, though she had no idea what had actually been said. It was amazing how body language and tone could convey a message. To say that she had reservations about throwing their final items overboard was an understatement, but Ember was a deep thinker above all. If the resourceful redhead was willing to do something so brash, she had to have some sort of logical reason, Brig'dha supposed. Besides, if Ember was ready to trust Brig'dha and go against her better judgment, choosing a path she had believed might lead to her death, then she would do the same. With that, Brig'dha pinched the oar between her legs, just as Ember had, and reached behind herself to begin tossing supplies.

The boat did rise ever so slightly, but the effect of the water rushing into it was beginning to counteract their gains as Ember and Brig'dha returned their efforts to rowing. Unfortunately, they had yet another problem. They were unsure of which way to row as the waves buffeted them about, disorientating them. The Sun had been obscured by clouds, though the strange towering cloud formation continued to present itself as an object of intrigue. The storm was to Ember's left, which she supposed was probably south. If that were true, that would make the white puffy clouds West. Ember began to wonder why the clouds were so different. How her mind could become analytical at a time like this was beyond anyone's understanding, and yet she kept thinking about the way the clouds moved.

In her mind, Ember imagined the clouds were a thick layer above them, moving south to north. To the East, the Sun's light shone down upon them from above, mostly blocked by the sheer density of the clouds. As she thought about it, she realized that clouds rising above the other, darker clouds would catch more of the unobscured light from above and reflect lighter than those below. That might explain why the puffy clouds ahead were lighter, but why would they rise? Then it hit her: all the clouds maintained what appeared to be the same distance from the ground, as best as anyone could tell. So, wouldn't that mean that the clouds ahead had risen because the land had risen? And if that were the case, would that not mean an island?

"Breeg'dha, row!" Ember screamed over her shoulder, pointing towards the puffy clouds ahead. Behind her, she felt a hand pat her on the shoulder, indicating that Brig'dha had understood. It seemed that going in a straight line had suddenly become the only viable option. So they rowed as hard as they could, the boat filling steadily with water until it rode so low in the water Ember began to fear with each wave that it would simply go under. Then, suddenly, a major swell came out of nowhere. It was the largest she had ever seen, rising at least twice her height and filling her with primal fear. If she hadn't been so wet, she would have felt the tears from her eyes as terror gripped her when the bow began to turn orthogonal to the wave.

"Row!" Brig'dha screamed from behind, dragging Ember back into the moment. The redhead leaned over the edge of the swamped boat, digging her oar deep into the water as she fought with muscles honed from her short life of grinding wheat and other rigorous tasks. Then, using all the endurance she had, she pulled the bow toward the wave. Suddenly, the boat began to ride up the edge of the wave is both women held on for their lives. The top of the wave started to break, but their diagonal course road along its break, sending them across the crashing wave and down the other side. As they cut across the crest, Ember caught sight of what looked like a stretch of land. It was very close, only obscured by the waves and the rain. That meant the water below them was no longer deep, the very reason that the swell had begun to break as waves did when they approached the shore.

Everything went black as the boat disappeared beneath the wave. For a brief moment, Brig'dha and Ember were entirely underwater. The water was a dark, terror-fueled void so cold that it stole their breaths. What monsters lay below those waves, ready to drag them away? A moment later, the boat emerged from the other side afloat once more, but only because it was wood. Ember looked behind herself and caught sight of Brig'dha, who was still holding on using her knees pressed against the sides of the boat to remain fixed in place, just as Ember had. Unfortunately, they were now riding level with the icy water and wouldn't last long.

"BREEG'DHA! INN'BRY'TH! ROW!"

Ember screamed as they fought against the swamped boat and the Greatest River to reach their destiny. Behind her, Ember could hear Brig'dha gasping as she fought to move the small boat. They lay just beyond the breakers, perhaps forty or fifty lengths of a man away. Yet, it might as well have been an eternity against the heavyweight of the boat. Ember's body was already growing numb in the water. That's when she realized that the only way to survive was to go all the way – to make the final leap and hope for the best. Ember looked behind her and caught Brig'dha's terrified look. She let go of her oar and gazed into the beautiful brunette's hazel eyes once more.

"Come!" she said, not knowing the word for swim. Brig'dha looked absolutely terrified, though, in the moment, her gaze conveyed understanding. She was being asked to let go of the boat, the oar, and everything she had left. It was a leap of trust – an act that would either kill her or save her. All around, the Greatest River's might grew by the moment with even greater swells clearly visible. The oar fell from her hand as she reached forward and took Ember's. They squeezed their hands tightly together, and with one final gaze into those foxy green eyes, they plunged into the icy abyss.

Brig'dha had never felt such cold before that day. It felt like thousands of obsidian arrowheads stabbing her body in every direction. The shock was so intense that she nearly doubled over, though she recovered more quickly because she'd already been dropped into the water once before. She couldn't feel her limbs almost immediately, and what breath she had was quickly stolen by the shock. The only thing she could feel was the cold embrace of the water and the tight squeeze of Ember's hand. She didn't feel it through her skin which had already become numb. Instead, she felt it deep within her flesh, closer to her bones where the nerves were still warm enough to feel. The pair kicked their legs and swum as hard as they could against the incredible current.

Brig'dha's vision began to darken as she felt herself running out of energy, or perhaps it was merely heat. Nothing stripped the heat from the body like water. Unfortunately, when the body ran out of heat, it ran out of life. She continued swimming as she felt the waters becoming more turbulent, Ember's tightly interlocked fingers holding onto her like a lifeline. At one point, she felt something brush her foot. Was it the ground or perhaps a monster? She was so far beyond even fear that she continued trying to swim, though her legs were beginning to fail her. Darkness began to overcome Brig'dha as her hand touched something beneath her, though it was so numb she only felt the impact deep within her flesh. She was numb and out of energy. All she wanted to do was fall asleep. It was time to let go, time to give up. The last thing she felt was Ember's hand still holding hers.

ᴐ ᴐ ᴐ

When she opened her eyes, she saw nothing but flame. None of the afterlife stories spoke of flame, and so she sat for a moment simply watching the fire dancing before her. It took Brig'dha a moment to realize that she was lying on her side covered with leaves, dried bark, and all manner of foliage. Beneath this, she was naked, but she was warm. Before her was a fire burning hot, and behind her, she felt what could only be a second fire. Slowly, she rolled onto her back and gazed up at the sky. There were still clouds, but what had been a stormy morning was now a clearing night. Brig'dha's body hurt. Her muscles ached, her skin felt raw in many locations, and her underarms hurt as though somebody had grabbed her and dragged her that way.

"Ember!" she cried out, suddenly remembering the radiant redhead. Slowly, she sat up as the leaves and dirt tumbled off of her bare skin. Her hair was still a little damp but mostly dry, and her clothes were lying by the fire on a small stick frame, drying. The last thing she remembered was plunging into the Greatest River. She remembered those emerald eyes which had compelled her to throw herself to oblivion and a hand that wouldn't let go. She had taken a leap of trust, and yet she lived. Brig'dha lay back down at the fire, still feeling extremely tired. She wanted to look for her friend, but she was simply too exhausted to move. Then from behind her, she heard the lower voice of her companion, and a deep relief filled her like the warmest drink.

"Breeg'dha good?" Ember asked with her thick accent, approaching with a new armload of wood. The redhead was wearing her clothing, though it still looked wet in a few places. She had obviously remained conscious, and Brig'dha had no doubt the daring warrior had dragged her from the freezing water to safety. Ember was just such a person, and she was simply too tired to ask.

"Yes, I am just tired," Brig'dha replied, though she was still fatigued. Near hypothermia had that effect, and it would be at least a day before she began to feel better. She supposed Ember had stripped her clothing and set up a fire. How could she have done this when she would have only been marginally better off? And that was when Brig'dha remembered how many times Ember swam in the icy waters to wash, even during the cold season. Somehow, the redhead was more tolerant of the cold, or at least to the shocking experience. Ember's esoteric ways had likely saved them both, though she shuddered to think of the cold. Looking about, she recognized the beach, at least in general. Ember saw her looking around and decided to ask the question she had been waiting much of the day to ask.

"Inn'bry'th?" Brig'dha was too tired to reply, but she nodded her head, yes. They were probably several days either north or south of her village, but this was definitely Inn'bry'th, and it even looked familiar, though she couldn't place it. Brig'dha lay still as the soft bliss of sleep began to overcome her exhausted body. They would need to repair their clothing and find food before they journeyed to find the Isen'bryn, but at least her heart still beat, and she still drew breath, which made those other tasks seem simple. Her last thought before she gave in to sleep was a strange memory of cold but velvety lips. If she had not known better, she would have sworn someone had kissed her, but the mind played tricks on itself with delirium.

EPILOGUE

Ember's goddess pendant, obsidian dagger, and her pouch containing the frozen water had survived, having been extra securely bound to her person. Ember had learned a hard lesson during a storm on the Great River, almost an entire harvest before. Unfortunately, the rest of their possessions had disappeared beneath the waves. Both women wore their basic clothing, which was easy enough to repair after it had dried. They had spent the first few days recovering and eating their fill of fish and small game. At first, Ember had taken care of Brig'dha, but eventually, the bashful brunette had recovered enough to help. Together, they quickly created the essential tools they would need to survive, such as a fishing spear and a crudely knapped stone blade for Brig'dha. Working together, they had become ready for the final leg of their journey in only five days.

It had taken three more days of walking before they had finally encountered a village. The settlement was actually three small families living close together and hardly counted as a full village, but that was more common in the lands of Inn'bry'th. Though it was difficult, Brig'dha understood their dialect enough to learn that she was only about four days south from her own village. To hear that they were so close had filled both women with a sense of excitement, returning some much-needed energy to their tired bodies. The pair walked steadily north another day before heading west along the coast toward Brig'dha's village, near what would one day become the city of Cromer, England.

As the Sun set low in the sky on the ninth day since they arrived, Ember noticed the first signs of a village. Near the water's edge stood drying racks left over from the cold season. Near the racks, wooden posts as tall as a man and carved with spiral designs stood like beacons of humanity. Ember was unsure of their utility, but their proximity to the water suggested that they were used to secure boats. For a moment, they stood before the closest wooden pole staring at it. Ember was simply curious while Brig'dha seemed to be evaluating it, perhaps determining if its markings were familiar. After a moment, she spoke, explaining the strange poles. This time, Ember understood more of her words. True to her word, Ember had worked much harder than usual to learn as much of

Brig'dha's language as she could. She wasn't interested in braving the Greatest River again, or at least anytime soon. So, she needed to learn the local tongue.

"They are called Geru'nas. You tie boats to them, but they also ward evil spirits and bring luck to those on the water," she said in a matter-of-fact tone. Ember still only understood a few words, but learning a language was a lengthy task. Ember's own people used much smaller boats which could simply be pulled ashore. But, judging by the strength of the mighty Greatest River and how thick the posts to secure the boats were, she suspected Brig'dha's people created much larger craft.

Up ahead, Ember noticed the white, puffy motes of smoke rising from what must be a village. It was a gentle column of smoke, the kind one created while cooking on a small fire. That was when they noticed movement on the rise, just above the shore. Both women glanced up and caught sight of a small child watching them. A moment later, an older woman joined the child, likely having come to see what they had found.

The old woman had long, dark hair with blue eyes and skin as brown as Brig'dha, though much more wrinkled with time. She wore a fur shawl decorated with feathers and bone beads to warm her upper body. She wore a thick leather wrap skirt that ran to the ground, adorned heavily with bone beads creating a beautiful white speckled pattern. Her face was red, smeared with ocher. After a moment, she lifted her hand and waved encouragingly. Brig'dha abruptly waved back, then turned to face Ember as her eyes began to mist.

"That is old woman Glea, the priestess of my village. I do not know the child, but they were probably born just after I left. I am home," Brig'dha said as she swallowed back tears. The two friends stood holding hands as they waited for the rest of the village to come and greet them. They had journeyed so long and so far, each wishing to reach the far West for different reasons. For Brig'dha, this was a return to her home after losing her husband in nearly her life. For Ember, this was her destiny foretold by the gods. She still didn't understand why, though perhaps returning Brig'dha was the reason. She supposed it beat making a pot or weaving something, but she still wished the gods had been a little nicer. Ember had left her home as a young woman, and now she stood far to the West as a warrior. She had no idea what the future would bring, but her fire was just beginning to burn in this distant land...

An ember of a new world to explore.

Ember with her fishing spear and a wels catfish

EMBER'S LANGUAGE

Neolithic languages are entirely unknown and will likely never be known. They were not recorded in any known way, leaving us to guess based on limited, often deeply hypothetical models. In the books, many cultures have languages the reader will encounter. This was done to provide realism, though it is important to understand that these languages are, at best, hypothetical, and mostly just educated guesses. Ember's language is entirely created by the author using a method of following root words from the oldest regional languages backward, examining how they changed, then extrapolating how they might have been. This method is called comparative reconstruction. Unfortunately, the level of unknown elements makes Ember's language so filled with unknown variables that it may be no better than a simple guess. Either way, the languages spoken in the series are internally consistent and follow strict structures and rules.

Ember's language follows a very loosely subject-verb-object word order. As an example, one might say, "Ember carries the rock," in which the parts of the sentence are: "Ember [subject] carries [verb] the [particle] rock [object]." In fact, the sentence can be used in other orders, such as, "The rock, Ember carries," and this may be done to emphasize the object or even the verb. Another interesting feature is the non-verbal aspects of the language. Often, head gestures indicate directions, while hand gestures indicate actions. This is often depicted in the book using brackets to describe the gestures: "The river [nods toward the East]" versus the modern, English equivalent of, "The river is to the East."

The use of the letter "h" in many words in the language indicates elongated vowels. While various markings are used in linguistics to indicate this, the author chose a direct, phonetic method to prevent the reader from needing to know this. For example, the word "Aneha," meaning 'blossom," would be pronounced, An-nay-ah, where the 'h' is used to elongate the e sound. Otherwise, the reader might accidentally pronounce the word as, Ann-ee-ah.

Adjective – Adjectives are often connected to a noun using a single quote. Example, "A big stick" would be, "A big'stick." When spoken, both words are pronounced as a single word with a brief pause at the single quote.

Adverb – Adverbs are often connected to a verb using a quote. Example, "He almost tripped" would be, "He almost'tripped." When spoken, both words are pronounced as a single word with a brief pause at the single quote.

Determiner – Determiners are usually not used, such as "a," "this," and "that." Example, "A tree is big" might be spoken as, "Tree is big". A head nod or non-verbal indicator may be included.

Exclamation – When a word is spoken with exclamation, the most prominent vowel is usually elongated. For example, sleep "sewep", would be exclaimed as, "seeewep!"

Conjunction – Conjunctions are often implicit, not using conditional words, like "if." Example, "If you eat this, you will be sorry!" would be spoken as, "You eat this, you will be sorry!"

Pluralization – Words are pluralized by adding a modifying sound. For words ending with an e or eh, an "a" sound is added. For all other words, an "e" sound is added. Example, the word for woman, "Geneh," would be pluralized as "Geneha, while the word for wolf, "vokas," would be pluralized as "vokase."

Preposition – Sometimes added before the word it affects using a single quote when the affect is significant or to be stressed. Example, "I saw her pass it to'them."

Pronouns – Female, male and gender-neutral pronouns exist, though most words are not gendered. Ember's language places very little emphasis on gender pronouns, often using a person's name or simply implying the subject.

Verbs – Verbs are often connected to a noun using a single quote. Example, "the cat ran" would be, "the cat'ran." When spoken, both words are pronounced as a single word with a brief pause at the single quote.

VOCABULARY

1	un	Close (near)	dhuak
2	dun	Dark	kar
3	tun	Daughter	daka
4	kuv	Dead	mordh
5	pun	Deer	vahen
6	ses	Drink/Eat	po'eh
7	sev	Do Not	maedhe
8	dukuv	Do	edhe
9	nen	Early	eu
10	des	Ember	kaelu
3rd Gender	wergene	Enjoy	turto
Agree	ya	Equal	sahm
Alive/life	giae	Far	kehl
Always	deleh	Father	patr
Am	kah	Fertility	aipe
Ash	kene	Festival/Ritual	kue
Ask	aes	Fertility Fest	aipku
Bad	duhs	Fear	deueh
Baby (Young)	kende	Feel	ten
Be/is/are	eshe	Fire	ehkne
Beautiful	wehnose	Fish	pehsk
Berry	marag	For/to	de
Big (Great)	meg	Forest	dahru
Bite	dek	From	aph
Bitter	deke	Fuck	aeeya
Biter	aeleh	Good	ehsu
Blade	akore	Hair	keris
Blood	esnee	Harm	derg
Blossom	aneha	Have	kehp
Blow	behs	Her/She	dehmoh
Boat	naulos	Hello	eleh
Bone	ohsdh	Help	kik
Bow	wehbueg	Hope	aeis
Buy (Trade)	kraeh	Hot	gehr
Cloth	keteh	I	ehg
Cold	ne'gehr	Is/be	eshe
Copper	aos	Join	ghed
City	meg'uek	Journey	deru
Char (from fire)	meg'kene	Kill	kerord

Know	ehuedh	Sit	sehde
Leather	lereh	South	sewh
Like (Similar)	ehig	Sorry	behunas
Little	pew	Star	sier
Look	spegh	Stupid	morehs
Love	wennus	Spirit	enesu
Make	kehr	Take	gheab
Man (Male)	wer	Textile (woven)	wheskeh
Marry	gheme	Thank you	ehshe
Might (Should)	dehmagh	That	en
Mother	matr	Third Gender	wergene
Moon	meneh	This	keh
My	ehg	Thief	meyus
My	e'(object)	To (for)	de
Me	eag	Thought	menh
Me (for/to)	(ki)eag	Touch	kreah
Name	nome	Tree	dehrue
Night	nehk	Try	dedhe
Neck	kopel	Until/till	dehe
Negation	ne'(object)	Us	es
Next	nes	Warrior	kor'ghe
New	neuh	Water	aka
Nothing	nehk	Wait	stehk
No	ne	We	es
Now	ne	Weave	whese
Obsidian	mehlek	Well	sueh
Of	apu	What	kehd
Our	wedh	Why	kehne
People	dau	Will	wit
Prepare	ekos	With	khu
Pottery	kort	With you	khum
Quiet	tas	Wolf	vokas
Question	pehkseh	Woman	geneh
Raven	aukrose	Word	aeg'lk
Ready	ekose	World	lenh
Red	errutas	Work	peh'os
River	denn	When	eome
Rock/Stone	ondah	Who	khas
Run	dremo	Year	ahden
Say	sehke	Yes	eya
Sharp	meg'ak	You	tuh (dhue)
Shut up	taseh	Vulture	veasehes
Sleep	sewep		

ABOUT THE AUTHOR

Ishtar Watson has an academic background in both computer science and archaeology. They live on the eastern coast of the United States with their super-smart spouse and a handful of cats. Ishtar has written several novels and LGBTQIA+ (pre)historic adventure-romance short stories and novellas. Their hobbies include archaeology, especially Neolithic clothing and adornment, astrophotography, model rocketry, weaving and spinning prehistoric textiles, nuclear physics (specifically gamma spectroscopy), mineralogy, archery, artificial intelligence, and writing.

Having Autism, ADHD, and Tourette Syndrome, along with many comorbid conditions, such as misophonia and dyslexia, Ishtar enjoys writing stories with neurodivergent characters. Their spouse is also neuro-divergent having ADHD and Autism – this mix of conditions forming the basis for many of the characters' neurodivergence and positive representation in the series. Ishtar and their spouse are both non-binary and proponents of neurodivergent and LGBTQIA+ people.

They have lived in western Maine, the Navajo Nation in Arizona, along the coast of Virginia, and a half dozen other places. They have traveled from Japan to the UK and many places in between. Their eventual goal is to become a Doctor of Computer Science and work with archaeologists – interdisciplinary collaboration. And yes, they love swimming, eating fish, singing, and dancing… and they loathe bullies.

Thank you for purchasing an independently published literary work. Writing, editing, and publishing a novel entirely by oneself is quite a lot of work (especially when the author has dyslexia). I appreciate you as the reader – you are why I write. **Please consider leaving a review and rating**, as this is the most important thing you can do for any author. Words cannot express how much a review means to an author.

~Ishtar ♡

AUTHOR'S NOTES

Clothing – Perhaps nothing is more critical to me than prehistoric fashion. Far too often, Neolithic illustrations and exhibits will feature Neolithic people wearing full-length tunics, often made from what appears to be almost modern cloth and design. White and even pastel colors are commonplace, as are design elements without an evidentiary basis in archaeology. These "white linen tunics" and similar inaccuracies are called the "white linen tunic" fallacy. Though it can be challenging to say if the cause of these depictions is some strange modesty-induced censorship or perhaps a wanton disregard for the evidence. However, we can be sure that full-length cloth tunics have no historical basis in the Neolithic and minimal basis in the subsequent Chalcolithic (Copper Age) and early Bronze Age. For those interested, I'd recommend Prehistoric Textiles by E. J. W. Barber, 1991 and Women's Work: The First 20,000 Years: Women, Cloth, and Society in Early Times, E. J. W. Barber, 1994.

Experimental Archaeology – Experimental archaeology is a hands-on approach whereby the researcher experimentally uses real aspects of ancient cultures to gain insight into the said aspect. Making clothing, wearing clothing, and maintaining clothing are all methods of insight. Do grass-stuffed boots provide enough insulation when walking in the snow? There is only one way to find out, for sure.

As an example of one of dozens of experiments I conducted to get my scenes correct: Leggings were not likely worn in humid climates during labor, which involved constant change between kneeling and standing. How can we possibly know such detail? Creating several examples of leggings using both recovered artifacts as examples (the leggings from Otzi the Iceman) and cross-cultural comparative analysis (examining the leggings of nearly a dozen contemporary lithic societies), and then wearing these leggings while performing the actual actions in the proper humidity and temperature provided the answer. The leggings would become stuck to the skin nearly every time, regardless of construction. Skin with hair was slightly less susceptible, but the problem was significant. As a result, a summer harvest depiction would be less likely to be accurate if the models were drawn with leggings vs. bare-legged.

Gender – As a non-binary person, I find the idea of being focused on gender roles very uncomfortable, and yet, the indications we have from archaeology are that gender roles were probably quite common though much more complex than the simple "man do this... woman do that" idea we see far too often depicted. Due to the likely importance of such roles and how they affect the protagonist, they have been included as best as I can recreate them. If you find prehistoric ideas of gender interesting, I suggest reading Gender Transformations in Prehistoric and Archaic Societies, edited by Julia Katharina Koch and Wiebke Kirleis, 2019.

Hair Stroking – Stroking of the scalp feels very good, and I enjoy it. As a derivative result, many of my characters do, too. There is nothing deeper than this, and I highly recommend letting someone with long fingernails give you a scalp massage.

Plague – The bubonic and pneumonic plagues were the cause of Brig'dha's companions' deaths. While these illnesses, the result of an infection from the Y. *pestis* bacterium, are often associated with the middle ages of Europe, research has shown they also existed in prehistory. In the 2022 paper, Emergence and spread of ancestral Yersinia pestis in Late-Neolithic and Bronze-Age Eurasia, ca. 5,000 to 2,500 y B.P., by Philip Slavin and Florent Sebbane, published in the Proceedings of the National Academy of Sciences, the emergence of Y. *pestis* is discussed in depth. Of course, my story's dates are a bit earlier, but I have taken some fictional liberties. I encourage the reader to research these interesting topics as presented by the experts.

Simplicity of Speech – The series' dialogue can be a bit plain, but this is due to a few factors. Firstly, a lot of the conversation occurs with physical gestures and shared implicit speech. The world was a simpler place 7500 years ago, and less background and supplemental information needed to be shared. Secondly, many of the series' characters speak to others with a very limited shared language, making complex speech problematic. Lastly, their languages are much less complex, favoring more plain-spoken sentences.

Skin Color – The coloration of skin in the books reflects the state of ancient Europe at the dawn of the Neolithic. Several genes are responsible for lighter skin color, a mutation with selective pressure caused by the need to obtain vitamin D, converted from cholesterol in the skin via sunlight. Lighter skin allows for vitamin D production, something needed when your diet changes from a healthy hunter/gatherer lifestyle into a cereal crop-dominated menu. Mesolithic people, like Brig'dha, likely had quite dark skin, as scientists have found by sequencing their DNA. Ember's people were about as light-skinned as modern ancestrally European people, though Ember is darker due to her half-Mesolithic heritage. The data reminds us how arbitrary skin color is and how foolish racism is. For the interested reader, I recommend, The Mesolithic in Britain, Landscape and Society in Times of Change, by Chantal Conneller, 2022 and Climate, Clothing, and Agriculture in Prehistory, by Ian Gilligan, 2019.

Mesolithic Textiles – Both Mesolithic and Neolithic peoples made textile items. In fact, one common misconception was that textiles were invented in the Neolithic. In her paper, Sensible Dress: the Sight, Sound, Smell and Touch of Late Ertebølle Mesolithic Cloth Types, 2014, Susanna Harris discusses approaches to interpreting Mesolithic textile material found in late Mesolithic Scandinavian sites. While I could write an entire book on just this topic (and enjoy doing it), suffice it to say that Mesolithic textiles were likely less sophisticated, yet present.

Wels Catfish – For a long time, the giant Wels Catfish was considered a native species of the Rhine River. Several years ago, this was challenged, and the poor catfish was relegated to being an introduced species. However, a few years ago, evidence was found that our favorite catfish might have lived in the Rhine natively, at least in some capacity. The 2009 paper, The Holocene occurrence of the European catfish (Silurus glanis) in Belgium, by Wim Van Neer and Anton Ervynck, discusses these findings and may be of interest to the reader.

- Cover Art, by Alexandra Filipek © 2022
- Kaelu with her bow, by Stiffler and K. © 2016, 2022
- Linear Pottery Culture Longhouse, by Alexandra Filipek © 2022
- Atlantic Sturgeon, by Alexandra Filipek © 2022
- A Typical Neolithic apron garment, by Alexandra Filipek © 2022
- Dugout boat, by Alexandra Filipek © 2022
- Fire bow, by Alexandra Filipek © 2022
- Pak, son of Ran, son of Torn, by Stiffler and K. © 2016, 2022
- Nettle fiber woven shoes, by Alexandra Filipek © 2022
- A typical adze, by Alexandra Filipek © 2022
- Ember's obsidian dagger, by Alexandra Filipek © 2022
- Ember with her fishing spear…, by Stiffler and K. © 2016, 2022

You can find more from these fine artists at their websites:

Stiffler and K.   FindChaos.com
Alexandra Filipek   Alexandra.Filipek.us

I cannot thank them enough for their efforts to bring my characters and story alive with their amazing illustrative talent.

~Ishtar

Suggested Reading

Below is a selection of books I have found of great use while writing the Ember series. I recommend these books, especially Dr. E. W. Barber's Women's work: The first 20,000 years. I hope this knowledge inspires you and brings you a sense of academic and scientific joy, as it has me.

~Ishtar

Amkreutz, L., & Vaart-Verschoof, S. van der (Eds.). (2022). *Doggerland. lost world under the North Sea*. Sidestone Press.

Barber, E. W. (1994). *Women's work: The first 20,000 years, women, cloth and society in early times, Elizabeth Wayland Barber*. W.W.Norton.

Barber, E. W. (2005). *Prehistoric textiles: The development of cloth in the Neolithic and bronze ages: With special reference to the Aegean*. Princeton University Press.

Baysal, E. L. (2019). *Personal ornaments in prehistory: An exploration of body augmentation from the Palaeolithic to the early bronze age*. Oxbow Books.

Conneller, C. (Ed.). (2022). *The Mesolithic in Britain: Landscape and society in Times of Change*. Routledge, Taylor et Francis Group.

Fowler, C., Harding, J., & Hofmann, D. (Eds.). (2015). *The Oxford Handbook of Neolithic Europe*. Oxford University Press.

Gilligan, I. (2019). *Climate, clothing, and agriculture in prehistory: Linking evidence, causes, and effects*. Cambridge University Press.

Gleba, M., & Mannering, U. (Eds.). (2019). *Textiles and textile production in Europe from prehistory to Ad 400*. Oxbow Books.

Heath, J. M. (2017). *Warfare in Neolithic Europe: An archaeological and anthropological analysis*. Pen & Sword Archaeology.

Insoll, T. (Ed.). (2017). *The Oxford Handbook of Prehistoric Figurines*. Oxford University Press.

Koch, J. K., & Kirleis, W. (Eds.). (2019). *Gender transformations in prehistoric and Archaic Societies*. Sidestone Press.

Lukes, A., & Zvelebil, M. (Eds.). (2004). *Lbk dialogues: Studies in the formation of the Linear Pottery culture*. BAR Publishing, Oxford, UK. Nelson, S. M., & Rosen-Ayalon, M. (Eds.). (2002). *In pursuit of gender: Worldwide archaeological approaches*. Altamira Press.

Tringham, R. (1971). *Hunters, fishers and farmers of Eastern Europe, 6000-3000 B.C.* Hutchinson and Co.

Whittle, A., Pollard, J., & Greaney, S. (Eds.). (2022). *Ancient Dna and the European Neolithic: Relations and Descent*. Oxbow Books.

A SELECTED READING

Ember of Life, book two of the Ember series
Chapter 23: I Will Name You Hullamu

(Warning – may contain very mild spoilers)

Brig'dha held her flax netted shawl tightly as she stood atop the building which housed the temple. Before her was a ladder that led down into a room controlled by powerful foreign gods. Part of her worried that stepping into such an unfamiliar and magically charged area could be dangerous. She hoped to learn more about the status of this amazing priestess named Aya'tar, and offer prayers to the local deities to appease them. The problem was that she would be slightly deceptive as she obtained information about the priestess, and she doubted the local gods would miss this. Would they inform the priestess, or would they simply strike her down? It was always a risk to be taken when standing before the most religious altars of foreign gods. Brig'dha took a deep breath and prepared herself for the task.

She carefully climbed down the ladder, a foreign task to begin with. Where she had come from, very few ladder-like structures existed. Most things were built on the ground. Access to a roof was performed with either a crude ladder or a pole with notches carved into it. This ladder was extremely rugged and made from aged and polished square timbers. The roof itself was plastered white with various designs all around the outside depicting what appeared to be religious events. She took a breath and descended beneath the entryway.

As she first stepped onto the cool floor, she was nearly blind in the darkness. It would take her eyes a moment to adjust, as the inside of the temple was dark, musty, and lit by two small fires. At one end was a wall decorated with symbols depicting birds from the sky carrying the departed souls to some afterlife. Before her was an altar to a fertility goddess, most likely Isut. At the top of the altar was a small stone statue of a plump goddess with an enlarged bosom and hips, a very common symbol to be found among fertility deities. Off to the right were several bullhorns connected to the wall as well as a small altar to what appeared to be a bull god. This reminded Brig'dha of the Moon Goddess and the Horned God.

The floor was covered with rush matting, and there were many stone benches and even wooden shelves connected to some of the walls with lots of small clay pots containing various substances held within. As her eyes adjusted to the darkness, she began to notice that the entire room was covered with religious symbology. In one corner sat a warp weighted loom, while in another was a large clay pot full of some unknown substance. Brig'dha felt tingles dancing up and down her spine, which she attributed to the magical energy in the room. This was certainly the temple of the powerful deity.

Hearing a slight noise, Brig'dha turned to her left toward the stone bench, suddenly realizing that there was a person on it, someone she had not seen initially as her eyes had yet to adjust. Brig'dha instantly stepped backward with a slight gasp. A long dark-haired woman lay upon a stone bench covered with skins and furs. She was also wrapped in furs and carefully nursing two young children. She wore copper bracelets and had an intricate ash pattern of black lines painted across her lower face, with a simple loincloth at her waist.

It seemed that Imkanar was right. She was absolutely beautiful, and her presence was undeniable. Her body was slightly heavyset, probably the result of her children, and exactly how he had described his beloved Aya'tar. Oddly, her beauty was almost secondary to her commanding presence, something Brig'dha noticed immediately. The woman regarded Brig'dha, quietly watching her, but said nothing. For a short moment, they just gazed at one another in curiosity. Brig'dha suddenly felt conspicuous, staring at the woman in what was probably her home, not just the temple.

"I... My name is Brig'dha of the Blue Sea People... well, the Isen'bryn before that. I worship the Goddess of the Moon, but I have come to pay my respects to the local goddess of the city, Isut?" she said clumsily and with a thick accent. The woman with the two children smiled back at her, patiently waiting to see if she would continue. Brig'dha found herself looking down, unwilling to make eye contact for long. Worse, she was absentmindedly holding some of the strings in her string skirt, tugging them, and feeling awkward. Something about the way this woman gazed upon her made Brig'dha feel a little inadequate. The long dark-haired woman was a fertility priestess, most likely, lying regally in the middle of a fertility goddess' temple and nursing two children. The symbolism was powerful and not lost upon Brig'dha. The fertility priestess was at her greatest power in this setting and might curse her if she misspoke.

"Are you the high priestess Aya'tar?" she asked, hoping the woman would say something. The nursing woman cleared her throat to speak, satisfied that it was now time to introduce herself. Usually, it would be considered rude to call her by the shortened version of her name before having even been introduced. Strangely, the exotic-looking brunette standing before her, and wearing an outfit which might be found on the ruler of a city, seemed so nervous and worried that she could not help but find her humorous. For some reason, while she was nursing the babies, she tended to feel exceptionally relaxed and had difficulty becoming angry. She took a deep breath and began to speak.

"My name is Isut'Sanup'ramu Aya'tar, high priestess of Isut and ruler of the city of Isut'na.

Milton Keynes UK
Ingram Content Group UK Ltd.
UKHW022029110124
435898UK00019B/252/J